PRAISE FOR KRISTY CAMBRON

"Based on true events, this exquisite tale impresses with its historical and emotional authenticity. Historical fiction fans won't want to miss this."

—*Publishers Weekly*, STARRED REVIEW, FOR *The Paris Dressmaker*

"In the timeless fashion of Chanel, Ricci, and Dior, Cambron delivers another masterpiece in *The Paris Dressmaker*. Penned with unimaginable heartache, unforgettable romance, and cheering defiance against the oppression the Nazis inflicted on Paris, readers will be swept away into a story where battle-scarred good at last rings victory over evil. *Tres magnifique.*"

—J'NELL CIESIELSKI, AUTHOR OF *The Socialite*

"Kristy Cambron's masterful skill at weaving historical detail into a compelling story graces every page of *The Paris Dressmaker*. A thoroughly satisfying blend of memorable characters, evocative writing, and wartime drama that seamlessly transport you to the City of Light at its most desperate hour. Well done!"

—SUSAN MEISSNER, BESTSELLING AUTHOR OF *The Nature of Fragile Things*

"Rich with evocative descriptions of Paris and harrowing details of life during the German occupation, *The Paris Dressmaker* satisfies on all levels. Kristy Cambron deftly weaves multiple timelines to craft a story as complex and romantic and beautiful as a couture gown. In addition, Lila's and Sandrine's strength and courage in a troubled world inspire us to live likewise. *Tres magnifique!*"

—SARAH SUNDIN, BESTSELLING AND AWARD-WINNING AUTHOR OF *When Twilight Breaks* AND THE SUNRISE AT NORMANDY SERIES

"Destined to delight fans of Melanie Dobson and Natasha Lester, *The Paris Dressmaker* is a well-researched and beautifully interwoven treatise on courage and conviction in the midst of oppression. Intricately weaving the lives of two women intersecting a world in turn luminous and treacherous, Cambron's Paris is one of descriptive art to balance the artfully crafted world of haute couture against looming betrayal and the encroaching shadow of war. Her delicate care and clear passion for the City of Light, its resplendent facades, and its indomitable spirit is a rallying cry to the power of hope to overcome the fiercest of occupations. Despite the looming darkness, the novel remains a wistful and romantic escape as readers roam streets that while desecrated and bombed retain their timeless and incomparable beauty."

—RACHEL MCMILLAN, AUTHOR OF *THE LONDON RESTORATION* AND *THE MOZART CODE*

"Cambron rises to a new level with this intriguing, well-written story of love and triumph. With real-life historical details woven into her fictional tale, the story pops off the page. I could've easily been Lila or Amélie. Readers will be thinking of this book long after they've read the last word."

—RACHEL HAUCK, *NEW YORK TIMES* BESTSELLING AUTHOR, FOR *THE PARIS DRESSMAKER*

"Stunning. With as much skill and care as the title's namesake possesses, *The Paris Dressmaker* weaves together the stories of two heroines who boldly defy the darkness that descends on the City of Light. In this shining novel, Kristy Cambron has lovingly designed and crafted a fresh perspective on a familiar war. Every word is expertly stitched into graceful lines in this seamless masterpiece of historical fiction. This is Cambron at her very finest. A luminous must-read, and a timeless reminder that light conquers dark."

—JOCELYN GREEN, CHRISTY AWARD—WINNING AUTHOR OF *SHADOWS OF THE WHITE CITY*

"[A] thrilling tale. Offering a strong reminder that first impressions do not always tell the whole story, Cambron wraps up her time-swapping series with this delightful portrait of a stately manor over the course of two centuries."

—*PUBLISHERS WEEKLY*, FOR *THE PAINTED CASTLE*

"Cambron once again makes smart use of multiple eras in her latest time-jumping romance. Cambron spins tales of resiliency, compassion, and courage."

—PUBLISHERS WEEKLY FOR THE LOST CASTLE

"An absolutely lovely read! Cambron weaves an enchanting story of love, loss, war, and hope in *The Lost Castle*. Spanning the French Revolution, World War II, and today, she masterfully carries us into each period with all the romance and danger of the best fairy tale."

—KATHERINE REAY, AWARD-WINNING AUTHOR OF THE AUSTEN ESCAPE

"Cambron's lithe prose pulls together past and present, and her attention to historical detail grounds the narrative to the last breathtaking moments."

—PUBLISHERS WEEKLY, STARRED REVIEW, FOR THE ILLUSIONIST'S APPRENTICE

"Prepare to be amazed by *The Illusionist's Apprentice*. This novel will have your pulse pounding and your mind racing to keep up with reversals, betrayals, and surprises from the first page to the last."

—GREER MACALLISTER, BESTSELLING AUTHOR OF
THE MAGICIAN'S LIE AND GIRL IN DISGUISE

"With rich descriptions, attention to detail, mesmerizing characters, and an understated current of faith, this work evokes writers such as Kim Vogel Sawyer, Francine Rivers, and Sara Gruen."

—LIBRARY JOURNAL, STARRED REVIEW, FOR THE RINGMASTER'S WIFE

"Historical fiction lovers will adore this novel! *The Ringmaster's Wife* features two rich love stories and a glimpse into our nation's live entertainment history. Highly recommended!"

—USA TODAY, HAPPY EVER AFTER

"Cambron expertly weaves together multiple plotlines, timelines, and perspectives to produce a poignant tale of the power of love and faith in difficult circumstances. Those interested in stories of survival and the Holocaust, such as Elie Wiesel's 'Night,' will want to read."

—LIBRARY JOURNAL FOR THE BUTTERFLY AND THE VIOLIN

THE
Paris
DRESSMAKER

BOOKS BY KRISTY CAMBRON

THE LOST CASTLE NOVELS
The Lost Castle
Castle on the Rise
The Painted Castle

STAND-ALONE NOVELS
The Ringmaster's Wife
The Illusionist's Apprentice

THE HIDDEN MASTERPIECE NOVELS
The Butterfly and the Violin
A Sparrow in Terezin

THE

Paris

DRESSMAKER

KRISTY CAMBRON

THOMAS NELSON
Since 1798

The Paris Dressmaker

Published in Nashville, Tennessee, by Thomas Nelson. Thomas Nelson is a registered trademark of HarperCollins Christian Publishing, Inc.

Published in association with the Books & Such Literary Management, 52 Mission Circle, Suite 122, PMB 170, Santa Rosa, California 95409–5370, www.booksandsuch.com.

Interior design by Phoebe Wetherbee

Thomas Nelson titles may be purchased in bulk for educational, business, fundraising, or sales promotional use. For information, please email SpecialMarkets@ThomasNelson.com.

Unless otherwise marked, Scripture quotations are taken from the Holy Bible, King James Version. Scripture quotations marked NIV are taken from the Holy Bible, New International Version®, NIV®. Copyright © 1973, 1978, 1984, 2011 by Biblica, Inc.® Used by permission of Zondervan. All rights reserved worldwide. www.zondervan.com. The "NIV" and "New International Version" are trademarks registered in the United States Patent and Trademark Office by Biblica, Inc.®

ISBN: 978-0-7852-4875-0 (ITPE)

Library of Congress Cataloging-in-Publication Data

Names: Cambron, Kristy, author.
Title: The Paris dressmaker / Kristy Cambron.
Description: Nashville, Tennessee : Thomas Nelson, [2021] | Summary: "Based on true accounts of how Parisiennes resisted the Nazi occupation-from fashion houses to the city streets-The Paris Dressmaker weaves a story of two courageous women who risked everything to fight an evil they couldn't abide"-- Provided by publisher.
Identifiers: LCCN 2020040338 (print) | LCCN 2020040339 (ebook) | ISBN 9780785232162 (paperback) | ISBN 9780785232179 (epub) | ISBN 9780785232186
Subjects: LCSH: World War, 1939-1945--Underground movements--France--Fiction. | GSAFD: Historical fiction.
Classification: LCC PS3603.A4468 P37 2021 (print) | LCC PS3603.A4468 (ebook) | DDC 813/.6--dc23
LC record available at https://lccn.loc.gov/2020040338
LC ebook record available at https://lccn.loc.gov/2020040339

Printed in the United States of America

21 22 23 24 25 LSC 5 4 3 2 1

For Jeremy—
Je t'aime, mon cœur.

And for Sandy Jean—
Our elegant grand-mère.

Be pretty if you can, be witty if you must,
but be gracious if it kills you.

—ELSIE DE WOLFE

CHAPTER 1

Look at the nations and watch—
and be utterly amazed.
For I am going to do something in your days
that you would not believe,
even if you were told.

—HABAKKUK 1:5 NIV

31 DECEMBER 1943
FORÊT DE MEUDON
MEUDON, FRANCE

If Lila de Laurent were discovered in the forest, she was dead.

Orphaned snowflakes drifted down, making the depths of the woods seem far more threatening in their desolation than the streets of Paris ever could. Floodlights grasped behind her, searching through the trees with skeletal shadows as she swept through undergrowth that frayed the hem of her ivory gown into damp strips. The sounds of patrol dogs barking in the distance echoed loudly, competing with her own drumming heartbeat as she ran through the snow.

If the Vichy police caught up to her, they wouldn't need an excuse to turn Lila over to the SS. And the Nazis would show no mercy. They wouldn't inquire why a *Vogue* fashion plate was trekking through the Forêt de Meudon on New Year's Eve. A bullet hole through her side and a pistol in her pocket would tell them all they needed to know about who Lila de Laurent had become.

The gloved hand she kept pressed to her side warned of urgency, blood seeping through the thin gabardine plaits of her ivory opera coat—a stain she couldn't hope to hide and an impediment she could not ignore.

"Il faut que je file!" Run! Lila gave herself the order through gritted teeth.

Even if it hurt to breathe, or move, or think from one moment to the next, she had to keep going. The Boche were as thick as the trees within the Forêt borders and the Maquis had a system of guerrilla fighters positioned in all directions spanning from Paris. It meant they couldn't account for one combatant's safety—even from their own guns—making the escape through the forest a foolhardy one if she was discovered and disbelieved by either side.

Her comrade, Violette, had repeated the warning with a firm grip to her arm seconds before Lila fled the Hôtel Ritz that evening:

> "To go through the Meudon is your only way out now. But be careful; it is overrun. Change your clothes. And cut your hair. If they learn of this, the SS will circulate a photo of you as the fashion princess with the trademark marron locks spilling down her back. You must not look like her. If you are to live, then that girl must first die."

With no time to shed the silk gown she wore or to see to the fallen chignon that now tangled in long ropes over her shoulders, Lila had already failed that instruction. So she avoided the cleared paths—which were likely host to buried mines at their borders—and kept to the camouflage of snowy places, following the trail set by Nazi-protected rail lines stretching through the trees.

A road curved round a bend and over a rise; château gates emerged.

Imposing towers of stone, twisted bramble, and ironwork stood as ghostly sentries guarding the thicket. Fresh tire tracks marred the road. In the distance a golden halo cut through the trees from candlelight glowing in the windowsills of a grand château. Scores of leaded-glass panes filled the front, beyond a lavish covered portico of burnished stone and the line of snowcapped autos that dotted the circular drive. Shadows moved across the windows as château guests passed by with champagne flutes and the blur of elegant, white-tie dress.

Lila melted into the trunk of a Scots pine to catch her breath, her slippers sinking against frozen pine needles at her feet.

A waning crescent moon hung overhead—near midnight.

An hour more trekking through the blistering cold wouldn't have tempted Lila to stop under normal circumstances, as the only châteaus left in the country still operating as manor houses were controlled by either the Nazi elite or *collaborateurs* in the Régime de Vichy. But peeling her hand from her middle was no longer possible—she'd be knees-in-the-snow from the pain and dead by dawn with or without the Nazis' help.

Her options were run and die, or stop, risk, and pray.

At a château of this size, there must be a service entrance round the back. Perhaps an outbuilding or, if fate smiled, a larder that may be stocked but not checked again until morning. A few hours' sleep . . . protection from the wind . . . even the hopeful promise of food—together they could prove the difference in survival versus not.

With careful steps to avoid the light, Lila followed the tree line around the back, watching for guard patrols that could appear, guns drawn, at any time. A cobblestone path led to the château and she stopped shy of it, behind a wagonette hoisted up by its broken wheel upon a pile of stacked bricks.

Snow fell, silent but drifting beyond a pitched-wood awning and heathered oak door that was warmed by the glow of an outdoor sconce. A beryl-and-rust-patched Renault idled in the alcove, its back doors ajar and motor spitting exhaust like cigarette smoke rising at a society party. The white text of its business name had faded on the placard, but enough remained that Lila could read upon its side:

BOULANGERIE
29 Boulevard Rouget de Lisle
Montreuil, Versailles

"Merci, God. *Merci."* Lila closed her eyes, her forehead pressed up against the rough wood of the wagonette for support as she drank in deep, steadying breaths. "Montreuil—only two kilometers away."

She could make it to Versailles from there. Meet her contact. Make the handoff. And then from Versailles . . . she didn't yet know.

"Allons-y!" A man's shout cut through the sputter of the engine, causing her to jump and look out once again.

Wearing wool trousers, an unbuttoned vest, and a white uniform shirt with cuffs rolled at the forearms, the man hopped down from the back of the bread truck and peered through the service entrance. He seemed to give little care for the bitter cold. Instead he focused on muscling crates in the back, then stormed through the door with such ferocity he nearly took the oak from its hinges. It swung wide in a ferocious clap against the château's burnished stone and bounced against the wall with a sluggish tremble afterward.

"Allons-y!"

The man disappeared through the glow of the servants' entrance, his calls of "Let's go!" dying away with him.

Lila scanned the scene. No movement in the front of the truck meant no extra workers to worry after. And she could just see crates and interior shelving in the back—enough cover to remain hidden. Fighting to stay alert through the ride into the commune of Montreuil, how she'd make it out of the truck unnoticed once there and whether the deliveryman might be friend or foe—those were the worries she'd confront as she came to them.

Each worry in its time.

Hoping the mass of snowy footprints around the entrance would conceal the addition of hers, Lila sprinted to the shadows beyond the Renault's back doors and climbed inside. She pressed her back up against the cold metal cage and slid to the floor like melting snow, landing against a wooden crate of baguettes and rustic sourdough boules. The only savior left was the tiny pistol in her coat pocket. Lila peeled her glove off and, in a last defense, curled her bloodied palm around the grip, holding the weapon tight against her lapel.

"Always putting us off schedule." The man didn't shout this time but grumbled a frustrated rebuke barely audible over the Renault's engine. He returned alone, muscling two empty crates stacked one on top of the other, and seemingly without the companion he'd sought.

In the light she could see he was of medium build, tall, and with soft brown hair that looked as though it had been parted and combed once but had been mussed by the dance of wind. The man lifted crates over the tailgate and slid them across the truck's metal floor. He braced hands on the doors to secure them . . . but paused.

Lila held her breath.

She could only pray the ivory satin of her gown hadn't shimmered in the shadows. But the action, however well meaning to save her, proved the opposite. The man surveyed the crates, then lifted a cautious boot to the tailgate.

With agility that surprised even her, Lila thrust the pistol up to shoulder height—hand only exposed—and extended it point-blank to his chest. *"Arrêtez!"*

Though Lila issued the order to halt with all the confidence she could muster, her bloodied fist trembled as pain pulsed through her. She anchored her arm tighter at the waist and firmed her grip, repeating, "Arrêtez," not a shout this time, but with what she hoped was an iron tone.

The man raised his palms and exhaled a fog of breath in the cold as he lowered his boot to the ground.

"*D'accord*. Easy . . . I'll not hurt you."

An ironic promise given she held the gun. But backing down was a good sign.

"What is it you want, mademoiselle?"

Perhaps it was the shock at being on the run for hours through the streets of Paris and a forest teeming with patrol dogs and Nazi guns, but Lila couldn't answer. No wonder her mind had chosen that moment to play its ill-fated tricks, telling her the deep voice that was so deceptively soft as it raked over gravel was one she'd heard before.

Many times.

The voice belonged to a dead man.

"*Bien*. Take it." He tipped his head to the thieves' hoard of bread in the crates, enough that the light caught his face. "Whatever you wish is yours. Just take it and go. I want no trouble here."

Lila stared back into his eyes, their unmistakable clear blue triggering long-buried memories. Though a few years older and thinned down, with an unshaven jaw, in caterer's livery rather than the posh tuxedos of her mind's eye, and standing at the tailgate of a broken-down bread truck in the Forêt de Meudon of all times and places in their busted-up world—nothing could mistake who stood before her.

"You . . ." Lila exhaled, a breath clouding on air as she held firm on her knees.

René Touliard flinched in a reflexive double take when she edged forward and the sconce light cast its glow upon her. If he was startled to see her, he kept hold of his composure—shoulders squared, eyes in constant communion with hers, his hands stilled on air as snowflakes drifted in a lazy waltz between them.

"Yes—*me*."

"I thought . . . you were dead."

"Obviously not. Very much alive." His manner shifted after he inspected the gun, a furrow marring his brow at Lila's crimson-stained palm and the traces of blood caked under her fingernails. "How'd you get your hands on that type of pistol? A Liberator. Thought only *La Résistance* were rumored to travel with those."

"They do." It was an offhanded remark born of pain and haste— one René wasn't supposed to read. She had no idea what the weapon was, just that it was her only defense.

"Oh no . . . Lila. What have you gotten yourself into?"

Lila shook her head. "There's no time. Can you drive?"

"I might. If you lower that. Out of courtesy to an old friend? I'm afraid I don't trust you not to kill me."

"An old friend. Is that what I am?" She lifted her chin a notch and kept the Liberator frozen in place as her heart processed the implication that the only man she'd ever loved had downgraded her to a mere friend in his remembrance.

"You were once."

"Then I wouldn't trust a friend not to turn this around and . . . use it on me. Not even you."

Lila's words tripped over pain, shock, or cold. Any one of them could have their fancy at the moment. She couldn't tell for certain she wasn't passed out in a Paris gutter somewhere and these might be her last terrible moments alive before her body gave her over to the grave—to see René in both her dreams and nightmares now too.

Footsteps scuffled behind them.

René darted his glance to the depths of the truck and back again. Lila nodded and descended into the shadows, their back-and-forth forgotten as she eased behind the crates. A younger man invaded the alcove in the next breath. He, too, was dressed in caterer's livery but arms void of crates.

"Alright. Here I am—Duckworth at your service."

"*En français, s'il te plaît!*" René snapped, the calm and cool serrated out of his tone. "And don't use that name out here. You know better."

"*Oui, votre Majesté!* Even if no one's about." The young man agreed, though with a ghastly bow and a little cheek about his air thereafter. "Listen, you're mad as a hatter to ask me to leave now. You cannot think to blame me for wanting to stay, not when the invitation to snoop on a New Year's party for the Nazis' top brass is so thoroughly . . . *je ne sais quoi.*"

"*Non.* But I do expect you to remember who you are before you get someone killed. If it turns out to be me, I'll be very displeased and will feel no guilt at taking it out on your arrogant hide." René clicked one of the doors closed so Lila was lost to the shadows behind him. "You wish to remain in your merriment, so stay. I have deliveries to make before dawn."

"And by then I should have all the information I need, as per usual."

"I'll return to fetch you in the morning," René said matter-of-factly, and slammed the other door closed.

The sealed doors muffled their conversation so Lila couldn't make out the rest. But whatever René had said was convincing enough that he opened the truck door and climbed into the worn leather driver's seat alone.

"What did you tell him?"

René sat, staring straight ahead into the darkness of the path that disappeared through the pines as if he, too, were trying to catch his breath.

"Nothing of consequence. Just to have a care until morning. The last thing I need is two problems to contend with tonight."

Was that what she was? A *problem*? Seemed like the bigger problem in France was uniformed in Nazi gray and pointing loaded weapons in their general direction.

"Why . . . ?"

Why are you here? Why are you alive? Why did you leave all those years ago?

Pain seared again, recoiling through Lila's middle so words died on her tongue. Of all the questions in the world she could have asked him now, she landed on the most hapless.

"Why are you delivering for a boulangerie?"

René glanced over his shoulder to her form doubled over in the shadows. Softness greeted her in the attention from his eyes, and heaven help her, from somewhere deep inside, Lila could still read that look and she knew what it meant. He was calculating—thinking a thousand things he wouldn't say.

"You're hurt?"

"Oui. I'm afraid I am."

"Here." He tossed a coat to the floor that grazed her knees in thick wool. "Stay warm, *Luciole*. I'll get you out of here." He kicked the truck into gear and it lumbered toward the forest's vast darkness as she pulled the coat over her shoulders like a blanket.

Luciole.

Lila wished she hadn't heard the nickname again.

It had been ages, not since they'd once seen the anomaly of fire-flies dotting a summer sky over the gardens of Versailles. And she thought she'd never hear that voice again or never see those eyes glance her way. Yet here he was—*her* René. Back from the dead just as he pleased. Like it was that easy to do. And casting a quick wave to the uniformed soldiers at the guard shack as they allowed the truck to pass through the château gates to be swallowed up by the ink of night.

Once through, the Liberator no longer seemed needed.

Lila allowed the pistol to sag and she went down with it, the cool metal floor welcoming as it met her cheek. She lay perfumed by the random scents of yeast, balsam, and him—from the collar of the coat—drifting as the pain finally came out of dormancy to its full fervor. She twisted her fingertips into a fist against the wool lapel and squeezed her eyes shut.

"Lila?" A pause, and then a shout. "Lila—*réveille-toi*! Do you hear me? Wake up!"

"I'm awake . . ."

Yet she drifted off, the crags and crevices in the forest road causing the truck tires to bump along, jostling her toward sleep like an odd sort of Pied Piper's lullaby.

"I can't drive and see to you at the same time. You must stay with me. Keep talking. Tell me, what in heaven's name are you doing in the middle of the Meudon? Do you have any idea how dangerous it is out here?"

"I think I've got a pulse on that."

"Might we table your wit for just one moment? How did you get here?"

No. We won't talk of yesterdays that led to today. Not now.

Best to keep focused on the task at hand. "I can't even say. But on foot through the forest as far as I could manage."

"From where?" He glanced over his shoulder, then back to the road, hitting her with glances that said he wanted an answer. "How did you venture this far south?"

"I'm bound for the village of Versailles. Château side. Surely you remember it."

"Versailles is swarming with military police."

Of course I know it is. I'm no ingénue now.

She exhaled, losing herself in the pain. "I know."

"Then you must also know there is no way for a rogue bird to fly over without the say-so of the Boche, let alone a bread truck to roll through the front gates of Versailles with a stowaway in tow. It'd be a death wish to try—yours and mine."

"I must . . . get there."

Lila breathed deep though the pain sliced her in two. She'd heard it from her father's experience in the Great War that men withered after taking a bullet—they fell down, bathed in blood, and remained silent, or gritted their teeth like they were chewing iron. Now she knew why. Either scenario seemed more favorable than the fire coursing through her at the moment.

Tears gathered in her eyes and she turned her forehead to the damp, rusted floorboards, refusing even then that he'd see her cry.

"C'est pas possible!" he muttered as he shouldered them around a tight turn against a snowbank.

"You . . . believed in the impossible once, didn't you?" Only the chugging engine answered back, and she knew she'd hit a nerve. "Tell me! Didn't you?"

"But we do not live in that world now, Luciole."

Lila slid her palm along the hem of her opera coat, searching for the lump sewn into its lining. She found the treasure safe. And for the moment so was she. That alone meant Providence still watched over them. Lila had made it out of the Hôtel Ritz. Out of Paris. And now it seemed she'd landed in the hands of the one person on earth she could trust to take her the rest of the way to Versailles.

"Perhaps not. But even if this is the end, we still have to try."

"The end of what?"

"My nightmare in Paris since the day you left."

The last thought that penetrated Lila's mind before she tumbled into oblivion was that even in the midst of their war-torn world, impossible might never be fully out of reach. After all, René Touliard had returned from the grave and that could mean everything. Lila could only pray she wouldn't find herself there in his stead.

"Happy New Year, René," she whispered, and let go.

CHAPTER 2

"Non. You cannot come in today."

Monsieur Mullins blocked Sandrine Paquet's entrance into his shop, his form anchored just behind the door, preventing her and Henri from stepping inside the boulangerie where they'd bought their bread for the past four years.

She stopped short so that her little son almost crashed into her backside and her oxford heel teetered against the uneven spot where the tile met the front stoop. Her reflection in the shop window of Le Fournier Boulangerie must have shown astonishment. Surely he was not turning them away. And without explanation.

"We can't come in? Whyever not?"

The old man's gaze flitted to the waspish-gray uniforms peppering the sidewalks and he shook his head—a tiny flinch side to side and a furrowed brow that said their safe association was no longer assured. "They are watching."

His whisper was so slight he might have only mouthed the words and Sandrine imagined the rest. Yet the terror in his eyes was real enough to send a chill over her that had little to do with the cold.

"You must leave, Mrs. Paquet. Immediately."

"Oui. Of course." Sandrine nodded. Fumbled. Swept a gloved palm over the front of her coat to smooth imaginary wrinkles and then gripped Henri's little hand tighter as she stepped back, and Monsieur Mullins hurried to close the door. The bolt locked hard into place, and the shade was drawn down tight over the glass of the shop door but a breath later.

"*Salope!*" A woman spat on the ground at their feet the instant Sandrine stepped down from the front stoop, the insult of being labeled a prostitute sending them from one shock right into the next. Spittle shone on the corner sidewalk in front of Sandrine's oxford heels, and she looked from the ground up to the pinched face of an old woman, who had narrowed her eyes to accusing slits.

Then the woman turned to stare at Henri—a mistake.

Through maternal instinct, the hair on the back of Sandrine's neck stood on end, and she curled her wrist around her six-year-old son to nudge him behind her skirt.

The woman pointed, waving a bony finger at her. "No wonder they refuse you service here. I have seen you with them, collaborateurs! *Allemands! Les cochons Vichy . . .*"

Collaborators. Germans . . . Vichy pigs.

"That is quite enough, madame. *Pardon.*" Sandrine sidestepped the woman as she secured the ration tickets back in her oxblood leather satchel, then led Henri down the sidewalk in the opposite direction.

"What did she say, *Maman*?"

"Who?"

"*Cette femme.*" Henri turned, looking back to the face of their accuser, the woman's nose and eyes still scrunched with fury under a faded navy day cap as she blasted insults.

"Put that finger away," Sandrine cautioned, though she kept her voice cheery. "Someone might think we carry tales as we cross the street. We wouldn't want that now, would we?"

Her son did as he was told, but that little brow that wrinkled in the same manner as his father's always had said Henri's curiosity would not die with a single sidewalk encounter. On the contrary, the encounter would only add to the many before it and cause his questions to grow. Where his coloring made him a caramel towhead with soft fawn eyes just like her, he was the mirror image of Christian Paquet in careful manner, reasoning, and deep thought.

Answering his questions could only be put off for so long.

"Where are we going, Maman?"

"We should find a boulangerie open today, mustn't we? For our New Year's tea. Paris has enough bakeries and they all accept ration tickets. We shall simply register at a new one." Sandrine straightened the satchel hooked over her elbow as they came to the street corner— more out of principle than actual need.

Henri was old enough now to have seen and done far more adult things than a child ever should in his first years. But there had to be some measure of normalcy, even in their world. They'd survived under the Régime de Vichy for nearly four years. Regardless of the growing sentiment of hatred against Marshal Pétain and his faction of appeasing collaboration, she and Henri were not ill-fated puppets who would slink about in the shadows created by her employers.

Paris was their home—they wouldn't be cast out, no matter the rumors circulating about them.

"But . . ." Henri slowed up enough that she had to stop or tug him along with her. "We've gone to Le Fournier since Pa-pa left us. Have we offended Monsieur Mullins in some way, that he should not allow us in his shop?"

Offend Monsieur Mullins?

Sandrine couldn't think about that now. Not when she wagered whatever had gone wrong went far beyond a mere offense. The terror aflame in the man's eyes explained more than anything else could.

When she didn't answer, Henri added, "He is a friend of Pa-pa's, Maman."

But your pa-pa is not here.

"Why not have an adventure and find a new haunt? I hear tell there is a *pâtisserie* in Montmartre that had croissants last month. Can you imagine? Would it not be like old times to have a croissant at our tea?"

Would Henri even remember the beautiful days of one's paltry concerns, like buttery croissants and teatimes? They were so long ago. Ordinary was a lost dream now.

"But I do not want a new haunt."

"You might not now, but once we find your favorite—"

"*Mais non.* I do not want to go anywhere except where my pa-pa will know to find us. When he comes back, won't he look for us at Le Fournier? And what if we should miss him? What if he . . . never returns and it is our fault?"

The question of a child's bleeding heart had the power to stop time around them.

The wind kicked up, toying with the sun in Henri's hair as he waited for her answer. Cathedral bells chimed somewhere in the distance. And the ever-present Nazi hornets swarmed the street corners with gray, watching Parisians like hawk-eyed beasts even though the street traffic was oddly silent on this day.

Sandrine eyed them as she reached out and squeezed Henri's little hand. "Nothing could be your fault. Not ever. And your pa-pa will return. You just wait and see."

Kneeling before him eye to eye on the sidewalk, Sandrine readjusted the blue-striped tucker around his neck. She smiled and dotted a gloved index finger to the tip of his nose, the merlot leather warm against his cherry cheeks and splash of freckles.

"Perhaps we will wait to go back when Pa-pa returns home. Hmm? As a celebration. But in the meantime, we shall buy our bread from another shop—perhaps one closer to Maman's work. It is quite a walk from Le Fournier to the Tuileries Garden and to the schoolhouse. Non? And I would not mind fewer blocks to travel when it rains. My favorite chapeau is looking quite sad these days because of it."

Henri missed every bit of an argument that was meant to convince him yet had zero merit with which to accomplish it. The corner boasting Le Fournier was on their way, of course. The blocks it took to traverse from their flat to the 1st Arrondissement would not have saved a scrap of time. Still, he seemed to accept her word on it and looked up at her once-prized violet cloche, the faux flowers faded and the style from too many seasons ago to count.

"Your chapeau is not sad," Henri whispered, his toothless smile offering a haven of innocence even in their war-torn world. "You said Pa-pa bought it for you."

Tears on the street corner would never do.

Emotion would have tumbled out had Sandrine not bitten her bottom lip in time. She must always appear gratified for the occupation in front of the Nazis. On the outside she must be muted and fashioned of stone, no matter the tender condition of the heart beating beneath the layers.

"That's right. Your pa-pa did purchase this chapeau. And I shall wear it proudly, *mon trésor*, until he might buy me a new one. But right now we'd best be off or we'll lose all of our festiveness for the holiday. You know *Mémé* will be waiting for our return back to the flat. The last thing we'd want to do is let your grandmother spend the holiday alone."

And she? Sandrine wanted nothing more than a good cry once they'd returned home—bread in their arms or not—and for a few precious hours, she could shut the door on the rest of the world.

———◆◆———

1 JANUARY 1944
16TH ARRONDISSEMENT
PARIS, FRANCE

Regardless of its pleasant chime, the echo of the doorbell through the flat caused them both to start. Sandrine looked across the room to her mother-in-law, her eyes flashing with immediate concern from her place by the hearth.

"I'll see to it." Sandrine smiled at Marguerite and placed her Bible on an upturned produce crate between them. "Not to worry. Probably a delivery come to the wrong door."

Sandrine rose and hurried off, heels clicking on the marble floor in echoes made sharper by near-empty rooms.

Once a beautiful flat her in-laws had owned in the fashionable 16th Arrondissement, it, too, had endured the ravages of war. Sandrine crossed through a library that had once boasted parties for the family's literary circle at Paquet Publishing, with glittering names like Ernest Hemingway and Joyce and Sylvia Beach on the guest list. Years later it housed only ghosts of yesterday with empty bookshelves, sparse rooms, and drapes drawn down tight at all times.

Caution was paramount. After more than four years of war, one never opened a door without being absolutely certain who stood on the other side. When Sandrine reached the door, she lifted the gold plate over the peephole, then dropped it just as quickly—catching her breath with palms pressed against the door.

Always, she must be the portrait of put-together before *him*.

Sandrine fiddled with the belt on her navy suit dress and straightened her shoulders, then unlatched the gold chain on the door. The hinges cried out as she opened it.

The captain stood in the hall, his six-foot-two-inch height in a uniform impeccably pressed as if ready for a normal workweek, instead of staring down the evening hours on a holiday. He tipped his blond brow in a nod and held out a bakery box—blush pink with a bow of ivory twine and the artful logo of the pâtisserie's name, Les Petits Galettes, curling over the top in rich gold-foil script.

"Captain von Hiller . . ."

"Josef—please. *Bonne Année*, Mrs. Paquet." He offered a faint smile along with the New Year's greeting.

She stared at the box. "What can we do for you?"

"I understand you had an unfortunate incident this morning."

"Oh?" Playing innocent seemed the card to lay down. Sandrine couldn't begin to guess how he'd known what occurred at the corner boulangerie unless he had spies skulking in all directions—which was possibly true.

"The boulangerie turned you away." His manner was always sharp, direct, and his words without mince.

"Closed for the holiday. Or perhaps they've a shortage of bread. The lines for food grow longer each day all across the city, as you know. I'm certain there was no ill will intended."

"You are too chaste not to come to me. That sort of unpleasantness will not occur again, I assure you. I've taken care of it personally. But as I know Henri enjoys them—here. A gift. Croissants, honey, and fig jam." He looked past her into their private world, scanning the shadows in the entry. "Is he about?"

Sandrine pressed her finger to her lips and edged the door closed, reinforcing the line drawn between their work association and the confines of her family. "Sleeping. I'm afraid the day has proved too much already."

"I see. Another time perhaps."

Those viridian eyes—knowing and so direct—stayed in candid communion with hers for two long, dreadful seconds before he shimmied the outstretched box for her to take possession. Sandrine reached for it, feeling a surge of warning when his fingertips brushed hers in the exchange.

"I've come to fetch you to the *galerie*."

Her breath locked in her chest at what that might mean.

In their haunted world of occupation, Sandrine envisioned the worst with every connection to the outside world, especially that which would summon her to the Jeu de Paume storehouse on a holiday. Every telegram could bring news of a dead husband. Every public radio broadcast spouted propaganda of another Allied defeat and imminent Third Reich victory. Every shipment they took in uncrated fresh risks for them all. Her worst nightmares could be confirmed in any manner of savage ways. Being summoned to the Jeu de Paume Galerie in this way—it was highly irregular.

And irregular was never comforting.

Sandrine eased into the hall, then clicked the door closed behind her.

Thank heaven—deserted.

She inspected the lavish rail of wrought iron along circular stairs that curled up and down, finding not a soul about to witness their exchange. No nosy neighbors to make their assumptions and toss evil glances her way. Sandrine breathed a sigh of relief and hugged the box in front of her, anchoring the cardboard as a shield between them. "What is it?"

"A shipment of degenerate cargo has been confused with art acquired from private collections in the city. The Rothschilds—a very important find of their vast collection. We are tasked to sort it out immediately." The captain remained glacial with the answer, which was characteristic for his apathetic opinion of art dubbed objectionable by the Third Reich.

"We were told the shipment would not be expected until after the new year. But it's here already?"

"*Ja.* Two vaults were discovered here in Paris and opened yesterday— one unknown until now. Trucks bearing crates of the valuables arrived with the others just this afternoon. The degenerates must now be cataloged and separated from the rest of the legitimate art. It is a matter of great importance to the Führer. He has assigned Reichsmarschall Hermann Göring to personally oversee the selection of pieces for the new Führermuseum collection in Linz. And today Baron von Behr has entrusted the honor of the day-to-day preparations of this request to me—or, to us."

The field director of the Einsatzstab Reichsleiter Rosenberg himself was involved, and one of the highest-ranking officials under direction of their Führer in Reichsmarschall Göring? It must be quite important to have such a rank and file of names that went straight to the top of the hill.

"I see. But what cannot wait on this evening?"

"There's an oddity in one of the crates and our curator has requested your presence to sort it out."

Mademoiselle Valland is there too?

That certainly put a different color on it for their curator to ask for her by name. When Sandrine didn't move, he cleared his throat. "I'll wait."

"Oh, oui. Of course. I'll just . . ." Sandrine nodded and fiddled with the string on the pastry box so she could grasp it one-handed and turn the doorknob behind her.

Before she closed the door on him—intent upon grabbing her hat and bag and writing a hastily scrawled note to poor Henri should he wake without his maman at home—Sandrine turned, catching the captain's eye.

"What is it exactly, this 'oddity'? Forgive me, sir. I'm certain Baron von Behr would have already shared this information with you. But it will help me to be prepared once we are there, to work as efficiently as possible."

"I'm told it is a dress."

"A . . . dress."

"Ja." He cleared his throat. Frustration or impatience—or who knew what was ticking through that mind of his—seemed to be irritating enough that he gave a curt nod and readjusted his hat, like he was done waiting and ready to be on the way. "I reminded Valland that the *Sonderstab Bildende Kunst* does not deal with textiles—we are only responsible for pictorial art. But I'm afraid she insisted in this case."

"She did. Very well. I won't be a moment then." Sandrine nodded and closed the door, leaving the captain—as she still refused the familiarity of addressing him as "Josef," as he was so forthright in suggesting—alone in the hall.

A dress?

A complication, more like it.

Sandrine hadn't any expertise in textiles. The paper and bindings of books she could manage without question. Even oil paint on canvas and wood she'd become a confident assayer of under Mademoiselle Valland's tutelage. But a dress meant she should expect this request to have more to do with summoning courage than assessing reams of satin or lace.

The floor creaked at the end of the hall. Her mother-in-law stood in the glow of light cast in the kitchen doorway, the once neat and refined woman of means pushing back stray wisps of gray at her temple as she fiddled with a leather shank button on the front of her paisley dress.

"What does that devil want with you?"

"Nothing, Maman. It is for work and that is all. I already said you needn't worry," Sandrine whispered, patting Marguerite's fidgeting hand as she walked by.

"Not worry? This is how it started before—they show up and demand deference as you do their bidding. Then they take people away. You more than anyone should know that one day, they don't come back. My husband and son are evidence of that, and now we are widows."

"I am no widow."

"You haven't an idea what you are anymore, do you?" Marguerite stared back, ice in her eyes. Sandrine couldn't decide if the statement was made for her benefit out of concern or to justify a forthcoming accusation. Perhaps both.

"Mademoiselle Valland is at the galerie and has requested my assistance. I must go."

"But you're going with *him*."

"I haven't a choice in the matter. You know this."

Marguerite's eyes narrowed, hatred burning in their depths. "Do you know what kind of game you're playing? What he will require of you? In the end he won't ask nicely. You know as well as I that they demand. And then they take."

Sandrine breezed by her and pressed the pastry box down as far as it could go in the rubbish bin, then covered it with the holiday treat of orange rinds and yesterday's newspapers. Even then the headlines cried death.

"Kiss Henri for me. I will return soon."

Pinning her navy hat over the blonde barrel rolls at her nape, Sandrine stared at her reflection in the entryway mirror. Tears tried to break free for the wreck of a woman who looked back from the glass. She forced them away.

This was no game, and she couldn't hide what was happening like tossing croissants in the bin. Marguerite did speak some version of the truth, as their neighbors would see.

The watchmen would part their drapes and eye Sandrine from all floors up, seeing the Nazi officer's car door open upon the curb—a car in a city of only run-down bicycles and worn walking shoes. They'd watch. Scowl. And judge as he held out his hand and Sandrine must accept it.

She'd climb inside. For Henri. For her accusing mother-in-law. For her dead father-in-law and absent husband, and for every single moment they'd been forced to survive Paris without them.

War didn't offer choices. And it sure didn't leave room for negotiation where the game was concerned. You walked a thin line between life and death, praying you knew which side was which when the game was over.

Sandrine may have shuttered her tears, but her heart bled as she stepped through the front door into the bleak Paris streets beyond and the waiting Nazi officer's car.

Christian . . . Where are you?

CHAPTER 3

1 JULY 1939
BOULEVARD SAINT-ANTOINE NO. 57
VERSAILLES, FRANCE

An artist's brush swept the sky beyond the glass, painting the horizon in stains of rose and plum as the sun dipped behind the château side of Versailles.

"*Le crépuscule* . . ." Lila parted the bisque drapes so she could gaze out at it—*twilight*—as she stood at the second-story bathroom suite window.

"What did you say?" Amélie's singsong voice floated over the crackle of embers on a garish marble hearth, its ornate bronze and irons fashioned as horses rearing before smoldering logs. "Except that it's July and perhaps only Elsie de Wolfe could make a fire on the hearth seem chic for a summer night."

"Nothing." Lila dropped her hand and the gauze floated back into place, the romance lost. "I said nothing."

Lila turned back to her friend, who'd abandoned the seam stitch she'd been tidying on a shock-pink satin cape draped over a boudoir chair by the fire, in favor of exploring their elegant surroundings.

"Oui! How could one think of a thing to say? We are in Elsie de Wolfe's private suite at her famed Villa Trianon. And with Marie

Antoinette's Petit Trianon a stone's throw away. It defies everything!" Amélie paced the bath with the graceful steps of a onetime ballet dancer.

The young seamstress ran her fingertips along the rich blue-green *boiserie* up to the fabric wallpaper, inspecting hand-painted peonies until wisps of her sugar-blonde hair—fairy-like and so opposite Lila's dramatic marron locks—blended in with the highlights of the pinks and blush whites around them.

"This villa is *très* chic and elaborate and . . ." Amélie sighed as if tossed in a dream as she turned back, golden eyes sparkling. "*C'est formidable!* Such a magnificent life Elsie leads. Even at eighty-one years of age."

"Her husband is Sir Charles Mendl, the press attaché to the British embassy in Paris, is he not? And Lady Mendl is American, so it seems our hostess's world connects oceans with ease."

"Oceans and palaces. She could care less for rumors. Instead, she artfully defies them. I believe that is the way to live, for a woman to decide how and with whom to enact her rich fantasies." Amélie paused, then said, "Have the important guests arrived yet?"

My, but Amélie had a knack for sailing her thoughts from outright shocking to schoolgirl innocent in a matter of syllables. Lila gathered the cape up from the chair, searching for the needle until her fingertips felt the cool metal against her skin. She sat on the edge of the marble tub to see to the stitchwork Amélie had abandoned.

"For a little garden party I believe."

"Such a tease you are, Lila dear. There was a procession of silver chariots at the drive to the Petit Trianon. Rolls-Royce after Rolls-Royce! Do you suppose *le duc et la duchesse de Windsor* are among them?"

"I should think the duke and duchess will be in attendance, knowing Wallis Simpson is such a close confidante of Lady Mendl."

"And what of the Rothschilds . . . Mary Pickford . . . even Coco herself? Did you know she is on the guest list tonight?"

"Of course. Isn't she always at a party covered by *Vogue* magazine?"

Lila smiled at her friend. "And she is Mademoiselle Chanel to us. We ought to remember we're climbing up from a bottom rung. *La Maison Chanel* as our employer means we are to blend into the background—not be a part of the big show."

"Speak for yourself, *chère amie*." Amélie gathered up her tiers of pale-blue lace and tiptoed to the window. She rose up on the peep toes of her heels, clicking her heels together like a little girl presented with her first china doll.

"Why, you beast!" She laughed and tossed a boudoir towel in Lila's direction. "They have brought the elephants out in a full circus ring in the center of the lawn. You could not think to mention that?"

"I must have forgotten a little nuance here or there."

"Nuance indeed. There are the bejeweled horses. And the torch throwers we saw setting up earlier. And I heard rumor—the pavilion down there was constructed under the direction of Douglas Fairbanks himself, just for tonight, with its striped awning and walls of windows shining out on all sides. Is that really a Waterford chandelier inside it?"

"Come away from the window. Someone might see you." Lila felt as though she were looking after a younger sister rather than working alongside a fellow fashion house seamstress.

"Tu me donnes une minute." Amélie tilted her chin down, eyes focused on the expanse of the grounds below.

"You need a moment for what? Searching for your young man, I take it."

Amélie bit her bottom lip over a smile as she surveyed the garden lawn. "Hector is not my young man. And he shall never aspire to be, thank you very much."

Lila raised her brow. "And does he know this?"

"Hector possesses little save for a winning smile. But he collects secrets like Cartier collects jewels, and that could prove useful. How do you suppose he found me tonight, knowing Lady Mendl needed a seamstress to mend a cape she'd snagged on her tiara? He hears the tittle-tattle from every fashion house in Paris. You would not believe the number of messieurs who slip a tip in his palm at these parties for a bottle of Dom Pérignon and a pair of crystal flutes. Why, he knows what happens in the boudoirs of France more than the fashion elite do, and that is saying something."

"And you'll use it all to write your memoirs one day, no doubt."

"Mais non. I intend to have books written about *me*."

A summer romance was one thing; that Lila could understand if not caution to tread carefully. But Amélie was not jesting. The combination of a wild heart and an angel face provided her friend ripe opportunity in their world of high-society parties and Parisian cabarets. It could prove a toxic combination if left unchecked.

Lila let her smile fade. "I'll ignore that comment, dear one, knowing that you do not entirely mean what you say."

"You sound like the older sister I never had."

"Then tell me, why could your love not be a member of the waitstaff? Or a gentleman from the mail room? If he's captured your heart and swept it away, surely that is a beautiful thing. Life is made of such treasures."

"You only say so because your dear René is on the guest list."

"Don't say that."

"One of those gleaming carriages out there belongs to him, no doubt." Amélie turned, as if the window had gone cold. "Not everyone is lucky enough to find what you have, Lila. A ring on your finger from a man with a mansion in his back pocket and an invitation to every fête in France."

"I have no ring. And he doesn't much care for these fêtes. I don't even know why he attends. He seems to detest the very society he's a part of."

"If that's true, then just why do you think he asked you here tonight, hmm? You may be the tender age of twenty-two and he only twenty-three, but that's quite old enough to be marriageable and for a young lady to flaunt a ring that says so. Wait much longer and you'll invite old maid status."

Lila snapped the thread with her pocket shears and exhaled as she stood, the skirt of her gown falling in a pool of champagne satin at the ankles. "I'd care not whether René were riding in the back of a car or driving in the chauffeur's seat. You know that. I hadn't a clue what his name was when I first met him. And I certainly wasn't angling toward any kind of marriageable status."

"Non? How convenient. *C'est un conte de fée.*"

"It's a fairy tale? I cannot think of it like that. Because this summer wouldn't seem real and it has to be. He is why I agreed to come tonight and why I wore this getup."

Lila gathered her nude mink stole along with their hostess's cape and turned round before the boudoir mirror on the wall. She clapped a palm to her cheek; the extravagance struck even her. For the sensible young woman she'd been reared to be, a fluff of mink and champagne satin—knotted at the shoulders and falling to lavish, liquid rolls down the back train—came at a king's ransom. Yet for this night, she'd plunked down six months of savings for the one outfit. "Oh, whatever was I thinking? It's far too dear."

"Couture too dear? *Phish.*" Amélie flicked her wrist as if the thought were already forgotten and began tucking folds of the train. "There is no such thing when it comes to men. Or fashion. Or the pride of the Parisienne. You have a rare talent. You ought to show your designs to Mademoiselle Chanel and be quick about it, before I pass them off as my own."

"Mademoiselle Chanel does not know I exist."

"Not yet. But she ought to, with the amount of orders flooding the salon for the autumn line. You could help plan next year's summer styles."

"And a war? What of that? Who knows where we'll be a year from now."

"Rumors . . . You forget, we have the Maginot Line. See? I do read more than just fashion magazines." Amélie patted the edge of Lila's long locks that trailed over her shoulder and softened the moment with one of her innocent smiles in the firelight. "Besides, war will never come. Paris will not stand for it."

Despite the blatant mash-up of a garden party as the world flirted with war, Lila was battling the same naïveté that such a nightmare was far off on some distant horizon. The French women defied war by sheer will and a refusal to carry the obligatory gas masks—who wanted a savior that would so clash with their couture? That was gauche. And not the way of the Parisienne at all. But even Lila could hear the pop of champagne corks in the gardens below and knew the luxury of avoidance would soon fade.

"Look at you—your pretty green eyes. They sparkle with *l'amour* tonight. And your smile? Perfect. So there. You are ready." Amélie pulled Lila's hand away from her cheek and replaced it with a quick kiss. "Marry him quick, chérie, or I might."

Though the night of a grand Elsie de Wolfe Circus Ball was an occurrence of epic proportion—and by some charmed miracle they'd managed an invitation to the grandest fête this side of 1939 Paris—darkness had settled upon the sky over the Villa Trianon. It seemed the fashion elite were gathering for an explosion of excess with their yards of satin and rivers of champagne, though it felt instead to the nagging pit in Lila's stomach like an odd sort of . . . good-bye.

They flipped the light switch and exited the boudoir, the fire left simmering behind the bronze horses on the hearth, with only a faint glow against the window. Even if René was to meet her here and ask a very important question out in the gardens below, Lila couldn't shake the feeling that something ominous was stirring.

Eventually every fire grew cold, and Paris had a thousand hearths at the ready.

———◆———

1 JANUARY 1944
61 BOULEVARD DE CLICHY
PARIS, FRANCE

Lila must be in heaven.

Nowhere on earth could boast such fragrances as the savory aroma of rashers sizzling in a skillet and the delicate notes of chocolate and caramel that clung to the air as in an upscale confectionary.

She blinked awake.

Sunlight.

Gold bled into the room from a high arched window. It warmed the space with a single door under a rounded arch and a table with four craggy, rustic wooden chairs. A small collection of ivory pillars sat half-burned upon the tabletop. A butcher's block and stove took up the plaster wall opposite, steam rising from the latter's surface until it clouded over exposed shelves and rows oddly stocked to the tall ceiling with foodstuffs. There was little else save for a closed rolltop desk in the corner and a small cot in which she lay pushed up against the wall closest to the hearth.

"It's good to see those green eyes again."

The greeting startled her, and she turned her head to find René at the end of her cot.

The winter sun glowed through the window where he stood, casting light on his simple trousers and work shirt with cuffs rolled at the wrist, hands buried in his pockets, and the very evident presence of relief in his smile.

He ran his hand through his brown hair, letting his palm catch at the back of his neck—telling. Soft. Simple. A little vulnerable, even. And unhidden between them. "I was beginning to wonder if you were ever going to rejoin us."

30

So last night really had happened.

A vague jumble of memories swam in her mind—the flight from the Hôtel Ritz. Snow drifting. Floodlights searching. Pain searing. The bread truck. An escape . . . and René. Through fits of pain and the lull of sleep she'd sought to hide from it, Lila remembered his face hovering over her—the first time ever reading fear in his eyes—and his arms gathering her up from the floor of the truck. She'd stared first at the ceiling of a starry sky surrounded by mansard roofs, then was carried through a maze of rooms similar to the one with beams and high arches they were in now.

René eased to sit at the foot of the bed, bracing elbows on his knees with hands folded in front of him. "Lila. Gunshot? I wasn't prepared for that."

She nodded. "I know. Neither was I."

"What in the world's happened to you?"

Too much to explain.

And far too many goings-on within her heart to feel she could tell him now. He wrinkled his brow like he used to when something had carved him up, those baby blues that had lost their easy sparkle instead waiting for her answer.

"What . . . ?" Lila's throat burned—too dry for rushing into conversation. She swallowed and tried again. "What time is it?"

"Classic. I'll ignore the fact that you just changed the subject. In that respect at least you haven't changed in almost five years." He rose on a sigh and poured a tumbler of water from a pitcher on the butcher's block, then returned to kneel by her side, holding it out to her. "Here. Drink. It'll help. It's been a battle getting water in you, so it's really the best thing right now."

She obeyed, the cool turned to heaven over the coals in her throat.

Without checking a clock, he offered, "I'd say it's just after three o'clock in the afternoon."

It was too late. Far too late. Lila had missed her Versailles rendezvous by more than twelve hours, and now no one knew where she was.

She sputtered over the swallow and held up her hand, rejecting any more. "Please. I must go."

"Go where? You can't even drink, let alone walk." When she moved to rise up, he edged closer, held out a palm to caution her. "Please, have a care—you'll pull your stitches. Do I need to remind you that you could have died last night?"

"Non, merci. You don't. I was there."

"Then at least tell me how you got into this fix. And how I can help you get out of it."

Sitting up was a capital mistake. Lila braced a hand over her middle when pain rammed her through, only then realizing she was wearing a long work shirt instead of an opera gown, worn seams buttoned over tight-rolled cloth from her waist up to her shoulders.

Somewhere between death and love, a girl still blushed.

Lila's cheeks burned and she looked up at him.

"I know what you're thinking, but I was a complete gentleman. There was a doctor and I swear I closed my eyes—" René set the tumbler on the table. He seemed to be making a valiant effort to ward off a smile. Always cheek with him, even years later, and smack-dab in the middle of a war. "Alright. They were closed almost the entire time."

"My clothes?"

"Burned in the fireplace. With your shoes," he said, then added a quick, "I'm sorry. We had to—the bloodstains. But I'll see about a dress for you right away."

"The coat!" A flash of ice water surged through her veins and Lila knotted her fist around the blanket. "My opera coat—where is it? Don't tell me you—"

"Calm down." He reached under the bed, pulled out a basket beneath her, and patted the woven lid. "The way you were holding on to it told me you'd want it back if you ever did open your eyes again, Luciole. Care to tell me why?"

The door on the far wall opened with a clamor, saving her from the brutal truth or the remembrance that a whispered "Luciole" could trigger.

The young man from the château strolled through the portal on a cloud of eccentricity—ebony crown curly and wild and his round wire-rimmed glasses perched dangerously on the tip of his nose. He nudged them back as he bustled to open the rolltop desk in the corner.

"The dressmaker's awake? Grand. Right smart way to start the new year, not dying at the start of it."

No mistaking the accent.

He's British?

He swept a leather strap out over his head and plopped down in a wooden swivel chair to open a cider leather messenger bag and center a typewriter on his work space. He emptied his pockets next to it: a tobacco tin, matchbooks, a pile of scraps of paper that he tried to lay out in some semblance of order, a tablet and pencil, and a bottle of sipping whiskey more empty than full.

"Did you hear a Nazi officer chucked it over a third-story balcony at the Hôtel Ritz last night?"

René bristled at the Brit's interruption. "Non. We did not."

"Where've you been, mate? It's all over the streets. Sounds a mite fishy to me though. He'd been shot first. You'd think if an officer was killed they'd shout it from the rooftops like they did last time this happened, to make a public example of the bloke who's done it—or at least to terrify the masses by executing innocent civilians. But no arrests and it's only whispers in the underground so far. I smell cover-up, but who knows for what."

Quite a forward notion to walk into the room with, as he tore open a box and began wrestling with replacing typewriter tape. Lila perked up, noticing the way René kept shifting uncomfortably and how the writer gave little notice to filtering his candor.

"I've about eight minutes to get this article started before I have to pull the next batch of macarons out of the oven. Wake me up from the keys if you hear the timer buzz, yeah?"

René tossed his glance back to Lila, giving her no clue as to why they were tracking the movements of their Nazi overlords. Though he had to expect the entire exchange left her properly confused. And interested.

"Uh . . . Lila de Laurent, this is Jean-Luc. Our assistant pastry chef."

"Manufactured names mean nothing to her. Paper may say Jean-Luc, but in this upstairs flat it's Sir Duckworth." He tipped an imaginary hat in greeting, then turned back to the typewriter. "And I prefer to go by the title of associate editor, if you please."

"Button it, Nigel."

Nigel paused, even though his fingers looked all too eager to blaze fire on the keys. He peered at René over the top rim of his glasses, then eased back in his chair, the wood creaking as he laced his fingers over his middle and settled into a casual laze.

"I thought you said she was your wife."

Lila connected gazes with René—only they two knew the real story where that was concerned. Or so she'd thought. Whatever Nigel was alluding to now was news to the would-be bride over a failed romance one summer before the war.

"She is. Or was . . . sort of."

"And you said we could trust her."

"We can." René ran his hand through his hair, frustration mounting. "Would you give her a moment? Lila just woke up and she has no idea what's going on."

"Neither do you, it seems. Your dinner is burning, mate." Nigel unscrewed the whiskey bottle cap and tossed it in a cluttered corner of the desk, then winked in Lila's direction before he downed a swig. "I thought you said this was on the level, if she was going to stay. That's what you told us when we agreed to this. You know the American isn't going to like it."

"It is on the level. And I don't care what Carlyle likes. I'll tell him to his face when he returns. She's with us, and this was my call. I'll take responsibility for it." René finally gave up, pulled the skillet off the burner, and waved at the smoke before he turned around again, his eyes tossing daggers at his comrade.

"Then shouldn't she know why she's here, René?"

"Enough!" Lila shouted and rose up, this time holding firm to the sitting position with a palm braced to her middle, regardless of the pain it triggered. "I'll thank you both to refrain from addressing me as if I am not in the room. I'm perfectly capable of stacking my own wits, thank you. And I hope you come armed with yours because I am *not* helpless. And I'm two full streets over from naive."

"*Est-ce vrai*, mademoiselle?" Nigel said, his accent drippy in over-the-top French.

"Of course it's true. Don't you think I've heard of the intrepid Sir Nigel Duckworth—reporter for the *Daily Sketch*, famous for mocking the Nazis' foibles with his British wit from behind enemy lines? He is hated in their parlors and talked about incessantly at their parties for how they'd enjoy nothing more than serving his head on the Führer's breakfast tray. But you, monsieur, are not French. Your accent is atrocious, you're wearing Algha spectacles, and you are drinking Glenlivet in the land of pink champagne. Give me a little credit by at least starting out with which hamlet of His Majesty's kingdom you're from, because we both know only the French write for *Résistance* and that is most certainly not you."

The men blinked for a breath. Exchanged glances. And the writer grinned wide, like the sun had just risen in his smile.

"Famous for mocking the Nazis' foibles with my British wit from behind enemy lines?" Nigel reached for a scrap of paper and scrawled something before he tucked his pencil back behind his ear. "Not a bad tagline at that. I am indeed Nigel—added the *Sir* and the *Duckworth* for a bit of panache in the byline. I am a humble servant of His Majesty, King George VI, assistant to our *pâtissier* here at Les Petits Galettes— mostly so I have a cover to write antifascist propaganda right under the grubby noses of the Boche—and am very pleased, I might add, to meet someone as clever as you. But how the boss man here managed to catch your eye is still a waking wonder. I'm afraid our American comrade will ask the same question when he gets a real look at you."

It seemed their boss man had reached his tipping point. René moved in front of her, facing the grinning Nigel with fists restrained at his sides, his temper having sparked a sort of shield-building action she didn't remember as part of his manner before.

"Enough, Nigel. This isn't a game. Anything you say now puts Lila at risk as much as it does us. I won't have you flapping your gums to feed your inflated ego. She's been through enough."

"And yet she knows about your underground publication of *Résistance*. Ask yourself, why do you think that is? In the meantime you've holed her up like a tart in the upstairs armory of a Paris pâtis- serie with Nazi officers crawling all over the dining room, and you still think she has a choice to make?" Nigel tossed Lila a contrary glance. "No offense, mademoiselle."

"Wait—we're in Paris?" She turned to René, suspending all belief until he confirmed it. "Your truck. It said *Montreuil* on the side. The boulangerie you're delivering for . . . it is in Montreuil."

"The truck is from Montreuil, perhaps. But Lila—this is war. I needed a vehicle to make my rounds so the Germans found me one. End of story. I don't know where it came from. And I don't ask ques- tions. I do what their pistols tell me to and live to see another day."

Lila stared at the door. "There are Nazis right down there."

"Oui. At least, there are every night when the cabarets open."

"And we're in . . . ?"

"Paris. That's right. Where else?"

"Montmartre. The windmill of the Moulin Rouge is right around the corner," Nigel cut in with a coltish tip of the eyebrows, as if that tidbit of information were somehow critical. "If you close your eyes and listen, you can hear the rehearsal music."

Lila's insides burned with dread far more than with physical pain. She'd done everything to get out of the city—taking a bullet in the gut because a Wehrmacht pistol had tried to turn her into a block of swiss as she ran away. It meant death to stay. And now, after everything that had occurred to free her, Lila was caught up in the spider's web again. Only this time, the stakes were so much higher: an officer was dead, and she'd been in the room when it happened.

In the end the Boche were sure to make her answer for it.

"You mean, you're working for *them*. The Germans."

"What choice do I have, Lila? We cater for the officers and their parties, and in turn they leave us be. The leftovers we give to the people in the surrounding neighborhoods so they can feed their children for another day. It's as simple as that."

Simple? Not simple at all.

In Lila's estimation the truth was harder to take than almost anything. René . . . a willing Nazi collaborateur? Working with the devils she'd risked everything to defy and vowed, almost with her life, to fight against? And all the while he didn't know she'd done it all for him.

A heartbreaking question triggered her to pause and shift gears. She considered Nigel—a Brit but also the would-be French character of "Jean-Luc"—and weighed something painful yet possible.

"When did you come back to Paris?"

René slid his hands into his pockets. Fast. And with far too heavy a sigh.

"Oh . . . Foolish, Lila. You never left."

"Non."

That one-word answer cut a fresh wound.

It meant that the time they'd spent at society parties . . . The tuxedos and champagne and his exquisite, perfectly timed smiles . . . Her girlish dreams for their future together in the summer of 1939 . . . Every single thing he'd told her had been a lie. At least he hadn't let it go too far back then. All she'd lost to him was her gullible heart. It could have been much worse.

Lila closed her eyes for a breath, pinching finger and thumb to the bridge of her nose, desperate to untangle her thoughts.

"Um, you were saying, Nigel—why am I here? Besides to be made a grand *idiote* for my illusions of the last four and a half years."

He shook his head and tossed a glare to René, as if sorry for something.

"Either war makes men out of boys or pastry chefs out of mystery men. That means you're up, mate. The answer is no-man's-land and it's not my minefield to cross. I'd rather face the parlor of Nazis right now than stick around for these fireworks." Nigel scooped up his typewriter and haphazard pile of notes to step from the room. "I think I hear the oven timer."

Lila turned to René when the door clicked shut and footsteps carried down the stairs. He stood by. Looking older. Weary maybe, and far more serious than her memory could ever recall.

"What was he talking about?"

"Lila, I don't know what design of Providence forced us back together in that forest last night or what happened to bring you to this point, but please know that whatever I did was born out of concern for you—the same concern I had years before. To avoid something like this at all costs."

"And what in the world does that mean?"

Those pools of blue that had once gazed on her with amour now only looked back with the scars of regret.

"It means war or not, I have no choice this time. We have to tell anyone who'll believe it that you're my wife."

CHAPTER 4

Sandrine vowed she'd forever despise that Édith Piaf song.

They passed the poster for *"Mon cœur est au coin de la rue"* as she and Christian stepped through the main entrance of the Gare de l'Est. The sultry melody played over in her mind, taunting with the lyrics of "My heart is around the corner," the gaiety more befitting a Sunday stroll through the Jardin des Tuileries than an anxious trek through a crowd, with train whistles and timetables ticking in the background.

Sandrine shook raindrops from her coat, defying the mist that had collected on the fur lapel of her bordeaux trench. Christian reached for her gloved palm, cueing in on the fact that frayed nerves must be getting to her because she was working to busy her hands—the chord of communion between their thoughts extending even to a walk upon a busy train platform.

He glanced up at the signage and slowed in the maze of people. "This is it—to board for Gare de Coulommiers."

Her heart thumped a drumbeat in her chest. "And then?"

"I'll go wherever the French First Army sees fit to send me."

Breathless, Sandrine surveyed the scene.

This was where they must say good-bye—a hapless corner with lovers and loners.

Newly christened self-serve buffets were left without enough men to staff them. Red Cross uniforms passed by, and soldiers bustled every which way as the country scurried to mobilize for war. They'd talked of it all the night before and Sandrine dreaded it come the dawn, waking in his arms as minutes bled away on the clock before he'd even opened his eyes. But now the scene was thrust upon them and these were the last precious moments they'd have as husband and wife before everything was poised to change.

Passersby bumped Christian from behind so his nose nearly careened into hers. And confound it—he smiled! He flashed that heart-stopping, boyish grin, and those soft brown eyes looked on her like he was courting her from across a social club instead of going off to war.

From trembling through every step as they walked past the Gare du Nord in the abysmal rain, to smiling and back again, they were an absolute mess. Of course Sandrine had to smile too. His attachment to hope was infectious and his ability to soften the rough edges made everything seem like it was not so dire.

Even if it was.

"Remember what I said. You and Henri will be safe with my parents. Don't attempt to leave Paris—not until we know what will happen."

Sandrine glanced around at his words, feeling the stab of regret that they could not go with him, even though his was a one-way ticket to the front.

"But some think that it may be the time to go. What if it—?" Sandrine sidestepped a man balancing a cart with two packed suitcases and a weathered steamer trunk—it was pause or get bowled over. "What if it gets worse?"

He nudged a thumb to her chin, bringing Sandrine from scenes of lovers parting—kissing and crying and embracing as rain misted the city—back to their own good-bye. "Do you trust me?"

What could a woman do but answer with her heart? Sandrine nodded.

"The Germans won't bomb the cultural sites in the city, not if they make it to France."

The thought hadn't occurred to her until that very moment. "You don't think that could happen, do you? What about the Maginot Line?"

"The Germans are swift. And smart, much as it pains me to say it. What I do know is that the arts in Paris will keep you safe, much safer than attempting to flee to the countryside outside the city. Keep the bicycle inside the flat, no matter how my mother complains. If this madness continues, fuel will be the first thing to go, and that bicycle will be worth enough men would kill for it. Don't go out after dark. Not alone. Not for anything. I'll send word to you once I'm settled and can get something to post. But . . . if I cannot get word through the army, go to Le Fournier. You remember it?"

"The boulangerie on the corner of Rue François Millet?"

"Go there. Ask for a Monsieur Mullins. He's the owner and can be trusted. I have made arrangements. And if I can send word through anyone, I'll do it through him."

"Why would you need to send word outside of the French Army?"

He didn't answer, just stared over her head at the crowd growing around them, reading it for goodness knows what.

"Remember the semolina I bought for you there, so you could make that bread from your grand-mère's recipe?"

"Oui. I remember, but what does that have to do with—?"

"Mullins says they have the best in Paris. Remind him of that when you go."

Small talk of war and semolina. How did we get here?

"Christian—I don't know about this. I've heard of what's happened in other places. The Sudetenland. And now Poland. Who knows what Hitler will seek to take next? It's rumored the German blitzkrieg is swift as bombs blow the countries to bits. And the people who are left standing? They begin to disappear. Those who speak out against the Germans are rounded up on trucks. Taken away. And never heard from again. Semolina would be a luxury when there is no food. No work. And they topple armies in a matter of days. Hours even. How can this be happening? Already it is a nightmare world."

"If there's any truth in it, and I pray there is not, it won't be you they come for. But here." He pressed an envelope into her hand. "Just in case, for you and Henri. There is help inside—an address you can go to and people who can be trusted. Keep it someplace safe. Don't open it yet. Not unless things get so bad you cannot turn back. Promise me."

The battle could be fought no longer; Sandrine let tears roll over her cheeks.

"Promise me?" The words were tender, far softer this time.

His request disarmed her fears. "My darling—forgive me. Please. Of course I promise. But I can't send you off like this, with worries of bread shops and bicycles. I'd planned in my head what to say a hundred times before dawn and now . . . I am a fool for trying to speak at all."

She shoved the envelope in her pocket and tore her gloves free, then pressed her hands to his face, desperate to feel the warmth of his skin against her palms. "We'll be strong, I promise. I will do everything you've asked. And we will be waiting. Just come home."

He gazed out over the tracks and the rise of steam from the train. Emotion caught in his eyes, showing in the choke in his words. The way he tried to look at the platform instead of back in her eyes. "Will you . . . tell Henri about me? I want him to know his father, even if I'm not here to watch him grow."

"I will. I'll show him photos. But you'll be back before he has a chance to miss you."

They both believed the lie as the train whistle blew, drowning out her promise with a screech that worked the platform into a deeper frenzy.

"I must go, Drina."

Sandrine joined the rest of the hopeless and became the crying lover—the pitiful wife haunted by the sounds of good-bye. She lifted up on her toes and pressed a desperate kiss to his lips, then buried her face against his neck, holding on to memorize the feel of his arms. "I cannot let go."

Another whistle. A final call. Scattering on the platform.

"Then don't. I will return," he whispered, the promise soft against her ear. "This is only good-bye for now."

Christian pulled back, those eyes that held such warmth glazing with emotion as they gazed deep into hers, asking for her to be brave. Trying to be brave for them both when neither felt bully for that.

"*Je t'aime*, Drina—*mon cœur.*"

And with that same good-bye he always gave when they parted, Christian pressed a hard kiss to her forehead just under the brim of her cloche and was gone.

The train swallowed him up, like so many others.

Sandrine stood with the rest of the ghosts on the platform as the locomotive pulled away, all haunted and staring with frantic searches of foggy glass partitions that rushed by, looking for their loved ones' waving hands through the open windows. Like the Édith Piaf song, it was another heart around a corner, and for Sandrine, a final look of amour as the rise of steam carried her love away.

———◆———

1 JANUARY 1944
16TH ARRONDISSEMENT
PARIS, FRANCE

Le Fournier was in shambles.

The chauffeur drove Captain von Hiller's auto toward the corner boulangerie and instead of shop windows painted over in the usual poppy-red lettering, the glass was shattered in a deep cut through the *u* of *Fournier*.

Sandrine stared as they rounded the corner to find the shop lying mournful and deserted—the horror of black ash and smoke stains clawing up the brownstone above the door and consumed windows devoid of glass, the swaths of singed curtains drifting in the wind. The front door, too, was burned black and hanging on its hinge like a bomb had exploded on the front stoop, with random sheets of charred paper and an overturned spindle chair blocking the front stoop.

Her gut twisted so she could scarcely breathe.

"I told you the matter was handled." The captain sat in the backseat with her, his elbow braced against the door so his fist cupped his chin. He looked straight ahead, not wasting a glance on the burned-out shop. "You did not believe me?"

The Nazis' reprisals when doled out were swift and severe. Sandrine should have known better. And she should have marked her steps with far more caution.

"Of course I did." She cleared her throat to set her voice in a stronger tone though her heart was racing. "It just seems a shame. When they had it, the brioche was good." Sandrine squeezed her fingernails into her palms so hard, she could feel the prick through her gloved palms.

What had become of Monsieur Mullins and his family? And she

was forced to comment on brioche when lives might hang in the balance. Heaven help them, wherever they were—and the poor souls who might be tied to the Résistance work they were supporting. She swallowed hard as the shell of the shop faded away and forced herself to face forward again with a veneer of apathy in place.

The view from the backseat through the front windshield was as Sandrine expected: a frozen city upon which night was quickly falling, La Tour Eiffel bathed in the darkness, and they the lone car on the road, to see it all past the nightly curfew.

The captain sighed. "You ought to consider moving closer."

His words crossed the border of familiarity she'd worked in earnest to put off for the last three years.

"Sir?"

"To a home nearer the Tuileries. Even if the garden views are taken up with vegetable production, it's still better than none at all. Or perhaps consider one of the streets near the Place de la Concorde, where the officers reside."

"Won't a flat come dear in that part of the city?"

"There is no obstacle for you to find a flat at an affordable price, not for an employee of the Einsatzstab Reichsleiter Rosenberg. And certainly not for someone who works for me."

"I'm thankful that working for the ERR should offer such opportunity. But my family is content in the 16th Arrondissement. You would have us move away from it?" They passed the shadow of the Eiffel Tower with its steel frame like lace punched in the night sky, and she said a silent prayer of thanks that it had flown by the window at just the right moment. "The Third Reich places great value on culture. Where else should I find more of it in this view as I cycle to the Jeu de Paume every day?"

"Today should not have happened." He finally turned, looked flat in her eyes. "Do not misunderstand. I have no complaint if you wish to remain where you are. But for Henri's sake, you ought to reconsider. I could . . . assist you in matters much better if you were not so far away."

"Thank you, Captain. I will consider it."

And of course she did, just not in the way he'd have imagined.

Sandrine thought of those last desperate moments on the train platform years before and how the lyrics of "*Mon cœur est au coin de la rue*" were so much less a curse now than they had seemed at the time.

They drove by nearly every memory she had in the city—past the bridges that traversed the River Seine, its current rolling with fury as red-and-black swastika flags invaded their Parisian sky. She'd walked across the bridges of Paris, hand in hand with Christian. He'd proposed on the steps of the Grand Palais—with no ring, no plan, just a blurted, "*Épouse-moi?*" in a breathless moment and twirled her around when she'd said yes. And the time Sandrine had told him he was going to be a father was as they sat in a little café in the Jardin des Tuileries. How it brought both pain and pleasure now to see it every day on the Place de la Concorde, to walk by the same café tables littered with Nazi uniforms instead of young couples in love.

The Galerie nationale du Jeu de Paume storehouse loomed before them—its classical visage and long Greco-Roman style cutting a regal form before them. High arched windows revealed a soft glow from its depths, enough that Sandrine could see soldiers carrying crates inside, and to her heartbreak, additional crates were carried out and tossed in a pile in the gardens. That meant even on the holiday, there would be no halt in protocol that was both immediate and fierce. Those employed at the Jeu de Paume would be forced to watch as "degenerate" works—paintings by the likes of Picasso, Dalí, Klee, Kokoschka, and Wassily Kandinsky—were doused in propane and torched with flames.

The car brakes whistled to a stop, drawing her back.

The captain waited until the driver opened their door, then straightened his uniform coat and surveyed the empty street at the same time he reached for her hand. Sandrine forced a smile in as faint a manner as would be acceptable and stepped out with him.

"Wait here," he said to the driver. "She'll need a ride back home."

"It's quite alright. I can—"

"There is a curfew, Mrs. Paquet."

"Oui. Of course." And that was that.

The captain marched past the guards at the museum's front entry doors, not even pausing to acknowledge their salutes but barking an order to a young uniform who crossed his path to take Sandrine's coat and be smart about it. She hurried behind, her steps matching his stride even as she shed her outer layer and unpinned her hat, then handed them to the young soldier.

Their curator, Mademoiselle Valland, came into view. She stood out as always, her own uniform of jacket, skirt, blouse, and the occasional tie prim and polished as the rest. With a tight chocolate-and-gray chignon at her nape, round wire-rimmed spectacles, and a no-nonsense manner with which she ordered the enemy to their tasks, her presence left little question as to who was in charge. The Nazis believed they were, and at first glance, that was true.

Sandrine knew better.

"Ah, Mrs. Paquet. We've been waiting." Mademoiselle Valland wasted no time in greeting, not even for the holiday. She turned a loose-leaf paper on her clipboard, scanned it for a moment, then gestured to a medium-size crate leaned against a wall. "Your crate is over there. A custom couture—1938 by my records. Another acquisition from the very important Édouard de Rothschild collection and sent over to us from the Hôtel Ritz."

Stolen from the prominent banking family's private collection, she meant but wouldn't say.

Sandrine unfastened the gold shell buttons at her wrist and rolled up her sleeves as she crossed the enormous open gallery space. "Oui, mademoiselle. And you wish me to do what with it?"

"Halt." The captain reached for Sandrine's elbow, grazing it just enough to draw her to do as he bid. He'd stayed close always—a most dutiful overseer—and up until then had been as silent as an owl watching from the hollow of a tree. "Is this not a waste of Mrs. Paquet's time? It ought to go to the garden with the rest of the degenerates."

Mademoiselle Valland broke in without hesitation, her heels clicking loudly against the high ceiling as she approached, authority in full force. "You are correct, Captain. While the Special Staff for Pictorial Art is indeed to focus on the paintings that come in, I told you when I requested you fetch Mrs. Paquet that my ledger states in that crate is a Chanel—this is *une robe française*. As I am certain you wish to see that everything is done in a proper manner for our records, sending a crate to the garden without due cause . . ."

Sandrine perked up. Their curator only used the phrase "due cause" to alert them when a prize was critical. So Rose must have found something in the crate that needed attention without the ever-watchful eye of the captain scrutinizing their every move.

". . . that is a scenario we must be ill prepared to entertain. Baron von Behr would not approve us cutting corners in procedure."

Sandrine bounced her glance between their master and the curator, standing toe to toe with him, she wearing a brilliant combination of subservience with authority in a brow raised over her spectacles, waiting for an answer.

"And neither would I," he snapped.

Of course. Nail him with propriety and process for his beloved Reich. He'll bow to it every time.

"Oui, Captain. We know this. It is why I am grateful for your leadership to guide us through such important matters. We must sort these crates if we are to stay on schedule before Reichsmarschall Göring's upcoming visit, and if your men are to get any sleep tonight." She looked up, dismissing Sandrine with a flick of her wrist. "Take it out of here, Mrs. Paquet, s'il vous plaît. There is an empty table in the archive room. This is beneath the captain's notice and we haven't time enough to fool with it."

For the intelligent officer that he was, the captain hadn't a clue he'd just been bested by a master saboteur playing the part of a humble art historian. He looked as though he considered changing the orders, but as the expert she was, Mademoiselle Valland had bolstered his ego enough that he accepted he must remain to oversee preparations for the Reichsmarschall's impending visit. She couldn't have been more in command if she'd checked her watch and tapped her toe to the floor while waiting for Captain von Hiller to follow *her*.

In their wake Sandrine nodded to the young art student who stood by. "Michèle? *Viens ici*."

The young woman was perhaps seen as plain by the officers' summation, with her mouse-brown hair and wide spectacles. Her eyes were ever doe-like whenever in the presence of their Nazi masters. But Michèle had over the last years of occupation emerged as a stealth weapon. Her petite form and diffident manner blended into every background, until she was needed, of course, and then she'd work under the radar of their notice with brilliant instincts employed.

They balanced the crate between the two of them as they hurried down the long hall, pretending that two were necessary to muscle such a load. But it was a crate light as a feather—either a dress was inside, or it hid something else entirely different, and Mademoiselle Valland needed it uncrated without the watchful eye of Captain von Hiller looming overhead.

They reached the archives and Sandrine flipped the light switch to illuminate several desk lamps, wide rows of shelves with boxes of whatnots, a random marble bust that owned a merciless break at the temple, file cabinets, and a large polished wood worktable spanning the center of the space. They deposited the crate on the table, and without needing to be told, Michèle clicked the door closed behind them.

"You heard Mademoiselle?" Sandrine asked without looking up, intent upon clearing books from the work space to a nearby sideboard as quickly as possible.

Michèle nodded, stacking spines along with her. "Oui."

"Did she find something in the crate?"

"Rose must have, though I don't know what. I was under guard by the soldiers as the crates were carried in, so I didn't see when she opened it. But the captain has been sticking to her like glue, and the only way to get him out of here was knowing if she requested your help, then he'd leave to go fetch you himself. She must not have been able to do anything with the soldiers around, or we wouldn't be in here now."

Though her insides quaked at being viewed as the pet of such a devil, Sandrine pushed the worry aside. They lifted the crate to the table and Sandrine drew in a deep breath.

"D'accord. Then we may have only a few moments to do this."

They sprang into action.

The crate had been started already, thank heaven—no additional tools were needed to pull the nails free from the lid. They lifted the wood to reveal an ivory dress box with *CHANEL* in bold black type. Unfolding the tissue lay bare its treasure inside: a gown in a tapestry of blush embroidery and brilliant tulle, a structured bodice overlaid by covered buttons down the back, and stunning plaits of chiffon that faded down to the tips of an exquisite, rose-gilded train.

"Lift it out carefully," Sandrine whispered as they pulled it from the crate, reams of blush chiffon and tulle falling in a shimmer over the rustic wood table.

"I don't understand." Michèle shot Sandrine a glance.

The bottom of the crate was empty—no painting hidden inside. No ledger or note or . . . anything. Just fresh planks of wood and a now-empty dress box.

"There must be something in the gown. Here—" Sandrine turned the gown over, running her fingertips along the seam at the back. "Go all the way down. Start at the end of the train and work your way up. If there is something to hide, it'll be much easier to conceal there than in the bodice."

They inspected the hem on both sides, working fast. Eyes alert. And ears listening for the clip of boots out in the hall as they ran careful fingertips over the stitches.

The unmistakable lump of something foreign ran under Sandrine's fingertips along the inside seam. She drew in a sharp breath. Paused. Then went again, slower. With fingertips smoothed over the edge she found it—*paper*.

Sandrine looked closer to find a hem with several stitches that had been loosed in too haphazard a manner to have been original on a custom-Chanel anything.

"Michèle?" Sandrine pressed her fingertips down, certain now she felt the torn edge of card stock sewn into the hem.

She looked up, eyes wide. "What is it?"

"Bolt the door."

CHAPTER 5

---

1 JULY 1939
BOULEVARD SAINT-ANTOINE NO. 57
VERSAILLES, FRANCE

Lila wove through the crowd of partygoers beyond the Villa Trianon's back doors. All around, frivolity reigned.

String lights laced the trees. Torches lit garden paths like fairies owned the night. Gowns shimmered in time with the sway of tuxedos and jazz music. Guests rimmed Elsie de Wolfe's grand circus ring on the lawn and an outdoor pavilion that encircled the trunk of an old oak. Lila passed waiters doling out the ever-eccentric menu of pork and scrambled eggs and a seemingly bottomless supply of champagne cocktails to keep the guests caught up in their revelry until the wee hours.

A tree-lined road lay empty beyond the back lawn, hugging the outskirts of the gardens. Behind it the Petit Trianon slept, hemmed in by a bed of perfectly manicured trees and hornbeam hedges.

Lila arrived to their usual spot first, sweeping her hand to brush off the stone as she sat on the fountain's edge.

A statue of cherubs danced with iron geese in its center, sanguine under the lullaby of trickling water and the party music in the background, as if the creatures hadn't a clue their tranquil garden could soon face the untold horrors of war. She dipped a fingertip to ripple the silver moonlight reflected off the surface of the water, tracing a figure eight through the light.

The crunch of footsteps on the gravel road drew her notice, and she looked up. René slowed to a stop several feet away, standing with bow tie dangling and his tuxedo jacket hooked over one shoulder.

"I know—I'm late." He looked sick about it, the usually dashing smile without its characteristic good humor.

Lila shrugged. "It's alright. I was too."

A breeze swept in between them. It toyed with a wisp of hair on her crown enough that it danced across the bridge of her nose. Lila swept it back behind her ear, then picked up her train to walk in his direction. "Lady Mendl snagged her cape on her tiara jewels. Imagine that."

"And they found the finest dressmaker in Paris to mend it?"

"They might have liked that, but it seems someone fetched Amélie instead. She has more flair than any ten fashion-house employees put together but can barely thread a needle. I had to help. Forgive me?"

He was supposed to match the cheek in her banter.

And he should have responded with far more enthusiasm when Lila stopped before him, pressed her hands to his shirtfront, and tipped up on her toes to drift a deliberately soft kiss to the corner of his mouth— their own unspoken *bonjour* a rhythm in place for some time now. Instead, even with the music and trickle of moonlight, his mood had darkened to pitch.

"While I hate to cover even an inch of that remarkable dress— here." He ignored the kiss, instead sweeping the jacket over her shoulders. "Can't abide you being cold."

"Why, this old thing? I'm surprised you noticed it." Lila half winked, saucy and light as she gathered her train in her palm. They both knew the champagne ensemble was couture and so had cost a king's ransom. "And how could I possibly be cold? I am wearing a strip of mink, you know."

He shook his head, deadpanning. "I could feel you shivering."

Maybe, but it was from the buildup of nerves instead of any real night chill. A jacket over her shoulders wasn't likely to soothe that.

"René . . . I know these parties aren't exactly your favorite notion. And this is the fête to end them all, apparently. But we don't have to stay. If you have your auto, we can—"

"I caught a ride tonight." He shifted his glance out at some lost point down the garden path. "In truth, I almost didn't come at all."

"Oh?" The train slid from her hand, rivers of satin pooling on the ground. "And why is that exactly?"

An explanation should have followed as to why he'd have stood her up, how he'd arrived at the Villa Trianon all the way from Paris without a car, and why he looked like the weight of the world had just broken from the sky and dropped down upon his shoulders.

"Because I knew what I must say."

"If it's the war, I've heard the rumors too. You wouldn't be out of bounds to show concern at a time like this. Even I've had a knot in my stomach since Amélie and I arrived, that this party is some great mirage of candor given the circumstances. But we have to hold on to hope, don't we? To trust that things are not as bleak as they may seem? This will all blow over and then we can get back to real life."

A simple movement. One sorry shake of his head, and it somehow explained the seriousness of what was battling inside him.

"We can't go back, Lila." Before she could question—even form words from thought to lips—he added, "I'm leaving Paris. Tonight."

"And you're coming back . . . when?"

"I don't know. Maybe never."

They'd first met at a similar party, turned circles on their own dance floor in those same gardens. It seemed so innocent now, meeting along the hedgerows. Walking and talking about everything and nothing. Dancing under the stars. They'd fallen in love under that summer sky, as Elsie de Wolfe shocked her guests with a sea of fireflies that had been shipped to France for one of her other special occasions.

Perhaps it was the schoolgirl in her, but Lila had fallen hard and fast for the dashing Touliard—long before she knew what that name meant. And those memories felt like a jumble of taunts now, knowing that other couples were lost in l'amour on a dance floor and they'd hit some sort of imaginary wall he'd built between them.

"Then take me with you," she blurted out, though when voiced, the idea sounded clawing and desperate instead of the least bit romantic.

"We both know I can't. Your parents need you here."

"If it's my reputation you're worried after—"

"I wouldn't do you the dishonor of suggesting such an arrangement."

"I meant that we could . . . get married. At least that's what I'd thought. It's why I spent six months of savings on this silly couture getup. When you asked me to meet you here tonight, I thought it was for . . . And then all the things we'd talked about. I know this has been a whirlwind few months, but what about our future?"

René flashed a quick look as a couple stumbled through the line of trees, laughing and thickheaded as they staggered onto the gravel road with their champagne flutes to guide them. He gripped Lila's hand, pulled her closer to the privacy created by the hedgerow, and dropped his voice. "You know my mother's family is Jewish."

"Oui, and your father was Anglican. What does that matter? You said you hadn't a care for all the posturing of society. And one day you'd stand up to your family if you must—if it came to it, you'd marry whomever you wished."

"What I want isn't important right now." His grip softened but still drew her closer. "There are rumors where the Jews are concerned— even half-Jews. You recall *Kristallnacht* last year? That, coupled with reports coming out of the territories that Hitler has already taken, is enough to confirm that this may only be the beginning. The Jews have become the fuse on a tinderbox in Europe. I shouldn't be telling you this at all, but if I don't do something now, it may soon be too late."

"What are you saying?"

"I have to get my mother and sister to safety, out of France."

"That sounds extreme. To where?"

He shook his head and stared out over the tips of distant trees, as if they held some unbidden answer.

"I don't know. London. Or New York. Wherever they can get a ticket—*if* they can get one. Even while France seems the only country willing to accept displaced Jews at the moment. We have an old textile factory just north of the city—on the edge of the *parc* at Georges-Valbon. My father closed it some years ago, but the building's never sold. By all accounts it's abandoned from the outside. But it has a freshwater source and a flat made out on the interior, and if there's no choice, we can remain there undetected until I can get my family to safety. It may be a failed venture, but I still have to try. Because whether we like it or not, war is coming. And eventually Hitler will extend his reach to France—to *us*."

She felt a laugh bubble up. "Look around you, René. This night. This party? Surely we're not ready for war. Most of these people will barely be able to stand in the morning. It's all glitz and glitter, and *Vogue* magazine snapping photos under the stars. No one's running your people out of France, not while they're attending to a champagne toast."

He looked on her with eyes in a slight squint at the corners—a wound he'd taken in at what she'd just said. "My people."

"René, I didn't mean . . ."

"I wish you could see more clearly what's happening beyond your world of runways and couture, Lila. If you did, then you'd know this is no garden party. If war does come, neither you nor I nor anyone else at this party will ever be the same."

"What does that mean?"

"It means you grow up and look past your naïveté."

Chastised, she bit back. "And yet you chide me when you're being naive yourself, and hopelessly stubborn. If you're serious about all this, you can't possibly think you can manage it on your own. Why can't we do it together?"

"It isn't safe. And I've—" He stopped short. Cast a glance to the lingering guests beyond the hedgerow, like their conversation was what? Taking too long? Or was he uncomfortable having others witness what had turned into a row? "I've said too much already. I can't involve you in this."

Can't nothing.

René Touliard was not the gutless type. If he was making a decision, it was because he chose it, full-stop. In that respect Lila knew him better than he realized.

Lila folded her arms across her chest, defying any soft answers from him.

"And yet you came all this way to . . . what? Lecture me for my innocence?"

His jaw flexed—never good.

"I can't marry you, Lila."

A million dreams died at the finality of those words.

He'd whispered as many promises in her ear over the months they'd danced, and talked, and sat nose to nose at café tables under the shadow of the Eiffel Tower. Amélie's girlish penchant for fairy tales had entranced Lila's heart to folly, and now she couldn't bear to have blurted out the truth, that she'd actually expected a proposal out of a whirlwind summer romance instead of what it was for him—a fling, and a horrible, unexpected good-bye.

Lila backed up, gripping the tuxedo jacket lapels in her fists.

"Luciole—"

She shook her head at the pet name, her heart seared by its mocking. "Mais non. You don't get to do that. Not until you tell me why."

"It wouldn't change anything. No matter what I might want, a future between us . . . *c'est pas possible.*"

"Impossible wouldn't have stopped you before. You said as much. What's changed?"

He stood still, his features frozen in the moonlight. "If I'm going to get my family out of France, I can't be tied down to a wife. And even when I do eventually marry, there are . . . certain expectations."

"Oh. I see." She stared blindly at the cherubs mocking her with gaiety from their carefree, moonlit platform. "And a merchant's daughter—a lowly dressmaker without a penny or a name—has the audacity to fall in love with a high-society prize that is vastly over her reach. So I may play foolhardy along with everyone else here tonight, living in some lavish dream, but if war really is coming, you'd rather go it alone. At least until you can find an heiress with the proper pedigree to take home to your mother. Do I have all the facts correct?"

"It's not like that. Not to me."

"Then perhaps you can enlighten me as to my imaginings. Because the excuses are beginning to stack up. René, you have never introduced me to your family. And mine has never seen you. They don't even know you exist beyond the mention of a nameless gentleman friend who's filled my dance card all summer. What's more, you always have us meet on the fringes of society, don't you?"

She looked at the fall of darkness around them as little clues began to string together. His furtive glances over his shoulder . . . The looks to the peering eyes of the elite moving about the party . . . The truth began to seep into every corner of her mind, and Lila couldn't fathom why she'd never seen it before.

"Even here. Tonight. We're hidden away in the gardens. Again. We've never even appeared together in public. After months, no one knows about us. Why?"

No softness remained in his features. René just stared down at her, offering no refutation as long seconds ticked by.

This was the way the world worked—his world of title and privilege and toffee-nosed society. And evidently, there was nothing more he'd say about it. Whether he believed in the impossible or not, he wasn't prepared to stand up for her through it.

"I have no choice. We have to end this."

"And if we do go to war, I thought at least we'd survive it together. I thought that's what this was, René—*you and me*. I was prepared to take on whatever the future would chuck at us if only I was at your side."

"If I could change this, I would. I'd do anything to change what is happening."

The hedgerow broke then, and a gentleman came round the corner at a pace next door to a run. His shoes slid to a halt on the gravel—sharp tuxedo, mussed hair in a deep burnished brown, and matching eyes that said he realized he'd walked smack-dab into the middle of a war that could rival whatever Hitler chose to bring.

The man eased up on the pebbled drive, clearing his throat with a cough. "I'm sorry, René. It's time to go." Then he looked to Lila, the oddest expression of remorse mixed with embarrassment covering his brow as he tipped his head to her. "Pardon, mademoiselle."

René nodded. "I'm just coming."

The man eased back, steps lagging in the moonlight.

"Your ride back to Paris, I presume?" Lila slipped his tuxedo jacket from her shoulders and held it out. "Here. Take it. I release you of any obligation where I'm concerned."

"Lila—"

"I won't make a scene. I can play the part of the chic debutante at least in that respect. I'll stay here in the shadows where I belong and let you slip away to find your next dance partner, or wherever it is you're being summoned to." When René made no move to leave, she added, "You said you have to go, so go. I can see clearly enough about one thing and that's how to find my own way home."

When he finally did take the coat, his fingertips grazed hers in a last pain-wracked connection between them. It forced Lila into the only thing a girl clinging to any last shreds of self-respect could do: she turned her back, squared her shoulders, and let him go.

What felt like an eternity might have been only a moment or two. She shivered under the starlit sky, arms frozen in a tight cross over her middle, too blitzed to cry or even breathe, listening long after the sound of the men's footsteps had faded away.

The twinkling lights in the gardens and the joie de vivre of the circus show were her companions now, along with the mocking sounds of gaiety on the grandest night Paris might ever see again.

War was coming; that was sure. But now she'd have to face it alone.

———— • ◆ • ————

1 JANUARY 1944
61 BOULEVARD DE CLICHY
PARIS, FRANCE

"Say I'm your wife? Then would you also say you've gone completely mad or just by half?"

René's reaction was far too reserved. He'd leaned against the fireplace, one leg crossed over the other, while he waited for her to reply to the notion that anyone in the room was actually skipping down an aisle. "Right. I can see you're . . . angry. Or confused. Understandable. Or what, actually? It's been a few years now and I'm afraid I don't know that face."

"Up until last night I thought you were dead, and now you—"

His face took a sharp turn and he stood out of his lean. "About that. Why would you think I was dead?"

Oh no. Backtrack. Fast. Or you'll have to explain far more than you ought.

"You broke contact, remember? German tanks rolled down the Champs-Élysées and from that point, I was on my own. You'd fallen off the face of the earth. But now years after the fact, I find out you're holed up in a Paris pâtisserie mere streets away, partnered with some overjuiced journalist and an apparently testy American whilst you feed Nazis crème brûlée in the dining room. How could you be this close and never think to come find me? Not even to see how I'd fared?"

"Believe me when I say I did everything I could at the time."

"Don't you think you owe me an explanation—a hundred of them, especially if you don't want me to gather my things and walk out your door this minute? Believe me, if it weren't for the fire burning up my insides right now, I'd already have gone. One tossed-out marriage proposal can't possibly change all that's happened. We've already been down that road and it's a disaster at both ends, even without a war to color it every shade of crazy. I haven't seen you in more than four years. What am I supposed to say?"

Always the thinker, she couldn't be surprised when René didn't respond right off. He'd simply listened to her tirade, remained calm as she blasted him—his eyes giving ardent attention—and refrained from commenting that she'd neglected to thank him for the very small favor of saving her life the night before.

He turned and pulled a spindle chair up to the side of the cot, then sighed as he sat, elbows resting on his knees.

"Even if I did deserve all that—which I'd concede I do—are you quite finished?"

"For the moment, oui."

"Bien. Because we've got a bigger problem to work out than my obvious shortcomings as a suitor. Last night I carried you from the street through the back door of this establishment, right past a patrol of SS guards."

Lila's glance sailed to the door—the only thing separating her from any number of SS who could walk through it, and who might recognize her face if they saw it again. "Why on earth would you do that?"

"I didn't have a lot of options, Lila. We were out past curfew, even for me to have justification with deliveries. They caught me lifting you out of the truck and that was before I knew I'd have to explain away a Walther bullet hole in your side. With that much blood, you wouldn't be walking on your own. So I wrapped you in my coat and carried you in as my wife. They bought the story that you'd had too much champagne at Le Chat—I did too—and had to see our sorry selves home from a night celebrating at the cabaret. After that, Carlyle went out to fetch the doctor and I kept you alive until they returned. And now here we are. But eventually that tale will get filtered up the ranks, and then they'll demand an explanation that is plausible or we're done for."

The last skip in the storyline seemed to trigger something in him. René cleared his throat. Pulled a gold watch and chain from his pocket, then snapped the cover closed and rose again. "It's getting late." He moved to the butcher's block, busied himself with arranging food on a tray. "You ought to try to eat something."

"I'm not hungry—" *Late.* Reality tumbled back, hitting full force in a string of reminders. Eating. Holiday. New Year's . . . *Oh no.*

"My parents! It's New Year's Day. They won't know what's become of me and they'll be beside themselves with worry!"

"I have to go out soon." René walked to the desk, brought over a pad of paper and one of Nigel's worn pencils. "Give me the address and I'll check on them."

"*You'll* check on them? Do you have any idea what the Germans are doing to Jews, right out in the streets? Doesn't that give you pause?"

"I go out in those streets every day. And I'm not immune to risk in this war. No one is—we just work to minimize it. So is there any reason I should worry that someone would come to your parents' home searching for you?"

"I shouldn't think so. They're staying in a flat owned by an acquaintance—I don't know the gentleman. Someone who fled at the start of the occupation and hasn't returned. It made sense as it was closer to Pa-pa's millinery shop, when it was still open. They could look after the flat and I decided it was safer to keep them hidden away there once I began . . ." Lila stopped, her thoughts drifting.

It would do no good to tell him the truth—she'd kept her parents hidden away, disassociated from her when she began working for the Résistance. One day, the Nazis could come looking for her, and she didn't want anything to point back to them—especially not now.

"Once you what?"

"Nothing. It's just, my father is a proud man," she said, and scrawled the address and handed it back. "What could you possibly tell him that he'll believe? I don't even know what to believe, and I'm the one in this mess."

He set the tray down on the chair by the cot. Bacon rashers, baguette, Anjou pears in a thin slice, hot tea—a king's hoard Lila hadn't seen in ages and wished like wildfire she could have stomached. But knowing they were Nazi-supplied rations, Lila would rather have eaten air soup than swallow anything that came off the back of one of their trucks.

"You just eat. Build up your strength. We'll work through the rest of this together."

"Together?" She ignored the tray's treasures, instead inspecting him. "I don't know how you'd propose we do that. Won't the Nazis wonder why all of a sudden you've produced a wife out of thin air? Won't they think that's a little convenient—or suspicious?"

"Not when they think I've been married all along. I wish this could be a romantic proposal, but all I'm saying is if we have to, you can pose as my wife in front of them. That'll explain a lot and it buys us time to figure out our next steps to get you home."

One might have wild thoughts when backed into a corner. Even wilder when the mind and heart and every frayed emotion were teetering on edge together as they were with the war. But it was Lila's heart that got caught up, tripping over something that might've been real. They hadn't seen each other in four, almost five years. Maybe he had fallen in love again—or for real this time—with someone else.

She swallowed hard. Looked at the shadow of her toes under the sheet. "And do you . . . have a wife?"

René waited until she dared to look up, then tipped his brow—just a slight measure that showed however innocent the question had felt, it hit the bull's-eye of a target she hadn't known was there.

"Non. I don't. But if I did, the story is she's been south of here for some time. Many left Paris in the exodus—too many never came back. I've made certain I'm forgettable enough that the SS officers don't care enough to inquire about my personal life. But I'm afraid that may change now with you."

René crossed the room to Nigel's desk, and with an expert nudge of the floorboards beneath one of the legs, he dislodged a plank. From it he pulled a book with a false middle, concealing a small stack of papers and, of all things, a pistol that glinted in the sunlight.

Lila stared at how confidently he handled the weapon and thought how until that instant, she hadn't known how in over their heads they both were. Orders had been levied where guns were concerned—strict ones that had come down almost immediately after occupation. All weapons were to have been surrendered in the first weeks. If the SS, who were so keen to float in and out of the pâtisserie, found where he'd hidden it, that offense carried a death sentence.

"Why do you have that?"

He didn't look up. "An insurance policy."

"I never thought I'd see you with a pistol. Seems an odd thing to keep hidden when we know the punishment if it's discovered."

The pistol he tucked back safe in its hiding place, lodging the book back beneath the floorboards. The papers, he gathered and brought to her.

"Not if it's to go with this. And I seem to remember you have an

FP-45 Liberator version of your own, although it isn't likely to help much if you get in a scrape. You do know you can only use it at close range?" René unfolded the papers and a small leather-bound book, then dropped them in her lap, the papers floating the remaining inches down to the coverlet. "You're here now, so we couldn't back out even if we wanted to. We might as well tell each other some version of the truth because we could be offering up our lives for it."

Lila thumbed through the stack and read, shock rebounding.

An identification card with his photo, stamped with *Federation des Maquisards* in blood red, with René Touliard and the *date d'entrée* inked as June 1940. On another: false identification papers with his photo, bearing the name Roman LaChelle.

"Where did you get these?"

"That's less important than what I have to produce. Remember the photo you gave me that summer in 1939? I've had it always."

Forget what that admission did to her insides. "I haven't thought about it in ages."

"Well, now we can use it to form a backstory for you. It could take a few days for us to manufacture believable identification *papiers*. Until we can work that out, we'll have to put your fashion career on hold and keep you here at the pâtisserie."

"I think it's on hold regardless." She shifted the conversation back to him and held up the Résistance card. "To get identification papiers, you said 'us.' Is this 'us'?"

He took a deep breath and those hands swept into his pockets again.

It was quite a tell, whenever René would look at her, that the one thing he was so clearly an expert at—peddling half-truths—was the very thing it seemed he hated to have done to her so many times over.

"You're a smart girl, Lila. I don't need to tell you the answer when you already know it."

"Then tell me something I don't know."

"I'll tell you anything."

Deep breath, and she dove. "Was any of it real?"

Without hesitation René edged forward and fired back as if her question had just lit a fire inside. "Would you believe me if I said every bit?"

"How could I? You talked of marriage and expectations . . . of leaving Paris and smuggling your family out of France. And all this time, you've been back here instead, working with the Résistance? It's too much to take in."

The question had tumbled from her heart straight out her mouth before any hope of a filter could catch it. Yes, she was sorry. Going-on-five-years sorry. For the guilt that had piled on and for the reasons she couldn't bear to look him in the eye for more than three seconds in succession. Sorry couldn't begin to go far enough, but her heart still begged to try to understand.

Lila's heart lurched somewhere inside, and she dared ask, "Tell me the truth. Who are you?"

He moved the tray to the end of the bed and once again sat in the chair opposite her. But this time, his eyes weren't distant. They were open. Honest. And it was as if no time had passed and they were back in the summer of 1939, once again naive to love and loss, and the ravages left behind when the two mixed.

"Are you sure you want to do this? Lila, if I open this door all the way, it cannot be closed again if you decide you're out tomorrow."

"Oui." One word she whispered, knowing full well what it meant.

"As far as the SS knows, I'm not a Touliard. And certainly not any part a Jew. To them I'm the subservient *maître* pâtissier here at Les Petits Galettes."

"How can that be? A pâtissier? It would take only one person to recognize you and report it."

"We bake bread too, you know. And who would recognize me outside of you? I spent most of my years in London before I showed up at Elsie de Wolfe's. Here I'm a part of an independent Résistance cell in Paris and with the Maquis in the Forêt de Meudon. We're an operative team of three. Carlyle—a captain in the United States Army who's been placed to work with contacts and feed intelligence information back to the Allies. Nigel and I are coordinating subversive communications from inside France."

"Subversive communications?"

"'Black Propaganda'—the shadow world. We collect, coordinate, and filter communications back to the American OSS through Carlyle. Nigel reports through Britain's Political Warfare Executive— the PWE in print, on radio, you name it—all to destabilize Hitler's movements in occupied France. And I contribute to the underground *Résistance* publication on behalf of de Gaulle's Free French here in Paris, and feed what I can back to his contacts in London. Our aim is to stir the Résistance through the spread of rumors and speculation, to embellish half-truths and diminish the German war effort any way we can. And to make certain we cover our tracks so the Boche won't know it's happening."

With the rush of information, words refused to come, so Lila nodded.

If it was truths they were telling, she'd rival him with hers. A fashion plate didn't run through a forest in the middle of the night, bleeding out from a bullet wound, and expect that she wouldn't have to give some sort of explanation if she lived to see the dawn.

"So what you're telling me is you're a spy?"

He shifted, crossing his arms over his chest like he'd just taken a dart in the bull's-eye.

"We arrogant Résistance fighters prefer 'operative.' But if you're asking whether we're employing the art of subterfuge to defeat the Germans, then oui. I suppose I'm a professional liar in addition to posing as a pastry chef. But as for the real René Touliard from that summer—the man you knew . . . ," he added, his voice treading toward a rough whisper. "He wanted more than anything to be able to tell you all of this. Years before. I can personally attest it almost killed him to keep it from you. It's why I wouldn't marry you. Never mind being a Jew, I couldn't let you tie yourself to me knowing what I was getting into."

He reached down and pulled her opera coat from the basket beneath the cot—the stained ivory an eyesore against his fingertips as he laid it over the papers in her lap.

"So, Lila de Laurent—I've trusted you with my truth. If we're really going to do this together as you say, at some point you'll have to trust me and share yours."

CHAPTER 6

27 JANUARY 1940
12 RUE FRANÇOIS MILLET
PARIS, FRANCE

Paris had been gutted of color.

Even around the corner from her in-laws' flat, Sandrine couldn't seem to find it. For all the hue and life and abundance of light that had once defined Paris to the rest of the world—even in the middle of a brutal, cold winter that had gripped most of Europe—it was evident by the street view that the City of Light had slipped into shadow.

They hurried down the sidewalk, Sandrine keeping up with her father-in-law's eagle-winged stride, dodging patches of ice in her heels and tweed pencil skirt, and doing her best to protect the last pair of seamed stockings she owned from brushing against anything that would snag the delicate silk. They passed shops of dingy cream limestone, with withered and frozen-out window boxes and signs in the windows indicating the presence of a bomb shelter inside. Roof after roof in mournful blue-gray zinc shielded the building-lined streets against a Parisian sky void of its customary singsong pastels. Only sad earthen shades seemed able to cling to their view, like a midwinter plague.

There was still no real belief by the populace that they were truly at war, save for the absence of so many of the city's men and the loss of the truly Parisian way of life. Only women, the young, and old men remained after the boys aged eighteen to thirty-five had been mobilized after the government joined Britain in declaring war. Food selection was already wearing thin. Prices continued a steady incline. And tensions rose as newspaper headlines screamed—the laissez-faire gaiety of the years before bleeding away as 1940 dawned.

Perhaps Paris was changing, but Victor Paquet would not.

Sandrine's father-in-law was known for his tall frame topped off by a gray trilby, his affable character, and the committed marriage he had to his family, his faith, his politics and the books he published about them. Hitler's Brown Shirts had been top on his list of objections for years. Now with the world in a slow crumble under Hitler's gauntlet, it seemed the same colorless canvas would paint the start of the next decade as well.

They bustled down the sidewalk through a world of gray to seek word about his son, and nothing short of an entire régime could stop him from finding it. A brass bell rang over the front door at Le Fournier as he opened it for Sandrine and led her inside.

Patrons marshaled along the blue-and-white-checked floor up to the vintage counter at the back wall. The people waited to make their purchases from a glass case offering boules, baguettes, brioche, and high-priced Lorraine quiche, though the view of baked goods was quite somber—only half of what it should have been and none of the pastries with their customary egg-wash or glazed-fruit finishes. No more delicate pâtisserie ensconced in the luxury of excess. Just flour, water, yeast, and salt baked into loaves, an easy fill for aching stomachs that seemed to arrive in a constant flow.

Sandrine fell into line at the back as Victor removed his hat—propriety, in his mind—and a firmness set his countenance that said worry had etched more than fresh lines on his face. If the way he turned his trilby in hand was any indication, the not knowing was eating him inside same as it was her.

Were Sandrine and her father-in-law here solely for bread, it might have been as doleful a Saturday morning task as any other. But months had passed. Agonizing days turned into weeks of checking and rechecking the post, only to find their lobby box empty of any word from Christian. It was only then that Sandrine could bear to tell her father-in-law the truth that though they suspected his only son may have disappeared somewhere into northern France, Christian had left behind a bread crumb with her. If necessary, they could go to Le Fournier and inquire, which was their intent now, her heart in her throat both for him and for herself the entire time.

Victor shifted at her side, impatience managing to paint over even the usual kindness in his visage with an iron jaw that shifted between looking up the line and making repeated checks of his wristwatch.

"You're certain they can help?" He stared ahead. Hopeful. Gaze darting between the counter and the snail's-pace movement of the line in front of them.

"Certain? I wish I was." Sandrine kept her voice deliberately low.

She sidestepped a woman who tugged along a little girl in a robin's egg–blue peacoat past them, the wrapped parcel of bread protected in her market basket like the woman expected vultures to swoop down from the sky—or the mob of anxious patrons lined up behind them to attack—and steal it away.

"What if we've been mistaken to come here?" Victor nodded to the woman, whose visage conveyed only "Hurry!" and "Don't talk to me!" as the bell chimed and she and the little girl bustled out of the shop.

"We couldn't be. It's one of the last things Christian told me at the train station. He said if he must, he'd send word to us through the owner here. We've had no word now in months. So our next hope must be to try."

"I meant that I should have come alone. I don't like the look of this. Everyone is on edge." He leaned down so he could whisper close and only she'd hear. But he kept alert, as if to shield her from an unknown threat that could at any moment seep out of the paneled woodwork. "Have you considered that Christian told you what he must at the time so you'd let him go on that train platform? To walk away from his wife having given her some hope to cling to, even if he knew it to be false? It sounds like my son to a T, unfortunately. He's sympathetic to a fault and would rather break his own heart than ever injure yours."

Sandrine gave a forceful shake of her head, the refusal to believe such a thing eager to bubble up from the pit of her stomach. Her body had been nagging at her for weeks, anxiety manifesting in the biting of her thumbnails and in startled reactions to sounds on the street, not to mention tension headaches that flipped her mind over itself, her thoughts telling her they must prepare for the worst. And she would have accepted the inevitable save for one thing. Her heart knew better.

It told her to cling to hope.

"Oughtn't we prepare ourselves?" He swallowed over a hitch on the last syllable. Hard. Over what must have been a lump of emotion trying to rise in his throat, and so he shifted his glance away from her to the counter. "Oughtn't we . . . think of Henri in all of this? He needs one parent to be assured in his life."

"You know as well as I that Henri is all I think about in coming here today—to find word about his father. But wouldn't we have received something if Christian had been killed? A telegram at the very least?"

Victor shook his head. "Who would send it? By all accounts Hitler has Europe in his grasp. If the French Army is on the run, who would have the time—or the method—to send word home to families about those men . . . killed in action?"

Killed.

The brutal finality of that word cut more than the truth might have in those moments.

Sandrine stiffened her spine. Her father-in-law might have been a limestone wall in nature, but what he didn't know was his son had married a woman with equal inner strength.

"It's getting worse—the panic. It's spreading like wildfire all over the city. All over Europe." Victor nudged her elbow, looking to the door and a crowd of patrons who'd begun to line up along the sidewalk. "Please, Sandrine? *Allons-y*. I will come back later on my own."

Sandrine surveyed the space behind the counter again. A woman in her midsixties at least doled out goods to the last couple of patrons in front of them in line with efficient hands and no smile. The shopkeeper himself nowhere to be found. And now a young girl emerged from the back room, from behind a velvet curtain drawn over the depths of the shop. She turned her back to the lobby, auburn hair hanging in a long braid that reached her waist as she unloaded sacks of semolina from a crate and stacked them in a neat little row next to jars of molasses.

War and semolina . . .

The thought sparked a memory of what Christian had told her.

"Just let me try—alone." For good measure Sandrine added a softer, "Please?" at the end. And where he ardently wished for word about his son, it seemed he could understand how different—and deeply felt—it was to long for word of a spouse.

"Alright. But I'll just be over there, oui?" Victor's impatience took him outside to a perch on the corner, where he stood and lit his pipe. He was watching with great care who came in the shop and went out and set a keen eye upon her through the glass of the shop window.

The woman next in line bought the last of the quiche and tucked a baguette in a basket hooked over her elbow, then breezed by until Sandrine was presented at the counter, with the cashier absent of charm.

"What for you?"

Sandrine hadn't even thought of an order. She tossed out the first thing she saw behind the glass. *"Une dizaine de brioche,* s'il vous plaît."

"A dozen brioche?" The woman eyed her, brow increasing its quizzical surveyance with each second that ticked by. "Quite an indulgence."

Sandrine opened her coin purse and thumbed through her money, took out at least three times what the purchase would fetch and slid it across the counter. "I believe this should cover it."

The woman cleared her throat and rang up the sale, punching keys on the antique cash register until the cash drawer pinged open and she dropped the money inside. "Anything else?"

Sandrine looked at the young girl, still stacking.

"I'd like to see some semolina," Sandrine whispered, tipping her chin to the flour sacks lined up on the shelf. "It comes highly recommended to us by Monsieur Mullins."

The woman stared back like a general, not blinking as she appeared to inspect whether Sandrine intended some level of cheek with the statement. "Monsieur Mullins recommended it, you say?"

Sandrine nodded and gripped her handbag tighter in her gloved hands. "I haven't had any in months and I hear it is the best in Paris."

"Do you now?"

"Oui. I should like to speak with the owner if possible, for the family of Christian Paquet."

"Paquet."

Sandrine swallowed hard. "I wonder if I may already have an order waiting in back."

The woman flitted her glance between Sandrine and Victor, who remained perched outside, checking his watch as his breath fogged in the cold.

"You and your friend out there ought to know that Monsieur Mullins is a reticent man. He doesn't take kindly to his name being tossed around. We are facing increasingly perilous times, madame."

"Oui. I'll tell him."

The woman snapped her fingers at the young girl. "Ana? A parcel of semolina for the family Paquet. See if we have their order in the back."

Ana nodded. "Right away, madame." She disappeared behind the curtain.

A gentleman appeared a moment later, a compact frame under a work apron, with bushy white brows and eyes that looked as though they'd enjoyed many smiles once but had tempered with time. He motioned her away from the line, to the end of the counter. Sandrine followed, noticing the line moved on and the rest paid her no mind as the gentleman boxed the brioche and tucked in a small bag of semolina.

"Mrs. Paquet?"

"Oui. I am Sandrine Paquet." She bit her bottom lip. Why the secrecy? There were no Germans about in France. No communists around either. Yet he acted as though spies were listening through every keyhole.

Why?

"I understand you are asking about semolina?"

"Oui. I am."

"We do not have an order for you yet. But I will watch the post to see when your next order comes in, and when it does, we shall be sure to hold it for you."

An order. The post. If word came in . . . they'd hold it for her, just as Christian had said.

It wasn't what a wife had hoped for, of course, but no word was better than ill news. So Sandrine nodded and opened her bag to offer what money she could.

"Non, merci. This is on the house today," he whispered, and pushed the box across the counter to her. "Your husband has been a good friend to us here. He once loaned me the money to get started in business, to open this very shop. And he stopped in often to see how we'd fared with the threat of the conflict coming closer."

"He did?" Embarrassed, as if she didn't know her own husband, Sandrine righted herself. "I mean, he never said anything, so I didn't know."

She'd known her husband was a good man, but often his kindness was something he kept to himself—even from her. Pride billowed at the thought Christian would help someone else, even as he was shipping off to war.

"Non, he wouldn't. He is a good man, and we owe him a great debt for his kindness. And I hope we shall see his family often at Le Fournier. I assure you that we will help you all we can. Now you know what to ask for."

There was no news on whether Christian was alive and yet Sandrine's heart began to beat with a surge of energy she hadn't felt for months.

It worked! Good heavens, Christian. That's what you were trying to tell me on the train platform.

As Sandrine accepted the box and excused herself to join Victor on the street, the only thing that kept going through her mind was the Édith Piaf song they'd heard at the train station that last day.

The lyrics of "*Mon cœur est au coin de la rue*" made sense now.

Strangely, they offered comfort, for her heart was indeed around the corner, in a boulangerie that might, if God had really heard her prayers, give enough hope to carry them through whatever was to come.

———— • ◆ • ————

1 JANUARY 1944
1 PLACE DE LA CONCORDE
PARIS, FRANCE

"Careful," Sandrine whispered, willing the even threads to remain in place while she pulled at the edge of the seam and the piece of card stock sewn in behind it. "We won't have time to stitch this up if it tears. And I'd rather not have to explain if it's noticed."

Michèle stood by the archive room door, hand working the knob, no doubt itching to unbolt the door. She peeked through the interior glass, through the window that looked out in the hall. "Hurry, Sandrine."

"I almost have it . . ." The satin gave, the stitches loosed just enough to release the treasure.

A note of heavy ivory card stock fell out in Sandrine's hands, torn down the middle at a rough edge, with *Hôtel Ritz* and *15 Place Vendôme* embossed in gold letters along the top. "There. It's out."

"What does it say?" Michèle asked, then in the same breath, "Someone's coming!"

Without time to catch anything more than that there were words scrawled in ebony ink across the front, Sandrine halved the card and pulled her right foot out of her oxford, then stuffed the note down in her sole.

Michèle took her usual cue to keep going in a seamless response and unbolted the lock to wing out into the hall. The archive door swung wide but she kept walking, as if she'd been given an order to hurry back to the crate sorting being undertaken in the grand storeroom space and was seeing to the instruction in the most dutiful manner.

"Captain," she said—loud enough that Sandrine could hear the warning—her greeting sharp and methodical as her footsteps echoed down the hall.

Captain von Hiller poked his head in, scanned the room. "Mrs. Paquet. You are finished?"

"Just," Sandrine noted as matter-of-fact as she could as she tucked chiffon back into the dress box. "I've sent Michèle out to help your efforts while I tidy up in here."

In her peripheral Sandrine could see he'd stepped through the door, but this time without his typical austerity in place. His hand lingered, fingertips toying with the knob Michèle had just abandoned. She waited until the stark *click* of the door snapped her attention up.

Never had he closed the door.

Never.

Not once in fact, whenever they two were alone. He was too married to his sense of propriety where the glorious uniform was concerned. He'd never breached the line she'd so carefully put up between them, even from their first meeting at the Trouvère bookshop . . . until now.

The card stock burned in Sandrine's shoe as he approached, slowing when he reached her side of the table. He trailed his knuckles along the table, moving in front of the crate.

"So it was a dress." He flopped a ream of blush embroidery over, giving the chiffon roses closer inspection with the pad of his thumb. *"Das Kleid ist sehr hübsch."*

He added a whispered something under his breath.

Sandrine had learned enough German in the last years to know he'd declared it favorable enough to be "beautiful" and that she didn't want to delve into any further conversation about the merits of the word—for a couture gown or otherwise.

"What would you like us to do with it?" Sandrine replaced the gown, pretending he wasn't right next to her as she sorted tiers of finery back into their box. "I agree with Mademoiselle Valland that it has been misplaced in the shipment to have arrived here at the galerie. And there is nothing else within the crate to indicate we ought to take ownership of it, unless you think it wise to send back to Mademoiselle Chanel at the Ritz."

"It feels a waste to have brought you out tonight for the folly of a dress and nothing more." His fingertip moved from the crate to dust the worktable between them.

"It's alright—this is my job."

Do it. Force a smile. Give him what he's after or he'll take more.

"I should have told Valland you weren't to be bothered."

"Thank you for the concern, of course. But I believe there is much still to be done and I should help." Sandrine looked up, parting her lips to a softer arc. "Shall we go join the others, Captain?"

Heart slamming in her chest, Sandrine calculated her only option of escape was to make light of the work out in the storeroom and to give the impression she longed for nothing more than to hurry back to uncrating for the Nazis.

A gross miscalculation.

The captain brushed his hand over hers as she attempted to whisk by, his fingertips issuing a gentle tug of the wrist to stop her at his side.

"Josef. Remember? I gave you permission to address me as Josef," he repeated, but this time with a softer entreaty that peeled back the layers of implication in what he'd asked.

Never. Josef *humanizes you, and you don't deserve it.*

He paused, a calculated tick of the head to the side, and offered, "Why don't you take it?"

"What?" Surely he could see her heart slamming beneath her blouse, or could feel the tremble of fear coursing through her as the corded shoulder strap of his uniform pressed into her shoulder.

"Take it—the dress. It is yours. Mademoiselle Chanel won't want it back now."

She cleared her throat. "I haven't a notion what I'd do with it. And there's no cause to wear it as my time is spent either here or at home."

"It ought not be shut up in a crate. It is . . . delicate. Too delicate for this war." He looked down on her with a connection that said there was more brewing behind the veneer than an encased wrist and shoulder nudge. "And far too beautiful to go to the garden tonight."

Heaven help her, but if Sandrine knew anything about men, she'd say he was very nearly searching for his words through a shot of nervousness. And that, perhaps more than outright affection or a blast of authority, made her spine stiffen like a shot. The coquetry in allowing her to see a shred of vulnerability was something he'd never come close to doing before.

"It would give me great pleasure if you would take it. A gift."

The gown shone in the light before her, its blush the haunting color of innocence. It was a symbol of everything she'd lived in the last years—of war, what it had stolen from the people of Paris, and how the women left behind were forced to smile as they endured the enemy's evil—just as she was forced to smile at him now.

The dress was supposedly a gift, yet the message was clear.

Sandrine stood silently, the skin of her wrist burning where his fingertips still held her. Refusing to accept it outright but knowing there was no clever way she could rebuff him and still keep him at bay in the future.

"*Das ist gut.*" He released her. "I will see that the driver puts it in the back of the car for your ride home." He left her then, alone with the dress.

Breaths hollow, door open wide, and insides reeling as his shoes clipped steps down the hall.

Tears glazed the corners of her eyes for how closely the encounter had flirted with forced submission. And how close Sandrine might come again if she was ever to find herself in the same room alone with him.

It was the first time Sandrine wished she could carry one of the crates to the garden. Given the opportunity, she'd have taken it out by herself, doused every inch of tulle and chiffon with propane, and not batted an eyelash as she watched the custom Chanel burn.

CHAPTER 7

4 SEPTEMBER 1939
31 RUE DE CAMBON
PARIS, FRANCE

Well, that's curtains, as they say."

Lila stood on the sidewalk in her cinched-waist Chanel suit along with Amélie, both staring at the *Fermée* sign that hung in the salon's street-front window.

Closed?

The floors of windows above the couture house lay quiet. Dreamy window displays that were always so swank had been pulled out, the characteristic pearls and mannequins in black-on-white palettes replaced by dark curtains drawn over the glass to block any view of the luxury parlors inside. There was no mistake about it— Gabrielle "Coco" Chanel had just closed her exclusive Paris salon, and along with every other seamstress on a bottom rung, they were out of work.

"How thoroughly disappointing. And it is nine o'clock on a Monday morning. What are we to do with our day now?" Amélie responded to her own question by straightening the cuffs of her blouse and tipping her rose-feathered chapeau lower over her brow to show what she thought of the news.

"It's war. This is simply the first wave of the unexpected that comes with it."

"This isn't war—it's a farce, that's what. I had three clients in my diary today. Who will telephone them to cancel? Shabby way of doing business if you ask me."

Lila stared up the street bustling with the ebb and flow of Parisians going about their morning.

The city was caught up in sunshine and a lingering summer before the calendar slipped headlong into autumn. Yet with glorious colors that had begun painting the leaves on the trees and the last blooms of the season holding tight to their window boxes, the city had gone gray in mood behind its usual veneer of gaiety. Now that it was true and France had joined Britain, they were a world at war—and on tenterhooks with what that might mean.

"Ah. *Regarde-la.*" Amélie tapped Lila's elbow, drawing her attention back by gesturing to a woman across the street. "She is not afraid, see? This is a Parisienne."

A vision of chic took her promenade down the sidewalk. Wrapped in a smart suit of canary yellow with a chapeau to match tipped down over her brow, perfectly coiffed chignon at her nape and full-seam stockings on display, she passed by them, composed—seemingly untouchable even without a gas mask—with her head high and a little puff of a teacup dog trotting at the end of the dainty gold leash in front of her.

"Mark my words: Chanel will return. And she will return for women like this."

They watched until the woman and the pooch had been swallowed up by the Lutetian limestone corner.

"You mean fashion is a matter of our national pride."

Amélie brightened. "Of course! You understand me completely, chérie, as usual. This is the time for Paris to rise and show the world that we will not take this lying down."

Perhaps not, but poise didn't do much to defy Hitler's bombs in the countries already under his thumb. Amélie's outlook was a positive one, and equally as infectious. But war was no garden party, regardless of how many young ladies stepped from the pages of *Vogue* to waltz by them on the street.

"Fancy a walk while we sort this out?"

"Oui," Amélie huffed, and hooked her arm around Lila's elbow to draw them away from the fading crowd. "And a drink."

They headed for a nearby café—the first one that popped into view on the corner. They'd gone there a time or two, sat at one of its *petites* tables under cheery, candy-striped awnings, with iron-grate balconies and red geraniums climbing four stories above the ground floor, and front doors that lay open, allowing the sea-blue tile of the interior to greet passersby on the sidewalk.

Amélie snapped at a waiter, "*Deux cafés,* s'il vous plaît," and slid into a chair at an outdoor table.

To sit and do something as ordinary as order cafés with war looming . . . it seemed defiant. Yes, chilling headlines splashed across the front of every newspaper, but the people were still promenading and riding along on bicycles. Buying bouquets from street vendors. Hooking wax paper–wrapped baguettes under an arm as they walked home from the boulangerie. And seemingly all affected in slight by a war that appeared a faraway trifle of a concern.

"I ought to look in on my parents. I haven't seen them in ages."

"You've been living your life, my dear. I'm sure they understand."

Understand, perhaps. What with fashion house parties and a full diary of clients herself, Lila hadn't time to spend with her parents as she ought. That had changed since René left though, and now with a calendar effectively wiped clean, the trek across the city to see them wasn't nearly as out of place.

No. Don't think about that now.

And don't think about him . . . Not today.

"I know. I've been so busy here lately. But they'll be unsure of what's happening with all of this. I have to help them."

"Oui, of course you must go. Give them my best, hmm?" In a breath Amélie shifted gears. Her attempt at sincerity was lost with her mind always calculating its next move. "I should telephone Hector, find out what that little scamp can tell me about the salon closing. If he knew about this beforehand and didn't ring to tell me . . ."

"Chanel believes that war is no time for fashion. I wonder now how many other houses harbor the same opinion and will close their doors as well."

"Let me tell you what is certain—the price of lipstick will double. That is the real tragedy in all of this." Amélie popped open her satchel and snatched up a compact to blot her nose, then swept a quick layer of raspberry rouge to her pout, kissing into her reflection. "What else is it our Mademoiselle Chanel says? 'If you're sad, add more lipstick and attack.' Well, I am not sad. Not yet. But I will attack if I must."

"I'd say we might want to form a plan of attack to find another placement. There may be a great number of those like us and all looking for work."

"You shall have no trouble—your creations are *magnifique*. Remember that custom Chanel gown you worked on for the Rothschilds last year? The blush satin and layers of chiffon . . . I still dream about it. It was the perfect dress. One day, I vow to get it back for us." Amélie smiled, staring up at the clouds, as if the gown-of-her-heart was drifting upon them. "If you can fashion creations like that, any designer would be charmed to have you in their salon. Or you could open your own house one day. Truly, I wonder if our former employer knows the value of the treasures she has just tossed upon the sidewalk."

"While I appreciate your devil-may-care attitude on the joys of filling clients' boudoirs with couture, I can't help but think of my father's caution after the Great War. He said the first things to fall by the wayside are the nonessentials. How does fashion survive if the people do not first survive to keep it up?"

"Who says couture is not essential? Fashion is a matter of French identity, non? You just stay here. I'll make quick work of this kind of talk." Amélie popped up from her chair. "Hector will know if there are any parties of note. We will go, and then we'll find a job worth our time—or a rich husband instead. Trust me."

Amélie shimmied off, disappearing through the front door of the café. She gave a little swish in her Chanel on her way to the telephone box and a smile at every gentleman she passed along the way.

Lila turned back to watch the street.

The Parisienne in canary was long gone around the corner of the limestone building. But others were cloaked under the same autumn sun, and the weight of what war could mean to them all. Secretly, Lila hated the ambiguity. The thought of darkness spreading over the City of Light was disquieting at best, but it was made worse by not knowing what was coming.

She could only pray it was not dressed in Nazi uniforms.

The waiter arrived, cafés in hand, and Amélie returned, a bright smile painting her face.

"*C'est très bien!* Hector has come through. There is a rumor of a party tonight in the 1st Arrondissement. Here is the address." She pushed a scrap of paper across the tabletop and picked up her café au lait, manicured nails shining bright against the white porcelain. "Success, non? We will don our finest and be ready to go by evening. Until then, we celebrate."

"Celebrate?" A smile—Lila's first one that morning, in fact. Her friend was just innocent enough to have seen a pink slip as a golden opportunity. "Amélie, I'm not certain celebration is the manner in which to approach current events."

"That is a broken heart talking, I think," Amélie countered, lifting her voice with a little singsong at the end as she dropped an extra sugar cube into her café and stirred it about with a delicate golden spoon.

Right. Maybe it was.

It had been months since her last words with René at the Circus Ball. And after, too many hours spent thinking. Some in tears and then scolding herself for falling to pieces over a man. Then secretly scanning every crowd for his face. Or at the handful of parties Lila had attended, peeking over the dance floor, needing yet still dreading the sight of him appearing with an heiress in his arms. And even as she tried to build up her self-respect once again, a little ping would hit her heart when she checked the post, just in case he'd broken down and sent her a letter.

But since July . . . nothing.

"If you're talking about René, he cautioned me about this—the war. He believed this would happen. I'd be the first one in line to go back to Elsie de Wolfe's garden parties, but we can't live in that world. Not now. We have to be sensible, don't we?"

"I know you do not wish to hear this, Lila dear, but you are best free of the Touliard sort. The money is devilishly attractive, but the way of getting it is rather gauche."

"You mean to marry a Jewish man?"

"I am sorry. Truly. He seemed an alluring choice to start. But I inquired on your behalf and though he has a name, few seem to know much if anything about him. He spent most of his years in London seeing to his father's business affairs, only to pop up again in Paris this past summer under a cloud of mystique. It is better to learn this now."

"Surely you don't mean that."

"Forgive me, chérie, but I do not believe you could have that association and a brilliant career in fashion too. I never understood the appeal. I supported you because you thought you were in love with him, but—"

"I was. In love with him."

I am . . . Oh Lord, I can't say it out loud.

"And why is that—really now?"

"Why? It takes a thousand chosen words to explain love. Because of the way he looked at me. And smiled across a party room. And held me while we danced. And he listened to every one of the dreams I had. They seemed important to him and ones he was prepared to support. He even wanted to help me care for my parents. What gentleman leads a romance with those words? But you know, it worked. I fell for it. Completely. And something just came alive in me whenever I was with him. I've never felt that before. And I've not met anyone like him since."

"I'll tell you what it was: an inheritance. That man had more of it than ten of these tables put together. And once you came down from that land of diamonds in the clouds, how long would you have been received at the parties had you accepted him and married into that kind? I say you are better off. And the sooner this Jew problem is fixed, the better it will be for us all."

Amélie was airy-fairy sometimes, but her opinions hadn't bordered such starkness before. And they were never cruel. Those words came dangerously close to both, especially as she toyed with a wisp of hair at her nape and stared off down the street, apathetic toward the entire group of people she'd just discarded.

And then the memory of the look in René's eyes when she'd once called them "your people" burned anew in her brain. The indifference Lila had once shown—it blasted her now with a layer of guilt that Amélie appeared immune to.

"You know, René was concerned after Kristallnacht last year. So much so that he was eager to find a way for his mother and sister to escape France. I don't know what's become of them now. I can only hope they got a ticket on a boat somewhere, before the Germans started taking out ships in the Channel. But I'd also hate for them to have to submit to hiding for the duration of a war. That's no way to live." Lila ran her fingertips over the address on the scrap of paper in the center of the table, thinking with her hand.

"For heaven's sake. Hiding from what? The boogeyman? And where do they presume to go? Into a well? Really now."

"Non—the family owns an old factory by the parc at Georges-Valbon. René said he thought he could hide them there if need be." Lila pinched the bridge of her nose, worries compounding. "Oh, what does it matter? Our paths aren't likely to cross again."

"Indeed." Amélie laughed, a generous smile painting her visage the shade of one clearly unmoved. "How dreary! A lost job or a lost man is nothing but an opportunity to find the next better one of each. We will not spend today lamenting an old beau's lot. That I cannot allow. So, what are we going to do? Cry in our cafés, or celebrate as true Parisiennes should?"

Amélie summoned the waiter and stared at Lila, the verve in her smile challenging with an unspoken *"Well?"*

To celebrate certainly was better than pining for a lost love, a lost job, or a world lost in the trappings of war. Salons may close and headlines may shout, but Paris was still Paris and the war was a world away. If there would be any opportunity for fashion to rise from the ashes of the conflict, they'd vow to be among the ones who would champion its cause.

"Celebrate. And why not?"

Whatever was coming, Lila may have to face it alone, but that didn't mean she'd face it without a smile.

"You know, I don't believe this café is enough. It is all about attitude, oui?" Lila glanced at the menu, scanning with her manicured index finger, then handed it back to the waiter. "We will have the raspberry mille-feuille, pistachio galettes, and the lavender-and-lemon macarons. Bring one for each us off the pâtisserie menu."

Amélie caught the waiter by the arm before he could hurry off. "I will take your best bottle of champagne, s'il vous plaît." She winked under the brim of her chapeau. "And make it pink."

———— • ◆ • ————

3 JANUARY 1944
61 BOULEVARD DE CLICHY
PARIS, FRANCE

Thank heaven there was a tub in the pâtisserie's upstairs washroom.

The water was ice when Lila dipped her toe into the filled claw-foot porcelain, but at least she'd been able to wash matted blood and dirt from her hair. And thank heaven the combination of stitches and bruising on her side wasn't as bad as her worst imaginings had tried to convince her before she'd actually seen it.

Lila dressed with care, slowly as she was alone, wrapping fresh bandages tight around her middle before she reached for the clothes René had left out for her.

A button-down dress of faded daffodil pin-dot—still yellow, but a good kilometer away from the canary vision of the Parisienne who'd graced the sidewalk years before. The yellow was pleasant and the fabric soft as she pulled it on. The cozy fisherman's cardigan paired with it had the added feminine element of pearl buttons at the cuffs.

But couture it was not.

Once upon a time, Lila might have turned up her nose at such plebeian attire. Now? She stared back at her reflection, the push-and-pull of her heart reminding her of all that had changed in the last years, even not knowing who she was any longer.

Fashion had once defined her. Or so she'd thought. Without it, who was she?

"Lila?" Knuckles tapped on the frosted glass of the bathroom door. She turned. *"Tu peux entrer."*

The door opened once she'd invited him to enter, hinges singing with age, and René offered her a faint smile in greeting. "Just me."

Lila stood in front of the medicine cabinet mirror and went back to cutting an uneven bob out of the last of her hair. She twisted to reach the mass at her nape—no good. Long locks fell wet down her back, tangling with the half that just brushed her shoulders.

"Need help?"

She gave in and nodded. "I think I'd better have, or it'll keep getting shorter. And then it'll make this war look like a small disaster."

René crossed the room, always with purpose, it seemed, behind everything he did.

"Here." He set a brown paper and twine–wrapped parcel on the sink before he took the scissors from her hand.

"What's that?"

"Fabric. Thread. Buttons. Needles. Measuring tape. Everything I could think you might need short of a sewing machine. The dress you're wearing was all I could find on short notice, but I figured if given the time while you're holed up here, you'd need another. And knowing you, I thought you'd rather make one of your own."

"Merci," she said. For all the peddling of propaganda and shroud of secrecy in their surroundings, she tried not to let the kindness of the gesture seep into her heart.

"Are you in any pain?"

"A little. But it's getting easier to move about."

"I'd wager you're hurting more than you'll say, but I brought extra pain medication for you too. From the doctor. It's in the parcel with instructions for taking."

"How did you find it?"

"Well, there's a lovely thing called the black market that Nigel knows a thing or two about how to tiptoe around, at least enough to get some of what we need."

"Oh. And you don't worry about the doctor having seen me?"

"Non. He's one of us. And he doesn't ask questions. We've learned that the less he knows, the better it is for all concerned." René ran a comb through the long hair along her neck, then made a clip near the top. The sound of the shears' cut echoed against the high ceiling—oddly sharp, and so final.

Lila closed her eyes for a breath, overcome by the emotion created as she felt the warmth of his fingertips graze her neck as he evened the line above her shoulder blades.

"I'm rubbish at it, but I can give this a straight shot across the back." Still no smile in his voice, but at least he'd managed to understand something of a girl's vanity and what she was losing with each cut. "I didn't realize your hair has so much wave in it."

"I can't remember it ever being this short, so I didn't know."

A cut. Another. And still another—the song of the shears kept playing, stripping away her old self, drawing her closer to tears with each lock that fell to the tile.

Lila was sure she'd have to mask the relief she felt to have him standing here with her. In the same room. So close she could see his unshaven jaw from that morning. And every thought of something so routine as a private moment between a husband and wife—the image of what they might have been—had died in her heart long ago.

She cleared her throat, desperate to talk about something.

Anything.

"Where did you learn pâtisserie?"

René did smile then. Obviously he'd expected her to lean into the depths of his activities in the Résistance. Or their SS officers problem. Or any hundred other things they needed to talk through.

Instead she'd chosen the most glaring.

"London." Setting the shears and comb in the sink, René stooped to gather hair from the octagon-and-dot deco tiles. He wrapped the evidence in a towel. "We'll have to burn this. All of it. I don't want it in the bin, alright?"

Lila watched him in the mirror as he tidied up their makeshift salon, until he finally looked back at her.

"London?"

He nodded. "A fluke. I had to leave Paris to learn about pâtisserie and picked it up in England of all places."

"You did say once that's where you lived before Paris. Were you there all the time—I mean, before you started showing up in a tuxedo at Elsie de Wolfe's parties?"

She shifted gears, taking them back to 1939 and the serious, smile-fading conversations he seemed to want to avoid. It was a subtle nod to the mystique surrounding him. He'd simply appeared at one of Elsie's parties and swept her off her feet—a mystery man with a past no one questioned because of his name and the size of his fortune. But she was questioning now. And in the silence between them, waiting for an answer.

"Oui. I spent most of my early years in London. But between there and Paris and building a textile business empire that spanned both, my parents just didn't have a lot of time for their children. And the only son and heir doesn't have a choice where learning the family trade is concerned. After my father's death, I had a responsibility to take over the business. But then with all of this . . . war meant I had a greater responsibility. So I came back to France in '39, that summer I met you."

"But . . . pâtisserie?"

"That. Well, we had a French cook." He shrugged. A little smile emerged—boyish almost, and just teetering on the edge of sadness, as if he was embarrassed to talk about himself during those years. "She was nice to me."

"Oh. It makes sense now, what Nigel said. 'War makes men out of boys or pastry chefs out of mystery men.' Is that you? A pastry chef, a mystery man, or both?"

A light laugh said he'd found a glimmer of humor in that instant and broken his serious character to embrace it.

"Mais non. I think that's all Nigel. Fancies himself John Keats reincarnate and has to be quasi-poetic with everything he says. But he actually enjoys the cerebral tormenting of the higher-ups in the Third Reich. The information we gather helps the PWE build the fabrications in material broadcast by 'The Chief' on GS1 radio. Nigel is one of his operatives on the ground. The Chief takes the information we send and puts his own color on it over the airwaves. Have you heard him?"

"I have, actually. That gentleman broadcasts some pretty shocking accounts over the German wires."

"Some undercover radio stations' transmissions originate from a thatch-roof cottage in a fishermen's village along the English coast, if you can believe that. But faux stations are popping up all over occupied Europe, so sly that even Hitler's armed forces have been fooled into thinking they're official broadcasts from inside Berlin."

"I'll have to remember to listen with a speculative ear next time I turn on the radio."

"Nigel's not likely to let you or anyone forget it. Hard drinking, hard smoking, and hard editorial—that's him in a nutshell. He contends we're the voice to countermand Nazi sympathizer "Lord Haw-Haw" and that's a noble undertaking. We have a time of it reining him in, but when he wants to be, he's a genius at what we're doing here."

"And the elusive Carlyle? What's he like?"

"A ghost. And clever, even if he does fancy himself in charge of the lot of us. Never stands still, that one. So the story goes, he managed to talk his way into a closed-door meeting between President Roosevelt and his cabinet at the Carlyle in '34, just because he'd overheard a conversation in a coffee shop between two old men who said it couldn't be done.

"He picked up the name after he was caught by the authorities and recruited into working for the American government. He's north of Paris for a bit, but I'll let his bravado introduce himself when he gets back." René sighed, the official air of spy talk turning a corner. "Look, I don't want to alarm you, but I went out for a reason that was more than what's in the parcel. We need to talk."

"Is it my parents—?"

"Non. I checked in at the flat and they're fine. I've told you I'll look after them and I will. That's a promise. But this is a problem that's developed here."

"Here. D'accord."

"There's a Wehrmacht—an officer. High ranking. A stickler for rules and regulations. He's a stone-faced tyrant if I'm honest, but his higher-ups like to entertain and have a sweet tooth the flavor of French pastry. He's come to rely on our catering for the officers' parties, and I've worked to build a rapport with him. Enough that we're given access—sometimes to spaces that can provide information we need to feed back to La Résistance, like the hunting lodge you stumbled upon in the Meudon. I made a delivery to his residence this morning. It seems he's heard about our little SS encounter on the street and has now shown interest in meeting my wife. And after an SS patrol has already seen your face, it's got to be you I present to them."

"I see. And when does this officer expect to meet her?"

"He could come in at any time. Maybe even today."

Her eyes must have gone wild, because he set the towel on the sink and with care eased his hand over hers on the edge of the porcelain.

"I promise—we can do this."

Of course, René thought he knew her, enough to say such a thing.

"You don't understand. I can't let them see me."

Perhaps the lost years between them mattered more in that moment than they ever had before, because he stood and looked at her with a calm, assured expression. It was as if nothing shocked him. He took in information, processed it lightning fast, and found a new angle to manipulate for the best outcome.

He gazed at her that way now—as if everything had shifted on a dime and he was ready to find a new path around a barrier. He'd assumed she was still the innocent he'd once known. Perhaps that façade had to crumble now too.

"Lila, if there's a reason the SS would be hunting a dressmaker with long hair and the telltale remnants of a Walther hole in her side, then you need to tell me now. And then we'll have to do our best to convince them that dressmaker is not you."

"What if it was me they're searching for?"

He edged a half step closer, stopping mere inches away. "Is that what you're telling me? The Ritz. The officer on New Year's Eve. That was you?"

Lila couldn't bear to look at him, but he was too close for her to turn away.

After a dreadful pause, she breathed out, "Oui."

"D'accord. Right." He sighed and leaned back against the sink, putting space back between them. Another problem accepted it seemed. "Did you kill him?"

How are we even having this conversation right now, so matter-of-fact about the snuffing out of a man's life?

"Non. But I am in part responsible for his death."

"We'll talk about which part that is later. But how do you know they're looking for you?"

"I don't. Not for certain. But they will because I'm . . . a *Résistante*."

If Lila had shocked him with the confirmation that she, too, was working in the underground, René didn't show it. Instead there seemed the tiniest twinge of . . . pride? He didn't blink at the admission, just moved on. Perhaps a spy with forged identification cards and a fondness for propaganda wasn't easily impressed in that way, not even from the innocent girl he'd toyed with marrying once.

"That much I guessed when you were bleeding in a bread truck. So you thought what? That I'd turn you in to the Jerries downstairs if you confirmed it?"

"Would you?"

"Non! And I hate that you'd even ask me something like that."

"The Paris network is infiltrated everywhere. Comrades are falling, being turned in by those they've trusted for years. The arrests are increasing every day. No one is immune to this risk, and I bring more of it with me. My presence compromises everything you're trying to do here."

"Well, that's where you're wrong. There is no safety with the Third Reich. Not anywhere in Europe. All we have is the grit to stand against the Germans. And I'm not afraid of them. So if we must, I can teach you to survive in their world just as I have. To blend in right before their eyes."

"But it's because of attempting to blend in that they're looking for me now. Eventually they'll find me, and when they do . . ."

"They won't. I won't let them. This is just one more task to work out in a series of many, that's all."

Lila shook her head. It couldn't be that simple.

If she dared run now, it could raise suspicion around him. But if she stayed, what was the cost? Her presence put René at risk in a way he couldn't fully understand—not unless she told him of the deadly mistake she'd made and how it had gutted her for the last three years. And that, more than anything, was impossible for her to do.

"I may look like someone you knew years ago. Maybe someone you even could have loved once. But the naive girl you danced with under the stars, she's gone, René. And the woman standing before you cannot go back from all that's happened since."

The pile on the chair in the corner of the room told the grim tale—a stack of soiled bandages, the threadbare shirt he'd loaned her, and the opera coat she kept close. Lila had almost died for what was sewn into its lining. She'd been ready to surrender everything for it. And now that she'd come so close to assuaging the guilt she'd carried for so long, there was nowhere left to turn.

"Look—whatever it is, I don't care. It doesn't change anything."

She shook her head. "But that's where you're wrong. It's changed *me*."

Lila crossed the room and lifted the coat, knowing he was watching as she split a corner of the satin and tore the hem free. She turned back, no longer battling to hold back tears. She let them fall free as she approached him, her fist closed around the evidence of who she'd become.

"You don't know me anymore. And you don't want to." Lila opened his palm, pressing a roll of microfilm into it. "Because they're searching for more than this—they want what's in my head. And they won't stop hunting me until they get it back."

CHAPTER 8

10 JULY 1940
8 RUE DE L'ODÉON
PARIS, FRANCE

Brakes squealed in the street, followed seconds later by fists pounding the heavy oak door to the Trouvère bookshop.

Sandrine looked up from reconciling columns in the sales ledger under the glow of the desk lamp as shadows of uniformed wasps flew past the bookshop's high arched windows.

"Ouvrez la porte!" More pounding and shouting from the sidewalk to "Open up!" and then, *"Maintenant!"*

"Someone wants in now? But it's not time for another quarter hour," Michèle tossed out from the kitchenette, from her usual place brewing morning café over the tiny stove in the back room. "What's all the racket?"

"I haven't a clue." Only Sandrine did. Or, her heart nagged that it did. It began to sink, for the orders were shouted in French as they would be for those inside to understand. But unmistakable was the accent with its *sh* and leaning on a hard *g* . . . *German.*

The Rue de l'Odéon had once boasted all the best stories on the Left Bank, and perhaps before the war it was true. But the Quartier Latin had been oddly hushed as of late—not bustling with the customary students, artists, and poets, or ardent intellectuals searching for their next inspiration. That was fast fading into a bygone world with each *librairie* that was boarded up along the street. It was rumored even Sylvia Beach's famed Shakespeare and Company was on the brink of closure—the 1920s fixture a haven for artists from Ernest Hemingway to James Joyce. Those names had popped into her in-laws' flat for their famed literary gatherings, before the war of course. But now, with each closure it seemed the Paris they'd known came closer to surviving only in 1920s novels and in the brave bookshops gutsy enough to continue with business as usual while the plague of Nazis encamped all around.

Now it was their turn.

Michèle emerged from the back, ducking her head under the low-hanging stairs as she stepped into the shop's front room, every surface laden with books—vintage and new—so alarmed she still held the steaming coffeepot in one hand. She braced herself against a stack with the fingertips of her other hand.

Sandrine stood as the pounding continued and the barks of "*Ouvrez la porte!*" grew more agitated, until she was certain the fists would simply tear the door from its hinges unless they obeyed.

"You must do exactly as I say." Sandrine pulled a cream cardigan over her poppy dress and hastily buttoned down the front. She eased the coffeepot and tea towel from Michèle's hand and set them on the desk, then pressed her palms to the young girl's shaking hands, staring her straight in the eyes. "Do not speak unless spoken to. Do you understand me?"

"Oui."

"You stay back here. I will go. And if the worst happens, run out the back door. Do you hear me? *Run*. And don't stop until you are home."

The walk from the little office desk in the back to the high arched glass and window displays—past walls of built-in shelves and the spiral staircase in the front room—seemed to occur in slow motion instead of the mere seconds it took her heels to click across the space.

Sandrine forced the illusion of calm, though the devil was knocking outside. She unbolted the lock and, with one final steadying glance back to Michèle's haunted visage peeking out from the back, turned the knob.

The wasps flooded in, a sea of uniforms filling all the book nooks and knocking spines to the floor with clanks and clatters from the butts of machine guns. Their ordered chaos was surely meant to intimidate and oppress any thought but total acquiescence. Sandrine knew it was their manner. She studied them, searching for whoever was in charge among the undecorated uniforms. And then *he* stepped under the low clearance of the door.

An officer with distinguishable rank appeared before her, an impressive show of gold litzen at his neck. He was young—thirty maybe. With viridian eyes far too direct and his manner a concoction of efficiency and matter-of-fact superiority that matched the firm jaw and close-cropped military haircut.

"*Où est le propriétaire?*"

His French was quite good, even the accent as he asked where the shop owner was.

"The owner is not here."

"Correct. Monsieur Hébert de Milles is not. And that is why we have orders to seek him out." The officer scanned a random stack of books, fingertips walking the spines. "You sell Kafka?"

They did. And knowing it, Sandrine and Michèle had hidden those books along with any Jewish author they could think of inside the fireplace grating tucked away on an upper floor.

"I'm not certain whether there are any editions of Kafka out for sale or not. We have three floors of titles here."

"And under new order of the head of the NSDAP Office of Foreign Affairs—Alfred Rosenberg—I have the authority to seize them all. Any Jewish assets abandoned prior to occupation or any shop selling degenerate titles surrenders its property to the management of the Third Reich. On both counts this shop is now closed. If and when de Milles does return, he must report to us immediately to offer explanation."

The whole of what "explanation" meant Sandrine couldn't guess, beyond that they were out of a job and de Milles was now a hunted man.

With the hammer of suppression already hitting the Parisian people—rations and curfews and laws meant to break the spirit as well as press them all under the thumb of German control—no job meant disaster if her family was to survive what could be coming.

"And who are you?"

She held her breath. "Madame Sandrine Paquet, sir. Shop manager."

"Papiers." He snapped his fingers, then opened a palm outward.

Sandrine moved to her satchel on the desk, feeling somehow that he was watching her every breath.

"Michèle?" She awoke the girl from a stupor. "Your identification papiers. Quickly. Please."

The girl obeyed, dipping into the back room and out again in record time, and they both produced them.

"And you"—he paused in scanning to look up, meeting Sandrine's eyes—"have an education?"

"Oui. English and art history. École du Louvre. And graduate studies at La Sorbonne here in le Quartier Latin."

Once he'd ascertained she wasn't a Jew, the education must have surprised him. The ice in his character fractured with a tiny flip of the lips that indicated interest.

"And Michèle Androit? Education?" He addressed Michèle, who seemed as though she would melt into a puddle if she had to speak at all.

Sandrine cut in, "Mademoiselle Androit is also a student at university. Art history."

"I see."

Sandrine flitted her glance between the commanding officer and the horde of soldiers making fast work of nailing boards over the shop-front windows, the light inside dimming as each one was hammered into place.

"Why do you work? Married women are not permitted. You should already know this." The officer noticed that his orders were being put into place with efficiency—the shop had become a cave of paper and spines in a matter of seconds.

"Oui. I understand that."

"Explain, then, why you are working in a bookshop with your education and marital status."

How much to say? What was too much and what was just enough to satiate the demand for information? She could say it was because she loved books. Or she loved her husband, and Christian loved books too. And being in the beloved little shop where his family had been dear friends with the owners all of their lives made her feel closer to Christian after the letters had stopped.

Sandrine swallowed hard, keeping her demeanor strong yet as submissive as she could. "My husband's family is in publishing. Monsieur de Milles is a colleague. We've been looking after things in the shop, as a courtesy while he is away."

The officer handed the papers back. But the pause that followed was not a welcome one. He surveyed her—however abruptly, it was there. His glance broke the authority he portrayed and dwindled down into the subversion of very real attention, of both her face and then the contours of her figure.

It was noticeable. Real. And alarming.

"It is a pity, such a beautiful woman forced out of her domestic responsibility to come to a place like this, owned by the scourge of Europe." He flitted a glance to Michèle, who dug her fingernails into the bookshelf anchored at her back as the steam from the coffeepot rose between them. "You are both free to go. Take only your personal belongings and leave."

And with that he was gone, barking orders to uniforms out in the street as the shop's wares were loaded into open vans parked on the curb.

They were allowed moments to gather their things—satchels and hats and Michèle's little potted violets from the window box. And then they were put out into the street. Sandrine wrapped her arm around Michèle's waist when she tried to turn around, leading them down the Rue de l'Odéon at a calm, even pace.

"Do not look back, Michèle."

"But the shop. What will happen to it? And Monsieur de Milles when he returns?"

"We must pray he does not," Sandrine whispered, keen to the feeling that they were being watched, ardently, by a pair of green eyes that followed them as they hurried away. "We must pray that God has delivered him safely out of Paris, never to return—not as long as the devil owns these streets. The world is not safe for a Jew."

For the strong young woman Michèle was, their first encounter with the Boche must have rightly blitzed her. Sandrine could feel her trembling, and she had to hold the girl up from falling after she nearly turned her ankle on a pebble as they crossed the street.

"The officer must have liked you." Michèle righted herself once they'd stepped up on the curb.

"Whatever are you saying?" Sandrine stared straight ahead, the rows of buildings sprinkled with the cold reality of boarded-up shops and cars with red flags proudly displayed over their front headlamps.

"Nothing. It's just that . . . he said you were beautiful, and then he let us go." Michèle stopped, garnering Sandrine's attention with a gentle squeeze to the elbow. "I only meant that you saved us back there. I've never been so scared in all my life. And I don't know what they might do now that they know our names—God knows. But you saved us today."

As Michèle dotted tears from the apples of her cheeks with the back of a shaking palm, Sandrine wrapped her and her pitiful potted violets in a hug. "Don't worry." She pressed a peck to her friend's temple. "All will be well. You'll see. Just go home. Stay inside. And tell no one what's happened here today."

They stood on the street corner, gathering their wits as sunshine and violets and tears were lumped together in a new world order. No, Michèle's words were not an accusation. They harbored no ill will, even if Sandrine knew what she'd said was true.

———— ◆ ————

2 JANUARY 1944
16TH ARRONDISSEMENT
PARIS, FRANCE

"What did you do for this?"

The accusations from her mother-in-law were bitter, fear laced, and nearly always ill timed. Sandrine had only just stepped back into her chamber when she was confronted by Marguerite, standing guard over the Chanel gown that had been hung in the boudoir closet.

"Do you not know me at all to ask such a question?" Sandrine breezed past her into the closet, taking the pin from her hair and stabbing it through the back of her chapeau before she set it on the dressing table.

Her accusations could be understood in earnest—Sandrine had witnessed the same atrocities as she, as it was the Nazi way to break the spirits of those they oppressed. Before the war a Parisian woman could not vote, work, or even open a checking account without her husband's say-so. To humiliate her now, propaganda posters fed the lie that she and her children had been abandoned in the basic necessities of life by the French men who'd run off to play savior by fighting a war they couldn't possibly win. Now it was only the German soldier who could save her. It was not by a blitzkrieg that Hitler sought to take over; it was by a prolonged, methodical effort to win the ravaged minds of the women left behind, and to appropriate all that was distinctly Parisian—the arts, haute couture, the very spirit of the French people—and repurpose it to become a higher form of the German ideal.

In all of this flowed the callous and crafty undercurrent of fear.

That fear now became the image of her mother-in-law, running her once-manicured—and now tired and weary—fingertips over the embroidered bodice of the blush Chanel gown Sandrine had uncrated. And she was so evidently intent on placing blame not on their uniformed oppressor, but upon the closest target she had: her daughter-in-law.

"This is not lipstick. Not bonbons or hosiery. This is different than the trinkets gifted to the officers' paramours. This is *couture*." Marguerite stared her through, eyes piercing in the reflection of the floor mirror positioned behind them. "You must have made quite a gesture to have received this in payment."

"This is enough, Maman. I am tired. I must sleep."

Sandrine collapsed on the ivory velvet footstool at her dressing table, ready to remove her heels, the scrap of paper inside one shoe still burning to be read. She'd had no time at the Jeu de Paume, nor in the car under the watchful eye of the captain's driver. This moment in the early morning hours had been the first—and only—she'd had for it.

"You did not go to the galerie."

And with that indictment, Sandrine dropped her foot back to the carpet—slammed was more like it—and stared back at Marguerite's reflection in the glass. "And how do you make that out, when I've been gone for hours on New Year's Day and forced to spend the holiday away from my son?"

"You went with him—*to* him! The devil who courts you. The job is a cover for your guile to get your pretty things. To remain in the class you married up to."

Marguerite stood in the shadows of the closet, and for the first time Sandrine saw what she held in her hand—a pair of shears glinted in the electric light that spilled out from the connected bathroom. She gripped them, fist white-knuckled, hand trembling slightly as she unleashed the fury of her accusations.

Sandrine turned on the stool, careful, with movements that spoke of calm authority. Weapon-in-hand and murderous thoughts against their overlords was a recipe for combustion, with her as the prime target.

"You don't know what you're saying. And for that, I shall forgive you. You look tired, Maman. Shall you give those to me and we'll say good night?" She stood and edged forward with her hands open to Marguerite—no sudden moves. Just calm, even steps.

Not sure what the motive of her mother-in-law was—mania? Fury? Pressure in a cooker that was about to blow? Any scenario could have fit the portrait of the woman, wild eyed before her, shears open and raised to a dress that to her was the symbol of everything that had caused the crumbling into their war-torn world.

"If my son were alive . . ." Marguerite leaned in, gritting her teeth as she raised the scissors toward the dress. "Christian would *weep* to see what his wife has become. I may be a remnant of the Marguerite Paquet I used to know, but at least I have my pride and my good name, which is more than I can say for you. You know what they call you in the streets? *Collaboratrice horizontale.* They whisper it as you and Henri walk by. And they watch from the windows each time you go out with him. They know what you are."

"Maman." Sandrine reached out, slow, to wrap her palm around the shears. "Give these to me, please. Let me have them and we will talk about this, hmm?"

Marguerite shook her head, her hair loosened from its haphazard chignon, gray fanning wildly at her temples. "You have destroyed your vows to your husband. To this family. To my husband's memory. And to God. For what? For lipstick and croissants. Rides in an auto. And pretty things to wear over your tainted body. If I could, I would shred every bit of that gown into a pile of rubbish at your feet."

If only her mother-in-law knew.

The truth? It was at her feet. Hidden in her shoe. The evidence that Sandrine played a dangerous, duplicitous game. To everyone—to her mother-in-law, to the hawk-eyed watchers in their building, to all in their neighborhood, and even to the Nazi authorities at the Jeu de Paume—Sandrine was a willing collaboratrice. A sellout. A French woman with a seared soul.

But to Mademoiselle Valland and Michèle, she was a comrade in arms.

They together knew the truth.

They together had already cataloged hundreds, perhaps thousands of pieces of art the Nazis had stolen—mostly from prominent Jewish families of Paris. And they together had decided to put their lives on the line to work for La Résistance. Not just to track the movements of the Rothschilds' stolen art or the bartered sales of pieces from the David Weill collection. This was not just for art. Or French pride. *Mais non*. For Sandrine, it was so much more.

It was a matter of the heart beating in her chest.

Christian was out there. Somewhere. Fighting to the teeth for his country, his family, and his God. Sandrine couldn't do what he'd done—go off to war. But she could fight her own version of it right where they stood. Defy in her own way. Battle the dark-winged figures of fear and oppression, biding her time until the enemy would fall.

Until she knew what had become of Christian, Sandrine could do no less than he. It was fight or die—wherever she could.

"Give me the scissors. *Now*." Sandrine held out her hand, bold and authoritative, as she demanded the shears from the broken woman. Once they were in hand, she let go of the breath that had been iced in her lungs and looked back, staring down at her mother-in-law through the shadows.

"You will not touch this gown, do you hear me? It belongs to the family Rothschild. I have taken ownership of it on behalf of the Jeu de Paume. It is my job to keep it in my care—unharmed and whole it shall remain as long as it is with us."

Sandrine took Marguerite in her arms as the woman crumpled.

For the loss of her husband. Her missing son. And the view of her entire world that had become the shadowed interior of a 16th Arrondissement flat haunted by coarse memories.

"Je suis désolé . . ." Sobs wracked Marguerite as the apology spilled out in guttural cries, over and over, through tears and lamentations that penetrated soul deep.

"Maman—you must trust me. We must trust each other."

"There is no trust left in me. It is dead. With Victor."

Sandrine held her as they slid down the wall to the floor, legs bare under their skirts, missing the Parisiennes' customary satin hosiery that was now rationed the world over and unavailable except for those who would do as her mother-in-law so callously accused. The scissors fell, bouncing to fall against a pair of Christian's dusty shoes tucked back on the closet carpet. And the dress made a blush backdrop behind them, painting their world in soft Chanel pink.

"Why must you read that book every day?"

The shift of subject came on the wings of instability, Marguerite's words muffled between anguish and tears.

"What book?" Sandrine tilted her chin down to look in Marguerite's eyes.

"*That* Bible! You are never without it. It is the only book left on our shelves, and yet its promises are hollow. My boy . . . and my husband . . . Why does He do nothing to stop evil men? Does He not groan over our cries of desperation? He does not hear us because He is not here. There is no hope left in the world."

"I don't have an answer—at least not one that will satisfy if this is truly what you believe. Except that it is not God's doing what is happening here. He is not indifferent to our pain. Men decide on their own whom they will serve, and if it is to court evil, God lets them go to it. I do not ask you to read the same book I do, but I will ask you to be brave. To trust me now. Without Christian or Victor or anyone else, we must trust each other to survive this darkness. Henri has no one but us right now, so we must work together to keep him safe."

Sandrine had already decided on the ride home from the Jeu de Paume, as the crate sat with her in the backseat—no matter what was to come, the dress would never see a burn pile in a garden. It was a symbol now. Of everything they fought. Of the war Christian was so bravely battling out somewhere far away. And in that closet, as his mother clung to her arms, they had only each other.

"I need you, Marguerite. Will you help me?"

"Then have me you must," she whispered, pitiful and quiet and staring at some lost spot on the carpet. "What will you do with it?"

"The gown? I will keep it safe."

The war would not best them. And the Nazis would never win. No matter what was to come, the dress would survive—Sandrine would survive and defy them to her core.

"But you will see. When this is all over, everything that has been stolen will be restored. I will hold this gown as part of that vow. One day, I will find its owner and we will give it back."

CHAPTER 9

14 JUNE 1940
8TH ARRONDISSEMENT
PARIS, FRANCE

Smoke drifted over the rooftops in the western suburb of St. Germain.

On 4 June it circled around points north at the Auteuil racetrack, Neuilly-sur-Seine, and the fashionable parc at Bois de Boulogne. Still more smoke painted the sky black after petrol refineries were blown up along the River Seine just a few days later, the government fearing the resource would fall into enemy hands. The French authorities declared Paris an "open city" and would not resist Hitler's advance, to protect the rich cultural treasures. Then they fled, and a frantic street carnival emerged as the desperate came out of hiding.

Parisians were forced to weigh the risk that more bombing raids were to follow. Lila had been among those waiting in barbarous lines at the boulangerie, with weary people lingering along the sidewalks outside every shop still in business. She, too, had been caught in the exodus that jammed city streets, watching as trucks and autos and even horse-drawn traps carried mattresses, the odd sight of suitcases balanced on weary travelers' heads, and any manner of raggle-taggle wares being tugged along by the fleeing.

With inadequate preparations by their crippled government—from too few shelters and the unavailability of gas masks to basic provisions wearing thin—it seemed all of Paris was caught up in a rush against Hitler's tumultuous advance. A mass of millions weaved out of the city on foot—or the fortunate, on bicycles—carrying whatever they could, from baskets to baby carriages. Discarded wares soon overtook ditches and refugees filled every high-priced corner at the inns as they encamped on all roads south of Paris.

All the while, the new breed of "refugee chic" emerged, with Parisiennes donning afternoon tea hats, gloves, and heels, and even in the sweltering summer heat, many had seen fit to layer on the best of their wardrobes to ensure they could keep all they could with the mad dash from the capital. Even Amélie had finally surrendered her grit and packed matching pink trunks with her best dresses the night before. She gave Lila a tight squeeze around the neck, tucked her white-blonde curls under an ivory straw chapeau, and rushed down the stairs from the flat they'd shared to climb in the front seat of a gentleman's car.

They fled in the millions and by 14 June, the city awoke to a subdued reticence without them.

The streets were oddly quiet as Lila hurried through the 8th Arrondissement that morning. It was as if a plague had swept through and consumed all of the living, from people to birds in the trees and stray cats on the street, leaving only a remnant of the few brave—or very foolish—who'd stayed behind.

A voice with a German accent repeated the same message over loudspeakers: A nightly curfew would be in force beginning at eight o'clock that night as the Germans moved in to occupy the city. Thereafter, the curfew would run from ten o'clock until five in the morning and apply to all Parisians. Lila hurried up the flight of stairs to her parents' new flat, chased by the automated overlord and the worry that she'd be too late to catch them before the day's events.

By the door a weathered crate caught her eye.

Nudged up behind a potted plant upon the landing, it sat covered under a swath of muslin. She glanced left and right down the hall. Empty. Not a soul stirred. Perhaps it was a mistake. Or someone's wares that didn't even make it out to one of the roads before it had been discarded in favor of toting something lighter.

She pulled at the cover and gasped—the crate was full to the brim.

There was no note, just a jar of honey and flour-dusted boules. Stalks of fresh celery and carrots, when the markets now seemed only to carry potatoes and a few wilted leeks per shopper. Rows of canned meat and sardines lined the bottom. A box of matches. Candlesticks. And a silver-plated Dunhill lighter balanced atop a small, metal jerrican next to it, presumably with the invaluable prize of petrol inside.

After slipping her key in the lock, Lila tucked her satchel in the crate and muscled the lot into her arms as she swept the door open.

"Maman, *tu es là?*" She called if anyone was there, then kicked the door closed with an ankle curled around its corner.

The flat too was quiet, as if no one was home to answer her.

The radio her parents so often kept chatting up the background sat idle in the front room, a muzzled guest in the dark. Dining chairs were snug in place around the table. China was put away, shut up tight in the built-ins against the wall. And bottles of unopened wine were lined up in their neat little row upon the sideboard, next to her father's chessboard that had been set up and forgotten, sitting in darkness under curtains drawn down tight over the street-facing windows.

No, no . . . Please tell me you haven't gone with the rest.

Not on your own.

Lila set the crate on the dining room table, the frantic pings of caution hitting her until she knew her aged parents weren't lost among the rest, walking some road of death outside the city. She bolted into the kitchen, then allowed her breath to release when she found her mother standing in her paisley dress and white apron, bent over the pale blue–enameled Deville against the wall.

"Maman. I called you. Didn't you hear me?"

"Oh, Lila. You're here. *Bien*." Ginette smiled and puttered with a matchstick in her fingertips, looking into the deep wells of the Deville's interior. "I was going to light the stove. Your father wants a cup of tea, but I can't find the right place. This flat just doesn't seem like home yet."

"It's alright now. You light it from the door on the side—here. May I help?" Lila took the match, struck it, and lit the kindling with the wood through the side door, then set the kettle on the hot plate in the center.

"Merci, dear. It has been a while since we've seen you." She patted Lila's hand. "Would you like a cup of chamomile?"

"Oui, Maman. I will stay."

How was it that in a year—one simple turn of the calendar—it seemed her mother had aged at least five or ten? She'd knotted her hair back in a simple gray bun. Those cheery eyes that sparked a warm gold and the visage that had always given off a youthful glow for her age had become etched at the corners and deeply creviced between the brows. She moved about slowly, rising on tiptoes to select rose-spray teacups from the cabinet.

"Did you know there was a crate by the front door?"

"Oh, oui. I must have forgotten with all the madness. Our new neighbor sometimes leaves *une caisse* for us if he has a good day at the market. But I think nearly everyone has left the building now, and I didn't want to open the door to anyone today."

"That's very kind of him. He must go to the market of kings. Some of these things I haven't seen in months, at least not without a price that would cost an arm and a leg to walk home with." Lila looked down the hall. Daylight shone under their chamber door, but that was it. "And where is Pa-pa?"

"Your *père* is shut up in his room. I'm afraid he is not handling this well—losing our home and our country at the same time."

Lila glanced at the windows. Drawing the curtains might shut out the sights, but the Nazis would still march down the street that day no matter how they hid. They'd still take Paris, and the rest of them would have to submit to whatever that meant.

"I know today will be difficult for him—it will be for all of us, Maman."

"It would have been anyway, but it was made worse yesterday."

"What happened yesterday?"

Her maman turned and crumpled, face buried in her hands. "They took the store."

"What? Who can come along and pilfer an entire store from its owner?"

"Who knows who they were. Some kind of French police. They said his leather goods would be needed by some provisional government and as a citizen of France, he must surrender them. But who really needs an old haberdashery, I'd like to know? Not Hitler. It is filled with fabric for ladies' frocks and yarn for children's jumpers. Why would they take an old man's life from him now, after all he's done for his country?"

A roar cut through the street below and Lila looked to the line of sunshine cutting down the middle of the curtains. It must be the procession outside. Only tanks and men by the thousands could make that kind of noise now.

"Oh, Maman. I had come with cheerful news in the midst of today. Though it doesn't matter now," Lila whispered against her temple, feeling the tiny shakes of a mother so overwrought with fear, it was coming out in all limbs.

Guilt chastened Lila for being a daughter so wrapped up in her own aspirations that she'd missed the lead-up to what this day would mean to her parents. To all Parisians. It was a nightmare.

"I was going to tell you that I've found a job at last. No more manning switchboards for a pittance or selling *parfum* for two days before another shop closes. This is a real job—Nina Ricci is reopening her house and I've been hired as a dressmaker for her new line. She says the women who fled Paris with all of this madness will return, and when they do, we must be prepared to dress them."

"A job. *C'est bien!* That should brighten this dreary day for your père. Why don't you tell him now? He'd like that."

"It doesn't matter at the moment. Not really. But I wonder . . . What would you think if I visited more often or even stayed on for a while? I could see to things and at least we'd all be together. And if I work, then we'd have some money coming in. Without the promise of any more crates being dropped at the door, it might help. What do you think?"

The door at the end of the hall opened with a bang, causing them both to start.

Her père stood in the light from the bedchamber, not weeping over his lost mercantile or searching for a cup of tea. Instead, Marcel de Laurent emerged in a horizon-blue uniform, the jacket and trousers impeccably pressed, with his French Army kepi cutting straight across a defiant brow. He was armed with an army-issue rifle tucked against his left shoulder, along with a swath of fabric bearing bars of blue, white, and red tied to the end of a broomstick shorn of its straw brush.

"Pa-pa . . . Where are you going?"

"To war."

"Pa-pa! You cannot." Lila rushed behind him as he bulled his way past. He went to the windows, threw open the curtains, and unlatched the door to the terrace that overlooked the street. "They will not let you fly that flag!"

"This is what the German kaiser sought, *non?* In 1914 he wanted Paris. He killed for his prize. And look—the Germans have finally won it for him!" He pointed to the line of artillery and the rows of men mobilizing down below. "They dare take the same route as we soldiers in the French Army when we marched home the first time?

They degrade France with this pompous action, and they spit on the graves of the fallen."

Their flat had a quarter view up the street, to a wide stretch of the Avenue des Champs-Élysées, where a sea of Hitler's soldiers had begun preparations for a victory march to the symbolic Arc de Triomphe. The road was lined with people on both sides, a brass band bedecked in uniforms had begun its setup beneath a grove of trees, and the plague of Nazi gray infected in a spread upon all the sidewalks.

"Look. You see, non? You see what is happening to us!"

"This is not the Great War any longer, Pa-pa."

But the words were somber—a weightless cry when she gazed at his face.

"How can you say this is not the Great War? This war is still ongoing. Our government? They have left us. Only the pride of the Frenchman remains."

For the few stories he'd told her and the many he had not, Lila looked at his tired face and could almost envision the ghosts of memories lingering there. Of brave boys dying in the mud at the Somme. Of trenches filled with men, old and young, prepared to defy the German kaiser's advance across a battle-torn Europe. For him to have survived when so many did not, it must have felt like the darkness had finally triumphed. And all the men who'd fallen at his right and been blown to bits at his left while he came home whole . . . In his eyes they'd all died for naught.

The world was right back where they'd started, only now the enemy had won.

"Frenchmen did not die in the Great War to see our country fall to the pigs. So you will move aside," he fired back, staring in her eyes with pinpoint precision. "And I will stand for the ones who cannot stand for themselves."

It was a small consolation that Marcel de Laurent, of the 37th Infantry Division of the French Sixth Army and veteran of the last

Great War, did not attempt to storm through the front door and single-handedly attack the German Army out in the street. Instead he stepped out on the terrace, head held high, confronting the enemy with his own brand of defiance.

"It is alright, Maman. Just, let him do this," Lila cautioned, as her Pa-pa raised the flag of the French Republic to wave boldly, splitting the sky out over the carved iron rail with its bars of crimson, white, and blue. "It will be alright. I promise."

In that moment Lila knew she must stay longer than for a cup of tea. They would never leave Paris now—at least her father would not go willingly, or he would never go alive.

Lila stood in the shadow of the terrace doors, her fist planted over her mouth as they watched the sun shine down on a beaten city and the Nazi sea flood the Paris streets below. Her father stood at attention—no salute but no fear either—his jaw fixed in steel and his eyes unafraid to shed their tears, as the parade commenced and the flag waved good-bye to the France they'd always known.

—◆—

3 JANUARY 1944
61 BOULEVARD DE CLICHY
PARIS, FRANCE

In Montmartre German soldiers flooded the shops come evening, when the pantomime of lights and cabaret music at the *maisons d'illusions* was in its full, riotous swing.

Armed with her new bob in waves cut to her chin, a pair of clear-glass spectacles, a simple gold band René had found for her to wear on her ring finger, and with a crash course in French baking that morning, Lila prayed it was enough to give her the unobtrusive air of a Parisian pâtissier's wife. Maybe she couldn't tell a *pâte à choux* from a puff pastry, but at least she'd eaten enough during her years of friendship with Amélie that Lila was confident she could box up any orders that came to the counter.

The other more pressing matter—how René was processing the existence of the microfilm—that was up in the air high as a hot-air balloon. He'd taken the microfilm and hidden it until later, when they could decide what was the best plan of action.

René had reminded her before they ventured downstairs, "Just stay busy. Show them you have nothing to hide. Be sure to look them in the eye, but only long enough for them to forget you exist as soon as they walk out the door."

Afterward, he slipped into some mode of focus Lila could only chalk up to the years of experience with this sort of nail-biting scene. He pulled on a white, double-breasted pâtissier coat and went to work, not connecting glances with her across the shop space even once. It wasn't until soldiers began flooding their way through the front doors and filling booths that René came up behind her as she stocked the few lemon curd tarts they had in the glass case and whispered in her ear, "Showtime."

René answered to "LaChelle" from several of the soldiers who appeared to know him. He held a common rapport, waiting on them with a balance of deference and distance. He never said too much. Never smiled unless appropriate. And he never let his hands grow idle. It was all work, work, attentive work. And for how delicate the situation, Lila could see the effectiveness of their play. For her part, it was a post behind the register though her side ached and she had to lean into the counter to remain standing more than once.

For the first hour she took the francs. Registered ration tickets. Gave change. And tried to be as unnoticeable as possible when she boxed up the luxury of pastries for the privileged and stood, calm-handed, and locked eyes with every Wehrmacht soldier who appeared across the counter.

René stepped over to her side, falling into the rhythm of a husband and wife as he brushed an arm around her waist and leaned in close so he could whisper in her ear. "The captain is not coming in. It appears he has an engagement tonight. That means we're spared, and you can go back up."

"D'accord," she said and unknotted her apron at the back, grateful for the reprieve.

René did smile then, a split-second grin that said he was proud of her and their little ruse was a success, at least for one day.

"We'll talk later? And lock the door behind you, just in case."

"Ah, LaChelle. Is this the one you brought in the other night?" A Waffen-SS leaned over the counter, breaking the moment in two. "You have a new flavor of tart in the shop. Is she for sale?"

Lila could feel every muscle tense in René's arm as the soldier edged around the end of the counter, stopping a foot away from the two behind it. He smiled through the reek of intoxication, eyeing Lila as he leaned against a pie case and reached for a cigarette from his pocket.

"Who is this pretty thing? I'd like an introduction. What is your name?"

"Avril LaChelle." She found her voice, the name foreign as it fell from her lips.

René edged in front of Lila, slow and steady. "She is my wife."

"You are married, LaChelle?" The soldier laughed, calling to a booth with a handful of uniforms and ladies in chic dress. All eyes turned in the general direction of the tension brewing at the counter. Hand gripping her wrist like a vise, he tugged Lila toward him. "Get this— the pie man here is married. Did you know? To a petite French tart."

Another uniform happened by on his way to the phone box in the back of the dining room and stopped, intrigued by his comrade's interest. "Ah—leave them. We haven't much time left before we have to be back at barracks. You want to waste it now?"

"I could share it, with the tarts at the front of the shop and at the back." His imbalance took over at a booming laugh, the cigarette drooping from his bottom lip. In swift reaction he tried to catch it but instead tipped the pie case until it gave way and shoved Lila's side against the counter as it crashed to the floor.

The force of the impact knocked the breath out of her, inflaming her wound until Lila almost couldn't stand. Her first thought was her stitches—they'd pull, she'd bleed, and the soldiers would know. But her second, equally frightening awareness was of the intensity that had taken over René's features.

He became another person. If he'd had their hidden pistol in his hand at that moment, Lila hadn't any doubt he'd have used it.

The tension spiked as René wrapped his grip around a cutlery knife hidden under the counter and the soldier's wounded pride showed with his uniform doused in lemon curd and confectioner's sugar. The throng of uniforms in the booth across the dining room edged to stand, and the ladies traded smiles, all noticing the ruckus that had stilled the back of the shop to silence.

Nigel swept out from the bakery kitchen at once and Lila looked up, time enough to see him wink in her direction as he carried a tray of fresh macarons and then promptly dropped them in full view of the shop. The clatter eased the tension in the dining room, creating laughter and whistles and applause from the jeering guests.

"Oh! Look at this. What have I done?" Nigel lamented with an overworked sense of woe akin to a silent film star and began sweeping the cookies in a rainbow of colors into the apron tied at his waist. "Free macarons, if any soldiers would like the ones left on the tray. My apologies."

"Just clean it up, Jean-Luc." René tossed a tea towel in his direction, which landed on Nigel's shoulder. "Be quick about it."

"Oui, Monsieur LaChelle. Right away." He turned to the officer standing off to the side, who had stopped midstride on his way to the phone box. "My apologies, sir. For the disturbance."

The officer rolled his eyes, waving him off as he ventured back to make his call.

Lila stood by, watching as the ruse played out and the perfectly capable British intelligence officer who was Nigel Duckworth handed out macarons to Nazis and allowed himself to become their definition of a bumbling French fool.

The display gave Lila a chance to peek down at her side.

Blood.

Drops had seeped through the pin-dots, with small but noticeable blotches of crimson. She did all she could think in that instant: brush up against a bowl of jam at the pastry station behind them, flipping the rim so it would upturn and spread a raspberry stain down the front of her dress.

"Je suis désolé." She was terse and firm as she turned and apologized to the soldier as the jam dripped from her skirt to the floor. "What a mess I've made of the counter. I'll just go clean this up."

Lila edged between the soldier and René, using her apron to hide the knife and wipe down the counter, removing shards of glass that had broken apart on its top as she went.

"A macaron for you? And your friend after he finishes his telephone call?" Nigel stepped up to the soldier, holding a rose-colored macaron with bright raspberry filling and colored cane sugar dusting the outside. "Or a dozen of them for your party? On the house."

"Ja. Das ist gut," he said, still staring René down as he swept his hair back over his crown with a cool palm, then brushed sugar and tart bits from his front with both hands.

"The front booth, oui?" Nigel urged.

The uniforms sat back down, defused by the promise of sweets and the eye rolls of their ladies. They waved the soldier back, laughing over his folly a moment later as Nigel swept them into his world of sweets.

Lila hurried upstairs, hands shaking until she reached the washroom. René followed a moment later, breaths ragged as he stopped in the doorway. "Did he hurt you?"

"You mean more than I already was?" Lila peeled the dress back by the button in her middle, turning to a three-quarter profile to show him the spots of blood that had seeped through her bandage. She braced her hand on the sink and hung her head. He was at her side then, arm anchored at the small of her back to hold her up.

"I'm alright. I think it scared me more than anything. That was close."

"Too close. But that was quick thinking on your part, with the jam." René shook his head, even releasing a relieved laugh while they both came down from the adrenaline rush that had spiked the encounter. "You can certainly keep your wits in check longer than I, at least when I see someone try to put his hands on you. Pretending you're my wife is proving harder than I thought."

Lila looked up, their eyes locking, her breath quickening, altogether swept by the fire of emotions branding the moment. They slowed, calming together with his arm still anchored around her waist.

"Is this going to be a problem, René? Working together? And trying to hide me at the same time I have to be seen? Because you know you can't fight every uniform in Paris."

"Non? I suppose I can still try."

"What about the macarons? Won't you lose out on them? You must be the last pâtisserie in Paris to have rations like that."

René smiled wide. "We'd only lose out if the Boche didn't eat them. Nigel makes it a point to spit in at least one batch a day. They'd have been wasted otherwise because we won't eat anything that comes off their trucks—on principle. This way, Carlyle and I get to linger and listen for information, and Nigel gets his daily revenge with enough of a boost to carry through his next article. Everybody wins."

Their clothes were painted with tarts and jam and the world was taken over by darkness right downstairs, but the moment didn't feel as foreign as it should. It was right and familiar to be in his arms again, to be locked at his side like the times they'd danced at the fashion elite's parties. To see the smile return to his eyes. To feel like the world hadn't really degraded into something they no longer recognized.

The flood of familiarity invaded her heart, reminding her of long talks at café tables. Of strolling the Paris streets until the sun set. The forgotten memory of who they used to be . . . together.

Everything might have changed, but somehow, everything was still the same. Lila was still at home, here, with him. The boom of laughter from a full dining room down below brought them back to the present and René released her.

"I ought to go back." He sighed, hands finding his hips. "Make sure Nigel's not going too overboard."

"D'accord. Of course."

"And we'll talk after? We pacify one officer if we must, but we make our plans to get you out of Paris." He turned to leave.

"But what if I should—?" Lila caught him with the start of a question and darted forward, only to bump headlong into his chest when he spun around at the same time. René's smile lit something in her when he looked down, and his hands, not knowing whether to wrap her up again or hang loose at his sides, had them bumbling together.

"If you should what?"

"What if I should want to stay . . . here? With you?" She turned the fake wedding band around her finger—she still wasn't used to the feel of it.

"As my wife."

"Well, as a member of your team. Oui."

"And you think I'd want you behind that counter any more than you have to be? After tonight? You said yourself you can't let the SS see you."

"And you said if I'm careful, they won't. What German soldier has really looked a Parisienne in the face, hmm? And a seamstress at that. They're not likely to remember a lowly dressmaker who was in servitude to their paramours, even if they did walk in those suites at the same time I was there. I may have been on the edge of every party, but I know enough about them to be able to filter officer names, to know some of the movements of the higher-ups at the Ritz."

He crossed his arms over his chest. "And if they're circulating a photo of you?"

"I've seen behind their curtain, René. I've seen things—heard things. For years. We should take all the information we have and use it to beat them. And I'd be careful. Stay hidden away up here. Whatever I can help with, we could do this. We could do it together."

"Together? It seems to be a thing with us."

"Save for the years we lost in there somewhere."

"Lila, do you realize what you're asking me? If anything happened to you . . ." He shook his head. Paused. And stared her through like only he could. "Why are you doing this, really?"

I can't tell you.

She inhaled deep, thinking of the weight she'd carried in the last years. It still bore down upon her. She knew then, the longer she stayed—close to him, remembering what it felt like to be at his side—the harder it would be to avoid telling him the devastating truth.

It would come. Truth always won out. And though she might lose him over it, the amount of time left between them was enough that she was willing to give up everything for just a taste of it.

"Because I want to do my part. I have to continue to fight, and this is the only way I know how. Would you really deny me the chance to do something important? To help you here, if I can?"

"You see my hesitation as though you're not qualified. Is that why you're trying to convince me right now?" He didn't wait for an answer, just nodded through a sigh. "The way I see it, Lila de Laurent, you might be more qualified than the rest of us put together."

"So I'm in."

"Oui. Against my better judgment."

"Bien. Then if you operatives should need my help at all until closing, I'll just be up here." She bit her lip over the breathlessness of it all—the little flash of cheek lighting up again whenever he looked at her, making her insides swim. "I suppose I could sew a new dress and plot to take down a régime in my spare time."

CHAPTER 10

24 October 1940
16th Arrondissement
Paris, France

The door to the flat burst open and slammed shut again in a breath. Sandrine and Marguerite looked up from their spot at the kitchen block, with little Henri standing on a chair as they taught him how to knead a proper dough for baking an authentic French loaf. They heard the lock chain slide into place and racing footsteps carried through the marble entry as Henri patted flour in the air.

"Victor must be home." Her mother-in-law checked the clock on the wall. "I wonder why at this hour?"

A shade past noon and he wasn't at the office.

The women exchanged glances at the explosion of noise that followed from the library—drawers being pulled open, something crashing to the floor, the unmistakable shatter of glass—enough that Sandrine thought she oughtn't delay to see to it, even if her apron and hands were flour dusted and they had fresh boules in the oven.

"Go on with your knead, Henri." She wiped her hands on a tea towel and flitted a steadying glance to her mother-in-law. "You stay here with Grand-mère. Teach her a thing or two about the art of fine French baking while I'm gone."

Sandrine kissed the top of his head, then swept from the room down the hall, quickening her steps as she neared the library door at the end. Shadows danced on the hardwood, the firelight revealing Victor, who seemed almost entranced as he moved about. He'd not even removed his coat, just darted from desk to fireplace, stepping on his hat on the floor and tossing reams of paper from an open drawer into hungry flames on the hearth.

"Victor? Whatever is wrong?"

"Come, Sandrine. I need you." He pointed to the drawer, overrun with a waterfall of paper. "Take this, feed the fire. All of it must go. I'll start on the file cabinets."

"Shall I close the door? Or surely you'd like to speak with your wife about this . . ." She looked down at the papers. Bills of sale. Contracts. Random company memos. What was all of it?

"Non. We haven't time." He'd poured a half tumbler from a crystal decanter on the desk and downed a shot. "I need you to listen to me first. I won't be able to repeat myself."

"Victor, you're scaring me." Sandrine melted into the leather wing-back by the desk, fear billowing in her as she held on to random sheets of paper, the flames licking at a pile thick for their appetite as her father-in-law bustled around the office.

"Is it the casualty lists? I've looked for Christian's name since they were first distributed in July. The missing and wounded . . . Please don't tell me a new list has come out."

He shook his head. "Mais non. It is not the lists. The SS raided Paquet Publishing today."

"What?" Sandrine dug her nails into the armrest—the shot of pain a reaction to tell her this was actually happening and not some terrible dream. "They raided the publishing house. Why?"

"Any number of reasons I could have predicted in earnest. The articles denouncing Pétain's grand radio speech from earlier this month and the rumored meeting with Hitler himself this very day, to outline their collaborationist aims. Or the *Statut des Juifs* this rotting government has just released—the laws they are proposing against the Jews are nothing short of barbaric. They are now limited in their professions. A Jew cannot serve in the military. Not in civil service. Not even in entertainment. They are taking all of the Jewish-owned bookshops, just like the Trouvère, but they are taking everything else with it. Their homes, businesses, even carrying paintings and books out the front doors of the Rothschilds' manor. I stood on the street today and watched it happen. Vichy police vans lined up along the Rue Saint-Honoré and drove off with everything from inside. Someone had to denounce them for it. And do it in a way that drew attention to their grievous actions."

"And that someone was you, I take it?"

"Oui, but I haven't time to explain further. They've already arrested all of the company officers. I was not in the office at the moment and good thing, or I wouldn't be standing here to tell you now. And if Christian were not already fighting for France, they would have arrested him too just for being my son. Praise be he's not here."

Sandrine looked to the windows, the drapes concealing the view of an abandoned Paris outside, the streets plagued by the silence of a curfew that would, at any moment, be cut by the sound of auto brakes squealing to a stop and the footfalls of military jackboots clamoring up the stairs to their flat.

"The SS." Sandrine lifted to the edge of the seat, the memos in her hand feeling like they burned without even having touched flames. "They're coming here for this?"

"Non. This is nothing. They are coming for me."

"Oh, Victor. What have you done?"

"I authorized the publication of articles denouncing their 'model' occupation, and in this climate that is quite enough. Burning these files is just a precaution, so I give them no names of associates. I won't be responsible for any arrests after mine. If they come to take Victor Paquet, they will take me alone."

He crossed the room, looking down at the memos in her frozen palm. He paused, even for the time he no longer had, the intensity of his features illuminated by flames dancing on the hearth.

"Have you opened the envelope Christian gave you at the train station that day?"

She shook her head. "I suppose I didn't want to tempt fate by doing so. He said to use it if things got so bad that I couldn't go back. That it was for Henri and me, an address of a place we could go should we need help. But it's felt so far like we're at the beginning of war rather than an end. I couldn't bring myself to open it, so I hid it behind the bureau for safekeeping. He told you about it?"

"He did."

Sandrine shot to her feet. "You mean you've heard from him?"

"Sandrine, non. I haven't. But I have learned that some soldiers from his unit were taken prisoner in a siege at Calais in May. Those officers who survived were sent on to a *stalag* near Sagan, Silesia. I've been able to confirm only that much."

"So he's, what . . . in Germany? In a prisoner camp?"

"I don't know yet. But I've been attempting to learn where and if I can confirm it to secure his release. It's why I've been so apprehensive for us to mill about for information. It is not safe given the circumstances of the publications. And while I can't say for certain where or how, I also believe Christian is still alive. And he is fighting to come home to you."

Tears flooded her cheeks for all the newspapers with their endless casualty lists and the letters she'd cried over that never came. Somehow, the papers in her hand became the connection to him she'd needed all that time. Sandrine gripped the memos, coiling them in a white-knuckled grip in her fist.

"You mean y-you can get word to him? Can I?"

"If Monsieur Mullins is working with an underground network to defy Hitler right here in Paris, and Christian said you can trust him, then continue to try through Le Fournier. Just be careful. Keep a low profile—ensure the SS doesn't know your name and the safer you will be until this war is over."

Victor eased the coil of useless papers from her hand, then replaced them with a book—a leather-bound spine with cracked edges and gold-rimmed paper that shone in the firelight. She couldn't tell him that someone did know her name. An officer had given considerable notice to it at the bookshop. She could only pray now the encounter hadn't caused anything to stoke true remembrance of her or the name Paquet.

"Here. Take this. When you do need to open the envelope—and you will know when the time is right—this will help you find your way."

She ran a hand over the cover, aged and worn and beautiful. He'd handed her the Paquet Bible? "I don't understand."

"You will. When the time comes."

"But this is yours. *Your* family's."

"And I'm sorry to do this to you now, but it seems I must. I am entrusting my family to you. My wife. My grandson. My son, when he returns. And my daughter, which you always will be." His finger-tips grazed the cover of the Bible, enough that he patted her hand—a paternal show of affection he'd never undertaken before. Always proper. A kind man, but a mite detached and business savvy. But now, she was his daughter? How could this happen again . . . with seconds to say good-bye?

"You are clever and resourceful, Sandrine. Use that. But always do what you know to be right—no matter the cost. Above all things, our choice to remain faithful in the face of uncertainty is sacred to God and He will honor it in His time. Do not give up on God; He will hold you fast."

Sandrine's breath locked up as he issued the affirmation that God was with them. That God was real. Present. And involved in their daily plight more than just a thought at funeral services or on holy holidays. What was this supposed to mean, when everything in Victor's manner was saying farewell and their fate was up to God?

Autos lumbered outside, competing with the pop and crackle of the fire eating away years of Victor's company—his life burning up in ash and smoke that trailed up the bricks of the chimney. And then automobile doors slammed. There were the customary shouts. And a chorus of bootfalls sounding like a specter's wail as it haunted up the stairs to their world.

"Promise me?"

Sandrine stared back at him, words seeming so feeble at the moment. But she nodded, whispering as if out of her body and hearing another's voice, "I promise."

Marguerite appeared in the library doorway, her soft eyes taking in the scene, which couldn't have been more appalling if an actual bomb had gone off in the room. Her view flitted from the hearth and the mound of paper drowning out the dwindle of flames, to Victor, who'd removed his coat and hat and was straightening his tie beneath his vest before he downed a last swig of liquid in his glass.

"What is this? We are baking bread for our dinner and you are here making quite a show of yourself with this mess. What have you done?" she demanded, hands on her hips, as if the rule of law in Nazi-occupied Paris was nothing compared to making a room untidy, and a mess a wife would have to clean.

"Do excuse me." Emotion claimed Sandrine as she slipped into the hall.

There was nothing to do but wither against the wainscoting, knowing the good-bye that would happen in the library.

Christian's parents would have a moment or two only, the time afforded a husband and wife to cap off a thirty-year marriage. And what did one say in those last breaths? Sandrine guessed it was much the same as parting at a train station, save for the warning she and Christian had been afforded the day prior.

She melted against the wall and listened first to the silence from the room.

It was followed by Marguerite's tears and furious anger and then a wail that was so guttural, Sandrine thought it would surely split the building in two. She hugged the Bible to her chest like a wounded little girl clung to her doll. Only for a breath though, as she remembered the charge she'd just been handed and picked herself up to hurry down the hall.

In the kitchen she found Henri, standing in his flour-doused apron, his little cherub cheeks tracked with tears through the white dust, for how could a little one understand war, or war that had found you even inside the safety of your home?

Sandrine held him as the front door erupted—the chain burst from the bolt and rattled about, and a bomb of wood splintered against the floor as SS officers swarmed into the flat.

She held him in the corner, rocking as uniformed shadows flew by and flour doused the gold pages of an heirloom Bible. Marguerite sobbed in the background as the bootfalls found their way to the library and the master of Paquet Publishing was dragged out to the street below.

The only sounds issuing around them: Marguerite's tears, the screech of an oven timer signaling the burning of French loaves, and a single gunshot in the street that proved the devastating accuracy of Victor Paquet's final words.

———— •◆• ————

3 January 1944
1 Place de la Concorde
Paris, France

"Well? What did it say?"

Michèle shot a glance down the hall at the pair of uniforms lingering beyond their office door, one sneaking an outlawed cigarette while the other laughed at a page from a pinup magazine butterflied between them.

"Don't worry about them. They won't notice a thing," Michèle whispered, crossing her arms over the middle of her mint sweater as she edged them into the corner by the window. "I knew you couldn't risk telephoning over the weekend, and I haven't had a chance to get you alone until now. But I've been beside myself wondering what exactly that note said."

Sandrine stooped as if to pull a book from the shelf beneath the window, running her fingertips along the spines until she selected one. Michèle joined her and they held it open for a quick moment between them.

"It's the oddest thing," Sandrine said, words fast and tone low. "Have you come across an 'LDL' before? A family name. Or a collection maybe?"

"Mais non. I've never heard those initials. Why?"

"I haven't yet had a moment with Mademoiselle Valland to ask, but it was a note on Hôtel Ritz letterhead. It said: *Rothschild and Touliard collections. Sold to art dealers: Zurich and Berlin. Catalog to follow. Send word to Trouvère.'* And then it was signed simply 'LDL.' I don't know what to make of it."

"That is odd. The name Trouvère. Maybe a connection to our bookseller from the shop?"

"I shouldn't think so. But it's a common word used in literary circles."

Michèle accentuated her doubt with a tip of the brow. "And how often have you used that word in a sentence lately?" She shook her head. "We've known for some time that La Résistance network sends messages hidden in clothing. I'll agree this is the first time we've seen it ourselves and here, but we must draw a connection somehow. Did you find anything else when you got the dress home?"

"Non. But you saw those stitches in the seam—perfect but

concealing a note that was scribbled as if the writer hadn't any time to do better. That doesn't make any sense. Who doesn't have enough time to write but can sit down and sew like that? Mademoiselle Valland requested us to find whatever may have been concealed in it before they did. But the question is, why was it sewn into a Chanel gown? And why send it here to us?"

"I don't know, save for the fact that we are housing art from the stolen collections of prominent Jewish families across Europe. If there's the slightest chance that even one member of La Résistance is here, then who better to receive it? Did anything from the rest of the newly acquired art say LDL or have the collection name on it?"

Sandrine shook her head. "I don't yet know. Our ingenious curator had quite a lot of film to make copies of in just a few hours' time."

"And she's not come in yet this morning. With Göring set to arrive any moment. You don't think they've found out what she's been up to . . . and taken her? What'll we do?"

"Do not mention the dress to anyone. Not now. I'll keep it safe at home until we know more."

The soldiers made a loud show of laughter, receiving a reprimand from an officer walking by. It startled Sandrine and Michèle back to work without another word, and certainly no backup plan to employ.

They busied themselves lining an assortment of gold-gilded frames. Oil paints, acrylics, watercolors, and sketches. The Impressionist works were less favored than those of Germanic origin, or those of artists they dubbed the "pure" masters. The less desirable works that survived the garden bonfires were filtered out—sold to any manner of shady dealers in France, Switzerland, or Germany. The room now boasted a private gallery of the prizes they'd most recently acquired from the days before: Vermeer. Rembrandt. Rubens.

The art was lined up in pretty little rows, in preparation for another visit from the greedy.

Though Reichsmarschall Göring had been through their doors

at least a dozen times in '41, and nearly as many in the year before, a fresh shipment and new vaults discovered meant another opportunity to decorate the walls in his own chalet, and also to hand-select pieces for the Führermuseum actively being planned for construction in Linz, Austria. Many of the pieces were to go there. If selected, they'd be crated and shipped out on the spot, and Valland's team would have but minutes to document the what, where, and to whom before the pieces disappeared completely.

Sandrine eyed the soldiers lingering outside the door. There was a shift to nervous energy about them—they'd stiffened. Doused their cigs. And hidden away their magazine so the rooms outside the showroom had fallen quiet.

Sharp footsteps grew louder as they echoed off the ceiling and Captain von Hiller stepped through the door. He surveyed the room, nodding outright and then half smiling when his eyes finally landed on Sandrine's stature in the corner.

"All in order here?"

"Oui, Captain. We are ready." Sandrine swallowed and folded her hands in front of her suit jacket, a model of precision for the task.

"The Reichsmarschall's car has arrived. I'll see him in." He looked around, skimming the art, glance jumping from doorway to doorway only to find them empty. "But where is Valland? She is always present for an official visit."

"Michèle?"

Always the quiet presence in every room, Michèle stepped away from her fixed point against the wall at Sandrine's request, pulling a pencil from her ear and readying it to a clipboard in her hand.

"Oui, madame?"

"Do inform Mademoiselle Valland that the Reichsmarschall is here for his viewing, and Captain von Hiller requests her presence in the gallery immediately. I'm certain the captain and I can handle this quite well for the moment, but as curator her assistance will be required."

"Certainly. Anything else?"

"If you would, please review the catalog for the collection pieces we spoke of this morning. That is all."

She nodded—efficient. Direct. And with a secret sparkle in her eyes when she turned her back to the captain, the ladies knowing it meant Michèle would hurry through any records they had, looking for the initials or the collection name on the note. "Right away, madame."

The air in the showroom felt as though it bled out when the stone-eyed Reichsmarschall Hermann Göring stepped in.

It was the first time Sandrine had led a selection meeting on her own, enough that she was required to pander. To grit her teeth behind a smile as the decorated officer came in, crossed batons shining out from his collar and insignia thick on the front of his uniform. She must offer him his fancy of champagne or port and then wait dutifully as he and the captain discussed the art.

Göring's gaze slithered over the canvases. He asked about any other Vermeers. And paintings of ponies—were there any? His daughter, Edda, so favored them and would like one of her own. And he much preferred Murillo, the seventeenth-century Spanish master of Baroque religious works, and would like to see recent acquisitions of them as well.

The captain looked at the back of the frame of one selected. "This is R1171, Mrs. Paquet."

"Oui. Of course. I'll write it down."

Rothschild, item number 1171.

Sandrine's breath locked up tight in her lungs as Göring next chose a Vermeer. Just like that. Snapped his fingers and ordered the priceless painting *The Astronomer* crated up and shipped out to become the prize of the Führer's private museum collection.

Jotting note after note, keeping meticulous records, Sandrine was aware that she'd become the only voice to protect the art in the room. And all the while, Victor's words radiated through her mind. She was doing what she must to survive in the moment with Michèle and Valland and the rest of the network—and behind the scenes, whomever LDL was. They knew the risk of the call that had been placed upon them. Sandrine knew to her core, watching Göring sip champagne and chat with the captain, there was infinite worth in doing what was right, no matter the cost or the debt any one of them may have to pay for it one day.

"Is what I hear from the captain true, Mrs. Paquet?" Göring addressed her with eyebrows tipped—the first time she'd ever seen his features regress into an expression that wasn't cold and subhuman.

"Sir?"

"You took receipt of a misguided Chanel gown here at the galerie? What a curious tale."

The captain stood by, showing no reaction to the fact that the gift between just the two of them was now common knowledge to one of the highest-ranking leaders in the land. If anything, the captain seemed genuinely pleased to have shared the matter so openly.

"I am looking after it, oui. But then, one never knows what we'll receive when we open a crate here at the Jeu de Paume. We are always at the ready for even the smallest surprise. And I can assure you, sir, we do our job here quite well."

CHAPTER 11

12 DECEMBER 1940
15 PLACE VENDÔME
PARIS, FRANCE

Elegance did survive in Paris, but it hit a crescendo at the Hôtel Ritz. The ornate interior boasted gleaming marble floors, crystal chandeliers, gold gilding and molded wainscoting, and fresh flowers perfuming the lobby. Bellhops and valets were dressed to perfection as they bustled about, seemingly in some dream world that appeared untouched by the war-torn streets right outside the front doors.

And then there were the uniforms.

Officers of the Third Reich, everywhere in gray with gold and blood-red litzen on collars, stepping off elevators and dining with pink-lipped females in the cocktail lounge. The Gray Mice—female German auxiliaries—whisked through the lobby, too, as if they owned part of it. And maybe they did. They'd arrived in Paris in late 1940, popping into the shops and nosing the wares of the street vendors who were left, plucking up French *parfum* and silk scarves still in supply, suggesting to the Parisienne that her city was theirs, and it was changing.

Lila's clientele at the fashion house of Nina Ricci were indeed the French socialites—the ones who also passed by her in the Ritz lobby. She was one who could afford the styles off the runway and still manage an invitation to the fashion shows that had sprung up again in autumn 1940.

Where the average Parisienne waited in daunting lines at the boulangerie or the local tailor's shop, the affluent might have relatives outside the city to provide foodstuffs already in short supply or connections to the black market where the Nazis' harsh system of rationing had not yet reached. The wealthy could afford the trips to the hair salons—the ones still in operation—and did not have to tuck their undyed locks under garish turbans that had become a fashion staple on the streets.

And among these privileged at the Hôtel Ritz, the paramour emerged.

Lila wasn't certain how to respond when the telephone call came in. She'd been pulled away from a client, pins in her teeth as she was piecing a new custom design to a dressmaker's dummy, and summoned immediately to the Hôtel Ritz that afternoon to dress one of the Nazi officers' young ladies in residence.

In a flash there she was—among the elite. In her crisp jewel-blue suit with split skirt and pert tam with smart peacock feathers splayed over her chignon. Lila had dressed to the nines, in the best she owned, for a meeting that was as mysterious as it could be lucrative.

The desk bustled with telephones ringing as the concierge, a tight-faced woman with a no-nonsense air about her, looked up and noticed Lila.

"Bonjour. *Puis-je vous aider?*" The concierge addressed her as next in line, though the greeting of "May I help you?" felt more like a nip at the ankles from a territorial poodle than a welcoming reception from a hotel help desk.

She stepped up. "I'm Lila de Laurent. I'm with the house of—"

"Ah. The Ricci dressmaker. We have been expecting you for some time. Mademoiselle in suite 3-D has called down twice asking where you are."

Lila would have explained that a bicycle ride across the city at midday was a feat that wasn't accomplished in the blink of an eye, especially not in such unforgiving winter temperatures. She'd stowed her bike, chaining it up two blocks away, knowing that though there were hundreds—maybe thousands—of bicycles now employed in Paris, it was not chic for her to arrive at the Ritz riding one.

"My apologies, but there was—"

"Never mind that now." The concierge snapped her fingers—a curt sign for a soldier to respond. "They will check your bags first, take down your information, and then escort you upstairs. You will stop here before you leave, where your bags and your person will be checked through again before you are released. Merci."

"This way." The soldier drew Lila to the filter point of a table blocking access to a great hallway, the arched windows allowing light to stream in on elaborate armchairs, elegant lamps on tables lining the walls, and crystal chandeliers twinkling in the sunlight—the long view revealing a bank of white marble stairs and elevators at the end. The soldiers emptied every compartment of her satchels, thumbing through swatches of fabric, pins, spools of thread . . . turning over every page in her sketchbook and thoroughly inspecting her identification papers before returning them with her clutch.

Finally packed up, she was allowed down the hall.

The hair on the back of Lila's neck stood on end as she passed officers who as a whole appeared hospitable when they'd first arrived. But Lila knew better. The gray ghosts had filtered into every aspect of their lives, and where they first seemed respectful to the Parisiennes they passed in the street, now they had a level of comfort to leer at passing women with a cunning smile and a glint in their eyes.

Lila kept her eyes focused on the back of the soldier's head as they stepped in the elevator and emerged on a private third-floor landing overlooking the lavish lobby beneath.

"In there." He pointed to the suite door before them, his posture indicating he'd be planted outside standing guard until she was through.

Lila swallowed hard. Straightened the hem of her suit jacket. Knocked on the suite door and waited while footsteps approached behind it. A maid answered, her eyes direct—soft brown, with deep flaxen locks pinned under a white cap. She stepped back, door opening wide.

"Bonjour, mademoiselle. Come in."

And with that Lila was granted entry into the inner circle of the Ritz's grand cavalcade of excess. It might have been a carbon copy of Elsie de Wolfe's world from before the war. More marble. Gold gilding. Wide-open windows and a terrace beyond. Rows of pink and lavender petit fours dotted a silver platter on the coffee table, with champagne bubbling in a flute and fresh roses festooned on the mantel.

Only this wasn't from before the war; this was sinking sand in the middle of it.

The chambermaid disappeared into the bedroom and Lila looked around, setting her satchels on a nail-head chair flanking a marble fireplace.

"Lila?" A singsong voice, familiar and playful, rang out from the bedroom as shoes clipped the marble floor down the hall. "Chère amie, you have finally arrived!"

Amélie . . .

A vision in lavender silk crossed the hall from the boudoir.

Her friend walked toward her with bouncy chin-length curls the bleached brand of Jean Harlow, golden eyes bright and hands extended to Lila. Amélie grabbed hold of her palms, kissing her cheeks before Lila could even wrap her mind around what this meant.

"Well, you silly girl. You cannot even say bonjour to your dearest schoolgirl friend?"

"Amélie—you called me here?"

"Of course I did! And for good reason. From the moment I arrived back in Paris, I said I must track down my dear sister Lila. But after a telephone call or two, I hear she is quite well and designing for Nina Ricci no less. Quite an improvement from our former lot as seamstresses, non?" Amélie stood back, surveyed Lila's suit, and folded her arms across her chest—authoritative, sleek, and impressed.

"Ah, see! You, too, are wearing the split skirt that is so popular with all the women of Paris. You look marvelous. I was just telling Violette in there—my maid—that I have a long list of the new fashionable items, and a split skirt is at the very top. That and one of the crimson Lanvin bags everyone is carrying. Have you seen them?"

"I have. They're made in a cylinder, for carrying gas masks."

"But who really does that? It's a question of what's fashionable. Like the split skirts. I simply must have a pair, even though I can't be bothered to ride a bicycle. Only the gauche do that now, oui?"

She drew Lila to the sitting room—all rose pink and mint and shiny gold gilding—to chairs opposite the fireplace. She swept into one, hand swiping up a flute of bubbly pink before she eased against the cushions and tucked painted toes beneath her. "Tell me—what have you been up to? And don't leave anything out."

And just like that, the dam of shock split wide.

If Lila had thought the lobby a display of frivolity, the suite—and the company in it—seemed wholly ignorant of what was happening in Paris. It was as if they no longer lived on the same planet, let alone in the same city as each other, to sit and tipple champagne and chat about their diary entries.

"Well . . . work. The fashion shows have started up again, which is good for bolstering the French spirits. There's little time for much else these days."

"Ah. I can imagine! Such excitement. And your parents? They are well, I trust?"

Something inside said to lie. Or cover the truth somehow. Lila didn't know why, but it felt necessary to keep things back—important things, like where her parents were existing in isolation while Paris struggled to survive. The woman sitting opposite couldn't understand that, not surrounded by her finery. Amélie had the same smile, the same pert profile and careful mannerisms, but something had changed. The temperature of the room felt a few shades cooler—icy and detached—and Lila was cautioned to heed its warning.

"They've, uh, they've gone."

"Not in Paris? I am so sorry. So many of our old friends have left. But you've been alone here all this time? What a pity, when we could have had our choice of parties to attend."

Gone to a new flat was all, but she paused in allowing Amélie to draw her own conclusions. Lila swallowed. And knew the answer before she'd ask, but she moved to the burning question anyway, somehow needing to hear the words said aloud.

"And . . . this is your suite?"

"Well, oui. I suppose. I have a man who thinks he owns it, but the woman really does, non? Until we can find something more permanent. My man is a touch on the . . . mature side. Fifty, and set in his hopelessly German ways, I'm afraid. I'm hoping a little youthful exuberance will mellow his sharp corners." Amélie drifted her fingertips over a petit four, selected one, and then pieced it apart with tiny picked bites while she talked. "What I need to know is if you are available."

"Available?"

"To dress me for a big event—a New Year's Eve reception at the German embassy for *le tout Paris*. It will be a night of celebrating the arts and the first I'm attending on the arm of my officer, so I wish to stand out. And you have the perfect gown to do it."

She leaned in, the characteristic sparkle in her eyes that Lila had so often seen but never imagined to witness in the circumstances that were presented her now.

"I remember your brilliant designs, the ones you never showed Mademoiselle Chanel." Amélie smiled like she had a secret, and it was good enough it could be coaxed out with ease. "She's here, you know. At the Ritz? I have seen her. We passed in the elevator, while I was coming in and she was going out. It is only a matter of time before we frequent the same parties. Just like I always said I would. Stacking up stories for the old memoirs, oui?"

This was a tsunami over Lila's head. Miles over, coming in waves with a current she couldn't hope to control.

The image of her father flooded her mind, standing on their balcony, pained and waving the French flag as German panzers swept up the Champs-Élysées. And the scores of Parisians who'd fled out on the roads south of the city. They'd learned later that German planes had bombed many or machine-gunned the refugees while they ran about like jackrabbits, desperate for cover in fields. While those stories had burned horrific images on her brain, it was the day-to-day life of the average Parisian she'd personally experienced under Nazi rule, and it was no less frightening to consider what they were capable of in streets as in fields.

And now, it seemed, Amélie had an amicable alliance with them whether she wished it or not.

"So, will Ricci let you go long enough to dress me?"

"I don't know that my schedule will accommodate such a tight deadline. My diary is near full, I'm afraid."

"But you could squeeze this in. As a favor to your dear friend?"

"Ricci has employed me to make their dresses and I'm not certain they'd wish me to dress the . . ." She paused, choosing her words more carefully than to spit out the phrase *kept women*. "Women outside of the label's official clientele."

"I see." Amélie coasted through the paltry explanation like a champion socialite would, thumb trailing a circle around the rim of her flute, eyes retaining their sparkle but only just, for she knew behind all the elegant pacification, she was being judged.

"And what if I should say what I really wanted was that custom Chanel gown you drew up years back, before Coco closed her salon—the blush pink one those Rothschilds got their hands on?"

"I'm sure I wouldn't know. It was my design but for Chanel's house. And I don't own it. I couldn't say what's become of one dress we sold to a client years ago."

Amélie shook her head, like a grand waste had been uncovered and it pained her to think on it.

"Then the emerald gown you no doubt have right there in your sketchbook. I remember all of your designs. And I should like to share them with others. So what if I said I wish to be a representative of Parisian culture at a German event? Surely you could find no fault in that, no matter what I choose to do in this suite—which is *my business*. I understand you are in business, too, the business of dressing ladies. I am such a lady willing to pay for your services, and if you like, we can keep it between us. But I assure you, with one simple telephone call to the ladies in all the suites at this hotel, you will have ten diaries full of clients wanting Lila de Laurent originals through the end of this silly war. And then you will have everything we always dreamed about—we both will."

Amélie nudged the silver tray of petit fours closer to Lila, as if she needn't answer. Offering to represent France should have been enough. "Here. Have a sweet. The raspberry ganache is to die for. They are too rich for me and will be tossed. Or I send them home with Violette here, to feed the rats in her building."

Amélie clapped her hands together and rose to standing. "Where do we begin? You need my measurements, non? Let's go in the boudoir. There is a floor-length mirror and much better light. We should hurry. You were a bit late, dear Lila, and I have a dinner date to freshen up for."

For all the schoolgirl notions they'd once had, of fairy tales and love and marriage to the men of their dreams—this was nothing short of a nightmare.

It was for Amélie, whose drifting from innocence crashed head-long into war, and for Lila, whose love had disappeared from her life just as the darkness of the Germans marched in. They'd each chosen a path, and it seemed if any Parisienne wished for a better lot than the one she'd been dealt, some twisted form of amour was available.

Available but hollow, and at a terrible cost.

They moved into the boudoir and Lila diverted her eyes from the maid, who'd busied herself spreading crisp sheets and a rose cover-let over the bed. They stopped in front of a floor-length mirror, the gold gilding shining bright in the afternoon sun as Lila unpacked her satchel of dressmaker's tools.

She looked up after a moment of silence, somehow feeling Amélie's gaze on her as she unwound the measuring tape, and stared back at the reflection in the glass.

There was so much to say, yet so much unsaid.

"War comes, Lila, and some buckle under. But we are not such women, are we?" Amélie stood tall, arms in an elegant former ballet dancer's pose, her face stone as she waited for Lila to stretch the measuring tape along her limbs. "We will survive because we are Parisiennes—gracious fighters. You in your way and me in mine."

The air was frigid and lifeless when Lila stepped out the front doors of the Ritz, dress order in a shaking hand and her heart nurs-ing too many fresh breaks to count. Some women did buckle under, she thought, as she unchained her bicycle from an iron fence. And some survived any way they knew how. Which path would she choose?

Lila walked home in her chic split skirt, wheeling her wares down the sidewalk. She held her head high—a little show of moxie as she passed soldiers nailing German signage up on the streets. They were staking their claim on her existence in more ways than one, and her heart cried the whole way home.

4 JANUARY 1944
61 BOULEVARD DE CLICHY
PARIS, FRANCE

"Alright—let's get down to brass tacks." René stood in the flat, keeping his voice low as he walked Lila around, inducting her fully into their shadow world.

"There's a loose brick in the wall here behind the door." He knelt by the door leading downstairs. "Third up, second to the right. Dislodge that and the rest will come down. Behind the wood planks there's a small cache of weapons—for emergency only. Easy access right here by the door. There's a map of the underground, should we need to reach the Résistance cells, tucked high in the plaster in the wall behind the bath sink. You can take it and run if needed. The identification cards and smaller pistols—your Liberator included—along with your microfilm are in the floorboard under Nigel's desk. And there's a transistor hidden in the ceiling grate in the bath. You have to reach behind the pipes, but it's there."

Lila scanned the room. It was a veritable arsenal of La Résistance, right here. It seemed like they could run the country from the little flat if they had a mind to.

"So what's on the microfilm?"

"A catalog."

He bounced back, "Of what?"

"Names. Places. Things."

"You mean you took a bullet for . . . an officer's ledger?"

René's question was valid, and she guessed he knew exactly how pointed it was.

In the grand scheme of the war and everything they'd set up to do with the shadow world of Black Propaganda surrounding it, he wasn't likely to see that the answer would mean much, not when lives were at risk. Until she unpacked the rest, where lives could be and were at risk—all of theirs.

"You're right. It's a little more complicated than that. There's a hoard of paintings stolen by the Third Reich. And documents concerning their sale both in and outside of France. I'd been tracking them—and the collection owners."

"Owners?"

Lila's heart seared at the edges to have to say it. "To learn the fate of Jews who've been sent away. Records of some of their prominent collections have come through officers staying at the Hôtel Ritz. I became aware of it and offered to keep a record of what I saw."

"D'accord. And you were gathering information in a suite on New Year's Eve. Who knew about it?"

They sat at the table in the late-night hours in the upstairs flat, voices muffled in whispers as Nigel pecked away at his typewriter, drafting his latest masterpiece on the rolltop in the corner.

Lila glanced over at him. "Don't you worry that someone will hear the typewriter?"

"The music is so loud from the cabarets that it's impossible to hear anything but that downstairs. I'd worry more about the soldiers overhearing this conversation if most of them weren't drunk or aptly preoccupied out in the street." He took a sip of coffee—hard, black, and keeping them awake. "Who can place you in the officer's suite that night?"

"Only three."

"Bien. That narrows it down for us."

"There's the officer—"

"The chap who took a nosedive off the terrace?"

She nodded, though how the terrace was involved was news to her. "Captain Scheel."

"He's not talking. Who else?"

"Violette—a chambermaid. But she's not what they think. She's been a part of La Résistance for years now. And she's been my primary contact. Up until this last time, she would take the information I gathered and hand it over to the network."

"Violette?" René shook his head, his brow seeming to test the merits of belief against what he knew about the depth of the networks entrenched in the city. "I don't know of any Violette placed in the 1st Arrondissement. Are you sure she's working with a cell, or is she rogue?"

"A cell I should think."

"How do you know?"

"She mentioned she reports to a leader by the name of Hedgehog. It's such an odd name and so specific that I had no reason to doubt."

Nigel perked up at the code name, stilling his typewriter keys. "You mean she reports directly to Marie-Madeline Fourcade? That's the largest network in France run by a woman. By jove, René—that's something concrete if anything is. She couldn't have made that up."

Looking between the two of them, René paused, as if something was clicking into place for him too. "Wait a minute. Violette must go by another name, a code name? Did she ever mention it to you?"

"She didn't. But I saw quite a lot when I was at the Ritz. And she saw as much. More, maybe. And reported everything out to the network. She's French but her father was German, so they placed her at the Ritz in the summer of '40 thinking she'd be more believable and would be accepted in employ as someone sympathetic to the German war effort. She was a chambermaid in some of the highest-ranking officers' suites."

"And speaks German, and so could understand everything they say."

"Right. It's her job to feed information about the goings-on of the officers there. Our paths crossed when I was dressing the officers' paramours for their social events. Those ladies are quite loose lipped when they have the combination of cocktails and a humble dressmaker's ear. They didn't know or didn't care to keep any secrets. Either way, I've been feeding information back too—whatever I could gather over nearly three years."

"And that's where the microfilm comes in."

"Oui. As a dressmaker I'd earned their trust. I could gain access to the private rooms when most could not—including a chambermaid. Violette tried but she was constantly watched. But I'd be given freedom in the boudoirs where the officers kept their overnight work—papers, briefcases, files from the German embassy—the things they kept on their person. Even some crates of stolen art came through the Ritz, if you can believe they were actually carried through the lobby. When we realized what was being kept in the hotel, Violette brought me the microfilm camera. She taught me how to use it. And it was she who set up the Résistance contact for me to get the microfilm out. But I wanted to make the handoff this time, instead of filtering it through her for translation. It took a bit of convincing, but she finally acquiesced."

René ran his fingers through his hair, a telltale action that something was agitating him from the inside.

"Something doesn't add up here. You said Violette and Captain Scheel both knew you. For a chambermaid to know you were there that night makes sense. But for you to see him take the bullet, you had to have been inside the suite. Is that what you meant about being in part responsible for his death?"

"I didn't see him go over the balcony, but I was in his suite. I was sent to the Hôtel Ritz on New Year's Eve to dress the officers' paramours for a party. After they'd gone downstairs, I managed to sneak back in and took photographs of documents in Scheel's third-floor suite—a list of everything on the trains and where it all was going. I'd then have travel clearance for twenty-four hours only—forged papiers would see me out of Paris."

"We found your papiers, bloodstained in the pocket of your coat. Had to burn them—they were more dangerous if they happened to have been found that way. But if you had made it through, you'd have gone where?"

"A café—Tasse et Soucoupe. My contact was to meet me there in the village and take the handoff the rest of the way, to see that it made it to . . ." She exhaled. Would they even believe her—a dressmaker funneling information to a general? "De Gaulle and the Free French in London."

"This goes up to de Gaulle?" Nigel had taken a pencil from behind his ear and was busy jotting notes on a piece of scratch paper, but after that question, he tossed the pencil and leaned fully into the conversation, skirting his rolling chair closer to their table. "How in the world did you make that connection? And begging your pardon, but why would de Gaulle care about tracking Jewish art collections when France is overrun?"

"It started as art. But I'd learned of something else, you see. One of the officer's women had too much champagne one night and passed out on the bed when Violette was cleaning up after a party. She told me that the woman started talking—going on about this and that in babbling gossip, really. But it evolved to something she'd overheard when two of the officers were meeting in her suite and they didn't know she was there. Something about leaving Paris if things went badly and the Germans did face losing the war. She claimed to not want to be here . . . when it's bombed flat."

Nigel whistled low, the ghost of cabaret music the only sound left to haunt the room thereafter. "Right. So what you're saying is, we could be in a bit of a tight spot before long?"

"Something like that, Nigel. If what she said is true, then there's a rocket in development—one the Germans believe will rival the V-1 and just might turn this war back in their favor. If not, they have Paris in their sights as a likely place to test it out."

René exhaled. "D'accord. Let's go ahead and assume that everyone in this room already knows the V-1 is what Hitler has used to pummel London—and other places. And we know about rumors of a more superior version having been in the planning stages. There've been whispers in the underground for months, but we hoped they were just that. So you say it's actually in development now? You're certain of this?"

"Oui. I can't begin to translate the basics of rocket science, but I do know something about what I witnessed in that suite. I'm not fluent but I know enough German to know what I photographed. On the microfilm is a ledger of the parts being made and transported for the V-2 missile construction, and it's happening right now. Scheel worked at the German embassy, and that paperwork was mixed together because the parts were on the same trains as some of the Jewish art collections I'd been tracking—all of it was bound for Berlin right away, in the new year."

"Blimey." Nigel reached for his bottle by the typewriter, uncorked it, and took a swig. "Then the Germans really are preparing to firebomb the world—starting with us. Seems you missed quite a handoff, Ms. Dressmaker."

"You might say that. Violette will have reported I fled the Ritz when all of this happened, but she wouldn't have known about the gunshot nor about you finding me and bringing me here. The SS may not even know about the microfilm, and the parts were surely shipped to Berlin by now. If the network even knew about this, they'd have to think I was either arrested by the Gestapo or dead by now and that the microfilm is lost."

"Then we'll have to ensure the network knows it's not. Your contact's name?"

"I never met him. I'm sorry, but I can't even tell you what he looks like or how I would have known it was him. Violette said he'd find me: 'Trouvère.'"

Nigel stopped cold, coughing over a swallow like it was his first drink. He pounded a fist to his chest until he could talk. "He's got a better code name than I do."

Lila glanced from one to the other. "That's a problem?"

"Trouvère. You see, it's a medieval epic poet from the area of Northern France—"

"And in the vein of Nigel's grandest aspirations," René cut in, unable to stifle a smile even by raising his fist to his mouth when Nigel looked like he might lose his lunch over the depth of disappointment. "I'm afraid *Sir Duckworth* won't be good enough to satisfy any longer. After this, forget the V-2. We'll have a bigger problem when we all have to change our code names to characters from Dante's *Inferno*."

"Shut it." Nigel tossed a crumpled wad of paper in the direction of the table, which fell a good foot away from grazing them. He turned back to his typewriter, pulled the paper out, and scratched through lines like a toddler scribbling in a picture book.

"Look, Lila. Nigel will simmer down and then he can send the microfilm out with his next article. We'll get it into the hands of La Résistance. We've just got to get our ducks in a row and—"

Before Nigel could tack on his two bits to René's plans, Lila shook her head. "I'm sorry, mais non."

"Non? Which part?"

"All of it. The microfilm is my job. I started it and I will finish. It has to be me to see it out and no one else."

René leaned back in his chair, arms folded over his chest. She could almost hear the gears turning in his mind, ticking off the calculations that always seemed so easy for him.

"Would you hand it off to the Americans as a backup if you knew the contact was trustworthy?"

"Oui. I suppose I would. This isn't the kind of information we can sit on. But it has to go from my hand to theirs, and I decide who and when. Period."

A heavy sigh said René knew her well, but not enough to refrain from arguing the point.

"And why is that?"

"Why should I need a reason to want to see something through? You said I'm part of this operation—well, this is the part that belongs to me."

"Alright. For argument's sake, let's say this goes into the category of 'personal for Lila.' I won't ask what you're not ready to say, but if we're going to get the microfilm to this Trouvère or to the Americans, then we'll have to put the pieces of all this together. You said three people knew you were at the Hôtel Ritz that night. Who's the last? If I need to be looking over my shoulder for an SS officer who's tracking you down, I should at least know who to point a pistol at when the moment comes."

Lila looked down at her hands, remembering that night.

Who would be the other? There was only one person.

Only the friend who had orchestrated Lila's grand rise to fashion stardom. It was Amélie who'd hidden in the suite one day listening in on the officers. And it was she who had carried a drunken tale of a rocket strong enough to pound Paris into its catacombs. She'd interrupted Lila in Captain Scheel's suite that night during a New Year's Eve party—and Lila hadn't known the full price she'd be required to pay in order to obtain the information La Résistance sought.

"I had a friend. You may remember we were close before the war. She was the . . . paramour of an officer at the Ritz."

René didn't bat an eyelash, just jotted a note and fired back with, "And which officer?"

"The first was a Baron Kurt von Behr—chief of the arts at the Jeu de Paume Galerie."

"Chief of the ERR. We know him well as we cater for his parties." René cast a pointed glance to Nigel. "Word on the street is his mistress is a Mademoiselle Puz."

"She is. But it's come to light that he's had many women in addition to his wife and . . ." Lila tore her eyes away from them. Leave it to René to inquire so openly about such delicate matters, even if they were in the middle of a war. "I can't talk about this, even with you. Just know her name is Amélie Olivier. And she will recognize me. No matter what I wear or how I cut my hair, she could pick me out of a crowd of a thousand. And she won't need a photograph to do it. If she decides to tell them who I am, then I'm through."

"You don't think she's turned you in already?"

Lila shook her head. "Cutting my hair, staying out of sight . . . it's just standard procedure. My guess is Amélie hasn't said a word to anyone. Or the SS is keeping a tight lid on it if she has."

Nigel clapped his hands together. "See! Cover-up. I told you. This proves it."

René was a little less enthused. A lot less, based on the way his face had drained of any emotion and he reverted back to the concerned operative who had a mind rattling with visions of V-2 bombs and the City of Light engulfed in flames.

"Why would the SS keep this quiet?"

"Because it would mean a massive security breach for the Germans. Amélie would have to tell them everything she overheard about the V-2, what she'd unwittingly spilled to the Résistance that led me to the suite that night and long before Captain Scheel's body was tossed over a balcony—and why she, too, was in the room when he was shot dead."

CHAPTER 12

17 JANUARY 1941
16TH ARRONDISSEMENT
PARIS, FRANCE

After months of lines and shop visits and waiting with a desperate tension pitting her stomach, Monsieur Mullins had finally come through.

It was a scrap of news Sandrine had longed for—a notice of Christian's fate.

Anything would have done after more than a year of no news, searching but dreading as they read name after name on the casualty and wounded lists, and as word came in of the thousands of men in the French Army who'd surrendered under Hitler's advance and were transferred to POW camps in Germany. Any word—even the worst—she'd prepared her heart to take. But an actual letter with *Drina* written on the outside, in the unmistakable script of his own hand? It was the greatest gift she could have received, short of having him home.

Sandrine hurried up the stairs to the flat, her heels clipping the marble with sharp echoes against the high ceiling. The envelope burned in her chest pocket, for she could scarcely wait to close the door behind her and tear into it to pore over her husband's words.

She turned the key in the lock and slipped in—the lights all ablaze from the entry through the parlor and back into the library. An odd feeling of alarm prickled over her, as she knew electricity was in short supply and now they must never waste it by burning all bulbs at once.

"Ah, Sandrine! You have returned." Marguerite looked as though a spring had been fixed beneath her chair and rose, nervous hands twisting in front of the waist pleats of her lilac dress. She swallowed hard. "Let me take your coat and hat, dear. We have a guest in *le salon* . . ."

"A guest?" Sandrine removed her hat and coat—the envelope still inside the inner breast pocket—and stepped through the entry to the double doors of the formal parlor. A uniform came into view, and then, the face.

The eyes.

Him.

The captain from the bookshop sat in a nail-head chair by the fireplace, the deep gray of his uniform foreboding against the cream furnishings. Back straight and hands calmly folded in front of him, he was at ease—here. Sitting in her own home.

More alarming, Henri sat on the floor near the captain's black boots, playing with toys on the rug as the fire crackled behind.

The captain rose, adjusted his jacket, and gave her a bow.

"Mrs. Paquet. Good day. I am Captain von Hiller." He paused, as if wondering whether she could still place him among all the uniforms in the city. "From the bookshop last summer?"

"Oui, sir. I remember."

And the French, which is remarkably accurate.

"We have been waiting for you for some time. I think your family grew concerned once the sun set. It is not wise to be out after dark, you know, even if we're not yet to curfew."

And that warranted some sort of explanation, she was certain.

"Um . . . my apologies. Had I known you intended a visit at

my home, I'd have made certain to be here," she said, even as Henri saw her and bounced up into her arms. She kissed his temple, then set him down again. "Henri, dear. Why don't you go find Grand-mère, hmm?"

"He needn't leave on my account. We've been enjoying his puzzles, haven't we?" The captain looked at Henri and Sandrine's heart flooded with caution. "Go on. Back to your play while I have a visit with your *Mutter.*"

She swallowed hard, looking down into the face so like Christian's, waiting for the direction to carry from her lips instead of the man's.

"Bien, Henri. You may go."

"What kept you?" The captain said and sat again, casual, as if they were old friends instead of strangers. She noted how he glossed over the fact that *they* were responsible for the callous death of her father-in-law and chose to ease into conversation as if he possessed the right to know the inner workings of her daily routine.

"The weekly shop," she said, and then, fearing he'd note there was no basket on her arm, she added, "But the lines have been too long so I've returned empty-handed. We will try again tomorrow."

"That is a shame. An unfortunate consequence of war, I'm afraid. But rationing has a purpose. Give us time to work out the particulars of a fallen government, Mrs. Paquet, and you will see marked improvement in conditions in short order."

"I see my mother-in-law has offered you some refreshment. Might I fetch anything else for you?"

There was wine in a glass on the low table in front of him, untouched. They had but one or two bottles left. Marguerite must have seen fit to open one for the officer's visit. How terrible for her to have served one of the uniforms who had only months before dragged her husband through that very room to be shot out in the street.

"She has, thank you. But I do not partake while in uniform, so with regret, I'm afraid I must decline."

He watched how she stood in the parlor and perhaps noticed how Marguerite had used the opportunity to melt into the background of the flat. Sandrine wouldn't have been surprised if she'd be found tossing suitcases onto the fire escape through the bathroom window or training a weapon at the back of the man's head from the shadows of the hall. Any scenario could have proved possible.

"Please. Do sit down," he offered, palm directing Sandrine to the chair that would place her between the officer and her son's place lying down, kicking his legs up while piecing puzzle blocks on the carpet. "It has come to my attention that the head of your household is . . . unaccounted for."

"If you refer to my husband, he was called to service in the early days of the war. But that is not irregular. There are a great many men away from home right now for service, including yourself."

My, how she hoped that wasn't seen as cheek. It felt right to walk a line with him, edging toward providing answers to questions—but just—and giving the most veiled of assurance that Sandrine knew her place and respected that the line drawn between him and her son could be seen.

"Mödlareuth will survive without me for a while. A small farming community outside of Berlin is not the same view as Paris, making home seem all the more . . . abiding. But I come on another matter. I understand your father-in-law was arrested for criminal activities against the Reich just this past autumn, concerning his now-defunct publishing enterprise."

Arrested?

Her insides churned like she'd swallowed fire. They'd gone from farming communities to her murdered father-in-law in a single breath. If the captain meant to intimidate her—to learn if they were carrying on printing anti-Hitler leaflets from inside their flat—it wouldn't work.

"My father-in-law is dead, sir."

And you know how.

"Hmm. I am but sorry to hear it came to that. And with the men of your household gone, you must need work, ja? How do you afford living here with no income?"

How indeed.

If he looked beyond the illumination of the parlor and the library, he'd have seen a completely different story. One where the mistress of the house had given up her furs and jewels and paintings—family heirlooms of generations—sold for a pittance on the street in order to put bread on their table. Where the captain sat was the last of the luxury to survive into 1941. But with the way things were going, such harsh rationing on everything from leather to yard goods, wood and glass, and even basic provisions such as sugar, flour, salt, and milk that had been in place since August of the year before . . . the forecast for improvement was bleak.

"We do our best, Captain, to live within our circumstances."

"I will come to the point, Mrs. Paquet. I am here because the Reich has need of your services. We have a matter of cataloging fine art across the city, and your education offers us the opportunity to fill a vacancy without delay."

"You're offering me a job?"

"Less an offer of employment than supplementing a need by the Reich. You will be paid as an employee of the Einsatzstab Reichsleiter Rosenberg—ERR. There is a Sonderstab Bildende Kunst or 'Special Staff for Pictorial Art.' The agency works out of the Louvre museum complex and we find that the Jeu de Paume storehouse is the best place to sort all of the reallocation of the art in the city."

"Reallocation of art?"

"To protect it, of course. This is war, is it not? The Führer is not without compassion, Mrs. Paquet."

Something slithered inside, the comment shocking for how it made her feel ill. Compassion for canvas but cruelty toward human flesh. Sandrine kept her mouth shut, gears in her mind ticking off the reasons she couldn't work for him and the reasons she might have to if she was to avoid the ruthlessness in his manner.

"Hitler puts great emphasis on the arts and would be pained if any were to be lost in this conflict. It is a primary reason why your city was spared a wave of bombs—to preserve the cultural sites. I've been tasked by the leadership of the Reich to manage the day-to-day operations of managing the flow of fine art in the city. And we have need of additional attachés who have education in this area of expertise." The captain looked to Henri, innocent and playing with his toys. "I thought for the benefit of your family and of your son here, this opportunity should go to you, Mrs. Paquet."

Sandrine knew it wasn't an offer of a job but a placement—one she could be forced into doing, without pay, and even without the veiled threat of keeping her precious son in the room as a reminder of how savage their masters could be to the noncompliant.

She must accept. Moreover, she must appear quite grateful as she did.

"Then on behalf of my family, I accept."

"Report to 1 Place de la Concorde Monday at nine o'clock. Both you and the girl from the bookshop. Tell them at the front gate that *Hauptmann im Generalstab*—Captain von Hiller—has approved your admission. They will allow you to pass through security to the inner offices, where I will be waiting to receive you."

Why was strength so elusive, so foreign feeling it seemed, every time she stood in his presence? Her legs fought a wobble even as he appeared ready to take his leave.

"And Mrs. Paquet—" He turned and stopped in the entry, steps away from where she'd first come in concealing a letter that could well have determined her to have the exact same fate as her father-in-law before her. "Some in the ERR cautioned me against this assignment because of the association to your late father-in-law's publishing activities. But I assured them that you are a model Parisian wife and mother, loyal to the Vichy and dedicated to the arts in Paris. I hope you can see me as your ally. If you should have any further problems with the lines at the local shops, do let me know. We do not wish for our ERR employees to report to work without the proper appearance. This is a model occupation and I should be displeased if you and your family do not receive the foodstuffs you need to remain healthy during this time."

"Thank you, Captain. I will remember that."

"You're very welcome. Until Monday." He tipped his uniform hat and, as abrupt as his nature from the bookshop, left without another word.

Sandrine stood in his wake, hand balancing on the telephone table until she was absolutely certain he'd gone. Her breaths raced in and out as the fire crackled in the parlor, as the lights blazed back to the library. She crumpled into the cushioned seat of the telephone table bench, sorting tangled thoughts.

Was she actually working . . . for the Nazis?

Marguerite came out of hiding, drifting through the doorway, her visage tracked with lines of worry. No tears, as was her way, but bitterness and fear. "What did he want?"

"It appears I have been ordered to accept a job. At the Galerie nationale du Jeu de Paume." Remembering the letter, she looked up at the door and rushed to it. She slid the chain, then turned the bolt into place. "My coat? Where is it?"

"On your bed," Marguerite offered, then spun on her heels as Sandrine fled down the hall. "I couldn't reappear before him, fearing I'd say something to that devil that would condemn us all to the same fate as my husband."

Sandrine ran into the bedroom, pinning her knees to the floor before the mattress, and reached for the letter from the pocket of the coat's mauve satin lining. She ran her fingernail under the sealed envelope flap, her heart lurching when she saw tiny sprays of blood splattered against the sealed side.

Out she pulled a letter, flipped it over. It was signed, *Je t'aime— mon cœur, Christian.*

Always, when they'd parted, the same words.

Tears flooded then, the joy close to overwhelming as it wracked from her core, crumpling Sandrine down at the foot of the bed. She clasped the inked pages between her palms, smiling, crying, praising what she'd feared was a silent God for all they'd gone through, now for the merciful provision of information about her love.

"What is it?" Marguerite dropped to the floor at her side.

Sandrine scanned the words, grateful, heart bursting as her fingertips ran over the beautiful smudged ink. His hands had held it, his thoughts had penned it, and he'd carried it, wherever he was— through fighting and death and who knew what horrors—until he could send a piece of himself back to her.

"He is alive," she cried, holding the letter out, grabbing her mother-in-law by the shoulders. "Do you understand what this means? Christian is alive, or he was two months ago. He was fighting in Calais. Oh my Lord. His unit was preparing to make a stand at Calais, for the soldiers at Dunkirk." She flipped the envelope. No postmark, of course. "It's from where? The North? Or a prisoner camp in Germany?"

"Can I hold it?" Marguerite's hand held a slight tremble.

"Oui." Sandrine pressed the letter into her palm, holding firm, staring at her squarely in the eyes, though they shed tears. "He is alive. That's what we focus on now—Christian is alive. And no matter what, he's fighting to come back to us."

Even without answers. Even with a forced invitation to walk into a devil's den and have to submit to his bidding the next week. As she and Marguerite shared the precious letter in their hands, Sandrine could do nothing in that moment but praise.

17 March 1944
1 Place de la Concorde
Paris, France

All Paris held its breath.

Sandrine did with it, as she crouched in a cutout between the street corner and a building's end, pressing her palms into the limestone wall with a band of strangers as bullets pinged the façade against the street.

She'd abandoned her bicycle on the sidewalk when gunfire erupted midride on her way to the galerie. It lay now with its straw basket crumpled against a lamppost, as stray bullets whistled and passersby tripped over the tires in their haste to run for the protection of the cutout between buildings.

"Baissez la tête . . . Baissez la tête!" A man shouted the warning over and over, as if they needed an invitation to duck their heads from an exchange of machine-gun fire between a band of Résistance fighters and their German overlords.

Tensions had hit a fever pitch as whispers of an Allied invasion permeated conversations at cafés and parks across the city. Rumors of German defeats on the eastern front had made their rounds the year before, though Paris was still cut off from news of the rest of the world and talk was hushed or quieted completely should any uniforms happen by. But Mademoiselle Valland had a pulse on news reports through her Résistance contacts and could confirm to their small number working at the Jeu de Paume that it appeared a tide was turning with the war, and the pendulum was swinging away from the Germans. They seemed aware of their régime's possible demise and had begun odd preparations, crating art for goodness knew what purpose.

The Résistance, for its part, grew restless.

Bold, even.

There were leaflet drops from rooftops. Rumors and speculation of the crumbling Nazi régime were printed in publications that were slipped under doors in the dead of night. Posters were nailed bold as brass on street corners—even outside the German embassy—and now it seemed random skirmishes would continue pinning Parisians down even in the midst of their morning routines.

It took a good half hour to make it out of the alley and more to make it through the resulting swarm of SS who took names and questioned onlookers. Sandrine was forced past the sight of bodies facedown in the street, with Résistance blood painting the pavement red, and it took the rest of the ride to the galerie for Sandrine's hands to calm in their trembling against the handlebars. Once she'd stowed her bicycle and made it through the front doors—quite late and tearing off her gloves with tam in hand as she hurried back to the offices—she hoped to go unnoticed.

"Mrs. Paquet?" The captain entered her office, no knock at the door as she was hanging her coat on the curl of a wooden hat rack in the corner. He flipped his wrist, checking his watch.

"Captain." Sandrine brushed back loose hair at her temple, tucking and tidying as she moved to sit at her desk and begin her workday, long after the ten o'clock hour. "My apologies for arriving late. It won't be repeated."

"I would like to speak with you for a moment."

He waited, his back to her until Sandrine stood and followed him to the windows. After a few seconds of silence, he motioned to the sorry sight of her bicycle, which had been tossed against a hedgerow bordering the gardens.

There hadn't been a thought beyond getting inside to work, and she hadn't considered until that very moment what it actually looked like. The basket was hanging off to one side of the handlebars, crushed and frayed at the seam. Two spokes were bent in the back wheel. And who knew how the tires were still intact, for the side facing them had the very distinct marks of bullet holes visible down the length of the metal frame.

"This is why you were late?"

She swallowed hard.

How close had she come to . . . being gunned down in the street? And now with the not knowing which direction a conversation would go, the words vanished right out of her mouth. Had he suspicions of Résistance rendezvous or clandestine activities that would result in a bicycle that looked as hers did? How close he'd be to the truth if he allowed his mind to trail too far in that direction.

"It was nothing to speak of."

"This was definitely something. What happened to you?"

"I was caught in a skirmish between two parties on the street on the way to the galerie, but I'm alright. None the worse for wear. We're getting used to it in the city." Sandrine squared her shoulders to the glass, stiffening her spine to put punctuation on it. "I assure you I am well and quite ready to work."

The captain stood in the sunlight, glaring at the bicycle as uniforms passed by the glass and activity going on behind them went unnoticed. He seemed transfixed, imagining perhaps what kind of incident could turn her bicycle into a holey mess yet allow her to walk away unscathed.

"You will have an escort from now on," he said, the statement rough, and paused, with an alarming tone of anger just barely restrained beneath the surface. He stood, hands anchored behind his back, jaw flexing to iron.

Oh no.

A Nazi escort.

An auto adorned with swastika flags on the front fender? Soldiers following her wherever she went? It was the last thing she wanted from him. An occasional automobile arriving as it had on New Year's was bad enough. But a clockwork association of this sort would not go unnoticed. And Sandrine feared, as she could not openly declare her alliance with La Résistance, it would not go unpunished by those with growing hatred for the Nazi tyrants.

The line she walked was already a string, and now thinning by the day.

The captain turned, for the first time that morning, and directed his gaze fully in her eyes. He looked down at her hands, reached for one and turned it palm up, then the other. She hadn't noticed the scrapes from the rough limestone until that moment. She must have gripped the wall tighter than she'd thought, as her palms were a raw pink.

"This is . . . unacceptable. I will come and collect you myself. Every day, if I must."

"It's not necessary." She coolly hid her hands behind her back, though her insides coiled at the implication he cared for her safety. "I am not afraid of my city. I am a Parisienne—we do what we must to survive."

"When I first offered you this assignment, it was on the predication that your family would be looked after. It was to help, not harm."

"And we are looked after, I assure you. My mother-in-law and I do quite well."

"Mrs. Paquet?" Mademoiselle Valland's voice cut down the hall, sure and sharp.

Sandrine turned, grateful and finally able to breathe when the curator walked in their direction. The captain dropped her hands and took a marked step away from her.

"*Excusez-moi*, Captain. I have been waiting for Mrs. Paquet. We have much to do today. Shipments to prepare for the train to Berlin and I need your note-taking skills, Sandrine. Kindly come and we shall resume our duties."

"Right away, mademoiselle." Sandrine nodded, a slight tip of the chin. More art coming in. Going out. Stolen. Sold. Picked over for the private homes of the Nazis' upper echelons. Or sent to burn piles in the Tuileries. It sickened her that this had become normal to them all. "Good day, Captain."

Bully for that. She followed her leader back to the offices.

Rose Valland had the instincts of a general but the air of a schoolmarm. Who else could have saved Sandrine from such an exchange?

"I'm certain I don't need to tell you this twice, but you ought to tread carefully, Mrs. Paquet," she whispered, not stopping in her hotfoot nature as they marched up the hall.

"I'm trying to. I've *been* trying to for more than three years."

"Well, try harder. You are a virtuous woman. And clever. This I know about you. But I am not unaware of the attentions he pays you—nor is anyone else here immune to seeing it. I will do my best to ensure you are assigned in other areas of the offices, but I would caution you not to be alone with this man. Not for a moment."

"I'm doing my best with it, I assure you." She sighed. "Now have you learned something else about the note or the Chanel gown?"

Mademoiselle Valland stopped sharply and stared her down from the top rim of her spectacles. "I will tell you more definitively when I know myself. In the meantime, take steps, Mrs. Paquet. Take steps to guard yourself before this gets out of hand."

Before this gets out of hand?

They'd left "before" behind some time ago. And so much for the girl talk about how to handle it.

Valland's warning was loud and clear, and not anything Sandrine hadn't been telling herself for months. It felt like dragging out a slow march to an execution spot, where she prayed she would not be forced to go. Between the bicycle, Paris's unpredictability in the streets, and the captain's steadily growing interest in her personal safety, Sandrine couldn't bear to face each coming day.

"Sandrine—"

She turned, unaware the captain had lingered after Mademoiselle Valland had kept going. He'd never whispered her name like that. Nor broken leadership character to catch her arm as she was rounding a corner and take the liberty to pull her back to him behind it, as if they had some private confidence.

She pulled her elbow free, softly, but with intention. "Sir?"

"There is an opening of an exhibition tomorrow evening at the l'Opéra National. To honor the Führer's contribution to the culture of the arts in Paris. Representatives of the ERR are expected to attend, and Baron von Behr insists that we go."

"*We* . . . go. You mean everyone?"

"For each of the officers, there is an invitation extended for us and one guest. I should like you to be my guest."

For reasons she understood heart-deep, Christian's face flashed through her mind. From that last day at the train station, it was the memory that had become the boldest, the one asking her to be brave. And Victor's, telling her not to do what was easy, but to always do what was right. And Rose, who'd been putting her life on the line for years, in order to keep their ruse going in the very gallery halls in which she stood.

Sandrine's limbs iced up.

If ever there was a time to summon courage on behalf of her husband and family—and herself—it was this moment. She'd managed to grit her teeth and hold fast to her wits while gunfire peppered the sidewalk that morning, but this was a different brand of terrifying.

No one refused a Nazi officer.

No one.

"I'm afraid I cannot do that, Captain."

"Why?"

"I am not free to do so." She cleared her throat. "My dance card is already full."

He looked back in the direction of the bicycle in its pitiful state, bullet holes reflecting as the spring sun shone down, and the flag of the Third Reich—a bold swastika cutting the blue sky—that waved from a pole in the gardens behind it.

"You see? That bicycle? It is what can happen if we allow the rabble to believe they've won. This is your duty. To Germany and to France. It is ours together to educate them. We must represent the best of Paris and what we are doing here for the culture in the city. So I will send a car for you tomorrow at six o'clock in the evening, and on every workday morning after that. You needn't travel in this city alone again. Not for a moment. You will be protected."

And to him, that was the end of it.

He nodded. As usual, with no room for negotiation as he began walking away, and with no time for her to give a rebuttal had she wanted to.

"Oh, and Sandrine?"

Her stomach pitted like a snake coiling to hear him take the liberty of calling her by name. *Twice.*

She turned back.

"Wear the Chanel."

CHAPTER 13

Production of the French *Vogue* may have been suspended in 1940, but the German-overseen publications to replace it were in full force the following year.

In matters of politics and the pseudo daily life of the Parisian, *La Gerbe* wouldn't have been a newspaper Lila would pick up. Its editors were defiant in leaving out mention of the real happenings across Paris—anything that was not pro-Nazi in influence—such as the bustle on the street in the days prior when it was rumored thousands of "foreign" Jews were rounded up by Vichy police and forced to register for transport, goodness knew why or to where.

The streets were rumbling over it all, but who would have known by reading *La Gerbe*'s latest edition? Lila had tucked it under her arm as she exited the elevator at the Ritz, open to a prominent article noting the recent visits to Paris of high-ranking Nazi officials, such as Reichsmarschall Hermann Wilhelm Göring, fêting with Amélie's Baron Kurt von Behr and young French society women showing off their exclusive French couture designs. One note in particular was of a "House of Lila de Laurent" design—the

171

reason she'd been dismissed from her employ at Nina Ricci just that afternoon.

Lila knocked on the suite door, only to find it opened by an SS officer coming out as she was going in.

Oh. This must be him?

But Lila thought better almost immediately. This officer was younger. Only thirty maybe. Haughty too. With impeccable grooming—a tight crop of blond hair and not a whisker of shadow could be seen upon his jaw. And when his sharp green eyes met hers, they made no effort to hide how he surveyed her black suit and matching tam tipped low over her brow, his gaze boring through her as she stood in the hall.

"Je peux vous aider?"

No greeting, just a barked question of whether he could help her with something—which didn't seem a warm invitation from a Nazi officer staring her down.

"Excusez-moi. I am the dressmaker, here for an appointment with Mademoiselle Olivier."

"Stop pestering her, Captain!" Amélie's voice floated from inside, retaining a note of obstinacy directed at the officer blocking the doorway. "She is not a spy. She is my dearest friend since we were girls in knee socks. And before you ask, there are no identification papers she must present to you for that. I will vouch for her. Come, come in, Lila. Step around the gate squad." Amélie ignored the officer and waved her to come past him.

"Bonjour." The captain gave so curt an agreement, Lila wasn't sure what to do. He strode out and was trotting down the marble stairs at the end of the hall before she could think twice about it.

Lila stepped in, thoroughly prepared to confront Amélie about the article but not knowing exactly what to do after. She closed the door, stepped into the suite, and was greeted by a gaggle of French ladies, all seated in a semicircle around the fireplace. They'd kicked off their heels and were smiling, having turned from cocktails and gold-rimmed plates of *entremets* to greet her with poppy-lipped smiles all beaming in her direction.

Amélie rose, approached in a cool dress of posy pink with gold ruching at the waist and sharp, structured shoulders, and kissed Lila's cheeks, her enthusiasm bright as her lips.

"He is a pain that one. We all agree on it, though if he ever did decide to crack a smile, I think one or two of us here might just swoon. Isn't he divine? But he's taken no interest in the ladies here—must have a Fräulein back home. So he came to drop off papers of some such nonsense today without a word to us, and now the baron will probably spend our dinnertime reading through the lot instead of going out to Maxim's with me. Honestly—men."

The parlor played host to *Belle Époque* ladies seated on a tufted chaise longue, shop bags, and candy-striped hatboxes bursting open with tissue paper on the pink paisley area rug. A mountainous pile of ivory silk lay in a lopsided fold upon an upholstered chair, illuminated by a gleaming chandelier hanging from a carved rosette ceiling in the center of the room. The vase of roses on the mantel had been replaced by a gold-framed painting of a still life with apples, the bright greens and reds accentuated by an active fire dancing on the hearth beneath it.

Amélie looked up with her, pausing to admire the piece in the room's glow.

"Oh, you noticed. Isn't it *très charmante*? Cézanne. It was from the lot of the discarded art no one wanted. But to be honest, I had to ask who in the world that is and why he painted a handful of apples dropped on a farmer's table. I'll never understand art."

True to form, she bounced from one thought to the next and clapped her hands together.

"Ladies? Attention, s'il vous plaît. This is our famous dressmaker from the House of LDL. Do show Lila your appreciation for coming out to see us today."

Lila swallowed hard and tried to put on her best smile, even at being caught off guard as the ladies twittered with polite claps and eager, dimpled smiles.

"Look at you—you are positively speechless! Don't you understand? My dear, all of these ladies are here to see *you*. This is Greta with the blonde waves and a fresh diamond on a very important finger. She wishes to talk about wedding gowns with you, no doubt. Camille is over there in the chartreuse—she always arrives in *vert*, and that little evergreen number you designed for me has been keeping her up nights until she has one of her own. Then there is Margot with the pearls and perfect ebony crown—our very own Hedy look-alike. The resemblance is uncanny, non? And on the end with the pretty smile and long legs is our sweet Adélaïde." Amélie leaned in to whisper in Lila's ear. "Who incidentally was just added to our number by a très strapping Captain Scheel from the German embassy who has lately taken up space on this floor."

"Bonjour, ladies." Lila nodded to them, who went back to their cocktails and layered desserts.

Amélie checked her over, finding only a satchel hooked over her elbow and the newspaper in a gloved hand.

"You didn't bring your sketches?"

"Non. You telephoned and said only to come for a visit."

"Well, I thought it should be understood, my dear. I have been talking you up to every female in this building. You should have expected they would all wish to see your work. And that pile of silk. Can you believe this? Parachutes! The baron found them for me. No one can hope to get silk at the moment, but they will be perfect for an opera gown and whatever is left over can become sweet little whatnots to go underneath."

Lila held out the copy of *La Gerbe*, folded to the photograph of the paramours smiling for the camera.

"It's because of this I came to talk to you."

"Oh, don't remind me." Amélie swiped the article, glared, and shook her head, then handed it back. The mixed display of disgust and annoyance played out with ease. "They never publish names and even when they do, they spell them incorrectly. I have been left out of mention too many times to count for their incompetence. If this continues, I mean to telephone the editor."

"Ricci let me go this afternoon because of it. Now I'll be hard-pressed to find work anywhere with my name out there as the competition."

"And I am sorry for that. Or I should say that I am sorry for *them*—they have lost a treasure. My dear, you don't need them. Your star is rising." Amélie swept her arm across Lila's shoulders, then squeezed her in a hug. "I have learned today that there is to be a performance of Wagner this autumn featuring the famous soprano Germaine Lubin at the Palais Garnier, and it is rumored that Hitler himself may come to see it, as she is a favorite of his. Every woman here will need a gown, and for all the parties in between now and then. You will rival Rouff, Valois, Dior, and certainly Ricci after this. With Chanel having closed her salon, you have become the hottest little ticket in Paris."

It once might have been every dressmaker's dream to hear those words, except now it felt like her worst nightmare. To have the opportunity to piece together creations that made a woman shine with confidence, to help her feel strong and capable and beautiful in ways she hadn't before . . . it was both Lila's passion and her gift. But in that moment, as Amélie looked on her with such ignorance of what was happening all around them, it bode more as a curse.

"Since you have not brought your sketchbook with you, we can use mine. I drew up an idea or two last night. Would you mind, Lila? My journal—lavender leather in the top drawer of the bedside table."

Amélie didn't wait for an answer, instead rejoined her entourage of smiles gathered around the mound of silk. It was as if the parlor were full of paper dolls dressing up for a reception at Marie Antoinette's court and they'd all been infected with apathy as they sipped cocktails from sugared rims and read fashion magazines that gave a glossy, Nazi version of truth.

The best to do was get through it. Look at the designs. Stay as on-the-surface as she could. And as soon as Lila walked out the front doors of the Ritz, she'd find work as a tailor or perhaps a shopgirl somewhere—try to rebuild again, even as she removed herself from Amélie's world.

Lila crossed into the boudoir, a chill running up her spine when she saw a mass of gray—a pressed and starched uniform hanging on the open door to the closet—as if their overlords had the omnipresent power to spy in every room. She hurried to the bedside table and opened the drawer, expecting to see a journal but instead . . . papers. Files of some sort. And a photo sticking out from a paper clip on the top of the stack.

And her heart stopped.

Lila ran her fingertips over a name scrawled in block letters: TOULIARD.

Tipping the edge with her index fingernail, she opened the file to find a ledger with catalog numbers and photographs, images labeled *Juifs—Touliard* that had to have been taken from inside René's family home. Their mansion was just down the street from one of the prominent Rothschild residences, in the fashionable district of the city. It had housed a collection of art from paintings upon the grand marble fireplace mantel in the entry, to ornate vases, a sterling tea service with a claw-foot tray held by anonymous uniformed hands, and even a delicate Cartier necklace, the teardrop diamonds winking back at her in horrifying snapshots of black and white.

Oh no . . . The roundup of Jews in the days prior.

If the Nazis had photographs from inside René's home, where was his family? And where was he, heaven help her? If all of their family heirlooms had been ransacked for a Nazi collection, what did that mean?

"Lila? Did you find it?"

To the melody of Amélie's come-hither call, Lila slammed the drawer shut and rushed to the other bedside table. She found the journal with a collection of ornate French parfum bottles and tubes of lipstick that rolled when she opened the drawer. Finding it wedged under a sapphire velvet–covered jewelry box tucked in the back—was it the same from the photos?—she swiped it up.

Amélie had to have known. She'd have seen the name alongside the necklace and been aware it belonged to René's family. Lila stared back at her and the faux existence permeating the parlor, with the ladies twittering over their couture dreams and she queening over it all.

Lila made a decision: If there was anything she could do to learn the fate of the Touliard family and help to change it, she would dress every single one of the spoiled ingénues placed before her. And if she could step into that suite again and find information that could help René in any measure at all, she vowed to play their game—even up to dressing Hitler himself—and win.

"I have it, ladies." Lila presented the journal to excited smiles in the room as she moved to separate out the reams of silk. "Let's begin."

---

17 FEBRUARY 1944
61 BOULEVARD DE CLICHY
PARIS, FRANCE

"Wake up, Lila." René knelt over her bed in the pâtisserie flat bedroom, patting her cheek until she focused on his face through the dark.

"Quickly. Wake up. We have to go out."

In the world Nigel and René had accepted her into, you sprang to action and asked questions while you ran. Lila had learned that well enough in the short weeks she'd been in Montmartre. René rarely slept, so he'd given her his room and dozed on the cot by the fireplace, as it seemed messages were always coming in and going out, and both he and Nigel were glued to the transistor in the shop's off hours, waiting for word from Carlyle on the movements of the Allies or poring over any transmissions they could take in. But if he was waking her now, when judging by the sheen of moonlight out the window it was not yet dawn, there must be sound reason.

"What's wrong?" Lila rose, sliding her stocking feet to the frozen floor.

He turned his back to her as she moved to slip into the pale blue dress she'd made—a serviceable frock of gabardine with stylish patch pockets and buttons down the front—that she hung over the end of the bed rail each night. How Lila wished it were a pair of trousers and a shirt like those worn by the Maquis women fighting in the countryside, but with the Vichy having outlawed pants for women in the city, wearing them put her too much at risk for being stopped and questioned.

"A call came in to the phone box in the dining room. Nigel's caught up by the Seine. My truck is one of the few allowed out for deliveries during the early morning curfew hours, so we can fetch him under the letter of the law," he said, and she heard the distinct sound of him loading and checking his pistol while he stood opposite her. "We don't have long before the sun comes up, but he can't take a chance to wait that long."

René turned back as she pulled on a wool coat he'd found for her, the aubergine color deep enough to keep her semi-hidden in the dark. She pulled on a scratchy wool beret and tucked her clipped waves up under it.

He handed over her Liberator. "Good idea to keep your hair back. You have sharp eyes and I'm afraid we might need them. If I have to get involved in something, I'll need you to bring the truck back."

"What you mean is, we need to look and act like shadows

tonight—secret propagandists on the move." Lila slipped the Liberator into her boot and readjusted the beret off her brow when she stood again.

"Something like that." He took a deep breath and picked up one of the crates of bread he'd set on the bureau—their cover, maybe, in case they were stopped. "The rest is loaded in the truck. Ready?"

Loading the other one in her arms, she nodded. "Let's go."

The city was pitch black and the River Seine roiled dark through it, like ink with a vendetta against its banks.

Their truck was stopped by the SS right outside of the Boulevard de Clichy in Montmartre, as René had expected. But it appeared he knew the guards and chatted as he handed over identification papers for a Monsieur and Madame LaChelle, then handed croissants in waxed paper through the open window to the group of SS posted on night watch.

"Destination?"

"First Arrondissement. To Sainte-Chappelle and then the usual deliveries at the Hôtel Ritz."

"Das ist gut, LaChelle. We'll call ahead for you. Be sure you stop at the security checks when you get there."

They were waved through, without even opening the back of the truck, which was something she'd seen all over the city on too many occasions.

"They certainly trust you." She watched through the window as the SS settled back to the checkpoint, sitting on a stone wall that rounded a street corner peppered with cabaret windmills in the background.

"They don't trust me. They just believe I'm a subservient fool and will continue to be so as long as I don't give them reason to think otherwise. They say they'll call ahead but they never do. We learned that the first year of occupation."

René kept careful watch over the streets as he drove, the truck chugging into the night, the cough of the old engine seeming the only sound left in a sleeping Paris.

"So, where are we really going?"

He heaved a sigh. "Sainte-Chapelle."

"What? That's in the center of the city! It will be crawling with SS. Why would you tell them where we're really going?"

"First rule of the shadow world is always make a lie as close to the truth as you can—it's easier to remember, easier to prove, and much easier to explain later if you're picked up and questioned. And we don't have a choice. Nigel is in it thick, I'm afraid. He went out to meet a PWE contact and got himself pinned down by SS patrols near the cathedral. We can get in under the guise of donations of bread for the hungry, and he'll be waiting on the riverbank down below the street. We get in, pick him up, and we're on track for morning deliveries before the sun rises."

Was it that easy to navigate around Nazi-occupied streets? Just swing by and pick up an undercover British intelligence agent as he strolled by the river? Lila breathed deep, willing the pit in her stomach to stop nagging her, even as the Liberator felt like a lead boulder down in her boot.

It certainly didn't inspire confidence in what they were doing if she couldn't get herself together for a drive through the city, let alone anything worse.

"Tell me you've done this before." She watched as shops and municipal buildings whizzed by the windows, alongside a cinema with Jean Grémillon's *Le Ciel est à Vous—The Woman Who Dared—* plastered across the marquee. The messaging was more than a tad ironic, given what they were about. She looked away. "Or maybe don't tell me. I don't want to think about you doing this sort of thing for the last few years. My heart is thumping a drumbeat just by doing it now."

"And how long have you been double-crossing the Nazi elite, mademoiselle dressmaker? Don't you think it gives me pause to consider someone pointing a gun at you and pulling the trigger? And that actually happened."

"Touché." She smiled, in spite of herself, and ghosted a hand to the nearly forgotten scar forming on her side. "So, tell me—how does one break into the espionage business? Is it more than being astute with languages and making pastries in your free time?"

"Something like that. But a little more cavalier to fall into. I met Nigel in London, after my father had died and I had become discontent with . . . everything at that point. But then came the rumor of war with the Germans and Nigel's association with the British government came to light with it."

"So you decided to fight with him. Just like that? Why weren't you called up by the French Army when we mobilized?"

"I wanted to, believe me. But I was convinced otherwise by a friend. Told me I'd be needed here and he could arrange something for me to still help, even if I stayed on." He smiled, maybe thinking back to more innocent days. "I'm afraid I've always been a bit on the rebellious side when I'm told I can't do something. Makes me want to set my sail into the wind, so to speak. So the opportunity to work against them and right under their noses—it was too much to pass up."

"And yet you did tell me going to Versailles was impossible. I wonder what happened to your sail then."

"I meant something else at the time." He didn't elaborate, just turned them down toward the river.

As the shadowed arches of the Pont Neuf came into view, quite without warning, René reached into his belt and pulled his pistol free. He eased the truck to a stop, brakes whistling through the dark. Rain misted the windshield, blurring the view bathed by the headlights into a watercolor portrait bleeding down the glass. But even with the obscurity, there was enough light to see it once René flicked the beams off.

An SS soldier blocked the cobblestone street and gripped a machine gun with the barrel fixed in their direction.

CHAPTER 14

14 JUNE 1941
1ST ARRONDISSEMENT
PARIS, FRANCE

Luftwaffe soldiers relaxed at a street-front bistro, sipping cafés and reading newspapers in their blue-gray side caps and uniform jackets, taking in the sights on the balmy morning. Sandrine and Henri had been caught up in the crowd they watched with passing interest, people flowing on the busy sidewalk, weaving around the line to the cobbler's shop that stretched paces out its front door.

The plight of the working Parisian grew bleaker by the day as rationing clamped down and the once-abundant wares like shoes or ladies' chapeaux or a dinner out at a restaurant that didn't cost more than two weeks' salary became scarce everywhere. Sandrine had enough ration tickets to have Henri's shoes repaired, but it was a guess what supplies would be available and whether they were in line early enough to leave triumphant in the end.

One of the soldiers eyed Henri as he balanced on the curb in front of Sandrine like a tightrope walker in a *cirque de rue*, the hole in his sole showing off his sock underneath as he danced on the wire.

"Come, Henri." Sandrine pulled him to her other side, turning her back on the soldiers.

They waited in the shade offered by a row of cherry trees, the gangly limbs stretching out along the sidewalk with only a few of spring's pink blossoms left to usher in summer's roll. Passersby moved on, weaving in and out of the line as patrons tried to keep their places assured. She held Henri close as bicycles sped by on their way to the Louvre or the Jardin des Tuileries, where the once-manicured gardens would be bustling with vegetable production in every square meter of grass.

It was still Paris, but not the halcyon days anyone remembered.

The line moved forward. The Luftwaffe were soon gone, replaced by new uniforms. And the clock ticked on as Sandrine edged out on the curb, craning her neck to find the never-ending start of the line.

"Pa-pa!" Henri bolted from Sandrine's grasp, running along the sidewalk. His little legs and sad, broken-down shoes were no hindrance. He ducked in between startled housewives and old men with canes as Sandrine lost her place in line to go after him.

"Henri? *Viens ici!*"

A defiant schoolboy running down a sidewalk, daring to cross over street traffic without looking, and shouting out for someone's papa was every mother's worst nightmare. Sandrine nearly lost her heel from running, the pointed edge getting caught in a sewer grate as she tried to rush past the street traffic.

Fortunate they were that Paris was without so many automobiles as used to clog up the streets, but the many bicycles and Nazi flag–adorned Wehrmacht service vehicles that did roll down every street weren't likely to stop in time for a wayward child and mother in pursuit.

A horn honked and Sandrine's heart nearly stopped as she watched,

Henri sweeping up the opposite curb as she was forced to wait for a break in traffic. Finally able to run again, she found him a ways ahead on the sidewalk with what looked like a Luftwaffe soldier bent at the knee, his back to her—odd, as if he were talking to her son.

And then he was gone—disappeared into the crowd like the rest, a newspaper under his arm and blue-gray side cap melting into the mosaic of uniforms dotting the streets.

"Henri! Why . . . ?" Sandrine glanced around. The soldier was long gone, just like her breath and her sanity. She knelt, midi skirt pressed against the rough pavement, looking him in the eyes. "Why would you run from Maman like that?"

"J'ai vu mon pa-pa."

"You saw your pa-pa? Where?"

Henri pointed as he stood in half pants and his little button-down oxford, a cherub finger extending out to the mass of the Saturday crowd moving across the Louvre plaza, uniforms and Parisians intermingling. Sandrine joined him, searching the sea of faces in motion, as crazy as it seemed to be on the street waiting for her lost husband to magically appear.

"You couldn't have seen him." She stopped short of adding, "You don't even remember what he looks like," for how long Christian had been gone from Henri's young life.

"What was he wearing? Not a German uniform. Did a Wehrmacht soldier speak to you?"

He shook his head. "Non, Maman. He just smiled."

A Nazi would stop to smile at a little French boy?

She shook her head. "You are imaging things, chéri."

"But the photo—"

"What photo?"

"By the bed." He pointed again in the direction of the museum complex.

There was a photo by her bed—the only one she had of them

together: of Christian smiling wide on their wedding day and she in a split second of bliss had looked away from the camera and instead smiled up at her husband.

"You saw your pa-pa, the man smiling in the photo I keep by the bed at home?"

He nodded, chin to chest, just as sure as anything.

Sandrine sighed, knees still on the sidewalk, hardly noticing as people brushed by. The cobbler's line was long gone for them—there'd be no shoes fixed that day. And the mercurial prospect of getting into any other shop wasn't a certainty. Not like walking in the sun, along a garden path, letting a little boy believe in something, even if she knew it was a fairy tale.

"If you saw him—your pa-pa . . ." Sandrine stood, brushed off her knees, and took Henri's hand. "Then show me. Let's go find him together."

They walked all through the 1st Arrondissement that day, along the waterfront where soldiers watched as ducks paddled and children played with sailboats in the fountain water, and through the Jardin des Tuileries with a harvest of fragrant camellias to perfume garden paths, until Henri's feet hurt and she picked him up, carrying him the rest of the way home.

She hated that a soldier gave her his seat on le Métro.

Sandrine didn't want to take it. Even that minor capitulation felt wrong. But Henri was lead in her arms and her feet ached, so she sat. She held Henri close and kept her chin high as she prayed silently; at least they'd kept a little glimmer of hope alive that day. And dreamed a little, of Paris before the war. Of what it was like when Christian really did walk down a sidewalk under the blossoms of the cherry trees or pick a camellia and slip it behind her ear. Henri didn't remember, but Sandrine did.

There were times when even the summer days were not so dark.

Would they ever return?

——— • ◆ • ———

18 MARCH 1944
PLACE DE L'OPÉRA
PARIS, FRANCE

Captain von Hiller placed a hand under Sandrine's elbow as they stepped inside the grand lobby at l'Opéra National de Paris, and she drew in a steadying breath.

The exhibition of "*Les Monde des Chimères*" was to be just what its name implied: a world of dreams. Only the vision it provided was more of a calculated nightmare. The gilded Palais Garnier boasted soaring ceilings of classical architecture alongside the temporary display of modern art dubbed "degenerate"—the deplorable state of the Jewish artist set against the backdrop of "pure," preeminent art.

"This way."

He led Sandrine up the grand golden staircase to the exhibition entrance beyond, where rivers of champagne flowed and high-ranking German guests mingled with the upper echelons of Parisian society. She scanned the scene, noting the women stood out against a sea of gray, their brilliant ensembles in elegant ivory or black, sea blues, and shocking cherry reds bedecked by diamonds and white gloves. Every angle boasted the enemy, their gaiety unrestrained as couples swayed on a dance floor, ladies sipped champagne, and the lot appeared to savor every delicious delight that Paris could serve on a gilded platter.

Sandrine lifted the train of the Chanel gown with her palm, sweeping the blush chiffon off the floor as they moved to the front of the party.

The captain weaved them through the crowd to a reserved table near the band, filled with their ERR chief himself, Baron von Behr, and two other officers—the men older, harsh, and decorated—with elegant ladies at their sides. Captain von Hiller saluted with a sharp arm in the air: "Heil Hitler," and Sandrine whispered the same, her tongue burning on the words. The baron nodded and his guest—presented as his wife—turned to talk to one of the others' wives, without a flip of notice to Sandrine.

"After you, Mrs. Paquet."

It felt like a slap, of all the places in the world for the captain to choose to say her husband's name aloud to the table, to imply she was a married Frenchwoman who'd arrived into their den, as if willingly, upon his arm. They'd see Sandrine as with him now, and he was making a very public claim to it.

The officers talked of the Führer's glory as the brass instruments sang their song, and of the steady victory that was bound to come from conflicts in the west. The conversation ebbed and flowed around the darkest of topics, their party both lamenting and mocking the scourge of the hook-nosed art around them, and declaring how the Jews' eventual demise was warranted for their subhuman existence. It then flitted to ladies' comments on the Parisiennes' fashions, lingering over the remarkable soft pink Chanel ensemble they didn't know Sandrine had been forced to wear.

She looked in her lap before a wave of nausea threatened to overwhelm her.

The shock of the captain's thigh brushing hers and his gaze stopping to linger on her jaw in profile locked up Sandrine's breath entirely—telling her the action was not a mistake and the attentions had great thought behind them.

"Let's dance." He eased the jeweled clutch from the vise grip in her lap and placed it on the tabletop.

It was his hand extended that made Sandrine want to cry. To slap him away. To fight the entire world of gray if only she could refuse and, like a madwoman, scream at the top of her lungs to shatter the garish nightmare sparkling around her.

The golden dance floor was peppered with couples, all officers she'd guess by the amount of litzen shining from uniform collars. The captain swept his arm deep around her waist, his strength pulling her close until the blush embroidery of her bodice was molded to him, and her cheek was forced to press the faint hint of stubble along his jaw.

"We don't have to come here again," he whispered after a few moments of swaying alone, breath warming her ear. "I can see your discomfort."

"Discomfort?"

He nodded. "I can feel it. You're rigid tonight—not like you. Are you scared to be out after what happened with your bicycle in the street yesterday? You know you have nothing to fear if I am with you."

"I would say I'm merely alert as one should be in times such as this. Do you not think it wise to be on our guard?"

"Ja. Of course. But I'd hoped . . . to talk."

"We talk every day at the galerie, do we not?"

"I wanted to have a moment with you before we were interrupted. Away from the rest. But I realize now that I don't want you to be forced to talk to me or to hurry off every time Valland snaps her fingers in your direction. You can say no to her."

A breath escaped her lungs as he continued.

Stop. I don't want to hear this. And I want to say no to you.

"I am not like those junior officers who go to the cabarets every night. I am older. I have seen more. Been responsible for men's lives in ways that they couldn't begin to understand. I know what I want. I come from a small village—the view much humbler than this. My Mutter still lives there." He smiled at the thought, lips a faint shadow against her brow. "I have written to her about you, you know. This war will end one day, and I will return a hero. And it is because of this that I should wish for you to desire my company. To say 'Josef.' To choose me as I choose you. I assure you I wish it. Very much."

"I . . ." Sandrine whispered, shaking her head, knowing she should form some reply, but her voice refused to comply. She looked up, her mind intent on marking the exits on all sides of the reception hall without a plan to actually flee through one. "It seems Henri is always on my mind. I can think of little else but him."

"*Das ist gut*. Very good." He backed up to look down on her, matter-of-fact. "He is French but you will see: When this war is over, he will become German. You will be also. And you will have shown yourself to be a model mother. Homemaker. And wife."

"I am already married."

"Are you? Where is your husband, Sandrine?" He artfully ran a finger along the barrel roll at her temple and took the liberty to sweep it back to the delicate skin beneath her ear before he let go. "And why am I here, instead of him?"

Sandrine's steps betrayed her.

She stumbled in their waltz, stepping on his toe. He released her, arms free but hands ready to hold her waist should she lose her balance and begin to fall.

"I'm sorry—I'm afraid I'm a little unwell at the moment." She stepped back. Forced a smile to her lips as she planted a palm to her middle. "Um, is there a . . . ?"

"Ja. Services for ladies." He tipped his head toward a frosted-glass window down a hall. "Down the hall. In the back."

"I'll just be a moment then. Excusez-moi." Sandrine hurried to the table, swiped her clutch without much notice from the rest of their party, and forced herself to walk to the ladies' room instead of run, so she could bolt out the first door she could find and stop the freight train that was speeding her into the man's vile intentions.

She rounded the partition. Hurried down the deserted hall, and before she could press her hand to the frosted glass of the ladies' room door, she felt the shock of a hand sweep over her mouth. She couldn't cry out, couldn't even move as a uniformed arm locked across her shoulders and yanked her back from the sounds of the crowd into the silence.

"Hush!" The voice plagued her, her captor ordering calm even as he dragged her down a side hall to a door at its end. "Hush now." He pulled them into the dark and bolted the door, even as she kicked and fought, her heel busting a stack of chairs while she tried to bite the hand that smothered her.

"*Drina*, sweetheart!" The arms squeezed hard and shook to get her attention. "Be still."

Sandrine froze.

Their breathing was ragged against each other, her shoulders pressing hard to his chest, trying to match the feel of the arms around her to something from her memory. She searched through the shred of light from under the door—his arms, hands, wedding ring—anything for an indication to confirm with her eyes that the voice really was from who she'd thought.

"I'm going to remove this and I beg you for both our sakes not to cry out." He freed his palm from her lips, then loosed his arm from her shoulders.

Sandrine backed up until the skin on the exposed back of her gown pressed the cool of the wall. He lit a tiny flame from a Ronson and held the lighter's flicker to dance between them.

"Drina? It's me."

The flame died on a heartbeat.

Knocked out of his hand and lost, the Ronson clattered to the floor—the same as they did together, Sandrine falling headlong into her husband's arms.

Chapter 15

22 September 1941
15 Place Vendôme
Paris, France

Amélie's suite was a bazaar of garters and lipstick and ladies with glamorous waves lining every inch of the bathroom mirror. A last fitting before a big opera event that night spelled hours at the Hôtel Ritz with a gaggle of preening ladies, and Lila fit to be tied as the one dressmaker among them.

"Over here, dear Lila. I'm ready."

Amélie dropped her day dress to her satin brassiere and girdle to step out of the pool of lilac on the tile in the mirrored alcove. Lila left Margot to put on another layer of lipstick while she moved back to dress their queen.

"Bien. Then let's see where we are." Lila held the opera gown out, helping her step in, and then shimmied the ivory silk up over her hips to see the fit over the deep V with lace and silk-covered buttons down her back.

Magnifique—even shoulders. Perfect drape. Clean lines along the hips.

Not wanting to pull too hard and risk a tear, Lila eased the button placket together at the back, finding it unyielding the farther up she climbed in fastening the buttons until . . . no close.

Impossible. Something's off.

"I took these measurements three times," Lila thought out loud, pulling and smoothing silk that refused to cooperate.

"Well, I may as well say it. It doesn't fit." Amélie's painted smile faded into a line as she lowered her voice. She tossed a glance over her shoulder to the ladies flitting about beyond, checking that they were still lost in their own reflections.

"I just can't think what my mistake was." Lila gave up, rubbing a palm to her brow as she calculated what to do. "But it's not going to button all the way up. That's certain."

"Non. It will not. So you will have to open the back and let it out as best you can."

"What do you mean? Not by tonight. Amélie—we haven't time. Not to redo this entire panel. The buttons and all the lace detail you wanted . . . it took weeks just to finish it. I can't possibly have this ready by six o'clock."

"And I am sorry to have put you in this position. It's dreadful, but it couldn't be helped." Amélie wavered, looking at her reflection in the mirror and placing a palm over her middle.

Kilometers away from the portrait of a blissful mother-to-be, Amélie stared back with her hand frozen on her belly, meeting Lila's glance. She gave a light toss of the shoulders in a shrug that didn't match the weight of her eyes welling with tears. *"C'est la vie."*

Lila placed a hand over Amélie's wrist, giving her fingertips a light squeeze of support that was hidden from the rest of the girls. "Are you certain?" she whispered, horrified when Amélie answered with a curt nod.

"I thought it was all those cocktails making rounds at the parties. You know, the new one that Chanel so favors—the Sidecar? Ghastly yellow concoction if you ask me. I prefer the bubbly. But lately nothing will suffice to keep a meal down, even with the high cuisine we have at Maxim's. If I see another one of those canary glasses come my way, I'm afraid everyone will know my secret before I'm poised to share it."

"What does the baron say?"

It was a gamble, even asking.

They'd not exchanged a word of confidence about the fact that Amélie had entered into such a dangerous liaison with a married man—and a boorish Nazi of high rank at that. But somehow, the tears in Amélie's eyes melted some of the ice Lila had locked around the situation. They were women—a collaboratrice and a dressmaker secretly sympathetic to the growing French Résistance—but both facing terrible choices and even more serious consequences. Yet it was as if they were schoolgirls again. Girls with sweet, romantic little hopes and innocence in their eyes. For l'amour. And family. And the fairy-tale lives they'd always dreamt up. But that was not in any way the vision cast in Amélie's eyes as she stared back from the kaleidoscope of mirrors. Hers was a visage haunted with regret in a grand Ritz suite.

"Men do not notice these kinds of things, Lila. You will learn one day." She lost focus, looked down, and toyed with pressing a fingernail to the scrollwork on the mirror frame. "They are blind, oblivious to anything unless it is right in front of them. And even then I doubt their ability to see much at all."

"What will he do?"

"You know?" Amélie sniffed over the rise of emotion and raised her chin in defiance. "I don't have the foggiest notion. That is the morose tale in all of this. This is where we find out the moral of the story, and how far the game of l'amour really goes, hmm?"

Lila swallowed hard.

Why was it all so complicated?

It should be straightforward, the lines drawn between good and evil. Doing what was right and battling against the wrong. But as Lila stood there, watching her friend blot the tears welling under her eyes and toss her Jean Harlow curls as if tomorrow could stick it because she didn't care, Lila saw how confounding war was to muddle with the shades of gray.

Bad choices didn't stop compassion, which tried to bubble up from deep within her. She wished they could turn back time and Amélie could be warned where they'd find themselves if she was not more attentive to the apathy with which she toyed. Love was not a game, and it appeared she realized it in that moment. But within a breath between them, the connection was gone.

Amélie sighed. Stopped crying. She turned her profile to the mirror, running her hand over her middle, and her vulnerability vanished.

"What about a belt? I could let out the back and just carry the V down, and then a belt would hold it so no one would know." Lila gathered the silk, adding a drape at the back. "See? That way, the back gets the notice and we'll add a layer of drape to hide the front."

"Oui, a belt for the opera. Something to show all these Germans that we are Parisiennes, non? A little trimming that screams '*Vive la France!*' louder than Hitler's little songbird. I've seen those styles with music notes on the runways, and just the other day I bought one. I want this gown to really sparkle and shine. Give those newspaper editors something to reconsider when making decisions about their feature stories."

"You're certain that's what you want?"

Amélie gave a single nod, the singsong back in her voice and the avoidance of reality her comrade once again. "Of course! It is in the closet. Would you fetch it? I'll have to think of what to do for shoes—a tragedy if I had to go out in those maladroit cork wedges all the ladies are wearing these days. Who even dreamt up that style, I'd like to know." She gave a mock shiver to underscore the fashion misfortune.

"But designers are incorporating wood and cork because they're virtually the only materials left not under such strict rationing. If it weren't for that, many would go without shoes altogether."

"Come, Lila. I can't believe it's as dreadful as all that."

"A lady can have but one pair of shoes per year and that's only repair work. Cork is less about fashion than it is about having a foot covering. It holds fast, and the sole wears down slowly over time and will last well into next year."

"And in the meantime, Frenchwomen have gone from light promenades to clodhopping down the boulevard. It's so sad." Amélie raised her voice, joining back in with the flitting ladies, gave a half turn, and reviewed her angles—tummy in, shoulders high, no doubt finding her poses to conceal a burgeoning belly that soon would be anything but hidden. "We heard a rumor that women are taking gentlemen's tired old suits and cutting them down to make jackets for themselves. And did you hear this, ladies? The rabble are shaving poodles—their own dogs!—to weave sweaters out of the hair. It's a riot!"

A chorus of laughter rose as the ladies, too, spun around in the mirror, their last primps before they also would slip into their evening gowns.

"Perhaps I should donate the curtains so some poor housewife can sew a new dress? Oh, the madness. We pray you can keep fashion on track, chère amie. Paris is desperate for you right now."

Lila set her pin box down on the edge of the vanity.

"I'll just go get the belt, then we'll try it together. See what we need to do with the gown. Alright?"

Trying to explain the plight of the Parisienne under the Nazis' harsh system of rationing was a lost cause in the making. Lila left the party in the bath and moved to the shadows of evening light creeping into the boudoir. She flicked the light switch in the lavish walk-in closet, illuminating Amélie's collection of gowns, day dresses, rows of shoes, and teeter-totter stacks of hatboxes, looking for the golden wink of a belt from the shadows.

The overwhelming feature, however, was not the harshness of Nazi dress uniforms hanging next to a row of furs or the rainbow of elegant tulle hems that kissed the carpet, but the shape and color of raw wood—crates, at least six—stacked in a rough hoard against the far wall.

Lila knelt and turned them out. Hands working fast. Eyes searching for labels or an ink stamp on the top or sides—anything that might say *Touliard*.

"What do you think you're doing?"

Lila froze.

She turned to find Margot standing behind, pearl teardrops dangling from her ears and silk slip rolling slightly at the shins as if she'd rushed and stopped on a dime. Their Hedy look-alike peered back, her glance direct in the way she inspected Lila's nudging back of the crates.

"Um . . . just fetching something."

Think. Fast.

Lila rose, straightened her dress, and popped open her palm, revealing the thimble she'd had on her ring finger. "Found it, little thing. They roll away so easily."

"Oui. I'm sure they do. But should you really be . . . back here?"

As if knowing that something was amiss—enough that she could have outed Lila to the other paramours in the suite bath—Margot crossed over to the closet. She swept up the belt and pair of gold glitter kitten heels from the top tier of the built-in shelf, buckles shining bright on the top as she held them out. "Amélie asked for the heels to match, but you'd already gone."

"Merci. I'll just . . ."

"I'll take them to her. She's fit to be tied, knowing you've not finished with her gown yet. You may be her friend, but you ought to hurry it up if you fancy your employ." Margot waved the heels back out of Lila's reach and stepped out.

Lila's blood curdled in her veins; that was close. Too awkward. And bound to make a story when and if Margot decided to get curious and mention how she'd found Lila nosing around in the closet of a high-ranking Nazi officer.

You must be more careful. You must think clearly . . . and plan better.

The split-second decision to give in to temptation and search without a plan could have been disastrous. Lila ensured the crates were stacked as they were before, not a splinter out of place, and flicked off the lights. She came around the corner to find the chambermaid standing with eyes intense in focus, a feather duster in one hand and a baby-blue shoe box in the other.

"Here," she whispered, pushing the box at Lila.

"What is it?"

"She'll have forgotten about these. That harridan buys so much she can't keep track. Tell her they were in the back of the closet and caught your eye. And next time"—Violette's glance flitted to check the movement of shadows from the ladies' turns in front of the mirror—"if you're looking for something, you might ask for help. You never know who may be of a mind to provide assistance to you, mademoiselle . . . or the family Touliard, if that is in fact who you seek."

"Is that so?"

"If you have need, I may be found at this address in future." She slipped a note in the front pocket of Lila's dress, then tucked in the dangling measuring tape to hide it.

"Merci," Lila said, as the maid nodded. Just once. And then turned to move about the boudoir, dusting the surface of the fireplace mantel as Lila rejoined the bazaar in the bath.

Battle lines, indeed.

The rest of the fitting appointment was spent with Amélie tucking artful folds of silk across her front and Lila pinning and restructuring her gown as the ladies uncorked champagne and passed flutes around.

Under the irony of Nazi rules and rationing paired with the glut of excess in the suite, it appeared to Lila that the noble art of subterfuge was still alive and well.

17 FEBRUARY 1944
PONT NEUF, 1ST ARRONDISSEMENT
PARIS, FRANCE

A pair of pistols brought to a machine-gun fight wasn't much to speak of.

Lila pulled the Liberator from her boot anyway and raised it against the truck dash. It might help to add something to their side, even if it was throwing a pebble at a speeding freight train. For his part the SS soldier didn't move, just stood as the rain misted down over his coat and field-gray cap, his weapon raised in what seemed a deadly game of who'd move first.

"He's too tall to be Nigel."

"I know. What do we do?" Lila breathed out, staring through the windshield as the glass fogged and rain blurred the figure into the arches of the bridge behind him.

In a slow, careful action the uniformed figure reached up with his free hand and grabbed thumb and forefinger to the bill of his hat, then tipped it in a nod to the truck.

"Did he just . . . ?"

"Tipped his hat. He did." René let out a sigh, then raised his palm for her to lower the Liberator. He slipped his pistol back in his belt and flung open the driver's side door.

"Where are you going?"

"Just sit tight." And he was gone, out into the night.

It wasn't a breath before shadows ran back to the truck and a man climbed up into the driver's seat, René at his heels.

"It's alright. Carlyle's with us."

So tall he had to duck head and wide shoulders under the frame, the man was all grit and gristle, an unshaven shadow on his face— not the suave stealth-talker she'd imagined. He looked more suited to a career as a chimney sweep than one in espionage. While he moved through to the back of the truck like an elephant in a Frigidaire, he wasted no time unbuttoning the Nazi uniform coat. René followed behind, closed the door, and looked out at the deserted street as he kicked them in reverse away from the river.

"Cheers, Carlyle. Is this the first time you've actually been in uniform?"

"You know it's not." Carlyle ignored René's cheek with a muttered insult from the back, then slipped on a plain wool coat and swept a hand over damp hair to slick it back off his brow, the sheen of deep chocolate noticeable even in the absence of strong light.

He rolled the coat in his arms, swaying back and forth with the force of gravity as René turned them onto a side street, then lifted the lid on a false bottom concealed beneath a row of the truck's shelving. He stowed the uniform, hat, and machine gun, then secured the metal hatch and covered it with a crate of boules.

"Fancy meeting you out here in Nazi central. What do you think you're doing wearing one of their uniforms without somebody giving us notice? Lila here was ready to take your head off until you tipped your hat, even if the Liberator wouldn't have been as bad as what you had in your hands."

"Not that way—there's a checkpoint at the end of the street. Turn here." Carlyle tapped René's shoulder, then coughed into his hand and rubbed his palms together. "Couldn't be helped. And I'm frozen stiff. Thought you were never going to show up."

As the van turned the corner, Carlyle knelt on the floor behind Lila's seat, looking past her out to the shadowed arches of the bridge growing smaller behind them. When the view was clear, he refocused his attention on her.

"Where'd you find a Liberator? That model is rare in these parts of Europe."

"Where did you find yours?" Lila cocked her head to the side, looking down at the concealed compartments. A lock of hair slipped free from her beret, maddening her with the chosen moment to drift down over her brow and remind him that she was a woman without place among their ranks.

She shoved it back behind her ear.

"Nice haircut. Looks different than the first time I saw you."

"It is."

"Well, we doubted you'd make it after New Year's. You bled like a stuck pig all over the kitchen table. And I had a time of it getting a doctor to come back in the middle of the night. People don't take kindly to being dragged outside with a curfew in place."

Nice to meet you too.

Testy Yank indeed. Lila stared back, unwilling to give an inch, no matter what he was trying to imply.

"And then Nigel filled me in on why you were in the state you were." He held out his hand. "We Americans give credit where it's due. Welcome to the team."

She took it, shaking his hand firmly. "Merci."

With the headlights flicked on and the night wearing thin, they rode in silence, catching their breath from an encounter that could have gone either way, to be sure. René rounded them back in the direction of Sainte-Chappelle, Carlyle melting into the shadows when they passed a car on the street—no doubt someone in the SS out during curfew.

René looked in the rearview mirror. "Alright. Spill. Why did I get a message to come and meet Nigel and find you instead? Tell me it's for more than him running off for The Chief's next broadcast, or I'm afraid I'll have to skin him alive for this latest stunt."

"It's more. We got wind of a truck full of weapons at the train depot last minute—the submachine guns we've been expecting. I helped create a diversion to get them over the river before the Boche knew they were gone. Stormie needed them in the 7th Arrondissement, so Nigel went with her to make sure they're delivered and to record it for the next broadcast."

René looked to Lila. "Stormie's our contact for cells around the Eiffel Tower, leading over to the Left Bank. She said they needed bolstering. Seems they've got it."

Light flashed by the windows, the odd play of moonlight cutting through. Lila noticed for the first time that Carlyle's eye was cut, swelling, and trickling a trail of crimson down his cheekbone.

"Carlyle? *Regardez là-bas.*" She tapped her temple and pointed to him.

He looked at it in the rearview mirror, ran the heel of his palm against the broken skin, and then wiped the blood on the inside seam of his dark trousers. And sort of skipped over the fact he had chided her for not knowing how she'd bled at their first meeting, and he was properly crimson faced at their second.

René tipped his chin up to look in the rearview, then turned to glance over his shoulder. "What happened?"

"It's nothing. A tussle with a member of the Waffen-SS. That's why Nigel called you out to pick me up."

"How is that nothing?" René nearly shouted, his voice laced with disbelief. "Did he get a look at you? Were there any more? You know they don't travel alone."

"We were meeting a contact down here and he happened to step out to relieve himself in the river, miserable fool. What was I supposed to do, just let him walk away with that information? Maybe got a look at me. Or probably not before I knocked him out and nicked his coat. I'd have dropped him over the bank into the Seine if a missing Waffen-SS wouldn't have raised an alarm. As it is he'll have a thick head in the morning if he doesn't freeze to death first."

"And if you continue to fancy yourself a war correspondent, you know you're not supposed to get involved. Not pulling rank and ordering where to take a cache of weapons, and certainly not tossing a Boche soldier in the river. What would Uncle Sam say?"

"Clever of you to recite the war correspondent's handbook to me, but we left him in the bushes. And you weren't there to talk me out of it. Besides, we've got a bigger problem brewing. It's why I stayed back to meet up with you instead of Nigel."

Carlyle reached into his trouser pocket, pulled out a photograph, and handed it up to René, who looked at it, closed his eyes tight for a split second, then slammed his fist against the steering wheel.

"I know this is a raw deal no matter how you look at it. We always search them for letters Nigel could use in the radio broadcasts—you know, to stir the Germans up with a personal 'Dear Frederich, from your angel Gunda in the village . . .' sort of thing. Well, no letters this time. But seems our little Frederich had this on him instead."

"Right. D'accord," René whispered, then handed the snapshot over to Lila before he angled them around the road, away from the looming cathedral windows of Sainte-Chappelle. "This changes things. I need to think."

Lila's confusion was replaced by dread in short order.

She gripped the photo of the *Vogue* fashion plate in her hands, the portrait of her own face staring back. She remembered when the headshot was taken, how Amélie had tugged Lila in front of the camera during an impromptu photoshoot in the Ritz suite drawing room. She'd styled her long locks in lavish waves over her shoulder, and bright lights had been set up so her eyes would sparkle just so. It might have been a glamour shot she'd never wanted, but it wasn't what mattered now.

All the SS needed was a crisp, clear image of her face and they had it.

"So they are looking for me."

"It would seem so. For a noncommissioned SS to have it on his person means someone has filtered it down to the lower ranks—at least in the areas around the center of the city. He probably doesn't even know why he has it, just that if you're spotted you're to be brought in."

"Or shot." The truth bled from her lips in a near-silent whisper.

Carlyle stared straight ahead, then looked as though he relented on something. "I'm sorry, but we'll figure it out."

The tiny nudge of acceptance said whether he'd have authorized or not, she was now a part of the team. Somehow it made her feel better. Until, that is, she glanced at René.

Lila took in the iron set to his profile and the way he drove without another word to either of them. To see him so changed—calculating and in his own head—she forced herself to remember the socialite side of him from Elsie de Wolfe's parties. His smile under the garden lights, the way he breezed her through every dance and displayed every bit of the posh manners that said he could handle himself with the upper rung of society. So different was the view from where she sat—the unshaven man with the handful of false identities and quiet strength, forced to carve out a shadow existence in the darkest spaces of Paris's underbelly.

Were there photos circulating of him too?

"Your call, Touliard. This one doesn't fall under my watch." Carlyle leaned back against the metal wall, crossing his arms over his chest. "What do you want to do?"

"Do the Americans know about this?"

"No."

"But they'll help. You'll help, right? A passport for her. Train out of here. Anything."

He shook his head. "Doesn't work that way. Beyond getting my hands on some travel papers—and even that won't be easy—there's not much I can do. Not while there's rumor the Allies are planning to come across the water and make a surprise visit on French soil. I wish we could, but we Yanks couldn't waste time on the plight of one Frenchwoman when there's a war to be won. No matter how much you'd want us to."

"Why haven't we heard anything of this in the underground? If there was a missing dressmaker toting top-secret Nazi information, our network would have heard something by now. We'd all be looking for her, especially given the handoff she missed—"

"If she wasn't right here in this truck," Lila finished, then handed the snapshot back.

René pocketed the photo and drove on, the gears turning in his mind seeming to have won in the battle to take over.

"D'accord. Change of plans." René checked his wristwatch and turned the truck north over the Pont au Change. "Can you make rounds to the officers at the Ritz? Lila can't go anywhere near it."

"I can."

"Bien. We'll have to ditch before we get to the 1st Arrondissement, let you take it from there, and we'll find our way back to Montmartre later. But if we're not back by sundown, send out a search party." René looked to her. "It's decision time whether we move to plan B and your microfilm goes to the Americans. That alright with you?"

A smile was out of place. Grossly. With the SS hunting her down, Lila hadn't a reason to do it. But the ghost of a smile lifted the corners of her lips before she could stop it. Trouvère—whoever he was—wasn't there. But Carlyle was. And in the moment that was good enough for her.

"If you think I was leaving this behind for one second, you don't know this Résistante very well. If things are speeding up, then we might as well do this now." Lila slipped her finger inside the seam of one of the pockets on the dress she'd made, opening a hidden pocket in the bottom until a tiny hole formed and the microfilm spilled out into her palm.

René beamed. "So the dress you made was for more than looks?"

"Of course. Why do you think I wear it every day? I wasn't going to waste an opportunity when you dropped it in my lap. This way, I can help transport messages for us. And if we're stopped, the Boche will spend a lot less time frisking an ugly dress seam than they would every inch of my male companions' clothing. Much as I hate to say it, if they underestimate a woman's intelligence and ability, we might as well use that angle to the full."

She turned to Carlyle, opened his palm, and slipped the tiny treasure into it.

"René trusts you, so I do too. Take it. Give it to London and Washington. And not to add a load of pressure, but if you boys don't figure out what to do with it soon, I'm afraid Paris will see the receiving end of a bomb to which we really don't desire an introduction."

Carlyle flitted his glance to René, as if half deciding, half asking permission. But he seemed to pocket the film without a second thought. "You realize you've just handed me the one thing that makes you valuable to them?"

"Good thing she's valuable to us even without it then," René whispered, and eased the truck to a stop down a deserted street, the slow drift on the brakes working to keep them from singing out to full intensity. He turned the keys in the ignition, deadening the engine. "Normal protocol for the truck returning to Les Petits Galettes without the same driver who went out in it. When we left, the first night shift guards were still on duty."

"And if they haven't already changed, then I'll relish the opportunity to talk my way out of it, as usual."

"Of that I have no doubt." René held out the keys, which Carlyle took in a quick shake of the hand.

"Watch your back, René. Both of you."

Lila's oar wasn't about to be left out of the water. She turned to René. "And where are we going?"

"We have an appointment to keep, Mademoiselle de Laurent. This one matters more than anything we're doing to upend the Germans, and that photo means it's just been bumped to the top of our to-do list."

CHAPTER 16

14 JANUARY 1942
1 PLACE DE LA CONCORDE
PARIS, FRANCE

W here is the film from yesterday?" Michèle dropped a folder labeled *Collection Göring: inventaire des peintures* on the desk before Sandrine, its insides laid bare. She turned her back to the officers in the outer office of the Jeu de Paume and sat on the edge of the desk to hunch over. "And the catalog of the paintings from Reichsmarschall Göring's last selections?"

"It's not there either?" Sandrine set her teacup down and looked up. "I'm certain I put it in the folder last night. It's the last thing I checked before I left, knowing how meticulous they are about the records, especially for the Reichsmarschall's collection."

"The entire list of the shipment sent out by train to his Carinhall hunting estate this morning—it's gone. The photos too. And if that train reaches Berlin and we have no record of what's on it, I don't know what will happen to us."

"Mademoiselle Valland is strict about how we catalog everything— you know that. And she is meticulous. I have never seen her make a mistake. There's no way this is our fault."

"She is strict, oui. But we also have an empty folder. I have to turn something in to Captain von Stickler out there in the next few minutes." Michèle peeked over her shoulder. The captain was in conversation with two officers in the outer office, not appearing to pay attention to the two whispering secretaries. "If my steno pad is bare, I'll have a lot of explaining to do. And to tell you the truth, he terrifies me. One look from those eyes and I think I'll melt into the floor. What do I tell him?"

"We can't say it's been shipped with the crates to Berlin."

"Are you mad? Sandrine, he'd self-combust right here, I know it. They're already in a perpetual bad mood now that the Americans have joined the war. I don't want to tip him over the edge."

"And if his little attachés were to say someone made a mistake and misplaced it?"

Michèle shook her head, then pushed her glasses back up the bridge of her nose. "*Mais non.* At best, he'd fire us. At worst, we'll end up guillotined in the Tuileries Gardens. For how vexing it is to have to 'oui, sir' and 'non, sir' through our days with the lot of them here, I can't be without pay or without a head. I'm quite attached to both, merci."

"And you're quite without worry about losing either. Not as long as I'm around. Just let me think this through." Sandrine turned toward the window, collecting her thoughts.

Mademoiselle Valland had been poring over the folder, taking her meticulous notes as always, when Sandrine had stepped out of the galerie the night before. In truth it's where she always was. Desk lamp on. Spectacles focused. Last one to leave. And officers moving about as she kept everything in precise order and then locked the drawer with the files secured inside.

Locked the drawer . . . Rose.

There was no other explanation but their intrepid curator.

Sandrine swept up the folder from the desk and stood. "Let me handle this."

Folder in hand, she strode to the outer office, the rows of carved desks and wood-coffered ceiling shining in the midwinter sunlight that streamed through the high arched windows. The officers were gathered around the captain—three of them, and without question they were not discussing the Jeu de Paume's array of fine art. More likely Casanova storytelling of a certain cabaret district in Montmartre the evening before, their smiles a little too easy and laughs too loud to have signaled anything proper.

Even though the captain appeared to show only marginal interest, how Sandrine was cheered not to understand the vast majority of the German language in that moment.

She cleared her throat. "Excusez-moi, Captain."

Captain von Hiller dismissed the officers with a nod. "Mrs. Paquet. What is it?"

"We have a problem, sir." She handed the folder over.

The *Collection Göring: inventaire des peintures* received its due notice when he read the label on the front, and the expected hardening of his jaw followed when he saw that its contents were missing.

"It appears we do." He closed the folder and handed it back. "And is there an explanation?"

"That's why I'm coming to you. I hesitate to critique the leadership in this galerie, as I know how you run this storehouse with efficiency. But I cannot continue to work with such sloppy record keeping, especially not after one of the Reichsmarschall's visits. I'm unable to do my job correctly."

"Isn't this Valland's area of authority?"

"Of course it is, and she does her job without waver. But she's out on the collection floor now, seeing to a new shipment in the gallery, and I won't bother her with something so trite." She prayed that was true. There was no scheduled shipment, so the bluff could be more than ill timed were he to call it. "I'm saying that the officers reporting to you ought to be reprimanded for this, before Baron von Behr and Reichsmarschall Göring find out that they let this slip through."

The captain glanced over at the junior officers, who'd found a few chairs to sit and continue their conversation, and she knew she'd touched a nerve. Mentioning the higher-ups to him all but assured agreement. The officers lazed boots up on the desks and smiled brighter than the sun streaming in through the windows, drinking from cups of coffee tippled with something from a flask, and ignored Captain von Hiller's notice of what appeared a very critical slight to their senior leadership.

"You wish me to reprimand the officers?"

"Oui. If you believe it appropriate. Their job is to see to it that we have what we need to properly catalog the items going on trains to Berlin. But as you know, they must sign off on the asset lists before we can do that. They obviously did not ensure the materials were cataloged properly, or that the photos were included." Sandrine nodded, ensuring that confidence read in her every movement.

She held her head high, folder braced against her plum blouse, and waited. "From now on, Captain, I wonder if I should handle all the film for Mademoiselle Valland and the requisition of art at the end of each night? I should hope this oversight would not be repeated."

"Ja. Very well, Mrs. Paquet. See that you include this task in your duties as of today and I will inform Valland that it will now be assigned to you."

Oh my heavens . . . it worked.

"Bien. I look forward to it." Sandrine turned on a dime and exhaled, not entirely sure how she'd managed to gain agreement, and for him to think it was his idea.

From now on, if what she suspected was true—and Rose Valland really was secretly cataloging all of the art the ERR was stealing from across France, then Sandrine had just signed herself up as the woman's second in command.

Whatever Valland was doing behind the scenes, both Sandrine and Michèle would have to keep secret. And without missing a beat, the captain had just handed her the keys to open every lock that stood in their way.

"Mrs. Paquet?"

"Oui, sir?" She turned, trying oh-so-hard not to show her fingernails digging into the folder in her hands.

"Well done." No smile—he wasn't likely to confer one of those. But the captain did give her a curt nod of approval before he crossed the room to run his leaders through their paces.

The last thought Sandrine had as she watched boots hit the ground and coffee cups quickly abandoned on the desks was that she might have dealt herself a new problem by seeking to fix another.

She'd just impressed a Nazi, and that was never good.

———— •◆• ————

18 March 1944
Place de l'Opéra
Paris, France

"Is it you? It's really you?" Sandrine felt through the dark and pressed her palms to his unshaven face. Her lips found his, drowning the need for an answer.

"It's me, Drina." Christian held her, whispering her name over again with his mouth against her ear and hand buried in the barrel rolls at her nape. "It's me."

Emotion packed his voice too. It wavered and died as he wrapped her in another kiss. They'd fallen against the door, lost together. The dark kept him shrouded in shadows when all she wanted to do was look at him, check him over, make sure he was whole and really holding her, and not some apparition of her nightmares.

"You're here," she cried, her hands desperate to hold him in the dark, her face sinking to nestle in the crook of his neck. "Where have you been all this time?"

"Everywhere. I wish I had time to tell you now."

They surfaced, and reality came crashing back.

Sandrine became altogether aware that her clutch had been lost. Her lipstick was no doubt smudged. And she realized they'd have but moments together before the captain's ardent attentions would have him looking across the dance floor, expecting her to reappear and in a put-together manner.

"I know. I have a minute, maybe two, before he comes looking for me."

"There's got to be a switch . . ." Christian fumbled in the dark, and she heard the clatter of what sounded like his elbow hitting against something before the overhead light clicked on.

The war had taken nearly five years between them and now, in the bat of an eye, had given a blessed moment back.

They stood staring at each other, blush Chanel against Nazi officer's gray, in a closet with red damask chairs stacked in rows on all sides and a bulb that hung high overhead.

"You're so—" She didn't know what to say.

Thin? Different? Older? Alive! Beautiful? Or hurt? He had a scar on his brow—she noticed it right off. An angry white mark healed over to the temple, peeking out from his hairline. She ran her fingertips over it, feeling the bumps as she brushed his brown hair back from the uniform hat.

He took the hat off and tossed it on a chair.

"Christian, what's happened to you?"

He grasped her hand and pressed a kiss to her wrist. Staring. Looking at her in the Chanel gown and shaking his head. "I can't believe it. I saw you across the dance floor. All the way across, and I thought, *This can't be true.* That God had smiled on me. And you're beautiful.

So beautiful you take my breath away, and I can't even believe you're here in front of me."

She looked past Christian to the door, still trying to catch her breath and wishing she could see through wood to the hall outside to know how long they had. And then to look back at him, to see that smile cover his face like old times . . .

"While I appreciate the compliment, my love, what in heaven's name do you have to smile about right at this very moment?"

"Here I'd been praying. Wracking my brain. Defying their blasted curfew. Slipping in and out of places dressed like this, trying to get you alone somewhere—to catch you on the streets even. At the flat. I went to Le Fournier, but it's gone."

"I know. I'm so sorry. I went to church and lit a candle for Monsieur Mullins and his family. But there's been no word, and I don't know what's become of them. I've been beside myself since I saw the state of the shop."

"It seems the Germans had been watching him for quite some time. Last I heard, he and his family were sent to a work camp somewhere in the east, for transporting messages for La Résistance." He looked at his boots for a breath. "I've been in Paris for weeks and couldn't find a way to tell you not to attempt to contact me through him. And then you walked in here. Tonight. On that captain's arm. And I thought every moment of the last years had been worth it because I could just see you again."

"I have so many things to tell you. About Henri. And I got your letter. Just one though. And your father . . . Oh, Christian. I'm so sorry. Victor. He's—"

"It's alright." He stopped her, brow pinched tight like an ache had shot to the surface that quick. "I know. I've known for some time."

"And after everything that's happened, to see me here tonight. You must have thought that I . . . Please know that being here with him, I'd never—"

"Shh. Drina, that's not what this is. I'm not accusing you of anything. I know enough about you to know that whatever you have had to do to survive, you did it for Henri. And you'd never dishonor me. Not me or yourself." He pressed a hand to her cheek, blotted a tear. "Has that man—?" He stopped. Swallowed hard over a flexed jaw. Held on with his palm to her skin as intense eyes searched her face. "Has he hurt you?"

A furious shake of her head, and she covered his palm with hers. "Non. He hasn't. I've managed to keep him at bay. But even this dress—I didn't want to wear it. It's of the Rothschild collection. I'd promised to keep it safe, to help Mademoiselle Valland make a second catalog of all the art they're stealing in hopes that we could one day bring everything back. And I didn't want to come tonight, but I hadn't any choice in the matter."

"I know." Christian nodded, emotion tight in his face. His brow wrinkled—he was in pain, of course. To even have to ask her such a question, and to have to wait for her answer. "Listen to me. You have to go."

She shook her head again. "Non. I can't. Not knowing you're here."

"Go back to him. But I need you to develop a headache. Stomachache. Anything. Just leave as soon as you can."

"But he'll drive me home. I know he will. I won't be left alone for a moment."

"That I expect. At least I know you'll make it safely across the city."

"And once at the flat? What do I do? How do I find you?"

"Wait for me. I'll come as soon as I can. Tonight, if I'm able." He pressed a thumb to her bottom lip, a butterfly's touch. "Do you have any lipstick?"

"Lipstick? I think so. Oui." She turned, looking for her lost clutch. She found it wedged under a chair leg and pulled it free. "I do."

"Better put some on then. I'm afraid I took it all off. Wait—" He pressed another kiss to her lips. Just once, but with shades of unbidden longing. He ran a palm quick over his lip to rub it clean. "Go. I'll come to you at the flat. As soon as I can. Stay put, alright? And stay safe. Je t'aime, mon cœur."

She turned to go and he flicked the switch, bathing them in darkness again.

Sandrine opened the door and slipped out, finding herself more than relieved that the hall stood empty. She opened her clutch, hands shaking as she grabbed the gold tube and rouged her lips while blending in with women who'd stepped out of the ladies' room all atwitter over something.

Once past the threshold of the hall, she slowed, careful with the chiffon trailing behind her.

A mask of serenity was all Sandrine could show in that moment, even though she felt as if she'd swallowed a truckload of fireworks. She whispered that she was unwell and as she expected, the captain responded without delay. Making their excuses at the table, carrying her clutch and retrieving her wrap—the stoic, dutiful Nazi overlord, so concerned for her welfare that she needn't feign nausea completely.

Sandrine walked slowly, scouring the room of people but not finding Christian among them. Looking in vain through the crowd of uniforms, all the way to the grand entry and golden stairs, she searched for the square of his shoulders and the scar at the brow and the eyes that she knew so well. And the lips that, if he dared, always seemed to smile when he gazed upon her.

Even now, as Paris seemed poised to crumble and she climbed in the backseat of a Nazi officer's auto to ride home, a new heartbeat took over in her chest. She was not afraid of what was to come—neither for Christian nor for herself.

Hope had awakened. And with it a fire from within to fight.

CHAPTER 17

20 OCTOBER 1941
15 PLACE VENDÔME
PARIS, FRANCE

The door to Amélie's suite was cracked open to the hall.

A soldier stood firm outside it as Lila approached. He didn't flinch like she did, even as the crash of breaking porcelain resounded all the way to the elevator, its passengers discreet and pretending not to notice the outburst until the doors closed and they were on their way up again.

"Is Mademoiselle Olivier inside?"

"For the time being, ja. You can go in. But if she makes any further disturbance, I'm to call downstairs and they'll drag her out, kicking and screaming if need be."

Oh no. Lila rushed in to find the parlor in shambles.

Hatboxes strewn about. Champagne flutes sat alone and sad on the little table by the terrace doors, next to an ice bucket missing its bottle and a meat pie for two that had long gone cold. The Cézanne was still upon the mantel, but it was half covered over with the spaghetti strap of a silk camisole that looked to have been chucked across the room. The hall to the boudoir was littered by odd shoes and dresses, like a bomb had exploded in the closet and the sad casualties were strewn upon the marble floor.

"Amélie?" Lila rapped her knuckles on the open boudoir door.

"What are you doing here? Come to say bonjour to the wayward paramour perhaps?"

Suitcases lay bare on the bed. The baron was nowhere to be seen, thank heaven, but Amélie was moving about in haste, drinking champagne straight from the bottle as she stripped dresses from hangers and tossed them in the direction of the bed.

"You're leaving."

"How clever of you to notice, darling dressmaker. I have been given my marching orders, me and the little cadet I'm carrying. We must be out of the king's suite here by this evening." She tossed a mink coat on the coverlet, then kept moving. "They think they've beaten me? Well, I do not bow that easily. I will chart my own course."

Lila sank onto the end of the bed, sitting on the one corner that wasn't covered over by satin or silk or piled with a mound of furs. "What happened?"

"You ask me what happened? Don't play innocent."

Amélie reached for a rumpled newspaper on the bedside table, then tossed it in Lila's lap and went back to folding dresses and tossing shoes.

The paper hadn't bothered to pin Amélie's photo on a back page. This little misalliance was front and center—the star of the show. The ERR high chief photographed with the Führer at the recent show of Wagner at l'opera in September—Amélie on his arm, sporting a couture gown by the 'House of LDL.' Her ivory silk and bright smile sparkled for the camera, but there was no belt to mask over the slight round of her middle, a flagrant display of her secret in a portrait splashed across the front page.

"You allowed me to be seen in an opera gown and belt embroidered over with notes from *l'Hymne de la Résistance*?"

"You knew Parisiennes are wearing music notes of the French anthem in the street. On their hats. Blouses. Shoes. Anything they can to show their support for Free France. You bought it—how could you buy it off the runway and not know what it meant?"

"I am not required to know! That is why I hired you. I cannot show my support for France like that while at a German event. I could wear a belt with a nursery rhyme. Or a Christmas carol, for heaven's sake. But not the tune of the enemy! I could have been arrested if it had gone badly. Fortunately, Captain von Hiller saw it, and as he is astute with music, he pulled me aside to notify me right there at the event. I told him it was a mistake, of course. A silly French sing-along that all the girls were wearing this season."

"They *are* wearing it."

"But not at an event where the Führer is the guest of honor!" Amélie slammed the champagne bottle down on the bedside table, the thick base of glass sounding as if it had split the wood in two. "You did this on purpose, hmm? To teach me a lesson about how to be Parisienne? Or how to be chaste like you?"

Lila wouldn't take the blame, nor the barb. She tried to keep compassion and fear in their box, if at all possible. "This is why he's making you leave, because of the belt?"

"Of course not. You are not that powerful, my dear. I removed the belt before the photo, as you see. But that little gown of yours could no longer conceal it, and when this edition came out, everyone else could see it too. It was bound to happen sooner or later—even if the baron does not wish his wife to know of his illicit rendezvous in Paris. I am still a Parisienne and, like our dear Coco says, I have a drawer full of lipstick left with which to attack. And I intend to do it."

Lila's eyes dared to glaze and she defied the tears, standing to keep her wits about her. If strength was the only thing they had left, she'd be of the gracious fighter brand or die trying.

"Don't you cry for me. I have a friend who's offered to take us in, thank heaven. Hector has proved valuable more than once it seems. And you'd better believe that I will be more informed to watch my steps when my path crosses with yours at the next party."

"Amélie—I never wanted this for you. For either of us."

"But this is what's happened. And as you seem so informed about the state of our fair city, here is something you don't know. There was that poor naval cadet gunned down while boarding a train at the Barbès-Rochechouart Métro. Remember? We now know the murder of this German cadet was at the hands of a dirty Jew—"

"It isn't known yet who is responsible."

"Of course it is! The Jews—you see what they've done? I warned you of this behavior long ago. This is only the beginning of what they'll do if we give them a long leash."

"How could the act of one individual be blamed on an entire group of people?"

Don't you see? The Germans have done far worse right before your eyes . . .

"Are you certain you know so much about your little Jew friends?" Amélie slammed her suitcase closed, a leg of seamed nylons peeking out from one side. She ignored it, instead crossing over to the bedside table and pulling open the drawer to retrieve a sapphire velvet box in her hand, the same that Lila had seen before—both in the back of the drawer and in the photos of the diamond necklace from the Touliard estate that first day she'd been invited to design in the suite.

"Well, this is my payment for the belt. Today, posters are going up across the city. You will see them for yourself outside. At the Métro. On park benches. While waiting in line for your pittance of bread at the boulangerie. They outline how the SS demands reprisals for that cadet's murder—hostages will be collected and shot if the culprit does not come forward. And the baron said they were looking for an excuse to round up the Jews, and this makes it nice and tidy. So the woman who owned this necklace will no longer have need of it. So I am taking it with me."

"What do you mean?"

"Hmm . . . let me think. There is an old textile factory just north of the city, I believe, on the edge of the parc at Georges-Valbon?"

"You didn't." Lila's heart sank, and she fused her fist to the bed rail to remain standing. "Dear God, Amélie, please say you didn't."

"There is a collection soon to happen, my dear, a roundup of little *Juifs* across the city. And I believe there is a once-prominent family hiding away in that abandoned factory. It was my duty to France to see that we all play by the rules, just like you wanted. So I told the baron where he might find your dear René and his beloved family. And within the hour, they will be picked up and packed off to some work camp in the east, where I hope they rot."

René. Your family. And you . . .

Lila's insides coiled. "How could you?"

"It is death for death, ma cherie. And war is cold with its selections." Amélie took the necklace and the haphazard suitcase and flung a fur over her arm. With her free hand, she curled her palm around the neck of the champagne bottle and turned her back on Lila, her shadow carrying down the hall. "See you at the next Ritz party. We'll catch up then."

Lila crumpled onto the end of the bed, shock giving way to pain. For her ignorance all those months ago, when she'd mentioned the hiding place while sitting at a little café table with her best friend . . . This was more than seeking out paintings and stolen heirlooms. This was life and death. This was her love and his family arrested—maybe even right at that moment—to be sent to a horrific camp where who knew what fate would befall them.

Her heart shattered. It was deportation.

It was hell on earth.

And it was all her fault.

—————◆————

17 FEBRUARY 1944
8TH ARRONDISSEMENT
PARIS, FRANCE

Carrying one crate of deliveries wasn't enough to warrant being on the streets before the morning curfew had lifted, and dawn was a couple of hours off at least.

René wove them out of sight, moving through the web of side streets along the Right Bank west of the Grand Palais, finally stopping in a niche carved out against a block of boarded-up shops. Water dripped from a downspout off the blue zinc of a low mansard; the journey of rain from the roofs to the ground was easily heard against the silence of the streets. Rubbish bins and crates from a café across the way littered the corner, making a rickrack tower up the wall of Lutetian limestone. A boarded window and ruddy, paint-chipped door were set off alone behind it, along with a single sconce of weathered brass that stuck out from the wall, gathering raindrops but offering no light with a busted bulb.

"This way." René hefted the lone crate they'd taken with them in one arm and grabbed Lila's hand with the other. "We can cut through the buildings without going out on the street."

"How do you know?"

"I've been here a time or two." He pointed up to a sad, dirt-caked marquee held up by rusty cables over the alley. "It's an abandoned theater complex—wide enough to connect through to a break in the buildings a couple of streets over."

"If it's vacant, how do you know we can go through? By the looks of it, the ceiling could have completely fallen in through the floors above."

"I said abandoned—that's not the same thing as vacant." René knocked. Then reached down and squeezed her hand, and they both waited.

A swatch of sullied burlap lifted at the edge of the window—no light, just movement. The sounds of bolts unlocking came next, and the door cracked open. René pulled her with him, nudging the door wide enough to slip through. They stepped into a long hall, the dankness overpowering, and onto a paisley carpet that seemed to have seen its better days a hundred years ago.

"It's a stage door."

"Used to be." He tugged her through. "For a cabaret long gone. They'll let us pass through here."

A woman in trousers and military jacket over a shirt and suspenders eased out from the shadows as they stepped in. She had a strong profile—sharp, elegant nose and curly hair cropped at the chin. She tossed out a *"Ça va?"* and *"Ou est* Carlyle?" before she pushed her submachine gun strap over her back and kissed René's cheeks in greeting.

"Stormie—this is Lila."

The woman eyed her, the flicker of the flame as she lit a cig from her front jacket pocket illuminating auburn locks and cat-like eyes in a domineering visage. "The dressmaker?"

"The dressmaker." René eyed the comrade, his glare firm. "Is that going to be a problem?"

"Non. Not if she's with you. And watches her step if she decides to move through my territory. I don't want the SS piqued if they happen to see her pretty face go south to the Left Bank." She blew smoke, smiling as she shook her head. "Where is Carlyle? I thought the American was transporting our reinforcements. Instead we get the journalist who is in love with his typewriter and drinks up our liquor stores. Not exactly a fair trade."

"Fair enough, I'd say, for a train car full of arms. Does that buy us passage?"

"Today it does. Tomorrow? Hmm. We'll see what mood I am in."

"Lila, let's go." René moved them down the hall, noticeably without a good-bye to their comrade.

"Who was that?"

"Stormie—our queen of the catacombs. Temperamental as they come but fearless. She grew up in the underground, if you can believe it. Her father was a municipal worker and she spent most of her youth under the streets while we were all above. But now she's with us, leading the charge of a cell that moves under the heart of the city. She won't give us any trouble. Just here to coordinate her weapons transfer, I'd wager. And likes to keep her ear to the ground in between times."

Without missing a step, René led them through a hole busted through a brick wall, the Maquis having tunneled through boarded-up shops in a system built from the inside. They emerged into an old dress shop by the looks of it, with changing rooms shed of their curtains, leaves collected on a rusted spiral staircase, and rose-striped wallpaper curling in water stains of putrid yellow and brown. The windows on the street front still allowed in the breaking dawn, though light had to fight with boards blocking most of the view.

"We'll need to have a care when we come out on the other end, but I think you'll feel a little less turned around when we do."

It was another couple of maze turns and then through a hole in the wall of an old *épicerie*, the grocer and his wares long gone, having left behind only scattered crates, busted brick, and a checkered floor buried under an inch of grime.

After tipping his head to a comrade nursing a hand-rolled cig in the corner, René led them out a door and they were back in the cold, the sky over the streets still shrouded in a veil of gray as the morning mist moved on.

It may have looked like any street in Paris, but Lila's breath caught in her chest when she saw the end of the alley and the leafless trees that shielded the Champs-Élysées beyond. She remembered the little café on the corner, the one that used to serve the best hazelnut-crème crêpes in Paris. Next to it, a bookshop she used to visit with her maman when she was a girl. And not far off, a boarded-up milliner's shop that would have once owned a sign marked with her father's name, and *Haberdashery* in the windows. She could see the old blue door, leaves blowing in the wind and gathering in a hapless pile on the front stoop.

Of course René would know where her parents lived—she'd given him the address that first day at the pâtisserie. But the way he was looking at her just then, with a mix of softness and knowing as she surveyed the memory of the street—it made her stomach spiral.

"Mind if we take the stairs? I don't trust elevators. I know you said no one knows where your parents live, but I still like to plan ahead for safety's sake." René squeezed her hand and led her up two flights, until they came to the landing with a sad potted plant in the corner and a familiar flat door at the end.

Lila paused. "I don't have my key."

"Here. Let me."

He swept in around her, pulled a key ring from his pocket, and slipped it in the lock, then turned the brass knob. The implication of what he'd just done broke through the surface and Lila stared up at him, knowing he must have seen the questions dawn all over her face.

"Go ahead, Lila."

Standing in the entry, door open to the landing behind, Lila peered inside to their flat.

"Oh, René. You gave me a start when I heard the front door open."

"Maman?" Lila looked from behind René to her mother, who'd slipped out from the kitchen already dressed in a woolen midi skirt and prim rose blouse, even for the early hour that it was.

"Ma fille!" She rushed forward, hands grasping Lila's face, holding on as tears and kisses were doled out, and "my daughter" and "You cut your hair, pretty girl" were whispered through tears.

"Maman. You two know each other?"

"Why, this is René—our neighbor. I'm certain I've talked of him before. He said you two are friends. You are, oui? You met in the fashion world. We gave him a key for ease of looking in."

"Oui, Lila and I are old friends, Ginette." René leaned in and pecked a kiss to her cheek as he held out the crate. "It's not as much as I'd hoped this month, but I did try. You'd like it in the kitchen?"

"Of course. I know you tried." She slipped her arm around Lila's waist and held on as René walked into the kitchen with the crate. "We were getting worried about you, Lila, having not seen you for some time. With the arrests increasing everywhere, I'm afraid your père has become more agitated. We see so many more trucks and tanks rolling down the Champs-Élysées. It does set our teeth on edge to see those gray uniforms so restless."

"It's cold in here. Can I light the stove for you?" René called from the kitchen, but the sound of a match flared and Lila knew he was already set about seeing to things she would have.

"You'd better warm up this flat, or we'll be wearing our chapeaux and gloves all day." She tugged at Lila's winter coat. "Can you take this off, stay for a while? René told us you've been quite busy with fashion across the city. We are relieved to hear it. So many looking for work these days and so little food about."

René walked back into the parlor after a moment, to the chessboard set out on the sideboard.

The wood pieces had taken the place of the radio they'd sold, the wine they'd drunk and never replaced, the china that all had to go in the first year, just to put food on the table—all save for the family photos still here, displayed as the winter sunlight just began to cut through the part in the curtains.

"We'll stay for a bit." René picked up the board, gingerly moving it to the dining table, careful to step around the chairs in the dim light. "Is Marcel up for a visit?"

"If he can see you and our girl, I'm certain of it. I'll go wake him, or interrupt him if he's talking to the Almighty. Perhaps his prayers have already been answered today, hmm?"

The casual way René moved about as they were left alone—like it was his home, too, instead of the one she'd shared with her parents—caused Lila to question everything that had passed in the last nearly five years.

Crates had appeared from those first days the Germans rolled in. They'd show up, stowed behind the plant, and then they didn't return for weeks. With no rhyme or reason and seemingly without pattern. And certainly with no neighbor's face attached—not the eyes she knew so well, the same ones so expertly deflecting looking at hers in that moment.

René removed his coat, rolled his sleeves up his forearms, and blew dust off a rook in the corner of the board.

"You've been here before?" she asked, but right away realized it was a ridiculous question.

He had a key. And a chessboard, frozen midgame. And of all things, her mother had greeted him by name and he'd kissed her cheek. Of course René had been here before.

"I've stopped in a time or two."

"Why? How did you know where to find them?"

"I kept an eye out. You know, just to see how you'd fared."

"Why didn't you say anything when I accused you of not caring enough to do just that?"

He blinked back as her pa-pa emerged from the hall, his face brightening to see them standing in the flat—her in one piece after weeks apart from them, and René, warm and holding a chair for her pa-pa with the chessboard at the ready.

Lila kept quiet through the visit, watching. Listening as Pa-pa asked questions of how close the Allies were that seemed to be on every Parisian's mind. And smiling as he proceeded to thoroughly route René at chess. Her maman made tea from the crate. And all the while Lila sat back, knowing why René had brought her and just how important that morning might become once they'd learned that her photo had been circulated among the SS.

In war, you'd never stake a moment on tomorrow, because tomorrow was a foe.

If they'd learned anything well, it had been that. While it seemed like it pained René to consider they might have a fight ahead of them, and who knew if any or all of them would survive it, he still meant for her parents to have something normal—even in the midst of war—and to make new memories with their only daughter.

They said their good-byes at the noon hour and promised to come again soon, even as Lila had her "dressmaker's work" across the city and René, for his part, said he'd return with any news to share of the Germans' crumbling control. It wasn't a subversive plan to advance Black Propaganda, or anything René could send on to the Americans in their ploy to undermine the Germans' efforts. But the morning had been something of a lifesaver—if only to her.

Lila closed the flat door, hand still holding the knob at her back as she leaned against the wood and faced René. "All this time . . . it was you."

It wasn't like him to be at a loss for words, yet he stood in the shadows of the landing, with the dam of her heart about to breach its borders if he didn't give her a straight answer soon.

He nodded with a light shrug of his shoulders. "I wanted them to get to know me. And I wanted to know them."

"And the rest?"

"The food is nothing. The Germans keep the pâtisserie in good supply and it's easy to shave off the top when you're not trying to make a profit." René made the customary boyish gesture of sweeping his hand through his hair and resting it at the base of his neck. "And the chess . . . not very clever, I know. But your father was growing agitated since not seeing you at New Year's. I thought it might be a good distraction until I could get you over here to them."

Lila almost couldn't breathe.

"You mean you risk coming all the way across the city . . ." She edged forward a step. Then another, emotion threatening to choke back her words. "To bring crates of food, for years. And to play chess with my pa-pa while the SS are shooting La Résistance out in the streets?"

"Yeah." He sighed. Hands sank down in his pockets, as usual. "I guess I do."

For all the sloppy spy work it took to carry a crate of food and play a game of chess with an old man while running with a cell of machine gun–toting Résistance fighters, Lila couldn't bear to have space between them any longer.

She blotted out the divide.

Her palms found René's chest and he responded, pulling his hands from his pockets when she leaned up to press a soft kiss to the corner of his lips—the way they always used to say bonjour.

"I don't think I'd realized until this moment. I may never have lost faith in God, but after all this, I'm afraid I'd lost all faith in man. Everything we're doing here, René . . . Everything I thought could no longer be forgiven in us, you have restored it." She wiped a tear from her cheek with the heel of her palm. "And I think I now have the audacity to hope again."

"I would give you everything I have. That's the truth, Lila. It's all I wanted from the first time I saw you across a dance floor. And it's all I live for now. Every single day, to try to build something up again. To restore what we've lost."

There was no light "bonjour" this time—no sweet kiss of greeting on the corner of his mouth. And no lamenting the time that had passed since the road at the Petit Trianon.

War made quick work of things like that.

Lila lost her beret when René pulled her to him, fisting his hand through the shorn waves at her nape, making up for every lost moment and kissing her like tomorrow wouldn't matter even if it did arrive. They forgot about being marked souls in a battle for France and instead fell headlong into the memory of a kiss and the rekindled notion that Paris was still the city of love.

CHAPTER 18

30 JUNE 1942
1 PLACE DE LA CONCORDE
PARIS, FRANCE

Sandrine walked along the colonnade at the Rue de Rivoli, noticing the difference in the crowd passing along the sidewalk in front of the massive arched structure.

Parisians still went about their business, living their lives. But by summer, the quiet optimism that had come when the Americans joined the war the previous December hadn't meant a hastening to end the Nazis' reign in Paris. In fact, tensions ratcheted up nearly everywhere as the Third Reich held fast its iron grip of Europe. And if all forecasts were accurate, it seemed the Jews of the city ought to be prepared to bear the brunt of the Nazis' campaign for continued domination.

They once might have walked by under the red-and-black canopy of swastika flags secured to the side of the colonnade's façade and no one would have known. But now all Jews were ordered to wear a bright yellow star on the left breast of their clothing, an emblem reading *Juif* legible from paces away. Now the stars floated down the sidewalks like the night sky, on dress plackets and suit coats, on women pushing baby carriages, and on little children's jumpers as they hurried by. An omen she feared would lead to the brutal reality Victor had warned of in the first dark days of occupation.

Quickening her pace, Sandrine held tight to her clutch and hastened to the front doors of the Jeu de Paume. After removing the pin from her navy sculpted toque, holding the hat in her hand, Sandrine walked into the outer office and looked around—no junior officers about. No Michèle yet. And no Captain von Hiller peering over her shoulder, heaven be praised.

She breathed a sigh of relief.

"Ah, Sandrine." Rose looked up from her place seated in Sandrine's chair and peered over the top rim of her spectacles.

"Mademoiselle Valland. Bonjour."

"Do you know what I have here?"

"I do."

Rose turned a folder around, showing that the detailed catalog of items in a collection they'd received the day before was missing from its insides. Sandrine cleared her throat. And without reservation hastened to open her clutch, unfold and replace the ledger back in its folder, and then stand before her leader for a reply.

"It has come to my attention that you have been privy to our . . . efforts. But you have not drawn attention to this. It appears we are of a similar mind behind the scenes and have been for some six months now."

"Oui. I believe that's how long I've known what is at operation here."

"Does the captain know?"

Sandrine tilted her chin to the outer offices. "If he did, I'd wager neither of us would be sitting in this room right now. When he asks for the reports in the morning, I find reason to delay them until you have returned with the film from the night before."

Her features iced up. "And why would you suppose I'm doing anything with the film?"

Rose was a remarkable woman, stalwart in the defense of the art she loved. Clever. Intelligent beyond any of the officers she routinely had to submit herself to. And in Sandrine's eyes, a true patriot of France if she was indeed working with the growing Résistance in Paris, as both Sandrine and Michèle had suspected for months.

The question was, how to test their trust in each other now when it mattered most?

"The captain does not pretend we are ignorant here, not even as women on staff. On the contrary, he knows us to be quite learned. Where he makes his most serious miscalculation, though, is pride. He believes that we are afraid—believes it so thoroughly that he assumes we would be pushed to acquiescence in all things. If we are afraid of them, we will not question. And we certainly will not act. But by all accounts, the film that should be in its folder very often is not. So it would seem the captain is unaware of our methods of . . . keeping a secret catalog of stolen art. If that's what you are asking me, of course."

"Have you anything else on your person that belongs in this folder?" Rose looked to the peacock-blue clutch on the desk. "Let me see."

Sandrine handed it over without reservation.

There were the few things every good Parisienne had—a compact. A comb for the spaces that saw wind kick up off the River Seine. Lipstick, if she could afford its high cost or had been wise and saved any back at the start of the occupation. Her identification card and Nazi-stamped authorization for working at the ERR. A tiny tortoise resin frame with photos of her husband and son. And one thing that would tell Rose where Sandrine's loyalties lay.

Rose pulled out an envelope, the cream card stock split by a letter opener having cut it clean across the top. "What is this?"

"A note my husband gave me on the train platform the day he left to join the French First Army. I opened it some time ago."

Rose paused, with a light wave of the card stock in the air. "May I?"

If it was what she wanted, Sandrine would agree.

It would not mean anything to most—and didn't appear to at first glance, as Rose removed a note from Christian and a page torn from the Paquet Bible out of the envelope. She unfolded the note and read. And then opened the page from the second chapter of Habakkuk and looked up.

"What is this? A note that says 'Habakkuk 2' and is signed 'Je t'aime, mon cœur'? Romantic, save for a page torn from the Good Book."

"I hated to do it, but I had no other option. My husband said to hold on to the envelope, to open it only if things got so bad that we could not go back from it. That there would be an address inside where I might find help for myself and our son. And the words on that page are precious now, and I intend to carry them with me until the war is over."

"Are things bad enough for you?"

"For me? Non. I am allowed no complaint. My father-in-law was executed the first year of occupation, and you know how. My husband is . . . somewhere, risking his life for France. And I see what is happening in the streets right outside this building, with the Jews. They don't know what horrors tomorrow will bring and neither do I. But working here, I am under the protection of our ERR masters, and I have the luxury of my life. No matter how inconvenienced I am to stand in line for rations or to be forced to walk or cycle to work each day, I haven't been asked to give much of myself in this war. Not really. And in the moment that I thought all was lost because I'd had no word from my husband in two years, he knew me so completely that he gave me this for the day I thought I couldn't go on."

Replacing the note and the page from the Bible back in the envelope, Rose folded her hands over the desk. "He gave you hope."

Sandrine smiled, for Rose understood. "Oui. Christian knew I would need it in order to wait. He reminded me it is the noblest call to be brave, especially when everything within us would have us give in to our deepest fear. He tucked an address in our family Bible, right next to this page."

"And what is this address?"

"It is for a pâtisserie in Montmartre, of all things. An address where he has made provision, where there is a friend who would help if I have need of it. It gave me comfort to know this, that there is a friend out there somewhere. I have not gone to them and I don't know if I ever will. Because God sees what is happening here—He *is* here in the midst of it. This is the call to be faithful with my life even as I question and endure my own doubts, until there is an answer to our deepest pain. Habakkuk 2: 'For the vision is yet for an appointed time, but at the end it shall speak, and not lie: though it tarry, wait for it; because it will surely come.'"

"You have been covering for me for six months as I take film, ledgers, and catalog numbers—slipping them all out overnight so I might make copies and bring them back by morning. All under the ardent eye of the Nazi captain who peddles the world's stolen art. And yet you were faithful, Sandrine. And never said a word. Why?"

Deep breath. Be brave.

"Because if you're working for La Résistance, then I will too."

Rose shook her head—a flat "no" as she closed the folder on the desk. "This is not a game."

"You think I approach this with a faint heart?"

"Non. But if you do this, what may be asked of you is something you must consider carefully. You have a son to think about."

"And Henri is why I must do it. I have been asking myself who I intend to be when this war is over—the woman with much who gave little or the woman with little who gave much. That is always the question, isn't it, when we walk through the fire in our lives? And I now know the answer."

Sandrine paused, the breath of time one last consideration for a decision she could never take back. "In the grand view of everything that is happening, the fate of art doesn't really matter, does it? Not when lives are at stake. But I cannot go and do what my husband can. I can't go to war. But I can fight. Here. Now. Within the sphere of influence God has given me. I am called to fight my own war against injustice, not anyone else's. If this is what I can do, then I pledge to do it. And do it with all of my heart."

The odd moment arrived when the captain walked into the outer office, saw them, and Rose did not snap to attention. Instead she handed the envelope back to Sandrine, and in the moment that passed as the envelope was shared between them, her face warmed in a return smile.

"You understand what work we have ahead of us together here at the Jeu de Paume, Mrs. Paquet? If there is any reason to believe a piece of art that has come to us is in need of special attention, you must see to it. We cannot allow any of the work to go to the bonfires—"

The captain perked up, his notice of their conversation piqued by the mention of the degenerate art, and looked on until Rose added, "Without *due cause*, of course."

Sandrine accepted the envelope, covering the word *Drina* written on the outside with her palm. "I understand completely."

"Bien." Rose stood, straightening her jacket as Captain von Hiller joined them in their office. She handed him the folder of the previous day's requisition and led the way to the gallery. "Then let us begin. It looks to be a very full day."

———◆———

28 MARCH 1944
16TH ARRONDISSEMENT
PARIS, FRANCE

For a split second, Sandrine looked for the nearest item she could use as a weapon, which turned out to be an iron sitting on the bureau.

When she came out of the bath and saw the figure in the dark standing over Henri's sleeping form in the bed, her hand started at the knot in her robe and ended wrapped around the iron handle.

He turned around when she gasped and pressed a finger to his lips.

Sandrine could have feared it was the night Victor had been taken all over again, that the SS had learned of her ties with Valland and La Résistance and were there to arrest her too. But the room was still. Rain pattered a lullaby on the glass of the terrace doors. She hadn't heard the sound of automobiles out in the street and no SS uniforms were in sight.

There was just a man in plain clothes, standing how Christian stood.

Hurrying to him, Sandrine melted against his side and laced her fingers with his.

"I almost gave up on you after the opera house. When you didn't come, I told myself I'd imagined the entire thing—seeing you there that night," she whispered, looking to the closed bedroom door, praying none of the neighbors had heard or seen a figure cutting through the rain, finding his way up to their flat. "How did you get in here?"

"It took some doing, but don't worry. I was a ghost." He wrapped an arm around her, like they hadn't lost years and he wasn't a stranger to the little boy in the bed. "Did you know there's a car down on the street?"

"What?"

He tipped his head toward the terrace. "A Renault. It's here every night. I think that captain is having you watched. Or, in his mind, protected. Either way, it's been too much of a risk to try at all. God bless the rain that helped tonight so I could slip in."

Christian paused, ran curled knuckles over Henri's brow, tousling caramel hair that was darker in the shadows. "He's grown."

"Oui. Quite a lot. He'll be tall, just like his father."

"I mean, he's grown in the nearly three years since I last saw him."

"Three years? How . . . ?" Sandrine's breath escaped and she remembered—the uniformed officer on the street. "You mean that was you? Outside the cobbler's shop that day? I didn't believe Henri, though he tried to tell me. I thought his wish to see his dear pa-pa got the better of his senses and carried him off. I couldn't let myself believe it might be you."

He nodded. Smiled a shade. And shrugged, like the weight of the world wasn't upon his rain-speckled shoulders.

"I tried everything to get to you. But it was too risky. I followed you on the street that day, but after, I was questioned when I ran into a skirmish between a Frenchman and Vichy police on the street. A few well-placed lies about my standing as an officer in the Reich and I only managed to make it out by the skin of my teeth. After that I had no choice but to go back to London until we could plan better."

"London? That's where you've been all this time?"

"I wish I could say so. We were caught up in '40, fighting at Calais. And then ours was the last unit to make a stand so the troops could make it out at Dunkirk. We waited until the final evac boat was about to leave and the rest of the Allied soldiers headed across the Channel. We knew we were probably fools but said we were in it to make a last stand together, so we were prepared to give the Germans the best routing we had in us. I wrote you a letter that day, thinking I wasn't coming home."

"Oh, darling—I received it from Monsieur Mullins. But your father believed you'd been taken prisoner, to Germany."

"He never knew I wasn't in Germany with my unit when they surrendered. I wrote that letter to get to you if something were to happen to me. I took shrapnel to the head as the last evac boat was preparing to take off. They didn't think I was going to make it, but they knew the boat of a retired commercial fisherman willing to trek across the Channel was my best chance. So a friend took the letter out of my pocket and they sent me back on the boat. I woke up in hospital in England days later. And I began working with the Free French in London as soon as I could stand on two feet."

She touched his scar again. "And that's what this is?"

He nodded, caught her hand. Kissed her palm. And then his face changed. Softened maybe, when he stopped thinking about war and death and the story of where he'd been and the horrors he'd seen . . . and instead looked on their sleeping child.

"He's so peaceful. Lying there like that, you'd never know what our world has become."

"He started sleeping in our bed right after your father . . . I think it makes him feel safe to see your photo. To know he does have a pa-pa out there somewhere. And that he's not alone in all this."

"He's not alone. He has you, and that brings me more comfort than you could ever know." He squeezed her hand. Watched as Henri stirred with a crack of thunder, yawned, and rolled onto his other side. "Let me?"

It brought tears to her eyes that he'd even need to ask. Sandrine watched as Christian slipped his arms under Henri's shoulders and legs and carried him in silent steps down the hall to his room.

"Should we wake your mother?" Sandrine said, as he returned and clicked the door closed again. "She'll never forgive me if she doesn't get to see you."

"I'll look in on her before I leave. But you know Henri can't see me. He won't be able to keep it a secret. No matter how he'd promise to, children shouldn't have that burden placed on them."

"I know."

"And if I don't . . ." He stopped. Started again. "You'll tell him about this one day, that his pa-pa carried him in and put him to bed, like a good père does?"

"Of course I will."

The rain fought the terrace doors behind them then, crying down the glass like a river as they stood, half a room apart. Sandrine looked to the dark city streets outside. If he went out, he might not come back. How was anyone to face that reality? All she wanted to do was stretch time like that day on the train platform, make the minutes with him grow longer, and the nightmare world fade.

"Do you have to go now?" She swallowed hard, eyes searching his face through the glow of light from the bath, nervousness creeping up from some buried place.

He shook his head, giving her a light smile through the dark. "I can stay for a bit."

Rain punished the glass, the melody ticking like a clock as time bled through the night.

And by dawn the sun shone again, but Christian was gone.

CHAPTER 19

18 JULY 1942
15TH ARRONDISSEMENT
PARIS, FRANCE

On the corner of Boulevard de Grenélle . . . past the Vélodrome
d'Hiver. The lower floor of the three-story building with the
blue door: No. 4.

The chambermaid's instructions were vague at best.

When Lila had attempted to go near the address, the city
had been in a general uproar at all points around the Vélodrome
d'Hiver sports complex. She'd had to wait two days for the long
lines of people—men, women, and scores of children herded and
packed tight together—as buses lined up around the indoor cycle
track. And even a day after the madness had ended, there seemed to
be SS guards and the remnants of the mass of people left on every
street corner.

Lila stepped around a discarded pile of suitcases and finally
made it down the concrete stairs leading to the basement flat to
the paint-chipped door with No. 4 hanging on its bottom screw.

Decaying leaves gathered in a low corner, as if the steps hadn't been cleared in ages. A window sat next to the door, the glass covered in a sheen of dirt. Odd, but there was a window box with the sad crimson of geraniums poking out of dry soil, as if they'd been planted years ago and were just teetering on the edge of clinging to color and life.

Lila glanced over her shoulder, up the stairs. No one stirred upon the sidewalk. No one to see where she'd gone.

Gloved fist to the door, she knocked. And stood back. Not even certain why herself, she straightened her belt and waited, hands resting at her middle. A man with a ruddy complexion. Tall but a hopelessly thin build. An unfortunate zigzag to his teeth. He answered on the first rap of her knuckles to the wood. He stared her to the ground, saying nothing.

"*Pardon*. I'm calling for Violette Caron, s'il vous plaît."

He raked his gaze up and down, from her wing-tip shoes to cerise skirt and blouse, up to her chic Paris topper, then closed the door in her face.

After she'd considered quite seriously turning back and hightailing it up the stairs, the door opened again, a crack this time, and then revealed the calm, quiet figure of the Hôtel Ritz maid with the same dark flaxen hair but in plain clothes. Her eyes brightened when she saw Lila on the stoop, and she opened the door wider.

Lila's heart started beating again. "Violette."

"Oui. Bonjour, mademoiselle. I am so glad you have come." She waved her into a flat that was equally humble as the entry. The gentleman stood behind, hovering on the edge of a hallway's shadows. "And do forgive Arthur here his skeptical nature when someone new arrives at our door. These are perilous times."

Though Amélie's misshapen comment about rats in Violette's building was certainly made without firsthand knowledge, it hadn't been far from accurate. The little natural light from the window shone on sparse furnishings: an amber sofa against the wall, its stuffing protruding from moth-eaten seams, clashed against peeling wallpaper in a horrid marigold and pea-green stripe. A lightbulb hung over a table and three chairs, and a bookshelf in need of dusting and a portrait of a horse running through a pasture served as the backdrop. A single brass crucifix hung on the wall, its edges corroded from musty, water-laden air.

"Come, Lila. Quickly." Violette placed a hand on Lila's shoulder and ushered her to sit. "*Maintenant.* We've been waiting for you."

"I tried to come sooner, but there was a large crowd in this area for the last two days, and Vichy police everywhere. I couldn't get through without authorization, not even to walk on the sidewalk. Whatever has happened here?"

The man hovered in the doorway to a hall, then looked to Violette and moved into the kitchenette to fill a kettle with water.

"You did not know?" Violette rested a hand on her arm, patting lightly. "It was the *Opération Vent printanier*—'Operation Spring Breeze.' A mass arrest. Vichy police rounded up all the Jews left in the city and kept them here for processing before they were sent away. We hear they are bound for work camps in the east. That is why I telephoned you to come when I was at the Ritz. I just learned of this."

"Work camps . . . Are you certain?" Lila looked out the window, the sad memory of the suitcases coming back to her mind, though all she could see was the grime on the outside of the glass. The haunted imaginings of the long lines of people patiently waiting for their death transport did unspeakable things to her heart.

"Your coquette friend—Amélie? She has returned to the Ritz. On the same floor, even, as she was with the baron. But she has a new officer now. She has usurped one of the paramours and moved into a suite . . . along with a young daughter. I was requested to come back as chambermaid for her, and it is rumored she and the officer are to be married."

Amélie has a daughter. And is marrying a Nazi.

"What is his name?"

"A cutthroat captain by the name of Scheel. You know him? Oui?"

Lila remembered the girl he'd had sharing his suite just the year before—sweet Adélaïde. The girl Amélie had dubbed as having the long legs and pretty smile. And who knew where the young ingénue was now.

"I know of him. I'd dressed his former lady for a party once. I hasten to say she had bruises covering most of her back—evidence of his temper. It took some doing to find a gown that would cover them." Lila shook her head. The secrets a dressmaker was made to keep were often in the same vein as those harbored by a chambermaid. "I wonder what's become of her now."

"Who knows. But he works for the German embassy and I was able to discern from your mistress Amélie that he was assigned to the oversight of operations here, for the grand roundup of the Jews. Our cell already had this house close by, to watch what was happening on this end of the city. It just so happens the address I gave you those months ago is adjacent to what happened here. We'd hoped to step in and help the Jews."

"And did you?"

"Non. I regret that we were too late. God save them now."

The horror. Watching as men, women . . . children were packed up and sent off to camps—the places rumored to be evil incarnate on earth.

"You were forced to watch yet could do nothing to intercede?"

"We'd have tried. We have men on the inside of the Vichy police, but we could not. There were too many of *them* about. But our contacts could review the transport lists for us. And I asked them right away to search out the names you seek. A mother, Esther Maude Touliard. A daughter, Patrice, aged twenty-two years. And a son, aged twenty-six—"

"Oui. René. So you found them. You found their names on the transport lists?"

"I am afraid so, mademoiselle."

Lila bit her bottom lip, such news something she'd never imagined could inflict such severe and immediate pain to her chest as it did when his name was confirmed.

"Where . . . ?" She covered her mouth with a gloved hand, pushing back tears, fighting for words. "And where have they gone?"

"The women were transported to a camp called Ravensbrück."

"And where is that?"

Violette's face sank, her chin given to a soft waver as she confirmed, "Germany."

"Here. Drink this, mademoiselle. It will help calm you."

Arthur brought a cup of tepid water—presumably weak tea—in a metal mug and set it before her. Lila accepted it, the heat coming through her gloves maybe the only thing to remind her that she was still alive and able to feel anything with the numbness of such news.

It was incomprehensible. A family gone. Wiped from the face of the earth because of her naïveté at the start of the war.

Lila gripped the cup tighter but couldn't down a drop. "And René Touliard? Please tell me—what of him?"

"We don't yet know."

"Then what can we do to track him? How can we know what's become of him—even to help him somehow? Please."

"I assure you, the network is doing our due diligence to find anything we can. And we will, soon."

For all the pain she'd caused and for such ignorance to have shared the Touliards' location with her friend—if there was any honor left in their topsy-turvy world, why was evil allowed to prosper? Lila thought of the stolen Cézanne on the wall of Amèlie's suite. Of the art that flowed through the officers in command at the ERR. And of the Touliard Cartier necklace—the family heirloom of René's heritage—which at that very moment could be clasped around the porcelain-skinned neck of a champagne-blonde shrew in a Nazi suite.

"What can I do? Ask me anything. I would do whatever is necessary to help them."

Violette smiled, in spite of herself it seemed. They both had taken in the news, and it had affected them both to know their countrymen were being shipped off to such hellish places. Lila could see it in the maid's eyes: Purpose. Action. Passion to fight back. She was not afraid, and that zeal was the one asset that seemed able to pull Lila from the guilt and help her fathom how she could go on.

"Much." Violette reached out, holding her palm out. Lila slipped hers in it and felt her fingertips squeezed. "There is much to be done. And much we can do to fight together in this war."

———◆———

5 June 1944
61 Boulevard de Clichy
Paris, France

René sat at the table in the flat above the pâtisserie, tinkering with the transistor radio by candlelight.

A balmy evening wind trembled the glass outside the windows as the sun set in a splash of raspberry and electric pinks across the sky. A burst of gunfire peppered somewhere in the distance—the new routine in the streets by summer, and then all was still again.

They'd lost electricity and with baking supplies wearing thin, there was no point in keeping the pâtisserie doors open through evening. In the worsening conditions for the German war effort, the loss of electricity seemed a more common occurrence. Rations were scarce. Basic municipal services had begun to break down. And the SS were focused on quelling insurrection from the increasing boldness of the Maquis in the rural areas and so doubled down on arrests of suspected Résistance fighters in the streets. It seemed all of Paris was teetering on a cliff's edge, in danger of sailing off at the smallest nudge. And they existed in the center of it, feeling the pressure of something that was coming, yet not knowing what it might be.

Sewing kit in hand, Lila pulled out a chair and sat beside René. He noticed the garment with pink feathers and tipped an eyebrow.

"Don't look at me like that—it's official spy business."

"Sure it is."

"Truly. Nigel brought it to me yesterday, asking me to sew a place inside these clothes for us to get messages out." She sorted through a handful of nude mesh, red sequins, and bright splashes of color on an evening gown. "But I have to wonder if these are going around the corner to the cabarets. They seem like show costumes to me."

Even in the dark she could see shades of amusement flash across his face as he tried to cover a smile.

"What?"

"Was Nigel's face pink as those flamingo feathers when he gave it to you?"

It had been, right up where his unruly brown mane tipped the tops of his ears, as a matter of fact. She turned the costume over on the table. "Maybe. How'd you know that?"

"I'd say you're using your dressmaking skills more for the benefit of his imagined love life than purely for our efforts here." He didn't try to stifle a laugh. "He helps one of our contacts smuggle information out of Paris, along with his stories to *The Sketch*. I think he's in love with her."

"Who is she?"

"Well . . . Josephine Baker. Heard of her?"

"Are you serious? What self-respecting fashion worker wouldn't have? She's a jazz singer—or was, before our occupiers outlawed the music. She's also an opera singer. And international film star."

"And an actress who's using her elevated position in much the same way you did—to get close to higher-ups in the Axis even as she smuggles messages for us across enemy lines. She's got beauty and brains, but she's also got guts, that one."

"You mean to tell me each time Nigel's come to me with a red face and feather boa costume asking for a patch job, I've been sewing places for her to hide Résistance messages as she crosses enemy lines?" Lila's hands tingled with the flash of the costume's sequins, and she smiled back. "I thought he had a secret sweetheart at the cabaret. But now that I know who it is, I don't blame Nigel a bit for being cagey with me about who the costumes were for. If she does all that, I just might be in love with her too."

"Which is more than I can say for anything I'm able to do at the moment." René's laugh at her cheek faded to frustration as he turned a dial and a high-pitched frequency cursed their ears.

"So you're trying to . . . fix it?"

"Trying to get it to actually give us something useful."

"We've heard chatter for weeks."

René gave up, tossing a screwdriver on the table, while the radio spit white noise between them.

"Chatter, oui. But nothing actionable. I can't get anyone to tell us something with certainty attached to it. Carlyle doesn't even know, and it's not a mark of confidence when the OSS keeps a lid on what's happening, even from their agents in the field. This battery won't last forever." René sighed and flicked the switch to end the static, then leaned back in his chair, hands braced behind his head like he needed a stopper before he sent the pile of junk careening across the room. "Old habits. I'm afraid I lean more to the impatient side of things. Sorry."

"Don't be. I remembered that much." She smiled, making her words intentionally edged in softness. "And we're all waiting for something, aren't we?"

The candle flickered a soft glow between them, and the stillness of the flat and the wind outside and the gunfire no one wanted to hear became unwitting companions. He looked over her sewing stitches and apprehension cropped up from somewhere within him.

"If I don't hear news soon, I'll have to go out. Find Nigel and Carlyle. See what they've taken in, if anything."

"I thought you might say something like that." Lila looked away from him, using her fingertips to dance along the edge of a row of costume feathers. It seemed safer than imagining him ducking gunfire after curfew, or worse, getting caught up in one of the mass arrests occurring with nail-biting frequency.

He drummed his fingertips on the tabletop so near hers, she could feel the brush of air it caused.

"You know, on second thought . . . maybe this contraption can do something useful after all." René flipped the dial, turning until the soft jazzy sway of the German-outlawed band music floated around them.

"Don't let Carlyle know I said this, but God bless the Yanks, if only for their music."

He stood and held out his hand to her. She accepted and they drew a slow circle that creaked the floorboards beneath their shoes.

Theirs wasn't a dance floor under the stars. No Versailles castles loomed in the background or high-society couples twirled around them. They were just two people, lost in a shadow world, he unshaven and in a shirt with a hole at the shoulder seam and she in the same boring dress she washed out in the sink each day. No jewels. No fashion and finery. No couture gowns or mink stoles in a saucy drape over the shoulder.

Just soft music and dancing.

"Who is this?" Lila pressed her cheek against his shoulder while he held her hand curled into his chest.

"Artie Shaw. Band leader in the US. This one's old though—'Deep in a Dream.' From before he enlisted. But seems they're still playing it over the airwaves."

"It's nice."

"You know, I once heard him play this live at the Blue Room."

She leaned back, looked up. "Where was that?"

"Took a trip to New York City in '38. He was there, at the Lincoln Hotel. But that was before Paris."

"'Before Paris . . .' Famous last words of a good many men, I'd wager."

He kissed her temple, and she could feel his lips press into a smile against her skin. "And in case you want to ask—no. I didn't dance with any other girl when I was there. My mother probably wanted me to. Make a match. All of that, but I refused."

"So what you're saying is, I'm the only girl you've danced with twice?"

"You're the only one I've ever wanted to," he said, the sway slowing, the clarinet carrying the tune off without them. "We're a long way from those summer nights at Elsie de Wolfe's parties, aren't we?"

"I'd be lying if I said it hadn't just crossed my mind. What's happened in the last four, almost five years, it's changed us. It's changed Paris and turned everything into a nightmare. When will it end?"

"Not all a nightmare, Lila. And nothing was impossible, not when I had you."

"How?"

He swallowed hard, seeming to search for words. "In your photo I kept in my pocket. Or put on the dash in the truck. I played every moment we spent in those months over in my mind between then and now. I wasn't supposed to fall in love—I wasn't allowed to. That was the first thing the Résistance taught us when I got in this game. It was the same rule Nigel lived by until this crush on Josephine Baker, and Carlyle with his Uncle Sam: *no women*. They complicate matters. And in war, that could cost a man his life."

Lila shuddered over a laugh. And women were seen as soft.

"How romantic a notion. *Merci beaucoup*, I'm sure, to be labeled such a temptress that we could bring down men with a mere thought. If that were all true, why, we could end this war tomorrow."

"Not exactly what I was trying to say. What I should have said—and did it poorly—is that I hadn't bargained on you. Or Paris. Taken together, those two things could change a man's whole life, and he'd be the better for it."

He paused their dance. Took a breath as they froze, standing together. And gazed at her in a way that instinct told a girl a boy was poised to do something brash, if it didn't seem too unbelievable in the middle of their current nightmare.

Lila could feel his heart beating and pressed her palm to it, wishing more than anything that he'd stop, yet still wanting him to go on if only to make the moment last a breath longer.

"I should have asked you to marry me that night instead of walking away, thinking I was protecting you. I've never regretted anything more."

Those beautiful words she'd once wanted to hear . . . shredded like a knife.

It was what torture felt like inside—she hadn't cried in months.

Years, maybe.

Life was all about survival and everything else was bottled. It was sewing gowns and tiptoeing around the Hôtel Ritz, and then it had evolved into something Lila didn't recognize, the obsession to find the next scrap of information about the Touliard family and trying, and fighting, and failing, to make her mind forget all that her eyes had seen. She'd have blasted a fist against her skull if it would erase a moment of the torture.

Lila pressed her forehead deeper against his shoulder, clamped her lids closed against the linen of his shirtsleeve. Not dancing. Just standing. And crying, her fingers grasping his shoulders and clinging to him for dear life.

"What's this?" René hugged around her, a cage of warmth holding her up. And when he gave a soft squeeze and realized she wasn't playing back, his embrace grew more serious. He held firm as she broke apart, rested his chin on the top of her head, and whispered, slow and even, "Lila. Why are you crying, love?"

"I never meant . . . for any of this to happen. I was never supposed to see you again. I could have lived with the regret—could have died knowing I was doing something for you. But now you're here. Standing in front of me. Alive. And open. And saying the things I'd have given anything to hear all those years ago, and I don't deserve it."

"You're not making any sense."

"I'm not doing anything noble, René. But it's the Touliard collection. Your family. That night at Versailles, you said you couldn't marry me—did you really tell me everything about why?"

"I told you I'd never lie to you. If it's what you want, I'm an open book."

"Then tell me the truth." She dared to look up, searching his eyes. "Tell me what happened to you between then and now. To bring you here, in this moment. How did you survive?"

"The truth . . . Nigel and I have known each other for some time. Met in London years back, through a mutual acquaintance who introduced us in a pub of all places. He's really Nigel Dunne—of the Yorkshire Dunnes—some small farming hamlet in Leeds. The son of a schoolmaster. Eleven brothers and sisters and he the oldest, just itching to get out and see the world. The way he tells it, from the cradle to the first boat dock he could find. And hasn't been home since."

René freed a hand, a butterfly's touch of his fingertips brushing a wisp of hair back at her temple and catching tears on the apple of her cheek.

"And Carlyle. We met him later, after all this started. He hasn't a home as far as I know. No wife. Children. He was a street-wise scamp the way he remembers. From boys' home to orphanage and back again, and living on the streets by the time he was eleven. That's how he made it to the Carlyle Hotel that day years later. And headlong into espionage for his country."

She exhaled low. "And what about you? What brought you to Paris that summer?"

"Carlyle would say I was the only one of us to legitimately come from something. With a family. A name. And a future worth anticipating. Maybe he'd have traded places like a shot. But that reality was a glass house, with deep fractures in our family that shattered when my father died. I was twenty-one years old and resented that I had to step in for a textile magnate who'd traded everything in order to build a small family mercantile business into one of the biggest fortunes in France. After years of being told what to do, how to live, and finally to whom I'd be married—to some New York heiress I'd never met—I'd had enough. I wanted the one thing those two drifters had: freedom. And I would tell you I'd have done anything to get it, including leaving home and responsibilities in London and tarnishing my father's legacy all to chase down what was a rumor of war."

"So you came to Paris that summer to do what?"

"To tell my mother I was on a crash course with life and I had no intention of falling in line. And I believe it broke her heart when I told her I was signing up with the French First Army. So I'd come back to Paris only to say good-bye and disappear into war. And find my way into some underground operation. But then I met you."

He stopped, the radio having moved on to some other lovers' song, and brushed his thumbs over the tears still weighing her bottom lashes. "And everything changed. I went to the first society party to meet up with a friend, but I kept coming back to them . . . for *you*. I wanted to imagine a life different than the one I was running from. One in which I could see responsibility not as a yoke around my neck but as a blessing. An opportunity to do good in this life, and to be proud of building something. Is that what you needed to hear, that you've changed a man's life?"

"Non. But I thank you for saying it. You'll never know what it's meant to me to hear it from you."

For the first time in the flat, René's face changed and read as scared. Not of SS guards or gunfire in the streets or the darkness that surrounded them. In the flicker of candlelight it seemed he knew the turn had been handed to her. And with the tears from a girl who'd never cried in front of him, he seemed to know something had broken open.

"When I learned your family had been arrested, I thought you were with them . . . I thought you were sent away to one of those death camps that are rumored about. It's why I believed you were dead. We got confirmation through the Résistance—the Touliard family. All killed. And when I heard those words, I died too."

"Killed . . ." He swallowed hard, and the silence that followed between them broke her heart. "You say confirmation. From whom? When?"

"All this time, I couldn't tell you."

"Couldn't tell me what? Lila, I'm done with the half-truths and the pocketful of names that don't mean anything. As long as I know you'll still be here with me when this war is over."

The ceiling could have crashed in and Lila wouldn't have felt worse than she did in this moment. It was tantamount to murder, the foolish ignorance of entrusting something so sacred to Amélie, and she'd done it on a whim, at a café table over a plate of pastries. Like the lives of his mother and sister didn't matter at all.

"I was crushed when I learned that you and your family had been arrested."

The truth bled out, the guilt ramming her like it had for the last years, relentless and clawing from her core.

"It's the reason I got involved with La Résistance in the first place.

And why I took a bullet that night at the Hôtel Ritz. I was looking for anything to carve out the pain I'd caused . . . You don't know this, but your mother and sister were transported to Ravensbrück—a camp in Germany." She drew a deep, shaky breath. "They died there. And I'm the reason why."

CHAPTER 20

※

JUNE 1944
1 PLACE DE LA CONCORDE
PARIS, FRANCE

"Where have you been?" Michèle eyed Sandrine as she came into the office from the hall, the third time she'd been to the ladies' room in the last half hour.

"Nothing—I'm just not feeling well is all. But forget that. What's happened?"

"Something big," she whispered, eyeing Rose, who was standing off to the side in the doorway, surrounded by uniforms.

The news that did trickle in through Rose's Résistance contacts said that the war was going far worse for the Germans than they'd ever let on.

"You know how the captain has stayed holed up in that office of his all day? Now a few moments before we're all set to leave for the evening, he begins ordering everyone around like the tyrant he is, but without a word of explanation. He just steamrolled through the gallery and barked out a decree for us to begin crating art. All of it."

"All that's left? It's mostly degenerate art that they didn't burn. They must have stopped thinking they have need of it, thinking

254

they could get some value out of it in the end." Sandrine stared out from the offices to the gallery hall, the long-distance view obstructed by mounds of crates, larger-than-life marble statues on wheeled carts, and stacks of canvas in gilded frames leaning against all the walls. "That could still be several hundreds of pieces. But what do they intend to do with it all? And the accumulation of the odds and ends of the Jewish homes and shops that have been cleaned out? It's a massive hoard. What will become of all of their belongings?"

"I don't know. But I don't think it's for building bonfires in the Tuileries. It smells like someone's losing a war if you ask me, and the hornets are going to try to pilfer everything they can before they fly out of the nest. We'll have to wait for our marching orders from Rose, but it doesn't look good—for them at least. For us this could be it! What if the Allies really are coming?"

"Will Rose get word out?"

The mention of La Résistance was kept to a barely there whisper between them, knowing the junior officers and soldiers could walk in at any moment.

"Of course she will. We haven't come this far to fail now. All I know is Rose was told to prepare the art for transport and she'll see that the information gets to the network. We have no train schedules or destinations, just a warning that we're to have the art ready. It's unprecedented."

"Where would they mean to take it all? Berlin? Or to Austria for the Führermuseum?"

"If they're still building it with a crumbling empire." Michèle shrugged, and the party dispersed around Rose, who walked their way. "I suppose we're about to find out."

"Ladies, we have been given a directive to prepare the art for transport. As a precautionary measure. We have no orders to send it off anywhere just yet, but we are to remain vigilant for any circumstance. We must ensure every piece is recorded with meticulous attention."

Rose dropped a clipboard on the desktop, then rested her hands—knuckles down—to lean her fists on the surface. Silent for a moment, as if the orders she'd been given were simply too much to entertain following, and everything in her was being summoned in order to obey.

"Bien. We ought to get to work then, ladies. And Sandrine." Rose looked her square in the face. "The captain would like to see you in his office."

Michèle shot to standing, a little fire under her shoes and doe eyes wide as she hugged file folders to her chest. "What does that mean?"

"It means that the captain wishes to speak to Sandrine, that is all. But I'm afraid if she does not come out of that office in five minutes with every bit of her unharmed, then I may have to go in there wielding a crowbar to retrieve her myself. D'accord?"

The maternal nature of the order was not lost, and Sandrine smiled as she stood. Their leader made the uncharacteristic gesture of squeezing her hand in solidarity.

"Oui, Rose. I understand. And I will hurry back. You needn't worry."

Sandrine noticed a breeze beyond the glass of the windows as she passed through the long hall to the office at the end, the windy evening wreaking havoc in the gardens with the random piece of paper or wrapper or summer bloom ripped from its hedgerow to be carried off.

"Captain? You wished to see me?"

He stood just inside the doorway, anchored by the window. His refusal to look up at her seemed an intentional slight, as he focused on something in a file he held in his hands. "Sit down, Mrs. Paquet."

Something is definitely not right.

For her to take a seat in one of the leather nail-head chairs in front of his desk, either he'd have to move aside or she'd have to get crafty in slipping around him. His stance was a boulder blocking the path from the doorway inside.

"Very well." She turned to the side to pass by.

The light brush against him was unexpected, and she was horrified to have the front of her suit press against the side of his uniform, almost like the night she'd been forced to step out on a dance floor in the Chanel gown. She breathed a sigh of relief when he left the door ajar but lost any sense of calm when those viridian eyes grew darker somehow as he settled in the chair opposite her. So straightforward were they in their surveyance that Sandrine's palms actually began to sweat as she twisted them out of sight in her lap.

"Was there something you needed, sir?"

"That all depends. Is there something you'd like to tell me?"

Spine ramrod straight. Posture perfect and legs prim and crossed at the ankles. Amiable yet terrified beneath her skin, Sandrine pressed her lips into a placid smile, doing all she could to project the image of innocence and composure. "And what would that be?"

The captain opened a desk drawer and closed it again, then set a Ronson lighter on the desk between them.

Oh, Lord, no . . .

Light from the desk lamp illuminated enough to show it was the same lighter Christian had with him at the Palais Garnier months before. She hadn't thought of it, and he mustn't have either, in their haste to slip out of the closet that night. It had been lost on the floor somewhere under a stack of chairs or in the corner. Rightly, all she'd been thinking of was the bliss of seeing him again and the hope of evading notice as she exited to the hall. It never occurred to her they'd been seen, or caught—especially without confrontation about it for weeks.

Sandrine looked at it, willing her face to remain unaffected.

"Does this help to stoke your memory at all?" He took the lighter, lifted and twirled the silver case in a slow spin against the desk.

"I don't see why it should."

"When I learned that you were seen coming out of a closet at the opera house with a uniformed officer on your heels, I believe that is something of note. Is it not? Do you think he wonders where this little trinket has gone?"

Shrug it off. Make him think there's nothing to it.

"I'm sure I don't know whatever you could be referring to, sir. But I assure you that you are mistaken."

"In which part?"

"All of it."

"Indeed? Very well then." He swiped it up, gave it a little toss in his palm, and checked his wristwatch. "It's getting late. And we have much work in the gallery. Gather your things. I'll give you a ride home afterward."

Sandrine walked out of his office, only able to give Michèle a fleeting glance and soft shake of the head—and mouthed *I'm okay* as she collected her satchel and hat and headed for the front gallery with him. He worked with diligence thereafter and she alongside, cataloging frame after frame he ordered loaded in crates stacked all around. And when the sun was just tipping behind the Eiffel Tower, he declared it was time to go.

The captain held the front door open for Sandrine, allowing her to walk through to the waiting auto, a cold silence his way of letting her know she was not at all in his good graces, and certainly not out of whatever dark woods she'd stumbled into.

The lighter had to mean one of two things: either he suspected she'd had a liaison with another SS officer the night of the exhibition, or worse, he suspected the truth. Could he have learned that Christian was back and working with the Résistance? If that were true, surely he now suspected her. Either way, escorted rides home drew her nearer to the apex of his control and the reality that at some chosen time, he would demand an explanation.

And what would she say?

The clock was ticking. Sandrine was backed into a corner and soon would be unable to hide the fact she was carrying her husband's second child.

CHAPTER 21

C amille? You in, chérie?"

Lila held her breath as the front door to Camille's Ritz suite opened without an ounce of charity and was slammed again as Amélie shouted her entry into it.

The ladies in the boudoir gave a collective jump at the intrusion and Lila nearly careened a pin into Camille's backside as what sounded like shopping bags and a tearstained baby lumbered together through the door. Camille froze, the gauze of the veil she'd been inspecting stilled in her hands as she looked down over her shoulder to Lila, kneeling at the train of the wedding gown.

"I will handle this," Camille whispered, removing the veil frosting from her chocolate waves. She stared over to the sweet little blonde newlywed, Greta, and the tight-lipped Hedy look-alike, Margot, the latter whose nerves had taken to wrapping and rewrapping her string of pearls around her index finger.

Amélie fiddled to balance an oversized hatbox of pink candy stripe on the baby carriage at the edge of their view through the bedroom door. She must have removed her hat and tossed it onto the nail-head settee a second later, as it flew like an ebony dart across the parlor.

"There was rumor of bombings in Rennes all weekend, so of course we couldn't get to our château." She paused with a *shh, shh!* at the baby, whose cries she continued talking over. "The Allies decided today was the day they'd punish the poor devils and bomb the countryside. So all the roads were jammed and our holiday getaway was ruined. We had to return to Paris under military escort so the men can plan some reprisal theatrics at Norwich the day after tomorrow. It was a bore, but at least I can show you what I bought."

Crying baby mixed with silent, terrified paramours and one Amélie, who entered the boudoir and finally spotted the would-be bride standing tall on a box in its center, with her lavish gown fanned out and her dressmaker crouched behind.

Lila stood and took the pins from her teeth, trying to offer the most unobtrusive smile she could summon.

"What is *she* doing here?" Amélie spat the question like she'd just ingested sour milk.

"Amélie . . . What a serendipitous surprise. We did not think you'd make it back in time for this. So sorry about the bombing, chérie. That is dreadful!" Camille's upbeat tone appeared to trip over her nerves as she stepped down from the platform. She lifted the bridal gown's satin layers as she approached Amélie in the doorway and kissed both of her cheeks. "But won't you come in? You remember our Lila? She is fitting my wedding gown. Didn't I tell you?"

"I seem to remember something about a wedding gown. But not *that*." Amélie shifted her glare to a little chambermaid hovering at the edge of the bathroom door. With hardly a welcome, she arched a brow as if the young girl should have already read her mistress's mind. "Well? This baby needs to be changed or she'll never stop bellowing. Take her."

The maid avoided eye contact with the ladies as she hurried across the room and took the curled carriage handle from Amélie's action of halfhearted bounces, cooing and shushing the baby as she rolled her away.

"What is she doing here? I thought the notorious 'House of LDL' was defunct within the circles of this hotel. What would Mademoiselle Chanel say if we were to engage with someone so inept at dressing the women here?" Amélie tossed her Jean Harlow waves, cocking a hip to accentuate a posh mustard ensemble with structured shoulders, patch pockets, and a set of sleek ebony travel gloves she was artfully peeling one by one from her fingertips. "And why is this little party going on here without an invitation having been sent to my suite? I am wounded, fair ladies."

"It's not like that, Amélie. It's just . . ."

So much for the help.

Camille darted her glance from Greta to Margot—no rescue there. They were suddenly struck mute. And then she looked to Lila, who'd been assured the bride could handle the finer points of the vixen's intransigence, at least until she'd begun to wither. Camille retreated back into silence under Amélie's toxic smile, swift as snow melting in the sun.

Lila stepped up. "Camille paid a retainer some time ago for a gown similar to Greta's last year. And I had a last-minute opening for today only. My apologies that you weren't here, but the scheduling oversight was mine—not Camille's." Lila blinked, waiting in the center of the room with measuring tape gathered in her hands, hoping the subservience would calm the wilder temperament.

"And we're finished. Oui?" The bride picked up on the paltry explanation and snapped a contrary look at their dressmaker, then hooked an elbow around Amélie's while they waited for her response.

"Of course. I believe I have just about all I need today." Lila began tidying—placing pins back in the pin box, rolling measuring tape, tucking scissors back in their travel case, and prepping delicate ivory tissue in the dress box for the gown she'd have to lay back inside it.

"Bien. Then I can slip out of this gown and we ladies may go to brunch. I've made a reservation at the lobby restaurant—crab cakes with lemon, berry compote, and blue cheese salad. And then you ought to choose our dessert and tell us all about your exciting trip. Truly, a holiday with bombs falling and you kept your lipstick to such perfection? Do tell us how you do it, my dear. We are each a willing student under your guidance."

Camille's smile weathered the cool in Amélie's reply—iron features and an aloof manner that built a wall around whatever she was truly thinking, in favor of playing the part of the posh alpha with ample forgiveness for the slight she'd received.

It was rumored Scheel was a living terror, as was his new would-be bride. It wasn't that the ladies were likely afraid of Amélie—she was more bark than bite in the end. But Scheel's influence hovered over them all, and his shadow dictated their behavior. His had a high-ranking role at the German embassy, and anyone with any smarts knew it wasn't a wise move to earn an enemy in someone who could make life uncomfortable for their own officers and, by extension, them. By the way they were all fluttering in welcome, the ladies were keen to buff out their mistakes in earnest. Amélie's fit of pique had worked wonders.

They were back in one another's good graces and Lila was back to being the hired help.

"Clean up in here, would you, dear Lila? And telephone my secretary when the gown is ready? She'll tell you when you may deliver it."

"It will be my pleasure, Camille." Lila dragged her feet after that, giving ardent attention to every seamstress tool she owned—taking an inordinate amount of time to move about the suite in silence—cleaning, straightening, and tidying up until the ladies were ready to venture downstairs.

The rocky road of female relationships was paved with crab cakes, apparently, as the ladies disappeared through the suite door but fifteen minutes later, leaving her alone. With the chambermaid employed looking after Amélie's daughter and Violette no doubt waiting in the service stairs for whatever information she might glean, Lila immediately flipped a switch in her mind to a mode of efficiency and tossed the remainder of her dressmaking tools into her satchel.

Listening with sharp ears, Lila heard nothing but the distant chime of the elevator bell, some inordinate laughter from patrons down the hall, and the desperate thumping of her own heart dancing a jig in her chest. With a deep indrawn breath, she sat on the end of the bed and, with less-than-nimble fingers, pulled the tiny microfilm camera from the hidden seam she'd sewn in her skirt and clutched it in her palm.

Did Camille's beau have anything of worth in the suite? The junior officer was under Scheel's command at the German embassy. Who knew what treasures of information he may have left behind? Lila couldn't guess but began opening drawers. Checking suit pockets. Looking for files in the closet, and finally landed by the desk, where she found folders in a drawer. With information she couldn't read, of course—all in German—but the emblem of the Third Reich was stamped on official letterhead and some sort of schematic for who knew what was included behind it, so she snapped photos of it all.

Her heart thumped with *click* after *click* of the camera, and she fumbled to arrange the papers back into the file and slip them unseen back into the desk drawer once she'd reached the back cover. But a shave of a second after, the tiny squeak of the boudoir door hinge sang out as someone entered the room, and she buried the camera in a closed fist just edged behind her back.

"Oh! Lila—you're still here. Bien. I have caught you." Camille sighed and rushed into the boudoir to wrap her in a hug.

"Oui. I was just making certain everything was in order before I go."

"Of course you were. And I am so glad."

Something broke inside Lila then, knowing she was clutching a microfilm camera tight in one palm hidden behind her back and embracing the naive young woman in an enraptured hug with the other.

Camille beamed, a smile accentuating a dimple in her cheek. "I couldn't go downstairs without thanking you for what you did in here." With her tone lowered to a whisper, she added, "I didn't want to fall out of her good graces. You know how it is. That is no place to find oneself, especially with her captain my Felix's commanding officer."

Camille reached for Lila's free palm and pressed a roll of *vingt* francs into it. "Here."

Lila stared down, the outside of the crisp banknotes covered over in the idiocy of the Reich's reimagined France, with visions of simpering women in colorful Aryan dress, surrounded by an abundance of food and smiles from a little cherub in their arms.

The money showed a perfect vision of the Nazis' utopia, handed to Lila from a woman in the complete opposite domestic situation than the Reich so fiercely advocated.

"What is it?"

"Why, a tip. What else? Not full payment for the gown, of course— I'll arrange for that later. Whatever price you put to it. But this is for *you*, Lila. For being a friend to us—all of us here agree. Greta, Margot, and me as well. You are keeping us in confidence with your discretion. My *mère* always used to say that a clever lady ought to keep her man happy, but a truly wise one keeps her maid happier. If you know what I mean."

"Quite." Lila forced a smile, the beaming bride-to-be Camille having no idea the size of the blinders that held her fast in that suite. "Merci."

"Think nothing of it. Just answer my calls first when I telephone for my next gown order, hmm? Well, I'm off to brunch then. And we have a final fitting next week? I'm so excited! Then I should like to see it all together—the gown, shoes, and veil. Felix won't believe it when he sees me. I will wear couture for my wedding, just as I'd always dreamed."

"I'll see to the scheduling of our next meeting myself."

"Marvelous! My dear, you are an absolute dream." Camille fluttered along with her, fawning and chattering on as Lila dropped the microfilm unseen into her bag, even carrying the dress box part of the way until she floated onto the elevator and waved with an "Au revoir!" as she went down to brunch in her mindless fog.

Lila hadn't much to relay to Violette as they huddled together in the service stairs that day. Just a roll of microfilm with documents that needed translating, and a random warning about the poor people of Norwich, England, being targeted in the sights of Hitler's bombs the day after next. The roll of colorful banknotes she didn't even bother to count, just handed over to be used in earnest for the cause of La Résistance—and the toppling of the pervasive arrogance entrenched at the Hôtel Ritz.

——— •◆• ———

5 JUNE 1944
61 BOULEVARD DE CLICHY
PARIS, FRANCE

"Say something, René. Please. Even if you only ask me to leave." Lila took a breath and ran her palms over the tear tracks on her face, bracing for the heartbreak she must take.

"I . . . What are you saying? My family . . . ?" He looked down to the floor and shook his head, a deep crevice between his brows. "Mais non. You're wrong. You must be."

"I wish it were not so. But Violette's cell became privy to the news of their arrest and transport that finally came in the Vél' d'Hiv

Roundup in '42." She took a step back, shame pulling her away from him. "I made a horrible mistake. I trusted a friend. I told her about the hiding place for your family before the war. But I never suspected she'd remember and use it later to wound you and me. Please . . ."

René's silence was worse than accusations. Far worse than anything he could have said or shouted—even screamed at her—was the pain etched on his face.

"Violette knew I'd have done anything in exchange for information about you or your family. Dressing the officers' paramours, attending their parties, photographing documents in boudoirs while they sipped cocktails in the parlor. It became my obsession. It was how I had that photograph taken—the one Carlyle found on the Waffen-SS? I knew it wouldn't bring you back, but if I could track the Touliard heirlooms that had been stolen, to find them and give them to any next of kin after the war . . . I swear to you, it was all I lived for. To try in some way to beg your forgiveness, even from the grave."

She turned, looked to the cot against the wall, knowing what was beneath it.

Lila ran to the basket, knelt to pull the opera coat from the night in the Meudon. She ran her fingers along the inside placket, all the way down the bloodstained satin and partially broken seam, until she felt the weight at the bottom. In a tiny pull, a tear, and a splitting of the thread with her index finger, the truth spilled out into her palm.

"That night, I went to Scheel's suite to discover any information I could about the V-2 bomb. But I stayed for you. To find this."

The radio had fallen into a soft static, the gaiety of American band music gone as Lila came back to the table between them. She opened her fist and set the Touliard Cartier necklace in the center of the rugged wood.

René's jaw flexed hard.

"I found it in Amélie's possession that night. I hid it in my evening bag and later, after I'd run from the Ritz, I slipped it in the seam of the coat alongside the microfilm—they being the only treasures I had left. She's probably forgotten all about it by now. She won't even know to look and see if it's gone. But for me? It was everything."

He nodded, as if sorting the facts. Processing betrayal. Maybe even disbelieving all she'd confessed until the truth was winking back at them in teardrop diamonds, and neither could turn away from the horror of what she'd done.

"So you have been living with this for the last two years, believing you have sent the Touliards to their death?" No words would come, so Lila gave a feeble nod and waited, hands knotted in front of her waist. "And you ask me what now, Lila—to forgive you?"

"Non. I know you cannot."

He looked to the necklace, then back at her, his eyes breaking her for the tears she saw building in them. "Then what?"

"I am asking you to let me go. Like you did at Elsie de Wolfe's Circus Ball. I've done what I came to do. The microfilm got out. And this I gave back to you. There is nothing left for me."

So good at hiding the thoughts that crossed his mind and adept at holding on to the things he wouldn't say, René hadn't given her a shred of reaction. He'd just stood there in the silence, listening as she bared the ugliest blots on her soul.

"No good, Luciole."

Fashion and frivolity were dead. All that remained was the consequence that lay between them. Lila looked to the floor to avoid meeting the pain in his eyes, staring instead at the scuffed work boots she wore. The haute couture she used to live by was now eclipsed by the choices she'd made and the woman she'd become.

"Don't call me that name, please. Not now."

"I meant no good, because I never could let you go. And I never did. Not all the way."

The floor creaked with his weight, and then he was there. Hands on the sides of her face, urging her up, lifting her eyes to meet him through the shame.

"Luciole? I am sorry."

"You're sorry—"

"Oui. I am sorry that you've carried this weight for so long. And that if the worst happened in this war, you would think that any of it was your fault. And that you'd risk your life for mine," he whispered. "I need you to listen to me now. My family is alive. We never used the factory. We never hid there, so it's impossible for Amélie to have sent anyone to find and arrest us."

"What? Your family is alive . . . How?" Lila gripped his arms, the unconscious reaction to the one unbelievable dream she'd had. It had been a hope, a craze that had kept her going—maybe they were wrong somehow, and the Touliards were alive.

"I was able to smuggle them on a merchant liner across the Channel before the occupation. They are in hiding in London and have been since the spring of 1940. We operate in half-truths and propaganda here. It was possible back then to manipulate passenger lists to camps in the east. All we had to do was feed the names. My mother and sister have had to endure the Blitz of German planes over Britain, but they are grateful. As am I, knowing what Hitler is doing to Jews in Europe. With great intention we left everything behind so as not to tip off the authorities by carrying valuables on our person. So my mother's necklace here, that you risked the love of my life to save, know that I am grateful, but it means absolutely nothing to me. Do you understand? I wouldn't trade anything in this life for you."

"But how would Violette have the information that you were dead if it was wrong—?"

"I'm sure she told you what she wanted you to hear at the time."

The shadow world wasn't so foreign in his eyes. René was quiet in knowing. And resigned to truth. And not at all surprised that the one sure contact Lila had in La Résistance was not so sure at all.

"What do you mean?"

"Since that first day you told us about her, something didn't ping right on the radar. Nigel felt the same and Carlyle dug into it. There's no Violette in the 1st Arrondissement. Not one that La Résistance is working with anyway and certainly not at the Hôtel Ritz. You said she's half French, half German? That may be, but I'd wager it means she's assisting both sides. And whatever she was doing to have you feed information back is anybody's guess now. They didn't need a photo to track you because she was doing that already. As much as I hate to say it, that bullet in your side on New Year's Eve may just have saved your life, because with it you were able to disappear."

Lila might have fallen in the strong arms that held her. She might have believed they could turn back time with the revelation, and the mercy and forgiveness she saw shining in René's eyes. But a door slammed down the stairs, and bootfalls sailed up.

Nigel ran in, winded and his spectacles askew. "Well? Did you hear it?"

René looked to Lila for a moment longer, then switched over to the frenzied reality of the Brit operative who'd just slammed his way into the heart of their private conversation.

"Hear what?"

"This—" Nigel turned the dial, the sound of static mangling the broadcast until the lilt of music notes cut the room. "Beethoven's Fifth. Been rotating over the airwaves for a while now."

"I know what it is." René ran a hand through his brown hair, the moment shattered. "Blast de Gaulle and his timing."

"Steady on, mate. It's just been confirmed through the network. This is it—what we've been waiting for! Better unload those bricks behind the door and get the stash ready. Curfew or not, I need the guns and the costumes because I'm going out. Carlyle is already stirring up a spot for us to use them."

"I don't understand. What does it mean? Get ready for what?" Lila asked as she gathered up the costumes she'd been sewing, looking from René to Nigel, the latter whose hands were busy fiddling with the strap on his messenger bag and shoving things from the rolltop down into his pockets.

Their clandestine journalist had missed the wink of diamonds on the table. And the moment between lovers was lost in a sea of frenzy as Nigel's enthusiasm sank in and the electricity pulsed back on, light filling the flat.

"It's a call to arms!" Nigel pulled the leather strap for his typewriter bag crossways over his shoulder and turned back, smiling—ready and eager—as he pulled a card from his inside jacket pocket. "Here, 'Dressmaker.' The SS dubbed you with a code name. And with the work you've been doing, La Résistance inked you in the ranks all proper like. Seems just in time too. Beethoven's Fifth Symphony is de Gaulle's warning that the Allies will land on French soil within twenty-four hours. And we're raising an army to liberate Paris once and for all."

CHAPTER 22

5 JUNE 1944
61 BOULEVARD DE CLICHY
PARIS, FRANCE

The cabaret windmills had been stilled and the hum of the neon signs extinguished. The hilled, cobblestone streets of Montmartre lay oddly sedate without uniforms to get lost in their usual Parisian gaiety.

The captain directed the driver to take their car through a maze of streets somewhere among the darkness. When the car brakes squealed to a stop outside Les Petits Galettes pâtisserie, with its candy-striped awning and prominent *Nombre 61* etched in gold on its façade, there was nothing to hold back Sandrine's horror.

"I thought we would make a stop tonight, before we venture back to Henri. See if it jogs your memory." He reached for her hand through the open door and she took it, her glove seared by the sharpness of his touch.

The wind toyed with the hair at her nape and lifted the hem of her skirt as Sandrine stood behind him on the deserted sidewalk. The counter lights were shut off inside the shop, absent any glow to show off painted glass and wooden shelves with fruit *tartlettes*, pastries, and too many empty spots to count. The door was locked, bars tight across the windows, and the tables lay empty—the shop shuttered tight for the night.

The captain rapped his fingertips to the door, the sharp *ping-ping-ping* like the solemn tapping of a persistent bird upon the glass.

"Here is the owner—LaChelle." He rapped the glass again to gain notice when a man trotted down to the bottom of the stairs to investigate the sound.

The man connected eyes with the captain and Sandrine standing on the sidewalk with the headlights of a running Wehrmacht automobile illuminating their forms. The pâtissier glanced over his shoulder up the stairs again, then rubbed hands on his apron front as he headed in their direction.

After turning a key in the lock, he opened the door to them. "*Je suis désolé*, Captain." The man's face softened as he apologized in the gap of the open door. "The shop is closed—the curfew. Supply trucks did not come in again, and I've had no electricity to bake this afternoon. Everything is from the day before I'm afraid."

"I understand, LaChelle. But I am here with an employee of mine from the ERR. I understand she is quite a fan of your pâtisserie—even more than I realized."

The pâtissier shifted his glance to her.

A tiny flinch of the eyes said something had triggered—a remembrance, perhaps, of a young husband and father who'd gone off to war in 1939? Surely if he'd left the address of a pâtisserie behind for her to seek help, he'd also notified the occupants inside it that she may, one day, appear on the front stoop. But not this way. They were here, staring at each other through the glass, Sandrine certain there was an invisible chord of connection between them but gutted that she could do nothing about it.

"Mrs. Paquet works for me, and as of yet, I don't know that she's actually ever stopped by this shop. Though I'm certain she knows it is here."

"I see." The man offered a tight smile in Sandrine's direction.

Something seemed to trigger in LaChelle as he heard her name, and it set Sandrine to wonder just how often the captain had spoken of her when buying boxes of pastries, and in what manner of familiarity. But it didn't matter now. Sandrine weighed whether she should appeal to the man for help.

Perhaps others were in the back room? Or on one of the upper floors?

Sandrine blocked the slight swell in her middle with her leather satchel and tipped her head in a nod to the pâtissier.

"Would it trouble you greatly if we chose some of whatever selections you have left? It's her son—Henri quite enjoys your pastries. And we are headed home to see him now."

The man looked at Sandrine, directly in her eyes, and she defied their wish to glaze with tears. Fear was splitting her in two as she considered that if things went badly, this might be the last man who would see her alive.

"Bien." LaChelle nodded and opened the door wide. "Certainly, Captain. Do come in. We can always make exception for you and your guests."

The man had light eyes not unlike the captain's, but his were a memorable blue and kind instead of cold. He flicked on the lights behind the display counter, illuminating brass, wood, and glass, and sparse pastry offerings in a wash of golden light.

"How old is your son, madame?" LaChelle asked, making small talk as he folded a flat box into a cardboard cube.

Find your voice.

Sandrine cleared her throat. "Um . . . he has six years, monsieur."

"And what are his favorites?"

"I'm sorry?"

"The pâtisserie." LaChelle raised gold tongs and waved them over the display case, cordially inviting them to have their pick. "Which has your son enjoyed most of the ones the captain has purchased for you?"

Sandrine hadn't opened a single box.

They'd all fed the rubbish bin from the first time the captain gifted them to her. She'd not even opened the boxes to see what had been inside, and now that gross error seemed to be coming back to haunt her in earnest. All she knew was what the captain had once told her— croissants, honey, and fig jam. There must be those.

"Oh, you know children. They do love their sweets." She prayed her voice didn't waver, smiling as she ran a gloved finger over the glass. "There—croissants. And *pain au chocolat* I think, if you have any left. Certainly anything you have that tastes of honey and fig, and chocolate goes over quite well with the petit ones."

The pâtissier crouched low behind the counter, selecting an array of sweets to fill the box to the brim. "I'll give you the rest of the lemon curd tartlettes too. They'll be no good after today. Someone may as well enjoy them."

The captain dug a wallet out of his pocket, and it sickened her how it looked as though he were paying for desserts on a date instead of terrifying a Résistante with his veiled aggression. And she had no idea the motive behind something so nominal as stopping to buy croissants.

"How much?"

"It's on the house." LaChelle closed the box with the gold-foil script and slid it across the counter. "My apologies for the quality. Please do come back and see us when the rations are in better supply."

"Ja, LaChelle. It is a problem, the blockades of the coast now making it difficult for those in Paris to obtain the supplies we need to keep our women happy. It is quite a task." He took the box and handed it to her. "But we are most appreciative, aren't we, Sandrine?"

"Oui. Quite." She took the box in hand. "Merci."

The captain turned to the door, easing his palm under Sandrine's elbow to lead her out. But he stopped short, turning with his hand on the knob. "You know, I just thought of something. It's been some time since I came by the shop and I understand you were going to introduce me to your wife. I should like her to meet Sandrine, if she's able." He glanced up to the shadows at the top of the stairs. "Is your wife here? Can you call her?"

"Oui. She is upstairs."

"*Das ist gut.* We'll wait." He held a hand out to Sandrine, offering a seat at a table by the window. He took off his uniform hat and set it on the table between them, then settled in the chair at her side.

LaChelle walked to the stairs and called up, "Avril? Would you come downstairs, s'il vous plaît?"

Sandrine sat and crossed her legs at the ankle, trying her best not to chew her bottom lip to bleeding.

The dominant thought that crossed her mind was how close she was to the door, and freedom, if she could smash a box of pastries over the captain's head and make an honest run for it. But the moment passed when she threaded the possibility with its more likely outcome.

Within a few seconds a woman descended the stairs to join them in the dining room.

The pâtissier's wife was striking—expressive eyes, deep-chocolate hair in waves clipped to her chin, glasses tipped over a pert nose, and a French-blue dress that softened her porcelain complexion and offset a charming spray of freckles. She looked to Sandrine, bestowed a delicate "Bonjour" in greeting, and stood at the man's side.

"This must be Madame LaChelle." The captain stood to give a slight bow in greeting. "Avril, ja?"

"Oui, sir." She looked to her husband, smiled, and gave a gentle fold to her hands in front of her waist.

"Ah, it must be a hard life after your time in the countryside, waking so early for all those Paris deliveries every morning. And then working all day here to keep us in supply of our pastries. Do the officers keep you busy?"

"It is what we're in business for. To provide the best for our customers."

"And we won't keep you from it. We have what we came for. But it is quite a pleasure to meet you, madame. LaChelle here is a good man. Quite good at his job as pâtissier anyway." He slapped the man's shoulder.

Sandrine's breath locked up in her middle—never did he stray so far from the strict confines of propriety as to chum alongside . . . anyone. The faintest spark of something seemed to tarry over the usually hard-pressed lines of the captain's face, and she didn't know what to make of his smile. It wasn't only out of character; it was terrifying from a man who only that evening had threatened her with a lighter he'd found—with the fact that he knew she was keeping secrets. But now, out of the blue, he was laying charm on a humble pâtissier and his wife at a very specific address, for some unknown reason playing the part of the world's chattiest and most charming Wehrmacht officer.

"I need to make a telephone call, so we'd best be on our way back."

"There's a phone box here, sir. In the back of the shop." The man motioned to a telephone booth wedged behind a table in the back. The captain followed the line of sight to the shadows in the back. "Just there. You are free to use it if you like."

"Sandrine? Go out to the car now. I'll just make a call and then we'll leave you, LaChelle."

There was nothing left to do or say, save to obey his order. He was, after all, the one with a pistol on his person. The pâtissier's wife kept her smile amiable but detached. Sandrine nodded through a forced "Au revoir" and turned to walk toward the door. Wondering if she'd just made the biggest mistake in her life by not appealing to them for help—or warning them that the captain was not as clueless as he seemed.

She climbed in the back of the auto as the lifeline of the man and his wife disappeared and lights were doused up the stairs. The captain made his telephone call. He exited moments later, cutting through the glow of the pastry-case lights with sharp, measured steps and an icy profile as he joined her in the backseat.

"To madame's flat, sir?"

"Not just yet," the captain barked at the driver, watching the shop interior with hawk eyes. "Wait here for a moment."

Sandrine gripped the pastel box in her lap, gloved hands over the gold-foil script on the top as the auto idled, the pâtisserie display case glowed through the dark, and the threat of his silence grew between them. He braced an arm against the door and tapped the Ronson to the sill beneath his fingertips.

"Do you know why I waited so long to approach you with this? It is because I value honesty. And chastity. And I wanted to give you the chance to come to me to confess."

"Confess . . ." She tipped her brow. "I'm afraid I don't know your meaning, sir."

Good. Act innocent. Make him think it's all in his head.

"*Nein.* You do not. And that is an oversight on my part." He turned then, to look at her with a parody of genteel affection as he pocketed the lighter. His eyes were sharp, staring her through. But his manner was controlled, chilling—not for lack of emotion but for the presence of a weak, manufactured smile.

"You know, Sandrine, war is a cruel provocateur. Before I came to Paris, I was stationed in Warsaw. Beautiful city—overrun by *les Juifs*. There was a day I was called in to manage an assault on a cathedral in the center of the city. There was a group of young Jewish boys who set upon Third Reich officers worshipping there, by throwing bricks through the stained-glass windows and setting fire to the nave. It was as reprisal for policies that had sent some of their people away to work outside the city. They just could not see what a privilege it is to have an organized method of records in this war. To keep track of undesirables. To provide for them in a ghetto that is orderly and safe. They did not wish to tell me the truth about who fueled this attempt at insurrection. But sometimes, Sandrine, finding the truth involves extraordinary methods of extracting information from an unwilling party."

He raised his hand, a loose fist with thumb in the air, and pressed it in a grip around her wrist—hard, with intention. So different from the coaxing way he'd once stopped her in the galerie that time. "You just need to know where to apply the pressure. I'd say that your husband's mother cares very much for Henri, does she not?"

"I would say so. She is his grand-mère."

"Hmm. Ja. And when I spoke with her of what I am sometimes forced to do in this war, she was forthright where the young men—and you—were not."

Marguerite . . . no.

What have you done?

"It gives me great pain that I had to go to her to find out the name of the officer who has wooed you with his charms. But instead, when I applied pressure to her secrets, I am given an old family Bible with the address of a suspected *Résistant* tucked inside. And what am I to do with this mess? Mistrust you because you did not share this with me before? Am I to call everything into question?"

The street opened up with a mighty roar.

Sandrine turned to the sight of headlights blazing through the back window as cars and a passenger van pulled up on all sides of theirs. Brakes cried out. Doors flung open. And uniforms swarmed the shadows under the candy-striped awning, like an invasion upon innocence. Sandrine watched in horror as machine gun–wielding uniforms stormed the pâtisserie shop's front door. Breaking glass and tearing the wood from its hinges. Overturning the table and chair she'd just been sitting in, in their haste to tear up the stairs after the poor unsuspecting pâtissier and his wife.

"I want his name."

"There is . . . no name." A tear squeezed from her eye, the tiny trail of salt tracking a line over Sandrine's cheek until it fell away off the bitter fix of her jaw. "I have never seen that lighter before. On my son's life, I have not."

The captain took care to place his uniform hat in proper place back on his crown, adjusting it so the bill was straight across the front. If he turned in her direction, the emblem of the skull would sear her. But he kept his profile sharp and determined, and did not bother to turn to look at her or at the shop again.

"It was a pity to stand and watch as those young men were shot that day, one by one, kneeling in the chapel they'd desecrated. To watch them cry. To vomit and wet themselves. One even called out for his *Mutter*. Do you see what this can come to, Sandrine? I am an accommodating man. But war can become very uncomfortable if people are not honest with one another. If they are not honest with *me*."

Breathing ragged in her chest and with gloved hands fused to the box in her lap, Sandrine couldn't bear to answer. She understood the horror of the implication. And in her silence, so did he.

"Gut. Then we understand each other." Captain von Hiller nodded to the driver peering out from the rearview mirror, his arrow having struck its mark. "And now we may go."

CHAPTER 23

31 December 1943
15 Place Vendôme
Paris, France

While a rainbow of gowns were hob-knobbing with gray uniforms at the exclusive New Year's Eve party in the Hôtel Ritz cocktail lounge, Lila had used the opportunity to slip up to the third floor.

With Violette's watchful eye keeping vigil on the service stairs, Lila was supposed to be gone a few moments at the very most—to find anything she could about the V-2 on a train manifest of a collection that had just been discovered in vaults across the city that day, including art from the Rothschilds and the prize of her heart, the collection Touliard. But in a split second, as she rummaged through boudoir and desk drawers, the plan shifted off axis and Lila's heart sent her into rogue territory.

A velvet jewelry case peeked out from under a pile of satin and lace in the unmentionables drawer. She opened it and inside, tear-drop diamonds winked back. Lila's breath caught in her chest—the Touliard necklace. She'd found it.

Lila whisked it up, clamped the case closed, and dropped the necklace in the evening bag still roped around her wrist.

Wardrobe to desk, desk to closet, she kept moving. But it was there a cascade of blush chiffon and the unmistakable rose-bedecked train of the custom Chanel gown—the one she'd designed under the Chanel label for the Rothschilds in 1938—called to her from the shadows, and Lila was helpless but to stop.

The memory of sewing the gown . . . of the honor she'd been given in her first high-profile assignment to craft a custom creation for the Rothschilds. How the gown had won her heart and, in the years since, become a symbol of everything Amélie had coveted for herself. And Lila vowed she would never have it.

Violette had told her of the practice of La Résistance sending hidden messages—sewn in clothing seams and smuggled across the borders of Europe. So while Lila hadn't a plan now, it was possible to send the gown somewhere safe, and if fate truly smiled, a message might get through. Lila had scribbled a note, sewn it in the seam of the train, and pressed a kiss from her fingertips to one of the roses as she'd closed it up tight—praying it reached someone who might take ownership of it until the war was over.

"Bonne Année, ma cherie."

Lila turned at the placidity in Amélie's New Year's greeting, from the crate she'd just closed up and tucked in with a stack piled against the wall. She breezed out of the closet without acknowledging the intrusion or that she'd been caught in the thick of it.

"I know what you're thinking. The gown. The dream Chanel? You saw it in there, non?" Amélie leaned in the doorway of the boudoir in an ivory fur stole and an ice-blue sparkler of a gown, nursing a cig that the German officers so frowned upon of their women. It seemed she didn't care about appearances—of that and a lot of other things. "I told you that one day it would be mine. And now it is. So is that why you're here, little dressmaker? To steal the gown back? I know it's not to wish me a happy new year."

"Non, it's not. I was just fetching something for one of the ladies. Do excuse me."

"Really. And what were you fetching in my fiancé's suite when I would not wear a House of LDL original if it were the last scrap of fabric on earth?"

I'm taking back all that you stole.

Words refused to come. It seemed only the truth burned between them, Amélie knowing her so well that Lila was certain the answer already showed on her face.

"You have no answer? It would seem you are not as innocent as you would have everyone believe. Our little French Hedy's interest was piqued when she caught you snooping in my old suite years back. And Margot's suspicions were interesting taken alongside Camille's mention of finding you behind her fiancé's desk the day I returned from my ill-fated country holiday. I knew then but still would not believe it. Not a tale about my Lila—my dear friend all these years. Roommate. Confidante. And a wide-eyed dreamer like myself, even for the Jew-loving dressmaker she'd become. I had waved off all suspicions and helped her rise to the pinnacle of the fashion world. I said that friend would never . . . *never* betray me."

Amélie drew out the last syllable as she stalked over to the closet, thumbed through the rack of gowns until she found a ream of ivory silk, and yanked it down from the hanger. She tossed it at Lila.

"Remember this from my little debut on the front page of *La Gerbe*? It's missing the belt, but I do have an opera coat to match. I could not allow you to be arrested in that shabby eggplant number you're wearing—not this season's hue at all. So I think you'll wear this to the German embassy. When they come to collect you, you will be the best-dressed Résistante they've ever seen hanging from the end of a noose."

When Lila made no move, only flitted her glance to the hall and the suite door, Amélie screamed out, "Put it on! The coat too."

With little to do but obey, Lila reached for the side zip of her gown, hand trembling as she tugged it down to change into the ivory silk. The air between them grew stark as Amélie's shout had disturbed the suite, and the stirring baby could be heard from the room next door, her howls growing painful through the wall.

"Should you . . . ?"

Amélie made no move toward the nursery, blowing smoke as Lila pulled the silk up to her shoulders and took the opera coat tossed on the bed to slip over her bare arms.

"Should I what? The chaste little girl is going to give me parenting tips? I do not think I need them from you." Amélie smiled—a visceral act that belied the poison in her tone and the gleeful spark of fire in her eyes. "But at least now we understand each other."

"Do we, understand each other? Have we ever?"

"It makes sense, why you were so eager to be employed by the lovely little sinners at the Hôtel Ritz—a world a lowly dressmaker may step into but will never fully belong herself. You wanted to be heroic and save your dear René, didn't you? But he's gone, with that *Juif* family of his. All dead I've learned, thanks to you. And look where it's gotten you, to chase after the forgotten? You attempt to supplant a world you will never understand. That Chanel gown in the closet is the symbol of everything that I am, and you will never rise to become."

"Even if you wore it, that gown will never be yours. It doesn't belong to you. None of the stolen things in this suite do."

"We'll see about that." Amélie crossed the room to the bedside table and gripped the handheld from its gold cradle. The switchboard operator chirped from the receiver as she stared back, eyes locked on Lila's. "Oui. The concierge desk, s'il vous plaît. It is an emergency, in the suite of Captain Scheel."

With but a split second to react, Lila hurled herself onto Amélie's waif figure, the surprise of darting hands and striking elbows overtaking her in a struggle for the phone. The push-and-pull landed them hard on the floor, the receiver clattering to the rug along with a lamp and a ferocious crack when it shattered to porcelain shards pinging off the wall.

Amélie pulled Lila's hair free of its coil, scratching her nails into the skin at the base of Lila's skull.

"*Lâchez-la!*"

The addition of a third voice resounded across the room, demanding that Amélie free herself from the fist she'd knotted in Lila's hair, but it was the pinpoint precision of a locked and loaded Walther P38 that spoke louder.

Lila scrambled free, eyeing Amélie, her own poppy-red lipstick smudged in a bleeding trail down her chin. With fury alive on her face but with nothing to do but submit to a Résistante and the gun she held in her hand, Amélie seethed over each ragged breath as she watched Lila stand but remained captive under Violette's trained weapon.

"This lazy beast didn't take the elevator like she usually does. Instead she crept up the marble stairs at the end of the hall, before I could reach in time to stop her." She turned to Lila, keeping the pistol firm. "You have what you need?"

Lila had what she needed personally but not for the Résistance.

She shook her head. "Non. Not yet."

"*Va-t'en*—go now, Lila." Violette tipped her head to the closet. "He is not like the baron was, keeping the files easily found in the drawers. This one hides them in a false floor tile in the back of the closet. Go. Find the documents and take the photographs. I can manage her."

The seconds ticked by as if in slow motion.

It took a breath to refocus, but Lila nodded, found her shoe tossed against the hearth, and slipped it on. She'd have to be prepared to run. But where? She didn't know beyond the map pinpoint of Versailles ringing in her head. The chambermaid holding the pistol was the only Résistance contact she had.

Lila tore at the inner seam of her eggplant dress on the floor and took out the microfilm camera she'd hidden there. She found the loose tile in the floor behind the crates, and just as Violette had said, she snapped photos of any official-stamped Reich document she could find, looking for *Zug*—German for "train"—and any numbers that went along with it. She hurried to pull the film out of the camera—a little black dot of a thing—and slipped it inside the seam of her coat, then tossed the camera on the embers of the fire, plucked up the treasure of her evening bag, and edged toward the door.

Minutes were all they had between the switchboard operator and the response from the concierge desk. When they heard the commotion or the swell of baby cries on the other end of the phone line, it would surely bring a sea of jackboots tromping off the elevator.

"You have it?" Violette stared down the length of her arm, barrel aimed in Amélie's direction.

"Oui. I do."

"Then go, now. We haven't time. You have a contact to meet, do you not?"

Amélie stared back in Lila's eyes, a cocktail of seething and fear mixing in them.

Violette was no fool. It had come to this, and she no doubt could see the conflict teetering in Lila's mind. One secret that killed a family had been traded for another, and a crying baby in the next room would grow up without her mother. It was a query Lila wasn't prepared to work out—how far the roots of evil had grown in her friend and how far they'd reached within her.

"This *prostituée* would turn you in. She would send you to your death and not think twice. And yet you believe I should spare her life?"

"I . . . don't know. I can't think." Lila hovered between Amélie's crumpled form shaking on the carpet and the closing window to seek freedom.

"What do you mean you don't know? This is done. She knows about the V-2, and that *we* know about it. Have you forgotten this fact?"

Amélie's eyes grew wild.

"And now that she knows what we've been doing in these suites all along, it is only a matter of time before the Nazis do too. As of this moment you are the hunted. The choice is yours—go and get that film to the contact. Or stay and we may all die. But I assure you it will begin and end with her. She will pay for her crimes, just as they will for theirs."

If her plan had become a showdown Violette had desired between La Résistance and a Nazi officer's paramour, it seemed her fortune had run out to see it through. The suite door opened and slammed, followed by the intentional footsteps of a Nazi officer thundering from the hall through to the boudoir.

"Amélie? The front desk called again. Can't your maid get that baby to stop screeching for one night—?" Scheel burst into the boudoir without time to calculate the sight of his fiancée kneeling in wrecked disarray on the rug, Lila frozen in stride between them, and a chambermaid pointing a Walther P38 at his chest.

The *bang* was the answer to his question—the shock of a pulled trigger seemingly the only thing strong enough to blot out even a baby's ardent cries.

The force of the blast pinned him to the wall, his eyes glassy and sliding out of focus as he slumped to the floor. Lila could only blink back for the first second or two, shock reverberating as Violette stood unflinching before the crimson blot on the wall and the Nazi officer bathed in his own blood.

Amélie pounded her fists to the carpet, sobbing as she crawled on all fours to the crumpled uniform melted against the wall. She gripped his collar, tugging the litzen and slapping at his cheek as he fell back to the carpet like a rag doll.

"You . . . you killed him," Lila breathed out, voice shuddering as she looked on. "An officer. Right here in this suite."

The shot was near deafening. And there was no rush-and-clean-up happening. If guests called the front desk for a crying baby, they were surely already ringing the switchboard off the hook for this.

They'd have seconds only to think what to do as Amélie sobbed and knelt her ice-blue gown in the rapid spread of crimson growing on the rug.

Violette tipped her head toward the hall over her shoulder. "Time to go, Lila."

"What? We can't just leave him here."

"Non, but you can go. Take the microfilm and get out. I need you to meet the contact no matter what. That's your job now. Here—" Violette pulled a small pistol from the inside pocket of her dress and forced it into Lila's hand. She grabbed her by the elbow as she rushed to move by, nails cutting into her skin with the force of the tug back.

"To go through the Meudon is your only way out now. But be careful; it is overrun. Change your clothes. And cut your hair. If they learn of this, the SS will circulate a photo of you as the fashion princess with the trademark marron locks spilling down her back. You must not look like her. If you are to live, then that girl must first die."

"Why would they blame me for this when you're the one . . . ?"

"Didn't you just hear the princess here when she threatened you? Her little paramour friends have already voiced their suspicions about you. When they find out about this, it is only a matter of time before those kittens show up at the prefecture of police to cry as they turn you in." Violette stared back, eyes sharp, cutting like she could see through to Lila's back collar. "Run, and don't you dare look back."

Lila hadn't time to decide a path of her own choosing. It was trust and leave Amélie in the hands of the Résistante as she backed toward the hall, or stay and all of them fall victim to the swarm of SS uniforms and trained pistols sure to flood into the suite within seconds.

Running down the service stairs, out the door, and down the stretch of hall became a dream world.

Even from floors up, Lila could hear the brass band play and the roar of gaiety from the celebration in the cocktail lounge below, the New Year's Eve party in full swing. All it would take was one uniform to distinguish the sound of gunfire from the pop of champagne corks, and the screams of a woman in peril in a third-floor suite, to cancel out the revelry. Just one, and the entire lot would swarm over her.

The lobby was no good—crawling with officers and a security checkpoint sure to be manned for such a party. Lila ran past the base of the marble stairs, winding down, praying she could find a back hall. Or door. Or service exit or window leading to a dark alley. Anything so she could disappear into the Paris streets beyond.

"Lila!" The guttural cry resounded from above.

The last vision Lila had as she glanced over her shoulder was the sight of a blonde paramour in blood-streaked ice blue, teetering at the top of the stairs.

Lamps glowed as Lila turned and ran the length of the long hall from the lobby, the evening bag and necklace clutched tight in her palm. Gilded mirrors reflected the golden surroundings, high arched windows, sparkling chandeliers, and cream walls. And bright-blue chaise longues stood guard all the way down to freedom, the lone witnesses of a dressmaker on the run and the searing bullet that found its target from the top of the stairs to pierce through her side.

---

5 June 1944
61 Boulevard de Clichy
Paris, France

"How does that captain know you?"

Lila didn't feign ignorance to René's question when they reached the top of the stairs. Nor did she misinterpret the speed with which he moved about the flat, erasing the evidence of La Résistance having been there.

"It must be from the Hôtel Ritz. I only saw him once, by chance, years before. At Amélie's suite the first time I came to dress the officers' women."

"Well, I'd say once was enough." He flipped the board beneath Nigel's desk to retrieve the documents they'd hidden there. All but the false papers declaring them Monsieur and Madame LaChelle were eaten up in flames when he tossed them upon the fire, then replaced the board to its seamless line in the floor. René pulled a chair into the bathroom, then stood atop it to ensure the rusty grate was in place and the transistor was tucked back in the shadows of the ceiling as far as it could go.

"I don't even know his name. He saw me for one second outside Amélie's suite—two at the most." She rushed up to him. "Maybe we're wrong. Maybe he doesn't know who I am."

"His name is von Hiller." René replaced the grate with nimble hands and expert calm. He moved to the sink, retrieved the underground list he'd tucked there, and stuffed it into a hollow in the sole of his shoe. He then took a towel and dusted the floor, erasing any impressions as he backed out. "Captain at the ERR. And it doesn't matter how long he saw you that day, he knows exactly who you are. There's no mistaking it—I saw it in his eyes down there."

"But what does that mean?"

René finally stopped after putting the chair back, with a pause that broke her heart apart. She glanced to the window that overlooked the street facing the cabarets, shuddering as fear swept over in a wave. She gripped the chair back in her fist.

The telephone box.

And she'd answered her own question.

"It means . . . he called them. They're coming for us, aren't they? Even now."

"Oui," he whispered. "We could have tried to fight our way out—which I know enough about you to be absolutely certain you'd agree if Nigel hadn't already emptied our cache of weapons. But I'd never have allowed it. Not if you'd be hurt. This way, there's at least a chance."

"We could go out the window. We could jump. I'll do it—let's jump." Lila flitted her glance back and forth between him and the glass, frantic that they might fade into the twinkle of city lights beyond.

"And fall two tall stories onto the cars that will surely be waiting for us behind the buildings? We'd never make it." He patted her cheek, pride shining in his eyes. "Look at me. I hate to ask this of you now, but I have to given the circumstances. We're still in this together, oui?"

"Of course. You know that."

"Then this—" René dug into his pocket and retrieved the necklace, holding it in his palm. "Do you trust me to take it, to keep it safe for now?"

Lila nodded, though how he'd manage it she couldn't fathom.

"Of course. It's yours. I . . . I got it for you."

René knelt and tucked the necklace in the hollow of his boot sole, patting down the outside edge for good measure, then rose again to her. It was a broken few seconds that they fell into each other's arms, Lila clinging under his shoulders and he turning his face down to hers.

"We have to stop parting like this—leaving, wondering when we'll see each other again. Next time we'll plan better. Alright?" He squeezed tighter around her waist as she trembled. "Listen to me, love. They're going to separate us."

"What? Non . . ." She shook her head, desperate. "I can't go without you."

"Our only hope is that the Vichy police come instead of the SS. If it's Vichy, they'll arrest us and they'll take you into custody with the other women they're holding."

"And if it's the SS instead?"

René didn't answer, terrifying her all the more.

The SS didn't ask questions. Nor would they show mercy. They executed even suspected Résistance members on the spot. They'd heard of it—seen the truth of it in the streets even, many times.

"Remember, you are Avril LaChelle. You are not their Paris dressmaker, no matter what happens. Do you hear me?"

"I can't do this."

"You can. You're stronger than they realize. They'll probably take you on to the La Conciergerie prison or maybe the closest prefecture of police. They'll question you, but they won't execute a woman. If things keep going for the Germans as they are and the Allies do come ashore to France, then our best chance is to wait for a prisoner exchange. With La Résistance growing bolder and plucking SS officers right off the street, it won't be long before the Germans try to negotiate a trade of prisoners like you for them." He pressed a quick, steadying kiss to her lips. The unbelievable sight of tears gathering in his eyes sent fresh waves of panic through her. "You'll be alright. I promise— you can do this."

"You said they won't execute a woman. But what about you?"

Glass shattered downstairs as the street-front door was split wide. Boots tracked up the stairs, even as his eyes stayed glued to hers.

"René! What about you?" She gripped him tighter.

"I have a hundred names in my back pocket, Luciole, but they'll never know the real one. That can be our little secret. They probably don't know about me yet. But if they do, what's killing another Jew to them? I'll die before I tell them anything about you."

René mouthed *I love you*, the warmth of his gaze fixed in a soft smile, even as the swarm of uniforms flooded in around them.

He stepped in front of her, arm hooking her behind his back until they were wrangled apart. Forced down, both of them side by side on their knees. A policeman smashed René's jaw with the butt of a rifle and Lila gritted her teeth over a sob as she watched him slam to all fours, coughing as he spit blood on the hardwood.

The last desperate hope Lila had was lost with the cold reality of gun barrels pressed to the backs of their skulls, and the darkness of Paris streets waiting as they were dragged down the stairs.

CHAPTER 24

Sandrine's prison had no bars, but hers was a world on tight lockdown.

The Renault that had once been sporadic in watching the front stoop of her building turned into three autos and never left her, Marguerite, or Henri alone. She was escorted to and from the Jeu de Paume each day and holed up in her flat on most others, with a guard posted outside their front door.

And as for the ration lines, they'd become frantic, long, and unyielding. From bread to eggs to milk, the unattainable luxuries of honey, sugar, and flour, and the pittance of meat—even the worst of gristly cuts—all seemed to have disappeared overnight with the Allies' arrival.

Abject scarcity coupled with searching the streets for Christian's face or waiting for him to reappear in the flat . . . they became the rhythm of her days. Sandrine's hope had begun to fade as the weeks ticked by and Paris fell into an even darker desperation.

It seemed the captain was ignorant of her activities with Valland, as the arrest of the poor pâtissier and his pretty wife on the night before the Allies appeared on the Normandy coast had been in reaction to learning of their suspected ties to La Résistance. If he'd known anything about what had been happening right under his nose—for years—he'd surely have arrested them all. Nevertheless, Valland had severed Sandrine's involvement as a necessary precaution.

They all knew hers was a sentence of being closely watched. And now the captain scarcely said two words to her and she was never alone. Sandrine stood in the gallery, the activity around them maniacal as art was crated and carried out by every pair of available hands.

"What's happened to you? Tell me quick before he comes back." Michèle nudged up next to Sandrine in the gallery and whispered, giving a pointed glance to the slight rise in her belly. "You're expecting?"

Sandrine nodded, shoving down a sob, keeping her eyes fixed on her clipboard in case anyone should see them in private confidence.

"Four months now."

"Why didn't you tell me?" She eased a hand in a soft grip to the fist in which Sandrine held her pencil. "Oh my word. I would have wanted to know if something had happened to you. Did he . . . ? I'll kill him. With my own two hands."

"There's no harm that's come to me."

"Then whose is it?"

"Would it shock you very much if I said my husband's?"

"Non, it would not. I have no idea how that is possible, but it would make me very happy indeed if it were true. And what's happening here makes sense now. The captain has had a claim on you from the start, and I hear he thinks one of the junior officers got to you. He's miffed as a hornet that's lost its nest. He even had one of them thrown in the brig and beat within an inch of his life when the soldier gave an answer the captain didn't particularly like. He thinks you've been seeing one of them behind his back, and I'd wager he's taken it as a great betrayal after all the special attention he's given you."

"But anything between us is imagined—scary and imagined—all in his head. I've never given him a single notion that I was open to wooing. It's been a delicate dance putting him off while not tipping him off to what we're doing at the same time."

"You think that's occurred to him? There's a very real possibility that he's been waiting for you these years. And in some offhanded way, he's decided he's not going to wait any longer. You can see it; he's positively seething over this." Michèle tossed a glance over her shoulder, checking that the gallery was still empty of soldiers. "Where is Christian now?"

"I wish I knew. I can't say where or why, but he's been back in Paris. Maybe even here right now, though he is in hiding. He's been working for de Gaulle and the Free French in London almost since the war began."

"The Free French you say? Doing what?"

"I don't know. But I keep glancing around every corner, expecting to see his face. Praying I'll see him so he can free us from the captain's prison. I wanted him to know about this child before anyone else figured it out. But if you've noticed . . ." She pressed a hand to her waist. "I'm terrified."

"It sounds like lip service to say it now, but don't be afraid, dear Sandrine. I have it on good authority that this is all about to come to a head for the captain and his ERR stooges," she whispered, wrapping an arm around Sandrine's shoulders in a quick hug. "I know something else that will make you happy too."

"What is it?"

"There has been a cell working with de Gaulle in London, to track the art stolen in this war. They've been working their way through France with the Allies, partnered with a team of historians and art experts from the US. They're called the Monuments Men, and they're chasing the Germans to get the art back. Sounds familiar, non? You don't suppose your Christian is working with them? If that's the case, he could be on his way here this very moment to rescue you like you've hoped."

"I hadn't thought of it before, but . . . oui. Perhaps he is working with them somehow. It would make sense."

"In the meantime we have confirmed: train 40044. All these crates we are packing up today—148 of them in total—Valland has learned where they are to be sent, and on that specific train. She's gone out to inform her contact—by name of Jaujard, if we come across the network ourselves—to tell him and de Gaulle's team how they can follow the art. And when she returns, we must be ready. We are not letting it go without a fight. And I'd wager the team leader tracking the art won't either. We've learned of his code name with La Résistance, and Rose asked me to relay this to you. I think you'll be *très content* to hear it too. Only he would choose the name of a bookshop that meant so much to you both."

Michèle slipped a scrap of paper in her hand and pecked a kiss to her cheek, then swept off to the other side of the gallery, back to her work sorting and cataloging crates.

Sandrine glanced around the gallery space—no captain. No Valland. Just a mass of crates and frames and soldiers hurrying about their own business. She unfolded the scrap of paper and her heart leapt.

Two words. A name only they would understand. And hope rekindled . . .

Le Trouvère.

CHAPTER 25

Paris had become a haunted place, its terror unafraid to bask out in the open.

As their arrest flooded from the unassuming Les Petits Galettes out onto the sidewalk, Lila craned her neck, following the top of René's head as far as she could until he was carried off by a sea of Vichy police and melted somewhere into the shadows of the cabaret buildings.

There were few passersby; none bold enough to step out in the street during an arrest, but Lila guessed the Parisians were there, peering out from behind drapes on the buildings' upper floors, or peeking through cracks in the closed doors of the Moulin Rouge and lurking in the shadows to watch as the Vichy seized the poor wretched souls before their eyes.

The nightmare threw Lila in the back of a waiting van, the doors final in their clamping shut. It was an empty cage save for the cold reality of benches welded to the floor, walls of metal, and a gray uniform who'd climbed in the driver's seat without a word to the captive locked in the metal grating behind him. She fought to sort the desperation flying through her mind, moving from the what-ifs to every she-prayed-not scenario that had Violette or Amélie or the steely-eyed captain appearing at a police station to confirm her identity, leading to the brutal torture and interrogation that was typical at the hands of the SS.

Lila tried praying. For René. For strength. For grit and grace. For . . . anything to see them through. But the words were muddled and incoherent, flying from one thought to the next. The one consolation was that she listened for—and thank heaven, hadn't heard—any gunshot in the street. That meant somewhere, René might still be alive.

An SS uniform stepped in front of the headlights of the van, directing the convoy to move on, and the driver chugged the motor to life beneath Lila's shoes. The van idled in place. Her chin quivered as she eased down to the metal bench. There was nothing to do but sit in the dark and fight to keep her wits sharp and her instincts strong.

"Our Father which art in heaven, hallowed be thy name . . ."

The passenger door creaked open and a second uniform—the terrifying sight of a Waffen-SS officer—swept into the seat in the front. Judging by his profile, he was determined, gaze locked on the street in front of them.

A line of cars flipped on headlights to lead the way and then the van jerked, thrust in gear to follow along. The officer gestured to an SS on the sidewalk as they drove by and barked something in German to the driver, of which she could only pick out the words *Saint-Georges* and *Pont d'Austerlitz.*

Lila's heart beat faster.

Pont d'Austerlitz . . . That's south. They're taking me to the Left Bank.

The van lumbered along behind the convoy of cars, and then somewhere in the dark, they soared over a hill and Lila was nearly sent off the bench to the van floor. Swaying under the force of picked-up speed, she gripped the bench tines beneath her knees and held fast, anchoring herself through the maze of twists and turns that took them deeper into the abyss.

A windowless world passed outside the van.

Lila could see nothing but the tiniest swath of movement through the front windshield. But the streets as they left Montmartre and the buildings to know for certain in which direction they traveled—they were a mystery. Perhaps they'd venture across the Seine to the Left Bank, but she wasn't likely to know. That or whether René was in a vehicle that moved with them. All that offered comfort in the tiny view she had was the sight of sleeping trees, limestone façades, and mansard roofs that told her they were still in the city proper.

Without warning the solemnity was cut by shouts from the driver.

"Nein! Nein!" The Waffen-SS soldier barked out what seemed to be orders in German, waving his hand forward as they rounded a turn, and he lifted a submachine gun level with the window.

The van screeched to a stop and Lila was thrown to the side, tumbling to the space between bench and floor, her cheek slammed hard against the metal grating that had seconds before been beneath her soles.

And then a blast in the street and another shout inside the van.

She hadn't any idea what was happening as the Waffen-SS soldier began shouting—near to screaming—in German. At least not until the driver squeezed his arm through the bars separating the front seat and the metal cage that held her and pointed a pistol in her direction. But the driver pulled back in a split second, the pistol instead trained through the front glass that had just shattered over his head.

Bang!

Was she hit?

Non. That was outside.

Instinct told Lila to wait. To play dead. To silence her breathing and, even though she could scarcely feel her own limbs tangled against the metal bench, to not try to move and assess whether she'd been shot.

Bang! Bang!

Lila swept into the shadows then, curling into a ball as small as she could, wedging herself under the metal bench for the only protection she had. She slammed her eyes shut as heat and sweat and humid air grew thick around her. Seconds ticked by in the dark . . . and instead of a close-range pistol shot searching for her in the back, it was the terror of machine-gun fire that clamored through the night air.

Fisting both hands over her ears, Lila fought for breaths as bullets pinged the side of the van—peppering over, under, sweeping by, and without a doubt some cutting through. The onslaught lasted for thirty seconds . . . a minute . . . who knew?

She fought for breath and words to pray.

Stop crying! Think.

How do I get out of this alive?

Bullets rained down, sounding as they pinged the fender. And then came through to shatter a side window, the shards of glass flying to Lila's tomb floor like razors cutting her skin.

The Waffen-SS in the front seat would no doubt finish her if he knew she was still alive. She bit her bottom lip against the will to rise, to pound her fists against the door and do anything to break the chains holding her in. But she stayed still, refusing to move a muscle as the eerie sounds of gunfire continued, with distant shouts and the occasional close call as bullets seared the van's metal side.

"Thy kingdom come. Thy will be done in earth, as it is in heaven . . ."
She mouthed the words. Begged them. Cried as she clung to them.

"Give us this day our daily bread. And forgive us our debts, as we forgive our debtors . . ."

And then, stillness.

The Waffen-SS lay motionless, catty-corner with the brim of his hat just tipping up over the edge of the bars. The driver? She couldn't see, but the engine still idled and the floor hummed beneath her body.

A swath of light beamed through the mosaic of fractured glass in the windshield. Beyond, an imposing red-and-black swastika flag was illuminated by a spotlight as it draped over the high front of a building with a row of Corinthian columns, the fabric rippling on the night breeze.

A drop of sweat rolled down her neck.

Lila bored her fingernails into the metal bench tine, listening to muffled voices outside, trying to discern German or French, waiting for what was to come. In the back of her mind, she considered that the Waffen-SS in the front seat might be dead, but even if it were so, hundreds more of them were out in the streets. And they could all have her photo.

The doors flung wide.

Lila squinted at the flood of light.

Two men—Waffen-SS—stood before her with guns drawn, but one with a tall stance, broad shoulders, and a relieved smile when he saw her—probably wide eyed and shaking and sweat drenched, but alive.

He tipped the brim of his hat.

"Carlyle!" Lila leapt from the van into his arms, hugging him tight around the neck.

"Good to see you too, fair Lila. Glad these Frenchies could get you back to us in one piece." He drew her down to the street, her boots unsteady beneath her as they landed. "I knew this SS uniform would come in handy. Come on. Hurry. Time to go."

Two men in street clothes closed the gap behind them, lingering on the street with submachine guns strapped over their shoulders, their gazes trained on the convoy of vehicles that had stalled in the center of the Place du Panthéon. Headlights illuminated the eerie scene: a tangle of two cars—one crashed, busted up, and turned on its side—and the bullet-strewn police van. Uniforms lay in the street. At least one body in plain clothes lay facedown in a pool that sucked the breath from her lungs. The Waffen-SS from the front seat lay askew, his boots hanging in a lifeless heap from the van's open door.

The figure of the Panthéon cut a looming stone frame into the sky behind them as they rushed her into a tangle of streets. Buildings. Darkness. Carlyle telling her when to run and stop and, at least once, pushing her head down behind a pile of crates as a car and siren sped past.

A train tunnel disappeared beyond the street and they eased down a hill on a trek between two buildings, the backdrop of pitch black swallowing up points unknown under the city. Moonlight glowed over stone walls and the lacy cutouts of trees against the sky as they ran, Carlyle watching the space out in front of them with his weapon raised.

Lila kept up, catching her breath to speak through a hitch in her side. "René? Where is he?"

"Don't worry. We've a plan for him too. And I'd wager if he expects you're here, then our boss man is but a few paces off. This way. Down here." Carlyle smiled, the gruff and grit still alive in him, but a tiny ray of care, too, as he patted her shoulder and led her down a set of stone stairs.

Carlyle looked to their accomplice, Lila having nearly forgotten the Waffen-SS who followed along a few steps behind. She turned to him, smacking into something in her distant memory. The burnished brown hair and eyes . . . the embarrassed smile as he'd pushed through the hedgerow at Elsie de Wolfe's party that night, pulling René away from her and into the darkness of war . . .

"I recognize you."

He nodded, a scar tendering his brow—that was new. But the other angles of his visage were unmistakable.

"You two know each other?"

"In a way. I'm sorry about our first meeting." The man cleared his throat and tipped the uniform hat, brandishing a smile behind the unshaven jaw.

"Well, if we're all friends here, that makes this a little easier. This is

Christian. He planned this little operation on a whim and, as a matter of fact, has been waiting for you for some time. Lila de Laurent? Meet Trouvère."

"Trouvère? So you've been in this longer than I realized. I'm afraid I'm a little late for our Versailles meeting, by about six months."

"And I'm the better for it, I hear. Very pleased to formally meet you this time, mademoiselle. It would seem my family owes you and René a debt of thanks for what you did on New Year's Eve, keeping the rest of us out of the hands of the Boche. They had a few code names they were trying to work out and put a face to—Violette and her man? No one could place her in the Résistance cells around the city. But they have heard of him: Arthur Le Grave. Sound familiar?"

"Violette had a man working with her. I believe that was his name."

Carlyle flitted a glance to Christian. "Mouth like a bicycle chain got ahold of it?"

"Something like that. But what are you saying—that he wasn't really La Résistance?"

"He was at one point. A valet at the Hôtel Ritz early on. But he went rogue, even as she—Violette—stayed on to feed information back to him. We learned that he couldn't be trusted for playing both sides of the Résistance while feeding information back to the Vichy police, the way one does when they're not entirely certain who the winner will be in a high-stakes poker game and they want to stack the deck on both sides. It was he who was waiting at Versailles that night, and he'd have known who I was if you'd shown up."

Christian extended a hand to shake hers, taking care to place his other palm over hers in a warm, double-handed embrace when she accepted. "We might have lost our entire team if you hadn't taken that bullet and found René when you did."

"If taking a bullet did all that—and I'm still not convinced it did—then I'm glad."

"We have much to talk about, I believe? I understand you sent some information on to us through Carlyle here, of the V-2 bomb shipments and the art being filtered through the Jeu de Paume. And more importantly, confirmation that these have been running together, all the way through to Berlin?"

"I did. Thank heaven. It seemed a comedy of errors how it all worked out. But oui—we got it where it needed to go in the end."

"Carlyle got the microfilm into our hands months back. And it was that information that brought us this far now. If the Reich does set their sights to bomb Paris as the Allies draw closer, then we've got an upper hand having been warned about it."

"I have more. I have a ledger. It's a catalog of the collections that came through the Hôtel Ritz, from '41 through December of last year. I may have photographed the art and the train manifest and handed off the microfilm, but all this time I worked with Violette to capture and translate the documents, and I kept a set back for myself. I have seen the catalog of every piece of stolen goods that we saw come through, and I copied it all."

Carlyle took a step back, and maybe it was warranted to have the propaganda king bested at his own game. "You mean you kept records of everything—all the lot in the officers' suites at the Ritz?"

"I did. Forgive me for not saying, but I thought I couldn't trust anyone but myself to see it through. I'd made a decision to go after the Touliard collection on my own after the war was over. But that was before I knew of René's fate. Things have changed now, but I'm hoping we can still use it."

"Bien. That's quite an undertaking." Christian smiled, almost as if overcome with something he'd kept to himself. "I know someone who has a similar idea about that at the Jeu de Paume. She, too, wants to give everything back, at great personal sacrifice. We should be quite proud of our Parisiennes and the lengths to which you'll go to do the tough tasks set before you."

"Right indeed. But we can talk shop later. I have strict orders to get Lila out of sight as soon as she arrived. And I for one would like to get out of the SS uniform before one of us gets shot. But first, here—"

Carlyle looked up to the streets on the bank above them and then reached into the underbrush against the train tunnel wall. He turned to Lila and thrust a pair of wool trousers in her hands, along with an ivory work shirt, worn leather suspenders, a felt beret, and military-style boots. A swath of fabric he laid over the top.

"An armband. We'll wear them when we go out to protect us from fire from our own. You're one of us now, so you might as well wear the official uniform of espionage. I know it's not Chanel, but where we're going you'll be quite cheered you have it."

"Steady on, Yank. I assure you that the state of my dress is the very last thing on my mind. You operatives should know me well enough by now to know that much. I'd rather you tell me where the weapons cache is so I can set my watch and be at the ready when the time comes to join the fight."

"See what I mean? René told you—fire." Carlyle nodded to Christian. "We'll get you a place to change and then someplace to sleep safe for the night. And tomorrow, Lila, we'll get started with tracking the collections. So we're ready to beat the devils at their own game, and Sir Duckworth can make fast work of reporting it."

Carlyle's flashlight illuminated the arch of a burnished metal door—ancient, rusted red, with moss-covered stones packed all around—looming in a cutout of the stone wall before them. He opened the door to the cry of rusty hinges to reveal a steep stairway . . . going down. "After you, mademoiselle."

"I'll take her," a voice cut in—the same deep gravel that had triggered her heart to recall a memory on New Year's Eve. Approaching through the dark from the other end of the tunnel, he appeared through the oblivion, cast in the glow of the flashlights they'd turned his way.

René.

"You're here." Lila ran forward and embraced him, shoes off the ground and arms flung around his neck, falling against him as he cupped the back of her head.

In the same plain clothes he'd been wearing an hour before, but a new bruise on his face from the place they'd smashed his jaw and a cut trickling blood from his eye, it was René. Alive. Well enough, she hoped. He'd run in her direction with Nigel trailing behind, and a group of uniformed Vichy police on his heels—obviously more than they'd seemed at the time—and was now holding her, the relief enough to make her feel like they'd been apart for five years all over again instead of for just an accursed trek across the city.

"Of course I'm here. You didn't think I'd really let them take you, did you? Without putting up a fight?"

"I wasn't prepared to let them take you either." Lila ran a hand over his broken skin, jaw already purple and swollen. "But your face? They did this to you."

"It doesn't matter." He caught her hand with his and pressed a kiss to her wrist. "They didn't bust up anything important."

"But how did you . . . ? The captain called us in to the Gestapo. The men in the front of my van were Waffen-SS. There was no way out of that."

"Of course not. It didn't take long to see the captain knew who you were, from the first moment he set eyes on you. And I knew if he used our telephone box to call it in, it was the best chance we had to slip through their fingertips."

"How?"

Carlyle smiled, revealing the grand game they so loved: to defy the Third Reich with wits instead of guns. He beamed, even through the fall of shadows.

"Why, La Résistance owns the switchboard, mademoiselle. It's a shame we won't have use of it again, but do you have any idea how much intelligence we acquired from that very box? The cabarets were a dream to loosen their inhibitions, and the fools didn't know they were handing their secrets over to—"

"Sir Duckworth and The Chief's GS1 radio, every time they picked up the receiver." Nigel swept in, placed a hand on René's shoulder as he winked at her. "And that captain sure didn't know La Résistance was listening in on every word when he called to report you. If anything, he did us a favor by tipping us off that you two were in a fix. We were able to summon Stormie and her cache of newly acquired submachine guns, and Christian put up a roadblock to stop the convoy in its tracks. Between the panic and the confusion about how we tracked them, I'd say my work here is done. I can have a new article punched out within the hour with all this fresh fodder."

Nigel took off his hat and bowed, as if offering respect at a funeral.

"Ah, she was the cabaret madame of every gent's dreams, that pâtisserie. A moment of silence, chaps. For we'll surely miss her."

René scooped up the stack of wares Lila had dropped when she'd seen him and, with his free hand, held Christian back at the shoulder.

"Christian? I need to talk to you. Someone who came into the shop tonight that you need to know about."

"D'accord."

"Come on, Lila. Let's get you underground first." René laced his fingers with hers and led them through the metal door, down the steep stairs to the watery grave of millions, and Stormie's kingdom of the catacombs beneath the Left Bank.

For some reason, though it was a comfort to have those she could trust on all sides, Lila's feet hitched on a step down into the darkness. The Allies could be coming, but what would they bring with them?

René squeezed tighter, whispering in her ear, "You alright?"

"You think I'm afraid with every step? Maybe I am."

"That's honest. You didn't change the subject this time."

"What does it matter if I'm afraid? Paris is waiting for her freedom, and she'll need all the help she can get to find it. Fear doesn't get to go down with us. Not tonight."

Lila walked a runway of stone that night, holding René's hand, as a Parisienne given the gift of worn trousers, a shirt, and suspenders. An authentic French beret and military boots that looked like they'd already seen a hundred winters. She decided as she dressed in the dark, *this* was the true fashion of Paris, more than Chanel or Ricci or any other name could possibly boast. The clothes allowed her to become a living part of history. A true Parisienne. A gracious fighter, and a woman stepping into the shoes of who she was always meant to be.

If there was to be a fight, for the first time in her life, she was ready.

Chapter 26

19 August 1944
1 Place de la Concorde
Paris, France

It's time to go." Rose's command echoed as she shouted across the empty gallery, and as gunfire erupted out in the Jardin des Tuileries.

They were holed up at the Jeu de Paume, a last-minute decision as they were closing the doors. They vowed to protect what remained in the galerie under close watch of their feeble team, until they could hand off what was left to the Allies.

"If you consent to raise arms and fight in your neighborhoods or right outside these walls, we send you now with the most ardent courage as you go. Or if you wish to go home where it's safe until this outbreak of violence is over, no one will think less of you. You have done your duty to this galerie and to France, and we commend you. But now that the SS is gone and the art with them, there is no reason to stay. So we are closing these doors within the hour."

Sandrine stood in the gallery among empty frames of gold littering the floor, hand pressed to her middle with her palm splayed against the rise under her Kelly-green skirt.

Breathe in . . . and out.
You can do this.

The crates that had been lined up days before, ready for transport to who knew where—now, they'd vanished. The carts holding marble statues, the canvases, works by artists such as Picasso and Toulouse-Lautrec, Degas, Renoir, and Gauguin—they'd all disappeared with them. Now what lay behind were the remnants of the last four years—walls that had seen the selections, floors that were picked clean, and workers who were the remaining witnesses of all the Nazis had done.

Sandrine watched as a few attachés and secretaries hurried through the front doors, and the eager old Parisian who was too aged for the French Army, but by heaven he could go out and raise arms in the street.

Rose looked to Sandrine and then to Michèle, who stood across the vast space. They said nothing. It was enough to stand firm along-side their leader.

"Your family, Sandrine? You ought to go while you still can."

"They are well and safe in their flat, mademoiselle. My family understands I have a job to do, and I will return home to them soon. At least let me help you close up here first. We cannot leave the Jeu de Paume at risk."

"My family understands as well." Michèle stepped forward with hands iced in fists at her sides. "I'm staying too. There are crates in the back of the storehouse. They appear to be the ones that were not sturdy enough for travel. But we ought to check through them, just to be sure nothing of value has been left behind."

"D'accord. Go see to it then. Fetch the boards from the extra crates." Rose smiled in a faint show of appreciation, watching as the few who remained made no move to the doors. She began a tense roll of her sleeves. "And those of us left here will start with boarding the windows, high as we can reach. We will barricade ourselves in and once we're certain everyone else is out, we will be the last to leave through the front doors. We'll need a hammer and nails."

"I've got them." Sandrine fled down the hall, watching the high arched windows as she ran toward the archive room, midi skirt catching at her calves if she attempted more than a half stride.

The SS had fled that morning.

Cars were already pulling away from the Jeu de Paume when Sandrine reached the galerie. She'd tossed her bike against the hedgerow, the tires flying at a skid as she ran to the front doors with enough time to see the last of the Nazi flags affixed to the fenders fade down the Place de la Concorde and disappear somewhere into the depths of the city.

It had been a swift end—the captain. Gone. And her prison bars decimated.

There was no escort that morning. Instead the streets were thick with the air of preparation for something—they knew not what, perhaps a fight, or the rumors were true and the Allies really were on their way. The one comfort she had was that Captain von Hiller had fled, and would shadow her and her family with threats no more.

The archive room was an interior space, thank heaven. A shell blast pulsed somewhere, or perhaps mortar fire from a street blockade? It was anyone's guess. Rose had been warned by her Résistance contacts that the streets would not be safe, as the Résistance was now organized and backed by de Gaulle himself, and they intended to make a stand.

Sandrine fled through the archive doors, flipped on the lights, and tore down the long row of aisles to the space in the back where they kept the cache of nail boxes. The last thought to enter her mind as she found the hammer and balanced two boxes of nails in the other hand was of Christian. And Henri. And Victor and Marguerite . . .

She curled her palm around the handle, realizing for the first time that the city was poised for a showdown with their captors, and in it, anything could happen.

"God be with us, Christian. Are we doing the right thing to fight?" she breathed out, still resolute in her heart, knowing this was right—not easy, but the right thing for all of them to do. But she couldn't reconcile the danger of fighting all around the galerie and the uncertain outcome were she to stay.

Would their children grow up with both parents, only one, or none at all?

Steady now, heart. She pressed a hand to her middle. *Steady.*

Click.

The lights died.

"Rose?" She paused. "Michèle?"

Another *click* . . . the door bolt slid from the inside.

The boom of mortar fire was the only response, as it shook the walls in a light tremble, made far worse by the absence of light save for what slid under the door. Her breathing tightened, the in-and-out shallowing as her sense of danger set alarm bells ringing in her head.

Her hand fumbled and the nail boxes fell, raining down in the clink and clank of metal scattering upon the marble floor. She let them go, righting her oxfords over the scatter of nails so she wouldn't slip and fall, and instead focused on drawing the hammer in an iron grip up to her chest. She eased into the dark, back fused against the shelf until she felt the metal burn a cold line through her blouse.

The racket of gunfire pinged in the distance. It should have terrified her, and would have if not for the blatant sound of footsteps—bootfalls—trekking in a slow, intentional cadence down the aisle, in her direction.

God . . . please don't let him find me here.

"Sandrine? I know you're here." The captain's voice cut the air, and she gasped, her palm stifling the sound. "*Viens ici*, madame. Now!"

She edged along the bookshelf, backing up, trailing fingertips behind her on the shelf surface so as not to turn her ankle on a nail. There were a few steps only—just three or four, perhaps—until there was freedom in the aisle and she could run toward the door. It might take a second or two at least, and she prayed if she made a run for it, the time would still be enough to flee around the worktable and unlatch the bolt.

Without sound she edged her foot in a slow circle on the floor, checking for the razor-sharp hazards of nails. It seemed she was well away from them. Sandrine pulled her toes free from her heels, one foot and the other in the silence, until her bare feet pressed the cold marble.

Run!

Through the shadows she blasted out of the aisle, her skirt constricting her movement as she tried—and failed, on a sob—to reach the door, arms surrounding her from behind and pressing her in a hunch over the side of the worktable.

"Put that down." Captain von Hiller tipped his chin to the hammer. He angled a pistol in his grip, pointing to the tabletop as his breath warmed her ear. "*Jetzt*—now! Put it down."

Sandrine lowered the hammer, allowing it to slip from her fingertips to the floor in a clang of metal to marble—heard, she prayed, by Rose and Michèle and the skeleton team left out in the gallery.

"You should not have done that."

"Or what? You'll shoot?"

He released her and she slipped to the side of the table, watching as the captain stood before her. His collar was undone. Hat lost. Hair mussed even for the tight crop he kept it. And through the darkness, she could see from the light spilling under the door that his eyes weren't the fearful wild of a caged man on the run from the Allied armies marching their way.

Worse. They were empty.

It was the blank stare that chilled her to the bone this time. She imagined it was the same stare he'd give an enemy right before he pulled the trigger. Or the stone-cold apathy with which he'd ordered the execution of a group of Jewish boys, lined on their knees before him, begging a devil for clemency when he hadn't any at all.

"You think I would hurt you, or your child?"

"Wouldn't you? You've justified murder. Sending innocents to their deaths. What is one more life in your eyes?" She stared down at the pistol in his hand. "You should have fled with the other officers. The art . . . it is all gone. There's nothing left for you here. And the Allies will be here at any minute—even now they could be filling that gallery out there."

"I do not want the art, Sandrine."

The coolness in his voice said what she'd already known. And how foolish to think that the man who had so passively threatened her—and her son—for years would let her win at the game he'd made in his mind.

Through the shadows she could see him eyeing the rise in her middle. She splayed both palms, butterflied over her waist.

"I want you. And I have never waited this long for a woman before."

"You wait in vain," Sandrine spat out, her voice stronger than she'd wagered it would be. "Leave us be. Go back to your farming village. Pray for forgiveness for all you have done here. And beg that God will hear you."

He took a step forward and she another back, the cadence keeping the same steps of distance between them.

"I can't do that. I sent the officers on ahead. I'll meet them at the train. And you're going with me."

"Going with you?"

With her muscles no match for his, he grasped her shoulders. Sandrine reared back with everything she had and spit in his face.

"You are routed, you proselytizing fool! Do you not see? The people—the Parisians—we are fighting back! Four long years of occupation . . . it is over. You are finished. And you ought to leave while you still have the chance."

Her breaths sailed in and out, hammer on the floor, out of reach as he picked her up off her feet. There was nowhere to hide and nothing to do, save for kicking and flailing into deadweight in his arms with all the bravery she could muster.

His jaw flexed, the truth having cut deep as she intended. "Whose lighter was it?"

"What?"

"Whose lighter!" He shouted the words through teeth gritted so tightly that spittle gathered on his bottom lip as he shook her, and it trembled there as he waited for her answer.

"That's what you want to know? Who bested you in your conquest? That's the prize you seek?" Sandrine shook her head. "Honor and virtue. Even humanity. These words mean nothing to you. This is not about the art. Or war. It is about the total disregard of human decency and the absolute depravity of the Third Reich. I would not tarnish the man's name by uttering it in front of *you*."

She stared back in his eyes, the darkness unable to hide his fury. "You are vile. I would rather die than go with you. And he would be *proud* of me to know I've said it to you at least once."

A blast shook the walls—so close, the Jardin des Tuileries must have taken the brunt. It shook them too, enough that he pulled her to him, hooking his fingertips around her arm in a vise grip.

The blast that followed should have been from his pistol.

Sandrine had expected it. Had prepared her heart when she'd seen the hollow, evil flash in his eyes. But instead the captain fell, slumped over her shoulder, and crumpled to the floor in a facedown heap after he was struck from behind.

Michèle stood over the captain with a bronze statue in her hands, breathing wildly, watching to see if he'd make an attempt to rise. She kicked the pistol, and it slid far under a shelf before she finally looked up at Sandrine. "Are you hurt?"

"Non. I'm okay." Sandrine's hands trembled as she stepped around his boots to get away. She rested a hand to her middle and the other to the table, trying to still the swimming of her head. "We're okay . . ."

It was a second before Sandrine looked back at her friend and registered what she held in her hand: a beautiful bronze sculpture of a little ballet dancer in a sanguine pose, hands innocently clasped behind her back and a ream of vintage tulle skirted around the middle in a soft blush hue.

"Poetic, don't you think? He always spouted off that the degenerate art had no purpose," Michèle said, a relieved sigh rushing out as she stood over the captain. "They must have thought this thing was worthless—a preliminary study for one of Degas's masterpieces. Well, I ask you."

"How did you know he was back here?"

"I didn't. Would you believe I found this in one of the offices? In a rubbish bin with crates stacked on top. I came back to show you, I was so excited. But the door was bolted from the inside, and I knew something was wrong. Fortunate we are that with all those times you had me bolt the door, I'd kept a key just in case. And it seems taken together with that, our dear Degas has managed to save the day."

Michèle reached for Sandrine's hand, grasping her palm tightly. "And if the Allies can take care of the rest of the SS, then we just might be getting somewhere with ending this war."

CHAPTER 27

Paris awoke to the stir of unrest on another balmy summer morning. The Free French were out there somewhere, under the same peach and rose and dusty clouds of the pastel-painted sky, moving fast through the arteries of Paris, gaining ground on the city as they nipped at the Germans' heels.

Lila leaned against the railway tunnel stone wall, arms crossed and listening to the innocence of birds singing their melody in the trees. The distant pepper of gunfire that had so marked the city over the past weeks wove into their song. She ran absent fingertips over the embroidered cross on her armband and the crimson, white, and blue insignia of the FFI—de Gaulle's newly formed French Forces of the Interior that unified La Résistance to an official military unit—displayed on her upper arm.

It was a new morning. A new calling. A new brotherhood she'd been inducted into.

Even if she'd already been carrying Résistance messages in the streets and continued helping René filter communications to the

Allies, it felt like holy ground somehow. There was a certain sense of pride to wear a beret and a band over a worn gentleman's work shirt, one she'd never experienced with a smart spring suit and matching chapeau. The irony was not lost that as a woman Lila could not yet vote but was now endorsed with a band that said she could fight to the teeth and give her life for her country if need be.

It was something she'd never fully understood when her father had come out of the flat and confronted the Germans in his horizon-blue uniform from the Great War, the day occupation had begun.

But now?

The armband awakened a flame within her.

From that day to this, it had been four long years. And her perspective on everything had changed. Who she loved and how. What men were capable of, both in fury and forgiveness. And how God might look at each heart and see both the righteous and the evil acts tangled inside its borders, even at the same time.

She'd even been given a new name.

What did the armband of an FFI fighter mean for the Lila de Laurent she'd always been, and who would the Dressmaker be by the time the last weapon was laid down? It hadn't occurred to her until that moment that she might have to take a man's life. There was no easy way through that. And no coming back from it either.

"Lila?"

She turned, warmed by the familiar sound of his voice.

René slipped an arm around her shoulder as he walked up behind, joining her to watch the break of dawn explode in color tipping over the mansard roofs on the street above.

"I was worried." The racket of machine-gun fire echoed in the distance, and he leaned in closer. "What are you doing out here?"

"If you dare say something like 'You know it's not safe,' I'm afraid you'll be sorry."

"The fact we're all holed up in a labyrinth of unstable tunnels that could cave in or flood at any moment, and the fact we're dodging German sniper fire in the streets every day, would make that an ill-timed comment. Not to mention a quite foolish one if I was talking about you, Dressmaker."

She looked up at his profile, he unable to hide the faint smile as he fired back with her official code name. "But with the Allied bombing at the Renault factory in Neuilly, and the uprising barricading themselves in at the prefecture of police last night, I'd say caution has been tossed out the window now. Parisians are waking to the reality that it's time to fight, and loyalists are rising all over the city because of it."

He didn't need to say it when she already knew—there was no turning back.

The battle for Paris had begun.

René caught her fingertips, stilling them as they moved over the embroidered cross. His palm warmed hers, and he bumped against her shoulder. "What's ticking through that mind of yours?"

"Everything. War. Fashion. Frivolity. Those parties before any of this started. And Amélie, if you can believe it. The choices one makes. And consequences. After all the things I thought I wanted to be back in 1939 . . . Do you remember that dress and the mink I bought to wear to Elsie de Wolfe's for the Circus Ball?"

"You're mistaken, love, if you think I'll forget a thing about you that night."

"For a time, it was all there was in the world. In all the haute couture and the finery that makes the French who we are, I don't see its place defined in my world any longer. And now I look at this band and I think it's the most beautiful thing I've ever worn. How is that even possible?"

"Maybe that's the point. Beauty changes as we change, doesn't it? The things we thought we were supposed to do and be once upon a time, they evolve as we do."

"Is that what we're doing now? Changing?"

He seemed to know what she was asking—what the next steps were. What they'd do. What de Gaulle needed and what France must supply to save itself.

"If you're asking me to fight, we're ready. Nigel's been pecking away at his typewriter at all hours so he could hit the streets first thing this morning. He always keeps his upcoming stories buttoned in his interior jacket pocket, and it's full of all we've been doing here. Stormie's been shoring up barricades around the catacomb entrances all night and ordering around everybody who's in earshot. And Carlyle's banded with the Americans. Got a tip-off before dawn that the Germans are trying to dig in around the Jeu de Paume. He's going to make a stand of it with the Allies when they get this far."

"And the train with the art?"

"Valland sent word to us through Jaujard. Before they fled, officers at the ERR ordered everything that was left loaded up for shipment— train number 40044. That included pieces from the Rothschilds, David Weill, the Touliard collection . . . and hundreds of others. It's all ready to go to Germany."

"So what does that mean for us?" She snuggled in tighter, leaning the back of her beret against his shoulder. "We go out too?"

"Do you want to?"

Lila turned, the sun streaming against them now, warming his face that had been bruised for her and the eyes she knew so well.

"I've been standing here thinking about why I even got into this war. It was to bring every piece of you back to me, not knowing you were still alive. And then I think of your family. I praise God you got them out in time. But what of the Jews who didn't—hundreds, thousands of others, who were lined up with their children for the Vél' d'Hiv Roundup two years ago? I was there. I *saw*. And I can't unsee now that I've learned what evil can do. Only God knows what's become of them now. I'm haunted by their memory as much as I was of what I thought I'd done to the Touliards."

"That's because you have a heart, Lila."

"I also have a catalog of the Touliard collection. And other art too. Maybe even what's on that train today. I don't know where Violette is or whether any of the SS are still hunting me, but I need that catalog. *We* need it. And I want to go get it, to give it to Christian before it's too late. I want to put it into his hand, like I was supposed to that first night all of this started." She swallowed hard and looked back in his eyes, willing him to understand that this request went to her core. And if need be, he'd have to let her go. "I can't keep it for myself any longer. Will you help me?"

"I could give you our options, Lila, but in truth every single one of them is for me to keep you buried belowground until it's over. I realize I did that once, walking away because I thought it would keep you safe. But love isn't safe. And I won't ask you to be less than you are because I'm terrified of losing you. So if you really need to do this—if you want to make your stand—then I'll stand with you. We'll do it together or not at all. That's my promise."

"Together . . ."

One word—*together*.

It was the one thing she'd wanted at the start, when they'd stood along the road to the Petit Trianon, and the chord that always seemed to elude them that he was now offering.

"We lost those years that we could have gone through this war side by side. I won't make the same mistake again, Luciole. So I'll go with you today, if you promise me one thing." He swept a hand up to her brow, gently removing her beret and running his palm over the waves that had fallen over her forehead. "You'll marry me when this is over? Rebuild what's been lost?"

For all the dance floors and tuxes and romantic gestures at the prewar parties when they'd first fallen in love, René couldn't have been handsomer in worn street clothes and a jaw marred by bruises. And she couldn't have loved him any more in that moment.

He pulled an armband from his pocket and slid it up his shirt-sleeve, affixing the FFI to his left shoulder.

"Before Paris . . . Remember?" She smiled. "Famous last words."

"They better not be. We have a future to build together, mademoi-selle, and today is step one."

———◆———

20 AUGUST 1944
8TH ARRONDISSEMENT
PARIS, FRANCE

"I never gave you an answer."

Lila crouched with René behind the fender of a Renault left catty-corner on the curb, its front wheel flat and door jutting into the street, as if its driver had made a clandestine leap from the moving vehicle.

"What?" he said, keeping his eyes trained.

They stared at the block of shops, the blue door and boarded windows of her father's old milliner's shop lonely on the street corner. An explosion boomed somewhere in the distance, the likely sound of mortar fire hitting in another battle far off. But that wasn't the same as being pinned down by sniper fire from the upstairs flats. If any German loyalists were up there, they'd pick them off first thing if they spotted the armbands.

"I said, I realize I never gave you an answer. I nodded, but that's not the way I'd ever imagined accepting a proposal. I thought I should at least mention it, if we're staring down meeting our Maker at the moment."

"And not the way you'd imagined me proposing, no doubt, while we're contemplating having a hair trigger aimed between the eyes." He slipped a hand up to her shoulder and gave a gentle squeeze at her neck as he peered up, checking the terrace windows over the street. "You didn't say non either, so I figured if we live through this, you'd be open to a little convincing if need be. I can be persuasive when I have to."

"There won't be any convincing necessary."

He kissed her temple. "Bien. Then let's just get in and get what we need, then get out of here. Nigel's set up to meet us on the other side of the river, with Stormie's cell just past the tower. They'll be on the lookout for us and FFI will give cover when we get there. You sure what you need is inside that building?"

"I know it is. I had nowhere else to put it. Every time I left the Ritz, I had to cycle past on the way home. And I couldn't put my parents at risk to have anything found in their flat—they'd have been arrested if they were discovered with it. Non—this was always the best place." Lila judged the distance from the Renault to the shop door, and it was a good twenty paces at least. "You want us to take it at a run?"

"*Absolument.*" He tossed a glance over his shoulder to check the sidewalk behind them. "Keep your shoulder square to the buildings. If they're above us, they won't be able to see the armbands at this angle. I don't want to advertise we're FFI if we don't have to. Best to look like civilians trying to go for cover inside one of the shops, alright? We'll worry about how to get out after."

Placing a steadying hand over the battle-proved leather messenger bag Nigel had loaned her, Lila exhaled deep and lifted her knee from the ground, ready to spring. "Say when."

Another breath, a break in the gunfire, and, "*Allez!*"

They ran at top speed, darting under low limbs of cherry trees lining the sidewalk, until they were at the blue door and René edged up behind her, his broad shoulders providing a haven at her back.

She turned her hand to the knob, not really expecting it to open. But the brass gave without a fight, the hinges creaked, and the door swung wide into the ghost of the old shop. All she needed to do now was crawl under the boards covering the front door, get to the counter, and find the journal she'd tucked up inside it.

"Lila? Is it really you?"

René turned on a dime, stepping in front of her, his Sten gun held out as their shield.

It was easy to see the woman was alone. No SS officer or German military uniforms trailing behind her. No Violette. No anyone but the shadow of the woman Lila had known all her life.

Amélie stood on the sidewalk behind them, hair mussed with tangles drifting over her shoulders, her porcelain cheek tracked with a smudge of dirt, staring back as she squeezed a tighter hold to a little sugar-haired girl in her arms.

"It's alright." Lila edged past René. With a soft palm to the elbow, she lowered the point of his weapon. "I'll talk to her."

Amélie's eyes were wild as she watched the buildings lining the street, and her shoulders jumped when the sound of gunfire erupted down a ways from the corner.

"Amélie," Lila said, she also cautious and watching the street. "What is it you want?"

The gunfire kicked up, the whizz of a sniper's bullet careening by, René acting quickly to pull Amélie and the girl to them, then ducking to cover Lila's shoulders from behind. They jumbled together, ducked through the doorway, and dove into the relative safety of the inside of the shop before pausing to catch their breath.

"I want . . ." Amélie fought for breath, then looked up, cupping a hand to the little girl's head. "I want you to take my daughter."

"Take your daughter? You must be joking," Lila spouted, incredulous.

"So, you are alive." Amélie stared at René, a shade of haughtiness still layered in her voice for the man she'd disapproved of so steadily when she learned of his family heritage at the start of the war. For his part René ignored the slight and held firm at the door, watching the sidewalk through the glass of the shop windows. He didn't say a word, just kept his eyes busy, connecting a glance with Lila only for a breath before looking away again.

"I wondered. Waiting nearby and watching for so many days. I thought if you ever did show up at your parents' shop, it would be with him. Somehow I knew it."

"Amélie, I'm in no position to take your daughter, especially not after what happened at the Ritz that night. It's against my better judgment to speak with you now—"

"Would it change anything if I told you that Violette is dead?"

"What?"

Amélie nodded, stepping around a wooden display table in the center of the floor, its top scattered with dust and leaves and old reams of fabric that had been left behind. She faced Lila, the sunlight streaming in through the shop window, highlighting her discomposure as she gave a frantic, winded explanation.

"The maid. Executed. By that Captain von Hiller. On the spot for killing an SS officer."

"She played a dangerous game. And if you look in those streets now, you'd see people are still dying. What is happening out there is as damaging as the years of indifference by those who aligned themselves with our occupiers. Maybe the apathy more so."

"Is it apathy to call truth what it is? I never knew the maid's motives until that night. I suspected you were searching for some clues to the fate of René here—in vain. You saw what she did, killing my fiancé. And she'd have killed me, too, if he hadn't shown up when he did. But all that time, I never believed what Margot tried to tell me, that you were actually working with *them*. Not until I walked into that suite."

". . . *you were actually working with* them."

The words burned through Lila as she stood behind the counter, hand pressed up under the wood on the top shelf, resting on the journal. Her fingertips squeezed around the binding in an unconscious reaction. To talk of truth and apathy, and then such callous words as an excuse? "Have you learned nothing in this war, Amélie?"

"Nothing except we each do what we must to survive." Amélie cast her gaze to René. "You could have let Violette kill me. But you hesitated, even after I tried to turn him and his family over to the Reich. You'd have saved me? Why?"

Lila refused to look at René. "I don't know."

It caused her to shudder, knowing how close both she and René had come to death. Even now, as he stood guard at the front of the shop, they could hear the peppering of machine-gun fire out in the streets. The FFI was engaged in a fierce battle—maybe even their own comrades—and it was something Amélie could never understand.

"But I regret pausing now. I saw you at the top of the stairs that night. You yelled my name—"

"Oui. To warn you!" Amélie stepped forward, as if to appeal to Lila directly. And heaven help her, but the sight of the innocent in her arms melted the antipathy she had so wanted to remain between them. "It wasn't me who pulled the trigger. It was that captain—he shot you. He dragged me away from the stairs and covered up what happened in that suite. The SS may have hunted you, but only we knew why."

Lila pulled the journal out of the hiding place, the precious leather and pages filled with the dressmaker's secrets she'd collected at the Ritz.

"This is what I've come for. And this is all we're taking with us. I am a Parisienne, but I am also FFI, and proud to be. I do not need your explanation of events that night. And I do not ask for it. When René and I walk out that door, I will not think of you again. Not ever after this day."

"The baron has fled with the SS—left his daughter behind," Amélie spat out, the truth sharp and cutting, even as she patted the blonde crown of the little girl in her arms.

"You're certain?" René looked away from the window and stepped forward, piqued by information they knew could serve the FFI as well as the PWE and the American OSS. "The SS leadership. They're all gone?"

Amélie nodded, hand over her daughter's back patting ever so slightly. "Oui. The cars lined up along the front of the lobby this morning, and I watched as the pigs were shuttled out with their litzen collars, tuck-tail and running, one by one. They left their Parisian women and babes behind. All of us."

A blast exploded somewhere down the street, causing the walls to shake and dust to fall from the ceiling like flour on air.

"Lila? They won't be able to hold position for long at the tower. If you want to get that to Christian, we ought to go." René tipped his head to the glass and pulled the strap of his Sten gun tighter over his shoulder as Parisians dashed by on the sidewalk.

"Right. I'm ready." Lila skirted around the counter, tucking the journal in her messenger bag as she headed toward René's place at the door.

"The Germans will fall, and when they do, I'm done for. I've come to ask you this not for me, but for Nicole. My daughter is an innocent in this."

"You wish to ask me what?"

"To forgive me."

The truth couldn't have been more of a shock than a barrel of ice water to the face.

"If you truly forgive what I have done, then when they come to arrest me, I ask you to take Nicole to my maman. In Chartres." Emotion leaked through for the first time and she approached Lila. Hand outstretched, she placed trembling fingertips against Lila's. "S'il vous plaît? She has a little farmhouse in the countryside. If it's still there, it is a . . . pleasant place to grow up. Not like the city you and I knew as girls and now are forced to weep in as women. I don't want her here to see what is to come, and I can't trust anyone else but you."

"Lila?" René placed a hand to her elbow, urging her away from the chaos erupting to a fever pitch outside. "We can't wait."

It might have been a moment of reclamation. Lila would have

considered forgiveness—the same complicated forbearance René had bestowed upon her that night in the pâtisserie flat compelled her to offer mercy now though the requestor was ill deserving, and standing before her with her head bowed.

But she hadn't time—a sniper's bullet shattered the glass of the shop window and tore through René's chest in a flash, arriving without an ounce of the mercy of which they spoke.

CHAPTER 28

25 AUGUST 1944
1 PLACE DE LA CONCORDE
PARIS, FRANCE

Do you hear that?"

Michèle stared at Sandrine as the *pound . . . pound . . . pound . . .* continued, echoing down the hall to where they'd holed up in the archive room. She stood, eyes wide, and their small team cut to silence as they all listened for what could be a shell blast or any manner of terrifying event happening outside the walls of the galerie.

"Is that honestly someone . . . knocking at the front door?"

After days of terrifying fighting that had erupted at all points around the Jeu de Paume, their little team had been warned not to venture out. Six of them—Rose, Sandrine, Michèle, two young secretaries, and one young attaché who took it upon his shoulders to see that the women were protected—had stayed put at the galerie with the little water they had in the washrooms and the meager foodstuffs abandoned by the fleeing Germans. They'd portioned the champagne and wine and feasted on opened tins of caviar, boxes of stale savory biscuits, and a bin of leftover apples, reserving what they could until either someone had to go out for more rations or they were liberated.

Either way, the moment appeared to have arrived for their weary band.

"Very well." Rose stood from her chair at the desk and adjusted her spectacles as she walked toward the door. She pulled a crowbar from a shelf, the searing cry of the metal catching until she had it in hand. "I will go."

Sandrine shot to her feet. *Non, you will not.*

It was the first crystal-clear thought to ping through her mind in days. All they could tell was that machine-gun fire had sprayed through the Jardin des Tuileries and tank shells had blasted around the Louvre until finally the terror had calmed by day six, and now all that could be heard was the distant sound of pounding on the front doors.

The walk down the hall could mean death in a heartbeat, with all the windows facing outside.

"Rose, you can't."

"Sandrine, this is my post. I am in charge, and whoever is at the door has the expectation to speak to its leader."

"Speak to its leader? But what if it's the Germans? What if they know what we've done with La Résistance? They'll execute you on the spot. You cannot go out there. It could mean your life."

"My dear, I do not believe the Germans have come calling today. They do not ask for anything, and they certainly do not knock. They have taken all they wanted here. All that is left is us. And as for this being any one of our lives"—Rose stiffened her lip but patted Sandrine's arm gently—"Our city has been prepared for this for the past four years, have we not? Would you have allowed anyone to stop you in your wish to fight them by working with La Résistance? Tell me, would you have said non to me?"

And that put truth to it.

Sandrine stood still, knowing Rose was clever but also honest.

She couldn't answer without the same, even knowing it could mean Rose giving up her life. Any one of them must be prepared to do the same.

"I would not have allowed anyone to make the decision for me."

"And we would not either." Michèle stood and brushed dust from her wool skirt. "It's why we stayed. All of us here made the same choice, mademoiselle. And if you're going, then we're going with you. All of us. Together."

They walked the long hall, all sober, purposeful, and quiet.

Sandrine moved with one hand buried in her pocket, holding fast to the page from the Paquet Bible with one hand and the other openly cradling her middle.

They moved past the windows with bullet holes having grazed the glass above the nailed boards, the sun-streaked shadows of their crackled circles dancing on the floor as they marched through. No one commented, just kept moving. Random papers were strewn about the floor. File folders spilt and dirtied with footprints. Frames discarded that had to be walked around, their gold busted but glittering in the streams of morning sunlight. And the lonely crate lid that had been tossed and splintered against the wall, the wood cut through a stenciled label for a piece of art it never had the chance to protect.

Their world was near empty, with only the remnants of the Germans' time in the storehouse left to the witnesses who remained. They rounded the corner, and Sandrine exhaled as one of the young secretaries squealed and the gentleman attaché of their number stood slack-jawed by the sight of a sea of green—a full contingent of American GIs—and armed FFI fighters crowding the arched windows on either side of the bolted doors.

"Rose, s'il vous plaît? I couldn't stand it if you—"

"I will handle this, Sandrine. You are in a delicate condition. You ought to stand back. Michèle? Keep her here, no matter what happens at that door."

Their leader straightened her suit jacket, prim and proper and giving every impression she wasn't the least bit intimidated by a horde of armed men demanding entrance into the front gallery. She moved with confidence, as if it were merely a walk across the galerie to open the doors for their first morning visitors, instead of to welcome an army of gun barrels to swarm them.

"Un momento, s'il vous plaît." Rose pried at the crate boards they'd hammered into the wall. One. Two. Three . . . They came down, falling as she tossed them in a pile on the floor.

Rose took a key from her pocket and unlocked the doors at the center, then said not a word as the massive portals creaked under the weight of being opened, and the arch outlined the outside world as they were split wide.

The men waited in silence, seemingly surprised that someone had been inside and with so much matter-of-fact about her had simply opened the door.

Sandrine looked to the sky beyond the front doors. Black smoke curled over the Louvre, and a row of tanks and military vehicles lined up in a shocking display of tank treads leading through the Jardin des Tuileries. The near-constant sound of machine-gun fire and loud rifle pops rattled off behind the sea of Allied men.

"Gentlemen." Rose stood firm as they raised machine guns to her. "Is this it? We are liberated?"

"Of a sort." An Allied soldier stepped forward, addressing Rose directly. "We are taking charge of these premises."

"Under whose authority?"

"The United States of America." The soldier raised his rifle shoulder height and trained it on the center of Rose's form. "Où sont les Allemands, madame?"

Michèle edged closer to Sandrine when they asked where the SS were, shoulder easing in front of her, presumably to hide her condition as the showdown continued. And Sandrine, trying to appear oh-so-inconspicuous, searched every face of the supposed liberators to see if Christian was among them.

She did notice a man in plain clothes standing a head taller alongside the American uniforms, with the noticeable band of FFI around his arm—an oddity that he had no weapon, just ardent attention and a no-nonsense demeanor alongside the Allied uniforms leading the show.

"My name is Rose Valland. I am curator. And if you ask where the Germans are, monsieur, we do not know. They are gone. Fled. The only effects left behind are the piles of rubble you see on the floor, empty frames stacked against the gallery walls, a team who stands with me, and one valuable item we have left that is locked up in the vault as of this morning. Other than that, they have left behind nothing. But you are free to look around as you like."

The GI surveyed their threadbare team standing tall against the guns.

"Is that so? Bien." He pressed the barrel's end against Rose's shoulder and gave a nudge. "Show me."

———— ◆ ————

"I didn't think being freed from the Nazis would feel quite like this," Michèle whispered to Sandrine as they walked in front of the sea of liberators with machine guns trained at their backs. "What do you suppose they want, marching us through the gallery like a bunch of turncoats?"

"They don't want anything. They don't trust us." Sandrine peeked over her shoulder as they walked down the stairs, following as Rose headed for the underground vaults. "We've been working with the Germans for years. They'd have to believe we're in league with them by now, if we're still alive. To them, we're collaborators."

"I see. And they expect to find what in the vaults? The *Mona Lisa*? Or an army of Nazis down there waiting to blow them away?"

"Maybe. Wouldn't you?" Sandrine closed her fist around the rail, descending behind Rose.

They reached the depths of the basement, and Rose stalked across the floor to the iron vault at the end of the hall.

"Go on, Mademoiselle Valland." The front of the group of GIs leaned in, machine guns trained on the iron target. "Open it up."

As Rose moved off, turning the gold five-spoke on the first vault door, Michèle kept tight to Sandrine, hooking an arm through her elbow. A GI stepped up, gun barrel intent on forcing them apart, perhaps not giving them a chance to fuse together should they discover a horde of Nazis in hiding. He raised his gun, dangerous and unflinching as the cold metal circle pointed to Michèle's neck.

"What say—they haven't done anything!" The plain-clothes brute stepped forward, and Sandrine didn't know what was more shocking— the way he slipped between Michèle and the eager Allied soldier's machine gun to shove it back or the distinct accent that marked him as an American even though the insignia on his arm said he should have been French. "Shove off. Can't you see this woman is expecting? And the rest are innocent? They aren't a part of this."

The GI's eyes flashed, but he held firm.

"Go on with you. See to your vaults," the brute spat, standing firm in front of their team as Rose turned the vault doors before them. He turned to Michèle, whom Sandrine could feel shaking at her side. "My apologies. Some of them are fat-heads, trying to be heroes now that they've made it into Paris. Can't relish the thought that some of us have been here fighting the Boche all along."

"It's alright, monsieur." Michèle whispered, even though the events clearly didn't seem to be sitting well with her. "But you are American then? What have you been doing here during the occupation?"

"You can call me Carlyle. And I'm afraid that's a long story, madame."

Rose turned the five-spoke on another vault. Tensions rose as guns were trained. And Sandrine exhaled, thankful they had at least one of the guests in their corner.

"My name is Mademoiselle Androit, monsieur—Michèle. And this is Sandrine Paquet, and the rest of our team left here at the Jeu de Paume. We're grateful, Carlyle, especially if your comrades would see fit to lower their weapons once the last vault is opened."

He flinched and looked back and forth between them, then glanced at the rise in Sandrine's middle. She melted a little behind crossed arms.

"Paquet you say? Any relation to a Christian—medium build, bookish type, goes by the very François Villon–esque moniker of Trouvère in some circles?"

The sun could have burst in the basement for how Sandrine's heart leapt. She could have hugged the Yank. Kissed him! Anything, knowing that he had fought alongside her Christian and must have some inkling of where he was.

"Oui. Christian is my husband. Do you know him?" And then in a wave of hopefulness said, "Is he here? Is he alright?"

"He's not here, I'm sorry to say. But does he know he has . . . a bit of a surprise to come back to?"

"He doesn't. Not yet. But we must say merci—whatever your story is, we should be very glad you're here, if only to see that everything goes smoothly in this prisoner exchange. I don't think I've ever been so cheered to meet an American as I am at this very moment."

"You're not prisoners." He smiled to Michèle, offering a softer-toned reassurance. "There are no prisoners here. I assure you, there won't be a prisoner exchange, not as long as I'm here with you. That's a promise."

Sandrine eyed his insignia, the cross and tricolor of the Free French, a bold statement in the sea of US Army green. "The armband—does this mean you fight with the French?"

"Not exactly. This is the French 2nd Armored Division under

General Leclerc, and the rest are the US 4th Infantry Division, save for the stragglers in the FFI who helped prime the city for the big show. This armband was loaned to me by a friend, as a matter of fact, who has to go see about some art on a train. One of these could protect us from being fired upon by our own or by the Allied armies while out in the streets." He looked to Sandrine, weary perhaps, with eyes that must have seen so much. But he smiled, as if gratified. "I was told to tell Christian's wife to wait for him, should I find her here on the premises. He says to tell you he'll be home soon."

"Very well. I will take that message." Emotion running high, for more than one reason, Sandrine nodded. "And I believe we have one for you gentlemen too, if you think you're up to the task."

Sandrine looked to the last vault as Rose turned the gold five-spoke on the door, and the item they'd held back for their liberators came into view—one SS officer tied to a chair, with blood tracked down the side of his face to a marked litzen collar, and deep viridian eyes that blazed defiance as he stared them through.

A bronze statue of a ballet dancer stood innocent before his boots.

The machine guns found a new target, and they trained accordingly.

Carlyle turned to Sandrine, brows lifted at the sight of the officer held under lock and key in the galerie vaults. She gave a final look to the captain and lifted her chin, gratified that he would have a chance to hear the truth from her lips.

"You see, we are La Résistance here as well. All of us, and we have been working under the command of curator Rose Valland these last years. We sincerely hope that justice can be enacted against those who have committed crimes upon the people of Paris. So we do have one piece of art and a prisoner to gift to you—the only things the Germans left behind in their haste to flee the Jeu de Paume."

CHAPTER 29

20 AUGUST 1944
8TH ARRONDISSEMENT
PARIS, FRANCE

Lila pounded on the flat door, shuddering as her fist stamped René's blood in half-moon prints upon the wood.

"Pa-pa!" she cried out, willing her arms to hold up René on his feet as he draped over her shoulder. "Hold on, René. Hold on, my love," she whispered, then, "Pa-pa! Open up!"

Marcel de Laurent cracked open the door, the barrel of his military-issue rifle peeking through the line until he spotted them and opened it wide. For the aging soldier he was, the spirit of nimbleness in battle appeared to have won over. He set the rifle aside without pause and shifted René's weight to lean into his shoulder, peeking over the top of them to the empty hall as he ushered them inside.

Her maman sputtered, standing off behind, asking, *"Qu'est-ce qui est arrivé?"*—What is it? What's happened?—over and over as they angled René around the furniture to the sofa in the parlor.

"I couldn't think where else to go. We had someone with us, but she had a daughter to save. So we tried to run on our own, but he's losing so much blood and I didn't know what to do except to come here."

"Come, René." He angled René down upon the chaise. "Easy, Lila, set him down. Easy now. We don't want to tear his wound."

Complexion falling more ashen as seconds ticked by, René gritted his teeth against the pain as her pa-pa tore the soiled shirt. He then pulled cloth from the dining table, knotted it, and pressed it hard to stem the flow of blood down his front. Lila swung the Sten gun strap crosswise over her shoulder, wishing she knew what to do to help, and more than anything aching to rewind the last moments in her mind.

They'd fled the shop and the sniper's bullet that found its FFI target through the shop window, only to run the block to the first place she knew to find help. Lila knelt at René's side now. Gripping his hand. Hating the stains of crimson as she laced fingers with his, the sight haunting as it was the same of her hands the night they'd come back together in Meudon. It was a moment to be dreaded—the helplessness of one who must stand by and watch as her heart broke apart before her eyes. For the first time, she understood what René must have feared when she had been brought in from the truck on New Year's Eve.

"What do we do?" she begged, heart thumping and voice shaking frantically. "Tell me what to do."

"Go to the bedroom. I need sheets. Or towels. Clean ones. Needle and thread. Scissors. Ginette? The brandy from the kitchen. And put on a kettle to boil. Hurry, s'il vous plaît."

Lila fled down the hall, tearing at drawers and opening closets, riffling through whatever was left in the flat to supply his need. She returned to see Pa-pa release the cloth for a moment and tear René's shirt wider, then pour the brandy to blot over the crimson flow.

"It's alright," René whispered, lips too heavy even to move with the words. He grasped her hand, pulled her off balance until her face came down to his. "Luciole. Listen to me. It's *nombre* 7."

"What is?"

He closed his eyes again, eyelids fluttering as he battled to keep them open. "Nombre 7. L'avenue Émile-Deschanel."

"Don't talk, my love. Not just now. Let us help you, hmm?"

"Mais non, Lila. *Partez*—" He pushed her back, fighting a bit as Marcel attempted to stem the flow of blood from his chest. René focused on pressing a hand against Lila's messenger bag. His eyes drifted closed and didn't reopen as he nudged the leather under his palm. "Go. Nombre 7. Christian is waiting."

Her pa-pa worked—she hadn't a clue how, as if he were a field medic caught back in the trenches of the Great War, and not the merchant tailor he was or aged Parisian who'd spent the last years of his life shut up in a flat in their occupied city. He asked for light and they brought him lamps and opened the drapes wide. Lila watched as René slipped into sleep, counting every up-down move of his chest as her father raised spectacles to his nose and focused in on threading a needle.

"Do you know what you're doing, Pa-pa?"

He peered over the top rim of his spectacles. "And where do you suppose I learned to sew, Daughter? War is a teacher of many things—some brutal, some useful." He pressed a hand to René's chest. "The bullet has gone through at an angle here, through the shoulder. He will need a doctor soon, but I believe this boy will live."

Lila allowed the dam of emotion to break free.

Tears tumbled as she rested her forehead on the FFI patch on René's arm and lifted up to press a salt-tracked kiss to his lips. He wasn't awake to scold her for her recklessness to venture out in the streets. And wasn't conscious to hear her give a proper answer to his proposal this time, no matter how she wished he was.

"Shh," Pa-pa whispered, hushing her cries. "Do you hear that?"

"Hear what?" Lila held tight to René's hand, slowing up the tears as she looked to the window and the agony of bullets and bombs in the streets.

"Outside."

Pa-pa rose, walked to the terrace, and stood before the glass. He took off his glasses, folded the metal, and slid them in his shirt pocket. Defying the fear of snipers' bullets or tank shells finding them, and without knowing what the outcome would be of the bloody siege that had taken over the streets, he pressed his palms to the handles of the French doors and pushed.

A song filled the flat as the doors swung wide.

In the midst of tank treads grinding down the Champs-Élysées and shells quaking the walls from the blast of nearby buildings, a melodic whisper cut through smoke and carried to the sky. It was faint but defiant, and growing through the pause of action down below, ferried through the trees lining the grand avenue. Up from the sidewalks to the flats and rooftops lining the streets, the words of a people echoing . . . rising . . . calling for liberation with a cry that carried all the way to l'Arc de Triomphe.

"Aux armes, citoyens!"

Pa-pa stood in the doorway, cutting a figure of defiance as the sun streamed in.

"Formez vos bataillons! Marchons, marchons!"

"Do you hear? They sing 'La Marseillaise'!" He turned, emotion cast over his visage. He straightened his back, lifted his chin, and raised his voice to sing along with the French anthem of Résistance. Maman joined too, a hand fused to the wood frame of the kitchen doorway, bracing herself to sing with the rest.

"Allons enfants de la patrie . . . Le jour de gloire est arrivé!"

"Can you hear, René? Can you hear the song we sing?" Lila whispered, lips pressed to his fingers as the melody went on through machine-gun fire. "This is my oui to your question. And I will come back to tell you in person. I promise. But for now, I must see this through." Lila swept the messenger bag with the journal to her back, fixed the Sten gun tight over her shoulder, and straightened the FFI insignia over her arm.

"I have to go, Pa-pa. There is something I must do. And then a doctor—I'll find one and bring him here."

"Wait."

Pa-pa might have tried to stop her, as her poor weeping maman did, but instead he ran down the hall to the room at the end. The sound of a distant crash—a drawer to the floor or something of inconsequence that had been knocked over in haste. He emerged into the hall again, the thick fabric bars of the French flag in his hands.

"Take it?" He rolled the Great War relic into a strip and tied it, looping the colors around her waist. "We'll watch over him, I promise. As long as you watch over yourself."

"I will." Lila nodded, mouthing *Merci* as she rushed to the door.

Watching over herself? It was not needed.

With a last look to her pa-pa and with the hopeful anthem of a people to be liberated carrying her down the stairs, Lila stepped out to join the fight as the Dressmaker, knowing that God would protect His own—the Parisienne she was always meant to become.

---

20 AUGUST 1944
L'AVENUE ÉMILE-DESCHANEL
7TH ARRONDISSEMENT
PARIS, FRANCE

A choking haze of gray wafted across the River Seine.

The wall of smoke drifted through the streets, obscuring Lila's view of the historic district of Faubourg Saint-Germain. The Eiffel Tower was hidden in the distance, its lattice climbing through a black sky, and trees tangling with bombs and armored vehicles that churned up the grass along the borders of the Champ de Mars.

That's it.

In the center of L'Avenue Émile-Deschanel, an Allied gunman rose above the hatch of his tank to pepper the upper floors of a department store building with machine-gun fire. A block down, a brave Résistant ran from the cover of a shop with a cigarette hanging from his lip and set to work swinging an ax to the trunk of a tall tree along the sidewalk.

Another Résistante moved in behind him, pinning combatants on the opposite corner with cover fire from her machine gun as the man continued chopping. After a few tense moments of sniper fire pinging the concrete around their boots, a small crew of FFI rushed out to push the weakened tree to its death across the street.

It crashed down with a furious *crack*—the smashing of windows and the blast of a bomb combining on the other side of the street as limbs and leaves of green hemmed in the tank from behind. If any German resistance fighting was to come through, it wouldn't be from any points north, and that at least gave Lila some opening to make a run for it.

Through the smoke: *Nombre 7.*

The gold number shone out from the limestone façade of a building but a few doors down. Nine meters maybe? Ten at the most. Oddly, she could eye the same distance on the fashion runways she knew so well, judging it would take her across the street to the two-story door of crimson wood and what had to be FFI guns poking out its shattered ground-floor windows. A Renault lay pushed on its side, the mechanical metal underbelly exposed, acting as cover for a horde of FFI guns positioned behind it.

Heaven help her, but Lila's heart soared when from behind the Renault, she spotted a familiar curly top with spectacles and a rope-tied typewriter slung across his side. Nigel popped up long enough to jam a rifle firm against his shoulder, fire several rounds, then duck back again.

"D'accord . . ."

Okay. They were in sight.

René said the team would be on the lookout for them and FFI would give cover when they got there. Lila just hadn't expected a pack of propagandists to have taken up arms until she saw it with her own eyes. And without really thinking of it until that moment, Lila had to assume they'd all have prepared for the notion that either she or René—or both of them—wouldn't make it back. So if they saw her beret appear through the smoke with Nigel's messenger bag flung over her shoulder, she prayed they'd know her and might hold their fire until she could get across.

C'est pas possible.

The odds were, of course, impossible.

And she might have believed those words to be true, but that's not why they flew through her mind. René had said that once, years before war had ravaged them, he believed in the impossible. He'd marry whom he chose. And he'd staked his life on impossibility never being fully out of reach in order to get Lila out of the Meudon and to get what she must into the hands of the people who could use it.

Now she'd do no less for him.

The call to finally hand off the journal and the greater hope of finding a doctor to bring back to René, they drew her on. Stiffened her resolve. And with a final swing of her submachine gun around from her back to her iron grip, she stepped out.

She ran . . .

She flew.

She tore across the street to the Renault with fire blazing her heels.

The man behind The Chief's broadcasts on GS1 radio became the story then. Nigel caught sight of her almost immediately. He shouted something as gunfire peppered the street and she ducked low, the smell of smoke and metal and burning cordite singeing her nostrils. He ran out behind her, providing cover over her back as they ran.

Her boots slid on tiny pebbles of gravel that sent her skidding behind the Renault's bumper and her cheek sliding to burn against the sidewalk. And then a face emerged in her tunnel vision. Christian peered over, eyes wide. Her bell had been rung with the rush of energy and the blast of a bomb behind them.

She shook her head, deafened, trying to hear him.

"Lila? Tell me! Are you hurt?" He grabbed her lapels, searching her under the front of the messenger bag bathed in a spray of blood darkening her side in crimson.

"Non—" She coughed. Felt her own limbs. Breathed in. And out. No pain. No blood darkening her clothes.

She nodded. "I'm okay. I'm okay . . ."

"Where's René?"

"Hurt. Shot." She shook her head again, desperate for words as she patted the blood-soaked bag. "I have the journal . . . but I need a doctor. S'il vous plaît? Help me. René needs a doctor."

He nodded and left her then.

Bolted out from behind the Renault without another word. Where to, she didn't know. But Lila picked herself up, dusting blood and debris from her hands, looking around at the FFI fighting alongside. She swept up her Sten gun again with no idea what she was doing— just responding to the need of putting something to fight with back in her hands.

Lila inched up as she'd seen the others do only moments before, leveling her gaze over the top of the Renault's side with her barrel trained out in front of her, thinking she'd have only a split second to prepare herself to take a man's life.

She'd have done it had the second not been long enough to see Christian dragging a dead man by his ankles, a trail of crimson blotting the street beneath the body and his mangled typewriter tripping behind.

CHAPTER 30

❦

26 AUGUST 1944
12 RUE FRANÇOIS MILLET
PARIS, FRANCE

Charles de Gaulle marched down the Avenue des Champs-Élysées as president of the provisional government of the French Republic, to both a rejoicing people and sniper fire that emerged to greet him.

Parisians swept out of their homes, flooding the streets with jubilance as their oppressors fled, to be replaced by the Allied vehicles that soon rolled in. It was the grateful lining the cafés and shops of Paris, filling all the sidewalks to bursting as they did outside the burned-out shell of Le Fournier. There they were singing. Dancing. Young Parisiennes offered wine and kisses to the GIs, waving posters with *Long live de Gaulle* and offering spirited shouts of *"Vive la France!"* to drown out the erratic gunfire peppering the background from the German-faithful Vichy still holed up in the city.

Bullets pinged the sides of buildings from rooftops and upper-floor windows, sending people to flee for cover, and machine gun–toting FFI would rush up flights of stairs to hunt down any combatants left hiding in their snipers' nests.

The people were grateful, but bloodthirsty, too, after the carnage of four years of occupation. They sought revenge even as the war in Europe was not yet over, their insatiable hunger fed through the *épuration sauvage*—the wild purge—punishments without trial that saw women pulled out of the crowd almost immediately, paraded in shredded clothes, and publicly shamed in the streets following their collaboration with the enemy.

Marguerite and Henri had stayed back at the flat, the streets still too unstable to travel. But after the events at the Jeu de Paume, Sandrine had no choice but to move through them, as quickly as her feet could carry her, weaving through the bystanders with her back to the clogged streets.

"La voilà!" a woman cried out, pointing at Sandrine as she attempted to bleed into the crowd unnoticed. But heads were turning faster than she could escape as the woman's shouts of "She is here—collaboratrice horizontale!" resounded on the sidewalk.

The woman didn't know her name. But she did know Sandrine's face, as she was the one who had stepped in and out of the captain's auto. For years. Seemingly of her own volition, once in a very elegant, very memorable couture Chanel gown. And now with the swell of a belly she could no longer hide, she'd been branded a willing collaboratrice for her fraternization with their fallen enemy.

"Collaboratrice!"

Another grabbed her wrist, a woman's nails cutting into her skin, but Sandrine twisted her arm to release the vise and picked up speed through the crowd toward the front stoop of her flat.

Fear and vengeance became her accusers in the form of neighbors. Strangers. And friends. They pulled her from behind, fists grabbing her hair as she tried to climb the stairs, the pain debilitating as Sandrine clawed at the rail leading upward. Her feet lost their shoes as she was hooked at the elbows and dragged back out to the sidewalk, scraping her heels near raw until they reached the burned-out Le Fournier again.

She saw the four spindle chairs set in a row atop a platform—built high on the sidewalk in front of the shattered glass and rough-nailed boards of the shop windows. She was forced into one, the delicate collar of her silk blouse ripped to near indecency. She was held down at the shoulders as a blur of nameless faces lined up to hurl their accusations at their row of caught women.

Spit landed on Sandrine's cheeks, running down her neck to wet her hair. The crowd became bolder as a line of women approached. They slapped her and smeared tar upon her cheeks. A woman burst forth and uncoiled a tube of lipstick, then held her chin in a vise as she drew something across Sandrine's forehead—likely the blood-red swastika that shone on the other girls' skin. Another woman's fist connected with the side of her mouth, and Sandrine closed her eyes to the brutal sting, turning chin to shoulder, trying to deflect the worst of another blow that could come after it.

The grinding of clippers cut loud, the echo of an automated beast crying out until she opened her eyes again, the sound strangely loud enough to be discerned over the eruption of celebration when the people saw its source. They cheered and Sandrine watched as the first girl down the row was selected. They ran the clippers over her scalp, shaving her clean.

Down the line, swift and fierce—one girl shaved, two, three . . . The rabble watched, friends and neighbors eating up the pleasure of enacting revenge after four long years of occupation.

Sandrine knew she could have cried out.

Perhaps she should have done so, to defend herself with the truth.

They hadn't a clue she was aligned with La Résistance, nor what the last days and weeks and months had meant at the Jeu de Paume, or the years of work for Valland's team before it. They didn't know that Victor Paquet had surrendered his life for his country so early in the war, and that Sandrine's own husband was still out there somewhere, saving the Jews' priceless works of art from Nazi theft. Maybe he was even among the number of the celebrating, rolling down the streets in an armored vehicle, heading home to Henri and her.

Sandrine searched the sidewalk, a desperate plea for Christian's face—for his rescue to appear in the crowd. But the street-court accused and doled out punishment before she could pray for his appearance.

No words were spoken when her turn came.

No tears.

And no saving.

Not for the years of fight the Parisians had all survived. And not for the eager revenge flashing in their eyes now. Sandrine held her head high, taking the clippers' swift roll of punishment as they skimmed against her scalp, feeling the blood drip from her busted lip to her chin, blonde locks drifting down over her shoulders as a summer breeze carried them across her lap.

She spread her palms over her middle in a defensive posture—the only reaction they'd get from her now—until they had won, and the crowd cheered as the locks of all four ladies were lifted high like a prize.

"*Arrêtez!*"

A woman's scream cut the air, so powerful it hushed the ravenous crowd and spread a small semicircle back from the chairs.

Marguerite stepped up, having commandeered a rifle from good-ness knew where, and lifted the weapon shoulder high as she positioned herself in front of the women. Sandrine sat, firm but dazed, staring at the back of Marguerite's form, her gray hair wild and shoulders squared against the rifle and the thick of the opposing crowd.

He shouldn't have been there to witness it, but Henri approached too. He buried his head in his maman's lap, sobs flooding out as he swept the hair off the round of Sandrine's belly onto the sidewalk, tidying the agony of the mess from her bare and bloodied feet.

"*Arrêtez . . . maintenant!*" Marguerite bellowed, her shoulders trembling with the force. "Now! Or I will shoot every last one of you."

No one wished for death on a day of liberation—not from a crazy woman with a gun. They had better things to do. Higher celebrations to attend. And more revenge to seek against the fleeing Germans and the other collaborators who were slinking back all across the city. They dispersed, fading out, tossing jeers over their shoulders as they left, turning their backs on the crazy old widow and the women who still sat in the chairs, their faces crumpled and tearstained, their crowns marked for the treasonous Parisiennes they now were.

Marguerite stood anchored there for the longest time, rifle raised as people passed by on the sidewalk and the sun beat down upon them. Even as the other shamed women slipped away, gathered by some nameless Samaritan who took pity to cover their nakedness with shawls and hurry them into a shop or flat somewhere to see to their wounds. But Marguerite stood tall, defying anyone in their neighborhood to look on her daughter-in-law as an accomplice, as long as it took to make the point that they were no longer under German rule and therefore would no longer behave like beasts.

You are quite grown up, my Henri.

So like Christian, she noticed, with the deep care in his eyes. The compassion and understanding as he seemed to have blocked out the people on the sidewalk. He untucked his shirt, tearing a swath of the blue-and-white checkered hem, offering it to blot the blood on her chin.

"You ought not do that, chéri," Sandrine whispered, hands shaking as she caught his in her own. "Your shirt."

"I'll get another, Maman." He pressed the fabric down with a sweet, soft child's touch. Her lip issued a sharp sting and she closed her eyes against it. Then when it eased, Sandrine exhaled and looked up at him. Oui, quite grown up he was now. And for the years they'd fought alone—or felt alone—Sandrine had never been more aware of God's presence than in that moment.

For every night spent crying alone in her bed . . . For every moment of terror that their actions at the Jeu de Paume would be discovered . . . For every second of brokenness and each moment of doubt, she didn't—couldn't—even in that instant, feel that God had abandoned them.

Not when love was so perfect in grace, right before her eyes.

"Just like your chapeau, remember? You have need of a new one. You wait and see. Pa-pa will return and buy you one for your beautiful bravery today, and every day since he and Grand-père have been gone from us." He brushed a palm against stray hair dotting her forehead, then slowly slid his palm down the side of her face to rest at her cheek. "I am quite proud to be your son."

Tears burned her eyes, but she took his fingers, curled them around her palm, and pressed them in a kiss to her lips.

"Je t'aime, Henri," she whispered. "Mon cœur."

"Grand-mère says she is sorry for all that's happened. And she would never let them harm you. Come, you and *le bébé*. Let us see you inside? You need to rest now."

And then we will rebuild all that has been broken . . .

Henri raised her with careful hands, lifting Sandrine's bruised body to standing. And she walked, barefoot, with Marguerite and her rifle as an anchor propping at one side and Henri lifting the other, heads held high all the way down the sidewalk from Le Fournier to a new life.

A new world.

A new Paris enduring the pain of being born.

CHAPTER 31

❦

27 AUGUST 1944
1 PLACE DE LA CONCORDE
PARIS, FRANCE

Liberation meant freedom from many things.

Paris was free of the intense fighting of the previous weeks and the oppression of the Germans for the last many years, but the war for France was far from over. The French 2nd Armored Division that had seen them through Liberation had moved on, pushing the Germans deeper into France and leaving behind American GIs, de Gaulle's new provisional government of the French Republic, and a city quaking with the debauchery of emancipation.

As she walked the long, tree-lined colonnade to the Jardin des Tuileries, a soft breeze rustled the Chanel gown Sandrine had draped over her arm.

The gentle brush of chiffon hit her bare legs at the hem of her frock and the hand she spread to protect the rise at her middle. It should have tousled blonde waves at her shoulders, too, but she was marked by a smooth crown and the trace of purple bruises that hadn't enough time to heal on her jaw and cut lip.

The Parisians passing her on the streets thought they knew who she was.

Most avoided her, crossing over to the other side of the road opposite the shorn woman on her way to the Jeu de Paume. They whispered and backed up as she passed by. A few thought they were standing up for the fallen, perhaps, by making open jeers and shouting, "Collaboratrice horizontale!" as she walked the garden path, with the evidence of what must be her crimes manifested in her crown and middle.

The little café came into view.

It was the one she and Christian used to meet at before the war, where she told him the first time that he was going to be a father. And it was the same she'd passed each day during his absence, when the gray uniforms of the Wehrmacht occupied all the outdoor tables. It was the same where she'd stood with Valland and the team as they were made to watch piles of degenerate art light the night sky with flames. And it was the nearby hedgerow where she'd stowed her bicycle before the last bloody battle for Paris, with its bullet holes to gleam in the sun.

She might have kept walking, hoping to forget such broken things, if not for the sight of a table at the end of the row. One table, one man sitting in a worn uniform of the First French Army, with a little boy in a torn shirt sitting at his side. They watched—and waited—for her.

Sandrine's breath caught in her chest as Christian stood.

It wasn't too far to see him take off his hat and turn it in his hands, or to witness the wind toying with his brown hair that had grown long and tipped over the scar at his brow. She froze on the path, waiting as he held Henri's hand and they came to meet her, their stride slow and intentional.

His eyes freely teared as he approached her broken condition. A bald crown. Lost pride. A busted face and what must have been a shock—a growing belly pressed up against the luxury of the Chanel . . .

What must he think of her now?

When Christian reached her, Sandrine was crying too. Half scared he'd reject what she'd become, even while relieved that the day they'd hoped and waited and prayed for had finally arrived. Christian hugged her in a wide circle, around the belly and reams of chiffon.

"Drina," he whispered, emotion cutting his words short so he had to stop and start again. "Je t'aime, mon cœur. I am home."

It seemed he couldn't speak beyond it.

Christian took the palm she'd spread against her middle, his fingertips curling it around his, and pressed the raw, shaking knuckles in a kiss to his lips. They found each other's foreheads, his to hers, softly, as he held a palm to her bare neck. She closed her eyes, pressing a palm to Henri's shoulder. Thinking she'd cry, only to feel Christian press a kiss to the cut on her lip.

"I've come to tell you that today a train was stopped at Aubervilliers," he whispered in her ear, pausing until she looked up in his face. "There was a Lieutenant Rosenburg who along with La Résistance led a unit to a packed train. No. 40044 still waiting on the tracks to be sent to Germany. We found it loaded with art. Picasso. Cézanne. Toulouse-Lautrec. Degas. Renoir. And hundreds of others—many paintings from the lieutenant's own family—the art you saved here and boxcars full of the beloved belongings stolen from the Jews of Paris."

She tightened her hold on Henri and the Chanel. How was it possible that in the mere instant it took to hear the news confirmed and to hold on to what had become the symbols of the fight in her mind, five years of their risk and toil at the Jeu de Paume had come to an end?

"Is Mademoiselle Valland aware of this?"

He squeezed his palm in a light caress against her bare neck. "It's she who sent me out here to tell you. Henri and I wished to meet you, to tell you the good news ourselves."

Sandrine didn't need to tell him what had happened the day before, that while all of Paris celebrated de Gaulle's grand procession into the city, war-weary Parisians enacted their own brand of justice. Or that she was doing what she'd said so long ago—returning the Chanel so it, too, might come home. Christian looked at the gown in her arms and smiled that same pain-wracked grin she'd seen on the train platform nearly five years before.

He seemed to know why.

Pride beamed from his face, and her chin trembled in acknowledgment of it.

She nodded, accepting him, and leaned against his shoulder until her bald crown rested in the crook of his neck. She took Henri by the hand and their family walked together, Christian's head held high over her, shielding the way to the front doors that were no longer held hostage by officers of the ERR or swastika flags. The crimson, white, and blue bars of de Gaulle's Free French had been hoisted over the front window arch of the Jeu de Paume, and the entry was guarded by the presence of American servicemen and the bold waving of their stars and stripes.

A GI offered to open the door for them, but Christian held up a hand. He stepped aside, too, instead looking to Sandrine.

"After you, Madame Paquet."

It was the first stone on the path, and the first step Sandrine could take in rebuilding the broken pieces of their lives. The page torn from the Paquet Bible had reminded her to wait—for years—that God would hear the desperate cries of His people. That He would prove faithful. And that though the day tarried, they must always cling to faith, for it would surely come.

She took a deep breath, wrapped her palm around the door handle, and stepped through the entrance of the Jeu de Paume, knowing at once that those words were true.

CHAPTER 32

It was rumored Coco had left Paris.

Her arrest came in August, and by September, she'd fled. Though it didn't look at all like her Paris shop was still closed, for American GIs had lined up all the way down the block from the once-bustling Chanel salon.

"What is happening?" Lila asked, as she and René stood on the corner, watching in wonder as military jeeps pulled up and were parked one after the other along the building-lined street, and GIs in fatigue green hopped out to flood the sidewalk in their happy swarm.

"Your former employer saw what is happening to collaborateurs across the city. And she is not stupid. Chanel has put a sign in her window: *Free Chanel No. 5 for American servicemen*, and it seems they all have wives and mothers who'd like a petite piece of Paris brought back home."

René paused at her side, scanning the street. One arm bore a sling under his suit jacket, but the other he'd hooked around the back of her raspberry-pink suit, perhaps protecting her from the ungodly reprisals were she recognized as Lila de Laurent—the dress-maker at the notorious Nazi House of LDL—instead of the active FFI member she'd become.

"Amélie once predicted that Chanel would be back after the war." Lila watched the bustle—men standing in the sun, nursing a cig or chatting back and forth in front of the salon's street-front windows, and the façades that still bore bullet holes. "Do you think she was right? Do you think Chanel will ever return?"

"Even when they find out that she spent the occupation in a Nazi suite at the Ritz Paris—who knows? But she just might be the most brilliant businesswoman ever to set up shop in this fair city. By the time she does come back, who would remember what happened during those years as they walk down the Rue de Cambon with their free luxury gifts?"

He was right. Reprisals had been swift, and those like Amélie had been caught up in the first wave of post-liberation arrests across the city. For reasons unknown to all, the women were targeted first and with the fiercest hand of judgment, even by men who'd openly collaborated in business for the past five years.

Lila had not been there to see the arrests, but she had delivered Nicole to her grand-mère at a Chartres farmhouse in the countryside outside of Paris, war-torn fields on all sides but the walls still standing. She'd learned later that the women were not so fortunate.

Amélie and her court of Ritz ladies were arrested and imprisoned alongside famous names like soprano Germaine Lubin, French film actresses Corinne Luchaire and Arletty, and dignitaries' wives who'd frequented the German embassy for events and raucous champagne parties at Maxim's every night.

Occupation now seemed like a depraved nightmare, but not so much unlike liberation as she'd once thought. Some were rightfully guilty—the women Lila knew and dressed while working for La Résistance had been active in apathy at best, outright collaborateurs at worst. But others, who really knew where the lines between collaboration and Résistance blurred? Many, even those who'd been active in aiding the Résistance, were sentenced to prison under the quickly formed *indignité nationale*—the sorting of crimes of what was dubbed "national unworthiness" after the occupation—which meant a loss of civilian status and marked some as traitors for the remainder of their lives.

They learned that Christian's wife had been unjustly caught up and endured a public attack at the start, even though Rose Valland had defended her in public. Rumor had it that de Gaulle's provisional government was organizing a commission to retrieve the art stolen from France, and the Résistance team that had worked under her at the Jeu de Paume was to continue that work in Germany for some years to come.

"I believe Paris will rebuild . . . and France will move forward. But not just yet. I wonder what kind of new war is stirring for the crown of French fashion. I hear Dior is already making a play at owning the Paris runways. That will be quite a fête to watch."

"And if they have an ounce of smarts, Lila, they'll hire you back in a thrice."

She lifted her chin, showing off a little moxie. "I've had a few offers I'm considering."

"And I support you taking whichever one you want after we're married, Luciole." René drew her away, to skip the Rue de Cambon and take another on their way to l'Hôtel de Ville. "But first, we have a promise to keep to each other."

"A promise. Oui, René. We do." She hooked her elbow through his good arm. "I can't begin to think what de Gaulle's government will require of a young couple wishing to get married even before all the smoke has left the sky. But you won't have a chance to get away before we find out."

"I should hope de Gaulle would be glad to see a request for a marriage license come through. Paris is still the city of love, isn't it? This proves it."

"First Paris. Then London, to return the Touliard family heirloom necklace, and anything else we can track down. And I wonder if we might stop in Yorkshire? I should like to meet the Dunnes of Leeds, to give them Nigel's typewriter. To bring back a portrait of who he was these last years and all that he did. Who could tell them more fairly than us?"

René looked away, staring up the street for a moment. "I can't believe he's gone. After all these years of working together . . ." He paused, emotion hitching, though he tried to hide it. "He was my best friend. And I never told him that."

"He knew, René. Of course he knew." It felt right to pause together, so Lila eased into his side. "And what would he think of it? Sir Duckworth, an international celebrity."

That made him smile and shake his head. "Now that it's known he was here and routing the Germans with his venomous pen all through the occupation? He stepped out in the street, brave fool. To save your life and mine, only to take a sniper's bullet in the end. But he'd have never lived a quiet day again once *The Sketch* articles were found in his coat, and he'd have loved every single moment of it."

"Then we'll take them back, to his family," she whispered, the sunshine and the beauty trying to return to Paris somehow poetic as they talked about their poet-friend. "And Carlyle? What of him? He goes home to New York a hero, or does he follow hot on the Germans' tails?"

"If only fate could see fit not to feed his ego anymore. I heard through the FFI ranks that he joined up with the first wave of Allied tanks that rolled through, and they're giving the Germans chase if they can, all the way to Berlin. I'd say there will be a parade in his honor if he does make it home one day, wherever home becomes. As for me, I'm now officially retired of trying to keep him in line. I'm afraid our streetwise Yank is on his own with both the end of the war and what comes after."

Lila caught her bottom lip with her teeth, suppressing a smile.

"What on earth are you trying so hard not to smile at?"

She turned to him, brushed the hair off his brow where the sun had lightened it. "It sounds like Carlyle—addicted to the chase. We'll have to go to the church and light a candle for him. But I think I'm smiling because I know you're not on your own. We're together in this. Remember? I can look at you now, René Touliard, and say *your* name. And hold your hand for the entire world to see it. And today, I smile because I get to make yours my name too."

"Come on then, love." He pressed a kiss to her lips. "Your pa-pa will have the chessboard ready and I want to beat him at least once before we leave Paris. That could take the rest of our lives if we're not careful."

Leave Paris?

Lila didn't hide a smile this time as they crossed the street, the Chanel salon fading in the background, and bricks and rubble being swept up from sidewalks.

They would never leave Paris. Not really. Not when she was a true Parisienne at heart and always the Dressmaker in her mind. Wherever their life and travels and future would take them, they'd be side by side, in a world determined to rebuild and a future that held a promise to give back all that had been lost.

Epilogue

25 August 2019
1 Place de la Concorde
Paris, France

So, what do you think of it?"

Flora Fontaine leaned on her cane to hunch down and whisper to the petite schoolgirl who'd stopped to admire the blush gown behind the display glass.

She paused, startled perhaps that an aged woman would stop to talk to someone so young. But Flora had stood back and watched for some time, as the school party moved through the exhibition in the Louvre's salon—young boys in blazers and ties and little girls in plaid skirts and knee socks walking by. The others in her school group had moved on, looking at other pieces of art on the walls and behind the glass cases spaced around. But this one . . . She had a sparkle in her eyes as her gaze drifted over the layers of tulle and chiffon and the long, flower-strewn train. She'd pressed her fingertips to the glass, even though it wasn't allowed, as if she wished to imagine what the reams of satin and roses would feel like beneath her touch.

The little girl looked back, ebony hair in a chic little topknot on her crown, freckles sprayed over the bridge of her nose and a tooth just trying to grow back into her smile.

"I think it is . . ."

Flora could almost hear the thoughts ticking through the little girl's mind as she crossed her arms over her blazer and surveyed the gown again. Perhaps searching for the right word because *beautiful* didn't go far enough and *exquisite* probably was not in her vocabulary just yet.

"Oui? It is what?"

"It is perfectly adequate, madame."

She chuckled to herself—the cheek! A custom 1938 Chanel was perfectly adequate.

"Oh! And what would you do differently, if you were the dressmaker? How would you create something that decades later people would still wish to come and see? It is a remarkable feat, non, to create something so beautiful that it lasts far beyond us, and people might still see its value enough to learn something new every time they come back to it?"

The little girl peered back, eyes taking in Flora's aged form. Perhaps she wondered what an old woman would know about such things as Paris fashion or haute couture. Or even vintage Chanel.

Flora smiled down at her. "You know, if you don't yet have an answer, that is alright. Because I believe that one day, you will. You will see fair the way you ought to go."

The group's teacher came by, scolding the little girl back into line. But Flora looked on, noticing the way the Chanel caught the light and how the little girl had seen it too. The gown had so transfixed her that perhaps, just maybe, another dressmaker was to be born.

"Grand-mère?" Manon slid behind her, bracing an arm under her elbow, her palm gently holding the lace of her frock's sleeve. "We were looking for you. They are waiting to begin."

Flora turned to watch as the school group disappeared into the vast crowds moving through the museum.

"Oui, I am coming, ma cherie." She patted her granddaughter's hand, shuffling along into their private salon.

Rows of chairs sat in an arc of gold gilding before a podium. The summer sun warmed the space as the people sat—Flora honored with a space in the front row. Photographers clicked away on cameras. The musicians stilled bows on their violins and cellos, the music fading as the curators came forward to the microphone.

"Bonjour, *amis et famille*. On this, the seventy-fifth anniversary of the liberation of Paris, it is our great pleasure to open the exhibition of *Les femmes de Paris*—'The Women of Paris.' We welcome the families of remarkable Parisiennes—Lila de Laurent-Touliard, Sandrine Paquet, and Rose Valland among the many honored here today—and mark this occasion for their very dedicated service to the Résistance effort in World War II, and to the ultimate survival of French culture. This custom couture gown, designed by *le Maison de Chanel* and sewn by dressmaker Lila de Laurent, is a benevolent gift from the Rothschilds collection, and in partnership with Ms. Flora Paquet-Fontaine from the Paquet Publishing family, who assured its survival during the occupation. It is our very great honor today to induct this piece of French history into the permanent collection at the Louvre Museum."

The crowd clapped and Flora beamed, looking back at the gown that had always been a part of the history of her family—the story of her parents and brother, Henri, during the war—and of the many who'd survived in the city she so loved. The blush cascade of satin and tulle and delicate chiffon stood behind the glass as the speaker continued, a marker to the lives that had been lived, and lost, and rebuilt as a result of the war.

More than that, she saw the dressmakers of the future—the bold, the unafraid, the petite schoolgirls—those so moved by the art behind a piece of glass that they, too, might see a brilliant future, and a foundation of faith blossom forth.

". . . It remains our great hope and ardent wish that the education gained from this endeavor will ensure that future generations understand the contributions of Frenchwomen during this war. And may each story we uncover of the Parisienne and her courageous dedication to her country be remembered forevermore. Merci."

— LA FIN —

AUTHOR'S NOTE

———◆≍◆———

It's Paris—summer 1939.

A line of taxis and luxury cars alike pull up the drive along Marie Antoinette's famed Petit Trianon for a party so exclusive, it's dubbed the most fashionable in France before it has even begun.

In many ways the 1 July 1939 Circus Ball of famed American decorator, enigmatic socialite, and onetime actress Elsie de Wolfe— by this time Lady Mendl, aged an impressive eighty-one years—was a last hurrah before the world slipped into the bleak reality of World War II. It was this image of light, high fashion, and French frivolity staged at de Wolfe's Villa Trianon contrasted against the colorless and dark brutality of war that so fascinated me for the subject of a novel. (And drove our creation of the cover art you hold in your hands.)

From the moment this story blossomed, I wanted it to paint a portrait of the women in Paris—the Parisiennes—in a block of complicated history from Occupation on 14 June 1940 until the Allied Armies' liberation on 25 August 1944.

Authentic locations in this novel, such as the Forêt de Meudon ("Meudon Forest"), Petit Trianon, and Villa Trianon (at Versailles), and in particular the Jeu de Paume storehouse, became silent characters in this story. The fascinating account of real-life art historian, La Résistance comrade, and French Army captain Rose Valland—who kept meticulous records of Nazi-stolen art at great personal risk during the occupation years—is at times merely touched upon, such as in the Valland-inspired character of Claire Simone in the film drama *The Monuments Men* (2014). It is the brave women such as Rose Valland (who really was marched to open the Jeu de Paume vaults with machine guns at her back) and singer, film star, and fearless Résistance spy Josephine Baker who should receive the spotlight here, even over the remarkable backdrop of the City of Light.

While this novel takes no definitive stance on Gabrielle "Coco" Chanel's collaboration with the Third Reich during World War II, that she spent the occupation in a suite at the Hôtel Ritz Paris for the duration of the occupation is historical fact, as is her highly publicized relationship with Nazi officer Baron Hans Günther von Dincklage— "Spatz," as he was more commonly known. As to any further conjecture about Chanel's rumored spy activity in aiding the Nazi régime under the agent pseudonym "Westminster," readers are encouraged—as students of history yourselves—to further investigate as curiosity directs and come to a conclusion based on the evidence you find.

While several locations were constructs for this novel, each scene was intentionally placed in an address across 1940s Paris that would have seen heartbreaking change, unpredictable conflict, and intense oppression under the occupation of the Third Reich and the French Vichy régime. Le Fournier (boulangerie), Les Petits Galettes (René's Montmartre pâtisserie), and the Trouvère (Latin Quarter bookshop), the latter whose name was intentionally chosen after the French word *trouvère*—a medieval epic poet—were all crafted from this author's imagination.

The fictional *Les Monde des Chimères* exhibition of pseudo-science and anti-Jewish art at the Palais Garnier—the name loosely translated from French as "A World of Illusions"—became the symbolic tipping point for Sandrine's character in this story. It's after this event she moves headlong into risking everything—not to do what is easy but to follow the path that core-deep she knows to be right. While this exhibition is fictional, many similar events took place before and during World War II.

A German exhibition at the Hans der Kunst ("House of German Art") in Munich took place in 1937 and applauded the Nazis' idealized view of classical and Aryan art as preeminent. In contrast, an exhibition of "degenerate art" removed from Nazi national collections was planned down the road from the first. It aimed at mocking modern artistic movements alongside the moral degradation of the Jews and Jewish artists, and it ultimately brought in more than a million visitors—three times more than the first. This rhetoric of Jews and art extended to Nazi-occupied areas, including a Paris exhibition on 5 September 1941 titled *Le Juif et la France*. This exhibition attracted some two hundred thousand visitors to view its grossly anti-Semitic propaganda, feeding this tone of abhorrence that would see the practice of Nazi-stolen art (including from prominent private Jewish collections) continuing through the end of the war.

In contrast to Sandrine, Lila experiences a slow transition from the glitz and glamour of the French fashion elite to the underbelly of the French Résistance, brought on by the quite personal trigger of the Touliard family's stolen collection. Lila's journey of survival evolves from the Hôtel Ritz to the catacombs—and the shadow world of René's "Black Propaganda" work—as she becomes an improbable fighter in La Résistance.

The Allies were involved in an intense propaganda campaign during World War II through the American Office of Strategic Services (OSS) and the British Political Warfare Executive (PWE), whose undercurrents flowed against the Nazi war effort by bolstering the French Résistance with rumors, speculation, and outright lies aimed at undermining Hitler's strongholds across Europe. With his opening line, "*Hier ist Gustav Siegfried Eins*," "The Chief" (actually a German exile in Britain by the name of Peter Seckelmann) began his broadcast on 23 May 1941 and would continue airing Allied propaganda for some seven hundred broadcasts. Information gleaned from newspapers and radio, prisoner-of-war interrogations, real letters taken off members of the German armed forces, and both British and American intelligence on the ground fed the broadcasts with their shocking "accounts" of ineptitude within the ranks of German leadership.

Lila's journey from light to a shadow world echoes the stories of many women in occupied Paris, each of which is layered and unique. Choices for Parisiennes were complicated, outcomes never assured, and consequences sometimes severe, as seen in the post-liberation *épuration sauvage* that marked the Paris streets after the bloody Battle for Paris from 19 August to 25 August 1944.

The actions of these "purges of purification" were particularly brutal against women who were Nazi collaborators during the occupation (those merely accused alongside the many guilty of collaboration *horizontale*). But in the vein of vigilante justice, those women who were innocent of an association were also among the punished—some even having risked their own lives to work secretly for La Résistance—such as Sandrine Paquet. The lopsided punishments of women over men (some who were known collaborators themselves) included outright execution, but more often public humiliation through head shaving and parading in public squares, beatings, degradation, and social and legal branding that lasted well into de Gaulle's reconstruction of France in the postwar years.

On 7 September 1944, the Third Reich indeed made an attempt to fire upon a liberated Paris by trying to set off two of the newly constructed pulsejet-powered V-2 missiles. Both of these bombing attempts failed, but days later the V-2 entered the war, being fired from an area of occupied Holland in bombings that would hit sites such as Porte d'Italie in Paris and the suburb of Chiswick, west of central London, England. During the height of the V-2 missile's barrage, England would bear the brunt of Germany's onslaught with some sixty rockets fired per week between February and March 1945.

Researching occupied Paris, its iconic fashion world set against the brutal restrictions of its people, and the heartbreaking part it played in the Holocaust (in which some 75,721 Jewish refugees and French citizens were deported to Nazi death camps, and more than 6 million Jews were the victims of genocide worldwide) is a time in my life I'll never forget. Reviewing photographs, poring over newspaper articles, watching endless newsreels, and listening to real-time BBC radio broadcasts of the events as they happened hit a nerve in a core-deep place. It made me rethink how to view history and how we, as the generations those people were fighting for, are shaping the futures of our own children and grandchildren.

We have a call to remember history as it was, to uncover the truth, to spotlight the savage consequences of sin, and to educate future generations so that those brutal mistakes might never be repeated.

For the lives lost, the lives lived, and the lives yet to come . . . may we never forget.

ACKNOWLEDGMENTS

⟡

*P*lay 'La Marseillaise'..."
There's a powerful scene in the classic World War II–era film *Casablanca* (1942) in which the French Résistance fighter Victor Laszlo approaches Rick's nightclub band and says those symbolic words.

The action unfolds as Laszlo's character (played to perfection by actor Paul Henreid) directs the anthem of Résistance to countermand the Nazis' own anthem by officers billeting in the club. What follows is a masterful display of French patriotism—and outright defiance—as one by one men and women, patrons of the club, begin to stand, and sing out, and shout, *"Vive la France!"* as their chorus drowns out the Nazi voices . . . and the German officers finally sit down.

Until I began research for this book, I didn't know this compelling imagery became a form of truth. As the Battle for Paris sparked on 15 August and then caught fire on 19 August 1944, the chorus of *"La Marseillaise"* could be heard in the western Paris commune of Neuilly—the song of the Free French rising, their voices carrying through the machine-gun fire and blast of tank shells to stir the Résistance to fight.

ACKNOWLEDGMENTS

It's the filmmakers' depiction of such a powerful image two years before it would happen, and the real-life courage of FFI fighters singing loud in the Parisian streets, that so inspired the characters' journeys I wanted to craft in this story.

Merci to the dream-defenders who made it possible.

To my editors and champions on this book: Becky Monds, I thank you, dear friend. Your dedication to beautiful storytelling is rivaled only by your support of those you love. I'm a better person for having learned about life from you. To Laura Wheeler: Thank you for your steadfast support of this story! You've helped craft this novel from cover to cover, and I find I've made a dear friend in the beauty of that process. To Julee Schwarzburg: My guide and ever-creative wordsmith . . . This novel creation is another journey I'll cherish because it's one where I've again partnered with you. To Jeff Miller at Faceout Studio and to Halie Cotton: For this cover art that stirs my soul like I've just stepped into the Chanel Paris salon for the first time . . . I thank you for using your incredible talents for the Lord! To Amanda Bostic, Paul Fisher, Jodi Hughes, Kerri Potts, Matt Bray, Marcee Wardell, Margaret Kercher, and Savannah Summers—a publishing team of my dreams: Thank you for supporting me at every step of this journey. I love you all. To Rachelle Gardner: You've redefined the words *mentor, agent, coach,* and *friend* and made a new category of excellence all your own. I'm so grateful.

The phrase *compagne de voyage*—French for "travel companion"— has taken on a new meaning for me in this season of life. My travel companions picked up suitcases for me during the writing of this novel, and it's for that genuine care, the battle-when-I-was-weary spirit, the pause to celebrate big wins, and the companionship to journey together in this life that I thank God for you each day: Katherine Reay, Sarah E. Ladd, Beth K. Vogt, Sara Ella, Allen Arnold, Sharon Tavera, and Maggie Walker.

A *merci* shoutout also to the real Mr. Duckworth from Yorkshire,

England, who stopped and chatted with me in the international aisle of the grocery, and to the real Stormie, who served this weary traveler some Starbucks and much-needed encouragement at an airport café while I was writing this story. I was delighted to name characters for both of you.

For my family: Lindy and Rick, Jenny, and my guys—Jeremy, Brady, Carson, and Colt—I'm penning these words because you believed that life is worth giving your all to, and you support me in that every day. *Je t'aime, mon cœur.*

As a woman of German, English, Welsh, French, and Native American descent, and as a longtime student of art history, I value the diversity of our humanity and am fascinated by the chorus of voices who have gone before us. My ardent thanks to those who help me learn, encourage me to stay curious, and help sort through every shred of information I can find to grasp a story. To Professor Anne E. Guernsey Allen, PhD, at Indiana University Southeast: For your mentoring that is now going on a quarter-century long (what?), I remain both in your debt and gratefully changed by your friendship. To Professor Charles L. Pooser, PhD, at Indiana University Southeast: Ardent thanks for helping me nail down the *Je ne sais quoi* of my French in this novel. (Those semesters in college all those years ago feel, well . . . all those years ago.) *Merci beaucoup!*

Now in a decade of experience and counting in the publishing world, I've had the opportunity to meet some remarkable, talented, and completely generous souls, from authors to booksellers to readers. The authors whose books we read write from an otherworldly place; theirs is a call that is woven into the fabric of who they are, crafted equally from threads of the soul, the gut, and the beating heart. But I've also realized that you and I—the readers—search for these stories from a similar place.

I pray that as readers, we would be so moved by the power of story that actions to build up the kingdom of God would be the spectacular consequence of opening a book's cover and traveling through its pages. If this—or any other story—has moved you to use your life for Jesus Christ, to build up the body of believers in the Church, to speak life and grace and truth over the brethren in a way that unburdens the journey of even one soul on this earth . . . love wins the battle.

To my Savior: It has all been worth it and I love You.

Kristy

Further Reading

Bouverie, Tim. *Appeasement: Chamberlain, Hitler, Churchill, and the Road to War.* New York: Tim Duggan Books, 2019.

Glass, Charles. *Americans in Paris: Life and Death Under Nazi Occupation.* New York: Penguin, 2011.

Jackson, Julian. *France: The Dark Years 1940–1944.* Oxford: Oxford University Press, 2003.

Mazzeo, Tilar J. *The Hotel on Place Vendôme: Life, Death, and Betrayal at the Hôtel Ritz in Paris.* New York: Harper Perennial, 2014.

Moorehead, Caroline. *A Train in Winter: An Extraordinary Story of Women, Friendship, and Résistance in Occupied France (The Résistance Quartet).* New York: Harper Perennial, 2012.

Rosbottom, Ronald C. *When Paris Went Dark: The City of Light Under German Occupation 1940–1944*. New York: Back Bay Books, 2015.

Rose, Sarah. *D-Day Girls: The Spies Who Armed the Résistance, Sabotaged the Nazis, and Helped Win World War II*. New York: Crown, 2019.

Scheips, Charlie. *Elsie de Wolfe's Paris: Frivolity Before the Storm*. New York: Abrams, 2014.

Sebba, Anne. *Les Parisiennes*. New York: St. Martin's Press, 2016.

Vaughan, Hal. *Sleeping with the Enemy: Coco Chanel's Secret War*. New York: Vintage Books, 2011.

Discussion Questions

1. Lila's journey through the war takes her from the frivolity of a prewar Paris fashion world, to dressing the Nazis' high-society women at the Hôtel Ritz, to eventually fighting with the Free French during the tumultuous last days of occupation. How did the years 1939–1944 change Lila's view of the world? How do these words describe what may have changed in her: *naïveté, passion, strength, hope, apathy, bravery*? What other words describe Lila?

2. Though he'd wanted to propose to Lila at the start of the war, René ultimately breaks off the relationship, thinking he is protecting Lila from the danger of what is to come. What might have been different about their journey if they'd married at the start of the war and instead endured the trials together? What is most important in relationships that endure through trials?

3. The dynamic of Lila and Amélie's relationship takes many turns throughout the war, including their choices to align with opposite sides of the conflict. Does Lila forgive Amélie for her anti-Semitic views, and for making poor choices that ultimately result in attempting to turn

René and his family over to the Nazi authorities? How do we continue to love others whose views oppose our own, especially when we don't agree with their life choices?

4. Sandrine's wartime experience is shaped by many aspects of her life, from being a wife and a mother to being forced to support and work alongside the very overlords she opposes. How does Sandrine attempt to hold fast to her convictions while fighting to protect her family at the same time? Why wasn't Sandrine spared from the public *épuration sauvage* events that took place at liberation, especially when she fought for the Résistance through the war?

5. When they part at the train station at the start of the war, Christian gives Sandrine an envelope meant to give her hope down the long road ahead. How do you think she chose the precise time to open it? How does what she finds in that envelope change her course of action?

6. Several "secret" items serve as an undercurrent for characters' motivations in the story: the Touliard Cartier necklace, Lila's journal cataloging the stolen Jewish art, the microfilm Lila smuggles out of the Hôtel Ritz on New Year's Eve, Christian's lighter found by Captain von Hiller at the Paris opera house, the page from Sandrine and Christian's family Bible, and the custom 1938 Chanel gown. How does each item impact the characters' journeys throughout the story?

7. Chanel's salon closure at the beginning of the novel sparks changes for fashion workers, such as Lila and Amélie. How is fashion used as a conduit for events in the novel? How did Parisian women use fashion to defy the Nazis and survive through their circumstances?

8. There are women in this novel whose choices set them on vastly different paths, from Violette and the women at the Hôtel Ritz, to Lila, Sandrine, Michèle, and Marguerite,

to the real-life historical figures who risked their lives to fight with the French Résistance, such as Rose Valland and Josephine Baker. How did Parisiennes survive, through either collaboration with or defiance of the Nazis, even with their everyday choices? How were the choices for women different than those for men?

9. In order to be good citizens, we typically believe we need to obey the government authority placed over us. But in times when we see evidence of what we know core-deep to be in conflict with our beliefs—such as when Lila witnesses the Vél' d'Hiv Roundup of Jews by Vichy police in July 1942—is it within our rights to stand up in defiance? When is it time to obey, and when is it time to question and even oppose authority?

10. In the World War II–era plundering of fine art of both public institutions and private Jewish collections across Europe, the Nazi régime determined what was dubbed "degenerate art"—particularly modern art movements with works by Picasso, Dalí, Klee, Kokoschka, and Wassily Kandinsky. Sandrine and Michèle worked alongside Rose Valland, risking their lives to save the art from theft and destruction. What defines something as art? How do we determine what artistic expression has value over what does not, especially when some would risk their lives to save it?

THE LOST
CASTLE NOVELS

"As intricate as a French tapestry, as lush as
the Loire Valley, and as rich as heroine Ellie's
favorite pain au chocolat, *The Lost Castle* satisfies
on every level. Kristy Cambron's writing evokes
each era in loving detail, and the romances are
touching and poignant. *C'est bon!*"

—SARAH SUNDIN, AWARD-WINNING AUTHOR

AVAILABLE IN PRINT, E-BOOK, AND AUDIO!

THOMAS NELSON
Since 1798

DON'T MISS THESE OTHER FABULOUS NOVELS BY
KRISTY CAMBRON!

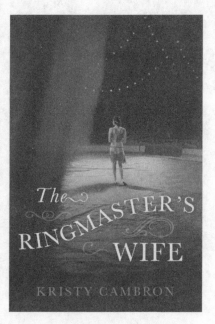

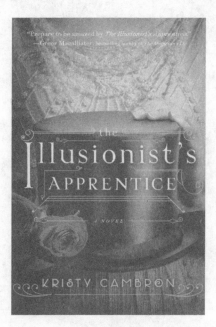

"A vivid and romantic rendering of circus life in the Jazz Age."
—*USA TODAY, Happy Ever After*

"Prepare to be amazed by *The Illusionist's Apprentice*."
—Greer Macallister, bestselling author of *The Magician's Lie* and *Girl in Disguise*

THOMAS NELSON
Since 1798

Available in print, e-book, and audio!

Also Available from Kristy Cambron, the

Hidden Masterpiece Novels!

A mysterious painting breathes hope
and beauty into the darkest corners of
Auschwitz—and the loneliest hearts
of Manhattan.

Bound together across time, two
women will discover a powerful connection through one survivor's story
of hope in the darkest days of a war-
torn world.

About the Author

Author photo © Whitney Neal Studios

KRISTY CAMBRON is an award-winning author of historical fiction, including her bestselling debut, *The Butterfly and the Violin*, and an author of nonfiction, including the Verse Mapping Series Bibles and Bible studies. Kristy's work has been named to *Publishers Weekly* Religion & Spirituality Top 10, *Library Journal*'s Best Books, and *RT Reviewers*' Choice Awards; received 2015 and 2017 INSPY Award nominations; and has been featured at CBN, Lifeway Women, Jesus Calling, *Country Woman* Magazine, *MICI Magazine*, Faithwire, Declare, (in)Courage, and Bible Gateway. She holds a degree in Art History/Research Writing and lives in Indiana with her husband and three sons, where she can probably be bribed with a peppermint mocha latte and a good read.

Connect with Kristy at: kristycambron.com
and versemapping.com.
Instagram: @kristycambron
Twitter: @KCambronAuthor
Facebook: @KCambronAuthor
Pinterest: Kristy Cambron